It's been just over a month since the innocent, green-eyed kid walked in asking for an interview. Mal pegged him as a reporter right away, got the kid to sign an interview consent form, which automatically protected the club — there was an airtight non-disclosure clause on that puppy — and called me in to give the kid as intense a scene as I could.

Which I did.

I'm fucking good at my job. By the end of the scene he was in tears and clinging to me, thanking me, something deep inside him opened to the light.

Of course, him being so affected doesn't explain why I've been dreaming of black leather around a pale-skinned cock dark with blood and framed by bright, fiery curls.

The thing is... when a sub opens to you like that, especially a newly discovered sub? It touches you, too. You can't pull that kind of emotion out of someone without putting your own emotion in.

As I held him that day, something inside me slipped.

My objectivity.

I have never become emotionally involved with a sub before. It's one of the reasons I'll have sex with them. It never crosses the line.

It crossed the line that night.

This is a work of fiction. Names, characters, places, and incidents either are the product of the author's imagination or are used fictitiously. Any resemblance to actual events, locales, organizations, or persons, living or dead, is entirely coincidental and beyond the intent of either the author or the publisher.

Velvet Glove Volume IV
TOP SHELF
An imprint of Torquere Press Publishers
PO Box 2545
Round Rock, TX 78680
Copyright 2007 © by Sean Michael
Cover illustration by SA Clements
Published with permission
ISBN: 978-1-60370-547-9, 1-60370-547-3

www.torquerepress.com

First Torquere Press Printing: December 2008
Printed in the USA

**If you enjoyed Velvet Glove Volume IV,
you might enjoy these Torquere Press titles:**

Chaos Magic by Jay Lygon

Deviations Series by Chris Owen and Jodi Payne

Hyacinth Club by BA Tortuga

Music and Metal by Mike Shade

Secrets, Skin and Leather by Sean Michael

Velvet Glove, Volume IV

Velvet Glove Volume IV
by Sean Michael

Torquere
Press
Inc.
romance for the rest of us
www.torquerepress.com

Velvet Glove, Volume IV

Table of Contents

Velvet Glove, Volume IV

Puppy Love

Dane Learns That Some Puppies are Human

D ane signed in at the front desk of the Velvet Glove, leaving an imprint of his palm. He was assured his suite would be ready for him and his new puppy.

Then he was asked to take a seat and wait for his escort. That would be Richard, the young man he had been in touch with on the universal 'net. The young man who'd told him about the dog that had been abandoned by his owner, left for they knew not how long in a cage. Unattended. Unfed. Unwatered. Left to die what was truly a horrible death.

It angered Dane greatly that people would do this, but it was not the first time he had seen it.

Of course, for every person who could be so cruel there was one like Richard, whose heart was bigger than his ability, who'd searched out someone to help this puppy when he himself had been unable to.

Dane watched as two men, one young and small, the other big, scarred and wearing special glasses, came toward him, holding hands.

They stopped in front of him.

"Hello, Dane?" The big man held out one scarred hand. "I'm Jean, this is Richard."

He stood and shook Jean's hand and then Richard's. "Hello. Yes. I'm Dane. Thank you. Thank you for calling me in. And for the rooms. That really wasn't necessary, but thank you. I assure you, I will help this dog. Tyg, wasn't it?"

The big man looked down at the little one, who nodded eagerly. "Tyg's been... badly treated. He's going to be sent away if someone doesn't help him."

"Yes, Richard sent me an account of how he'd been left by his previous owner. Shameful, really."

The little one — Richard — took his hand and tugged, leading him toward the lift.

"Yes, everyone assumed the man had taken Tyg with him. The police are looking for him, in fact. Tyg was left behind to die."

His heart broke for the poor dog. "When they find the abusive bastard, he should be left in a cage with no food or water as well. It's no more than he deserves."

The lift traveled quickly upward.

"Yeah. Andy and Bear have been taking care of Tyg, but he's aggressive, angry, unsocial." The lift door opened and he was led down a long hall, to a door marked kennel.

He nodded. "Yes, that makes sense. He'll have branded all men as users and abusers. Only time and patience and being well-treated will convince him otherwise."

The door opened, a lean man in leather answering, a naked young man at his feet... barking... "Richard! Jean!

Is this the man interested in Tyg?"

He blinked. "Yes. I'm Dane. I sent my credentials with the animal rescue shelter to Richard a few days ago — he said he'd pass them on..." Dane was fascinated by the ... well, dog-boy at the man's feet. He had a... a tail coming from his ass.

"Excellent. Come on in, I'll introduce you to Tyg." He was led into a long, sunny room, one bright kennel after another with a...

He blinked.

Men.

Men with tails and mitted hands and one or two with dog masks on.

Men that were barking.

Surely this was a joke. After all, if it wasn't, if this was for real, then Tyg was also actually a man. Oh, no. Someone had not left a man in a cage... no. It couldn't be. It couldn't possibly be.

"My name's Andy, I run the stables, usually, and Bear trains the puppies, but he's a little stressed over Tyg, so he's talking a break. Poor guy, he gets so involved. Have you worked with many dogs like this? It's a rare kink, but there's nothing like having a pup love you."

Dane cleared his throat. "I have worked with many abandoned and abused dogs, though I do believe this is a unique situation." This Andy was quite serious; this was not a joke or a game. Dane knew of the Velvet Glove, of course, any gay man living on the colony did. They catered to all tastes, and this had to be one of them.

He would no more make light of this... kink than he would hurt an animal. And he would not abandon the dog that needed him, even if this dog was actually a man. Perhaps especially as he was.

Thank the gods Richard had insisted on setting up rooms for him. They would be equipped with everything he needed, which was a good thing since he didn't have the first idea where a real dog's needs left off and a... man-dog's began.

Andy nodded. "He was badly treated. Physically he's well, but emotionally he's lost, untrusting. I had him muzzled and sedated this morning when we knew you were coming. He's still a little off-center, but he's pissed and awake."

They came to the end of the hall, to a man wearing a muzzle, sitting on his haunches and glaring. This man had no collar, no tail, no mitts — nothing that the others had. The man had a dusting of dark stubble, huge, dark, lost eyes.

Oh. Oh, Dane knew that look. Had seen it more times than he could remember and it broke his heart every time. And it scared him — some animals could be saved, some not, but it was always the ones with the lost eyes who were most at risk.

He stepped forward, holding out his hand to be sniffed. "Hello, Tyg."

A low growl sounded, then Richard moved up, fearlessly going to the huge dog... man... dog... and giving Tyg a hug, petting the strong back. Tyg relaxed, actually allowed Richard to move him, bring him closer to sniff and smell.

He let Tyg sniff his hands and then he reached back. "I'm just going to take the muzzle off, Tyg. Let you get a proper smell."

He didn't like muzzles, didn't believe in them. If you had to use a muzzle to get close to a dog, then you were mistreating it. And if the dog had already been mistreated, you needed to earn its trust, and that could not happen if you muzzled it. He figured it probably worked the same for man-dogs. He'd find out soon enough, he supposed, if he was going to be able to trust his instincts and experience or if he was going to have to seek out advice.

The big man with Richard spoke up. "Richard? Should you be in there? With him? Is it safe?"

Andy's voice was gentle. "Tyg won't hurt Richard. He loves that boy dearly. Tyg's a good dog, he's just scared."

Those eyes watched him, then the pup turned, pushing into Richard's belly.

It really was too bad Richard wasn't taking the man-dog himself, they obviously already shared an affinity that Dane was going to have to build from scratch. Still, it was proof that the pup wasn't completely lost.

"There's no such thing as a bad dog," Dane said softly, giving Richard a smile as he took off the muzzle. Richard was scratching the dog's neck.

The strong muscles were trembling, the dog scared, stressed, nervous, soft whimpers just audible.

He sat on his haunches, bringing him closer to eye level with the dog. "My name is Dane and I'm going to take care of you, Tyg. This seems like a very nice kennel, but there's a lot of dogs to care for here and you need special attention, don't you, Tyg? I'll be that special attention. I'll be able to devote my time to you constantly. We'll learn to know each other. Learn to like each other, too, I think."

He reached his hand out again, slowly, gently petting Tyg's quivering flank. "I won't hurt you."

The dark eyes rolled, head in Richard's hands. Andy's voice sounded again. "You'll be able to keep him with without a cage? He reacts... poorly to cages."

A low growl sounded.

"No cages." He continued to pet the man-dog. "He doesn't need a cage or a muzzle. He just needs care and love, attention. Poor love." The touches seemed to relax Tyg, the man-dog slowly easing to the ground, cheek on Richard's lap.

"Oh, that's so sad..." The huge scarred man sounded as if he would cry.

"Yes. I'm glad you called me, Richard. And so is Tyg — he can tell you care for him and wouldn't hurt him, that's why he trusts you."

Richard kept petting the dog's head and Dane kept petting his flank.

"Can you tell me all the problems I need to know about?" he asked Andy. "Has he been eating? Lashing out at the other... dogs? What exactly comprises anti-social behavior in your mind?"

"He eats very little and never where we can watch. He attacks the other dogs quite fiercely. He has only recently allowed himself to be handled at all. He never speaks, sleeps most of the day. He will not allow grooming, which is why we keep him shaved. He has been mitted up until the last few days — he tore at his skin. The doctor believed that he should not be kept as a pup, that perhaps he wanted to stop, but I see no evidence of that."

"Well, if he doesn't, he'll let me know, I suppose. But he probably shouldn't make any decisions either way until he's not so traumatized. What do you say, Tyg? Richard's arranged for some lovely rooms for us. Will you come and live with me?" Dane had no clue what he was going to do — a real dog-dog wouldn't have the voice to make a choice. Tyg did.

Those eyes lifted, staring at Richard, who nodded, stroking his face. A soft whimper sounded, the man-dog nuzzling into Richard's hands.

"Come, Tyg. You must try, pup. He's a good man. I checked him out myself and I'll check on you every day." A new voice sounded, a huge man filling the hallway, the other pups raising a ruckus at the sight of him.

Wow. This had to be Bear. He was a little relieved to discover that the man didn't seem to be role-playing as a bear. Dane nodded to the big man, but returned his attention to Tyg, letting the pup know that he wouldn't be distracted by newcomers or other dogs.

The pup shifted, reluctant, slow, moving toward him, head bowing, touching his thigh. He petted the bowed head gently. Poor man. Pup. Poor pup.

"Come on, Tyg. Richard will show us to our new home."

Andy reached down to pat Tyg and a low warning growl sounded. Andy sighed and pulled away. "Best of luck, Dane."

"Thank you, Andy. Don't take it personally — he doesn't trust anyone right now. Except maybe Richard." He stood. "Will the halls be cleared for us? I won't use a muzzle on him."

"There is a wagon. If you'd rather, we can have him delivered," Andy said.

He shook his head. "No. That's too close to a cage — I want him to come willingly."

"Then I'll have the halls cleared." Bear stepped away, grabbing a comm from the wall, speaking quickly.

"Thank you." He turned back to Andy. "Was he one of yours to start with?"

"No. No, the two of them - Tyg and that... thing - came together. We'd never met before he was found." Andy shook his head. "We would have kept tabs on him, assured his safety. We care for our puppies."

"Oh, I didn't mean to imply you didn't. I was just hoping to know a little bit about how he was before he was left, what his favorite things were. We'll work it out, though."

"We have the things that were in his cage — a bowl, a blanket, a col..." Tyg snarled, growling, teeth bared.

Dane dropped back to his haunches, petting Tyg's head. "Sh, sh. We won't mention it again, Tyg. Hmm?"

The growling eased, Tyg relaxing a little, panting. Poor thing. They'd figure it out, though. Already they knew any mention of the cage upset Tyg.

They'd get there.

He headed for the door, hand on Tyg's head, encouraging the pup — it was going to be easier if he just thought of the man as a dog, as it seemed these people thought of each other and themselves — to follow him.

Richard followed, the big scarred man behind. The pup growled as they passed the other kennels, Andy shushing the pups, Bear murmuring and petting.

"It's okay, Tyg. We're going somewhere quiet, no more pups except you. You'll have all my attention, pup."

The hallways were quiet, still, the pup's whining and shaking becoming more distinct, stronger as they moved.

Dane kept petting the pup's head, murmuring to Tyg, promising him water and a soft bed, a quiet place, but not alone. When they got onto the lift he went to his haunches again, stroking the quivering sides, nodding to Richard to join him.

The lad did, petting Tyg, crooning softly and rubbing his cheeks against the pup's. Tyg eased, leaned toward him and Richard, eyes closing, panting quietly.

"Very good, Tyg. We're almost there." The elevators door opened. "Come along."

The pup followed him, muscles working, shorn head hanging low. They soon came to his rooms, Richard pointing them out, and he put his palm on the reader, relieved when it opened for them. "Come in, Tyg, come home."

Richard was the one who led Tyg into the quiet, sunny rooms. They were simply furnished, warm, clean, huge windows showing the city.

"Oh, this is beautiful. Peaceful. I think we can be happy here."

He wandered the rooms, making sure there was nothing there Tyg could hurt himself on. There was a large bed, low to the ground. It would be easy for the pup to climb up. He nodded. Good. He went back to the living room, finding Richard in the middle of the floor with Tyg's head in his lap.

Jean was watching out the window, obviously trying not to hover. Tyg was no threat to the lad, face peaceful, quiet, eyes closed.

He went and sat with Richard, being sure to make quiet noises so he didn't startle Tyg. "He likes you a lot, Richard. I'm glad you found each other. It would have been a shame to lose him because he was abused."

Richard gave him a smile, the trust and hope in the young face palpable.

"Richard has a healing touch." This from Jean, along with a smile.

"Yes, I can see that. I hope I can call on you if I need you." Like if Tyg wouldn't respond to him. He hoped it wasn't too late, hoped Tyg would accept someone other than Richard for comfort.

Tyg's eyes opened, watching him, searching his face. He reached out slowly, petting Tyg's flank. Sweet pup.

He chuckled at himself silently. Oh, he was already thinking of this man as a dog, and he was already in love. He always fell in love with the hard cases.

The huge dark eyes slowly closed, the pup relaxing, trusting him enough for that.

"When do you have to go?" he asked Richard, trying to work out a plan for their first evening.

Jean moved to sit upon a sofa, the pup's eyes flying open, then closing again. "We are supposed to meet Noel for supper at eight bells."

"Good, good. I'd like you to help me set a few things out for Tyg. A bowl of water, a few glasses of water, so he has a choice. Some food. Dog food, regular food — fruit, nuts and stuff that can sit out. And then we can go through the blankets, help him find some he likes."

"We'd be happy to help, right, Richard-love?" Jean nodded, offering him a smile. "You're taking a huge concern from Richard's mind. He wanted someone to take Tyg so badly."

"Yes, I can see that. He's a sweet, loving young man. You're very lucky."

"Yes. Yes, I am." Jean smiled. "How can I help?"

"You can do the water? And set out the food — all in the kitchen. Richard can help me with the blankets, help me show the pup where the bathroom is and to choose the blankets."

He stood. "Come along, Tyg."

The pup raised his head, watching him, then slowly pushed up onto all fours, dragging, moving slowly.

Jean tilted his head. "Will he get a collar and a tail like the others?"

"If he wants. He doesn't have to do anything he doesn't want." He slid his hand along the shorn head. "He'll find his way. Time and love. In the end it's what we all need."

Tyg moved with him, watching, learning. He pointed out the bathroom, Tyg's tension easing, eyes lingering on the tub before they headed toward the bedroom.

He and Richard went to the cupboard and pulled out the blankets. "We'll both sleep here, Tyg. The bed is big enough for six, let alone two. Oh, I'm going to take this red blanket. It's so soft and warm. What ones do you like, Tyg? You can have one or two for in here and another for the sitting room, if you like."

Tyg came over, vibrated, watching him closely. Each blanket was nudged and sniffed, then a deep blue blanket, puffy and warm, was separated, Tyg curling upon it with a soft sigh.

"Just the one? I guess that'll do."

He had Richard help him make the bed with flannel sheets that were wonderful, blissfully cozy, and then they added a bunch of pillows and his red blanket. Instead of putting the rest of the blankets away, he piled them in the corner so that Tyg could get to them easily if he wanted another.

"Can we move your blanket to the bed, Tyg?"

Tyg lifted his head, eyes meeting his, almost surprised. Then the pup nodded, responding directly to him.

"Good. Here." He pushed his blanket so it took up half the bed. "There, lots of room for you." Taking a corner of the blanket, he tugged gently, giving Tyg an opportunity to help him if the pup wanted.

Tyg didn't help, but instead climbed onto the mattress, nuzzling into the sheets, waiting patiently for the blanket to cover him.

He and Richard spread the blanket out over Tyg, and then he sat and petted the pup gently. "You going to sleep now, Tyg?"

Tyg curled into a ball, eyes closed, cheek coming to rest close enough for him to feel Tyg's heat. Then the pup nodded again and gave a quiet, peaceful-sounding sigh.

"All right. You sleep. If you need anything, you help yourself, or you find me. You can wake me if you need to — I'm here for you." He petted Tyg's head and then looked up at Richard.

"You know, if you can bring me my bags, I think I'll unpack my clothes and maybe do some reading in bed. Just to be close."

Richard nodded, gave him a happy smile. The pup settled further, relaxing, beginning to snore softly.

He took Richard's hand. "Thank you, Richard. For finding me for him. For bringing us together. I will do everything I can to heal him."

Richard beamed at him and gave him a hug and kiss on the cheek.

This wasn't what he had expected, not at all, but somehow he was committed, somehow he belonged.

Somehow, it felt right.

Tyg and Dane Together

Sleep.
Safe. Warm. Right.
So quiet. So soft. So...

Tyg opened his eyes, head lifting, the world quiet and dark and blue.

He was not in the kennel. Not in the hospital. Not in the cage.

Someone shifted next to him, turning and settling and breathing softly.

He lifted one edge of the blanket, waiting for his eyes to adjust so he could see. Look at the person Richard had chosen for him.

The man was older than Richard, with short, dark hair and a round, kind face. Red lips were slightly parted and a book was open on his chest. Yves had been pale and sharp, free with the whip and the shocking collar, and had never let him sleep on a bed. Never let him relax. Never came back for him.

Left him to starve.

Tyg backed away from the sleeping man, slinking to the floor. The bath.

He would hide there.

The man shifted, made a noise and then called his name. "Tyg?"

He froze, looking about. The bed. He pushed himself beneath, made himself as small as he could.

The man got up and he could see feet as his new...

owner? walked around. "Tyg? You in the kitchen?" The man padded away.

He waited until the man was gone, then bolted, heading for the bath, for the safety and water.

He could see lights go on and off through the other rooms, heard his name called several times. Was that worry in the man's voice? Or anger?

He relieved himself, then crawled into the tub, curling in the bottom, shivering, waiting.

The light came on in the bathroom and the man made a soft noise. "Oh, Tyg. That can't be comfortable." The man crouched next to the tub, hand sliding over his sides. "Come back to bed, pup."

Oh.

He whimpered softly, rippling under the touch. Not angry? Not hurting?

"Sh. Sh. Sh. It's all right, Tyg. Nobody's going to hurt you. It's just you and me and I will never hurt you. I want you to be happy."

The words sounded unreal, too good to be true. Still, Richard had given him to this man. So he let himself slip from the tub.

"There we go. Come on, pup. Do you want something to eat or drink first?"

He shook his head, but his stomach disagreed, growling furiously.

The man smiled. "Well, I'm hungry. You can go straight back to bed if you'd like, but I'd like it if you kept me company while I ate."

He followed, partially out of curiosity, mostly because he didn't want to sleep in the bed by himself. It felt... disobedient.

There were water bowls and water bottles and a bowl of dog food and a bowl of fruit and another of nuts in various spots on the floor. The man walked around them easily, going to a cooler. "I'm going to have a beef sandwich. Would you like one?"

His stomach growled furiously. Beef. Oh. Oh, meat. He whined, licking his lips, heading over to lap at the good, clean water so that he wouldn't be punished.

"Do you prefer it cooked or raw? I have some raw ground beef you could have, or some of the shaved cooked beef I'm having in my sandwich." The man didn't sound angry.

He lifted his head, eyes fastened on the sliced beef. He could smell it. Moving forward, his nostrils twitching, his hunger overrode his concern. The man smiled, holding several pieces out to him.

Tyg whined softly, carefully taking the meat and taking it to the corner to eat it, groaning at the flavor.

So good.

Oh. Oh, it was so good.

"You can go into the fridge any time you want for food that's not out. Or come to me if you're hungry and let me get it for you. Once we've figured out your favorites, I'll make sure we keep them stocked." The man's voice was quiet, gentle. "Here, I took out too much for my sandwich — have a few more slices." The man put them down about a foot from where he was and then backed off, eating his sandwich.

Tyg ate those and then went to eat some of the fruit, drink some water. Oh. He could have anything he wanted from the refrigerator.

Anything.

Milk.

Oh, he liked milk.

He crept over to the refrigerator, keeping an eye on the man. The man was eating his sandwich, half turned away from him — not watching. He nudged the door open, reaching up with one paw toward the bottle of milk, pulling it down to him. In seconds he was drinking from the bottle, throat working, gulping.

So good.

Cold.

The man made a soft, sad noise, but when he froze and looked, the man was still eating, examining the last bites of sandwich.

He licked his lips, belly full and stretched, then held out the half-full bottle, offering a drink to the man.

The man smiled and stepped closer, taking the bottle from him and drinking from it before returning it. "Thank you."

He nodded, breathing in the good, clean smells.

The man washed his hands and then petted him. "Well, Tyg, what would you like to do? We could watch a vid or play or go back to bed. Oh! Or have a bath — you like the water?"

Oh. Oh, yes. Yes. He did. He liked baths. Not the hoses, like in the kennels, but a real bath.

He barked once, nudging the man's hand, then stilled, his voice startling him. He hadn't wanted to bark for a long time.

The man laughed. "I'll take that as a yes. You were asleep a long time and there's no reason we have to follow conventional timetables. We're both awake. Let's go have a bath."

The man headed back to the bathroom. "It's more than big enough for two — will you let me share?"

Tyg gave the man a curious look. Let him? He was the man. He could do as he would. Still, Tyg liked baths.

And milk.

And quiet.

He slid into the bathtub, leaving room for the man.

"Excellent, excellent. You like the water hot? I like it fairly hot, but I can adjust." The man stripped out of his linen pants and turned on the water. "How about bubbles? Do you like bubbles? I was reading up on the club this evening as well and there are private pools. We could reserve one and go swimming. If you like swimming."

He blinked at all the questions, settling on a nod. Dogs didn't speak. Dogs never spoke. Surely this man knew that only bad dogs spoke or stood.

He'd had the bad dog forced out of him.

The man poured something into the water and suddenly there was a whole bunch of bubbles, making the man laugh as he climbed into the big tub.

Tyg blew at them, grinning as he watched them float. The water was hot, surrounding him, so good that he wiggled, moaned.

The man settled in, groaning. "Oh, that's good. I can't remember the last time I relaxed in a bath."

Tyg nodded, stretching carefully, toes and fingers curling. It was good.

"What else do you like besides the water and beef and milk?"

He blinked over. He liked to play. He liked his new blanket. He liked Richard and scratches and pineapple and swimming and running in grass.

"Can't you speak?" the man asked him. "Or do you just not want to?"

He tilted his head, blinked. Confused. The man wanted his voice?

"You know, speak. Words. It would be easier to know what you liked and disliked if you could just tell me." The man smiled. "I'm pretty good with dog body language, though, so I suppose I'll muddle through if you won't speak."

He whimpered, licked his lips. "B... b... bad dog."

The sound of his voice scared him, made him tense and wait for the blows to come.

"No, Tyg, you aren't a bad dog — not at all."

Oh. Oh, he liked that, too.

Not a bad dog.

The man came close, hands sliding over his head and down his back, petting him. He closed his eyes, the sensation terrifying and good all at once.

"Such a good dog, Tyg. All you needed was someone to treat you right, isn't that right? That's why you like Richard, he's sweet and he sees you and he loves you. Not that Bear and Andy don't — I'm sure they do, but they've so many pups, don't they? Poor Tyg. You're not alone anymore, though, no, you aren't." The man had a nice voice, low and gentle, soothing.

He was caught between needing to relax and needing to be safe, protect himself. But Richard loved him, was good to him. Brought him here.

Tyg found himself relaxing.

The man's words slowly came to an end and the man just hummed instead, hands moving in gentle patting motions over his head, his back, his belly. It was the nicest thing he'd ever felt, the heat and petting and full belly and safety, all wrapped together. It was perfect.

Tears slid from his eyes, emotions refusing to be denied.

"Oh, Tyg..." That was all the man said, hands continuing to slide over him, so gentle and caring.

He stretched, then curled up, leaning into the man's touch.

"There we go, Tyg. Just you and me and peace, hmmm?"

He nodded, looking up into those warm eyes, holding the man's gaze.

The man smiled at him, hands coming up to stroke his muzzle, his head. "Such a good dog."

He liked to hear that, pushing into the man's hands, a

low sound vibrating inside him.

"Yes, such a good dog. Such a pretty purr. Good boy. Good boy." His neck was gently scratched and his belly petted again.

Tyg wasn't sure what to think, what to feel, but he just took the sensation the man offered. Good. He was good.

They sat for a long time in the water, the man's hands petting him, occasional words of praise for him. Then the man said the water was getting cold and they had to get out.

He grumbled. This had been perfect. So perfect, and he didn't want to lose it, but he obeyed, slipping out of the tub and shaking. Hard.

The man laughed and then started wiping him down with a thick, white square of cloth. He got almost dry, then grabbed the cloth and ran, leading the man on a chase. There was that laugh again, the man running after him, stumbling and bumping into walls and following him.

He hurried into the room with the couches, turning, spinning, looking for somewhere to go.

The man burst in and lunged for him.

Something inside him snapped and he bolted. He was not going in the cage again. Never. Never getting caught again. Freedom was outside, out the window, out of here, out of this place. Never going in the cage. Not a bad dog.

"Leaving you," Yves had said. "Leaving you here. I should never have brought you here."

He ran full-force for the window, running from those words, the disgust in those eyes, the smell of shit and starvation, the pain and bugs and fear.

The world went black like the night sky when he slammed into the glass, face-first.

Tyg and Dane Begin to Discover Each Other

Dane screamed as Tyg threw himself at the window. The pup hit it hard and went down, landing with a thump. He scrambled his way over, cursing himself. Damn it, he'd let his guard down, broken his most important rule — he'd forgotten that Tyg was damaged.

He knew better than to believe that first flush of success. He *knew* they spooked easily, especially at the beginning.

With Tyg, though, he'd wanted it so badly that he'd believed a bit of food and a few kind words would be enough to heal who only knew how much damage.

He checked for a pulse and checked Tyg's face. The nose was broken, bleeding, but otherwise Tyg was relatively unscathed. If he couldn't wake the pup he'd call the doc, but the last thing Tyg needed now was another stranger poking.

"Tyg. Tyg, I need you to wake up."

A soft whimper answered him, a hurt whine.

"It's all right. I'm going to get you a spray for the pain. It's all right."

He pet the pup's belly and then reached under the couch, grabbing the medkit he'd stored there — he'd spread them out around the place before going to bed.

"Keep your eyes closed and don't breathe for a moment," he ordered and then sprayed Tyg's face with antiseptic anesthetic. Tyg listened to him, relaxing as the painkiller did its job, soft whimpers fading. When the pup's eyes opened, they were huge, scared, worried.

"Oh, Tyg, sh, sh, it's okay. You broke your nose, but it'll heal." He pet Tyg's head and belly.

Tyg shivered, watching him."B... bad dog?"

"Well... I don't want you to do it again, but no, you aren't a bad dog. A scared and hurting and confused dog, but not bad."

Tyg nodded, curling up, cheek on his thigh.

"When you're feeling up to it, we'll move to the bed," he murmured, gently cleaning Tyg's face with a swab. He put a bit of tissue up each nostril to stem the last of the blood flow, and then returned to petting, murmuring.

Tyg panted, breath warm on his bare skin. Every so often a tremor would rock the pup, cause a soft sound.

"Are you still hurting somewhere?" he asked. He didn't want to have to bring the doc in, wasn't sure it wouldn't upset Tyg even more, but if there was something else wrong...

The pup shook his head, blinking slowly. "S... sorry."

"Just promise me you won't do it again, that you won't try to hurt yourself, and it'll be forgotten."

"Did... Sc... scared. W... wanted out."

"I'm not going to hurt you, Tyg. You don't have to be scared. And it's my turn to apologize — you're supposed to have a safeword, aren't you? A word that stops everything when you say it."

Tyg's eyes went wide, the pup nodding.

"What's your safeword, Tyg?"

"Scissors." The pup swallowed hard, poor voice so raw, so unused. "Scissors."

He pet Tyg gently. "Okay, there — you see? Next time you're scared? You say scissors and no matter what, everything will stop, all right? I just want to help you get better, Tyg."

"I want to." The tears started again, slow and steady, soaking his skin.

"I know... I know... " He just kept petting. "Sooner or later you'll start to trust me, Tyg. Because I'm not going anywhere."

"Won't leave me here in a cage?"

"Never. I don't believe in cages. I don't believe in muzzles. I don't believe in choke leashes." He was adamant about those.

"I was in a cage before." Those eyes were devastated, full of sorrow.

"I know. I wish I could change what happened to you." That lost puppy look just killed him. It always had, but with Tyg it was all so much more devastating.

Tyg nodded, eyes beginning to bruise, to swell. "Name?"

He frowned. "Your name is Tyg, I won't try to change it. Oh! You mean mine!"

Tyg almost smiled. "M... master?"

He shook his head. "Not unless that's what you want. My name is Dane."

A chuckle sounded, real and rich. "Great Dane."

He blinked and then started to laugh. Those eyes were dancing, laughing, suddenly alive. His laughter faded. Oh, Tyg was lovely with happiness on his face.

Tyg looked at him, head tilted, curious. "Good dog?"

"Oh yes, Tyg." He stroked the pup's head. "Very good dog."

Tyg shifted his head, licking his fingers. He hummed happily, but didn't lose himself in it like he'd done before. "Are you feeling well enough to go back to bed? It'll be more comfortable to sleep there than here."

Tyg nodded, moaning as he shifted, head hanging a little. "Blanket. Bed."

"Are you still hurting? The anesthetic should still be working, but if it isn't, we'll use more..." He was worried Tyg wouldn't tell him, trying not to cause trouble.

"A... aches."

"Okay, let's get you into bed and I'll give you an analgesic for the pain."

He headed for the bedroom, hoping Tyg would say something if he needed help. Tyg nodded, following and climbing up onto the bed, curling into the soft blanket with a soft sigh. Dane found a couple of tablets and a glass of water, helping Tyg take them. Then he tucked the blanket around Tyg, stroking the shorn scalp.

Tyg purred again, eyes closing. "Good. Good Dane."

"Thank you, Tyg." He leaned forward and kissed Tyg's forehead softly. "Sleep well."

Tyg yawned, scooting so they were almost touching, then slumped, sound asleep.

Poor love.

Dane settled down next to Tyg, hand sliding absently along the pup's flank.

Time and patience. Luckily, he had plenty of both.

Tyg was getting used to waking up surrounded by a blue blanket, the scent of Dane close and warm and familiar. The day after his nose got hurt he had stayed in the bed, every motion making him whimper and ache. The second morning was better, but he spent the day with his cheek on Richard's lap, letting the lad pet him.

The third morning he woke feeling good.

Hungry.

Awake.

Alive.

He stretched, groaning a little, muscles rippling.

Dane's hand slid over his head and then down along his side. "Morning, Tyg," murmured the man, sounding still mostly asleep.

He pushed into the touch, then slid out of the bed, heading to relieve himself and play in the bathtub.

Play.

In the tub.

In the water.

He grinned at himself.

Some time later, Dane came in and relieved himself and splashed water on his face. "You look like you're enjoying yourself, Tyg. I need caf — do you want any?"

He rolled over, sliding in the bubbles. He was having fun. Much fun in the hot water. Caf, though? Bitter and nasty like medicine. Milk was good.

Dane chuckled. "Bubble baths are probably a nicer way to wake up than caf. Still, I'm tired enough this morning, I need the stimulant. I don't know why, it's not like I haven't been getting enough sleep."

He thought maybe the man was talking to himself. Dane seemed to do that a lot. Still, that was okay. Dane was good to him. Friendly. Kind. If Dane wanted to talk to himself? That was fine.

Dane came back a little later. "Tyg? Are you still in the water? You're going to turn into a prune."

He peeked up from over the edge of the tub, blinking innocently.

Who?

Him?

Dane laughed and crouched by him, hand sliding over his head.

"I should check your nose, Tyg."

He whined softly, forcing himself not to pull away.

"I know, I know, pup, I'll try not to hurt you."

Dane put a hand beneath his chin and raised it, moved his head from side to side. "Actually, it looks like it's healing well. I don't think there'll be any sign of the break."

He ducked his head, licking Dane's fingers, nuzzling them, hips wagging.

"Mmm, such a good dog."

He beamed, grinning. Good dog. Good dog in the bathtub.

Dane grinned back at him. "Come on out, Tyg. Let's have some breakfast."

Oh. Breakfast. He liked breakfast. He slid from the tub, shaking himself dry.

Dane laughed softly and toweled him off gently. "Do you like bacon and eggs? Pancakes? I can't do French toast or waffles, but I could call some up from the kitchen."

"Bacon. Eggs. Milk." He licked Dane's wrist in thanks. "Mmmmmmilk."

"Mmm, I'll have to make sure we keep the cooler stocked with milk. Your favorite, yeah, pup?"

He nodded, belly rumbling, following Dane eagerly. Bacon. Eggs. Milk. Breakfast.

"You prefer cups, the bottle it comes in, or dog bowls to drink out of, Tyg? And how about eating?"

He blinked, thinking. He'd never had an option before.

"Can I tell you what I'd like, without you thinking you have to do that rather than what you would really prefer?"

Tyg nodded. Yeah. Yeah, he could handle that.

"I'd like you to eat with me — it doesn't have to be at the table, it could be on one of the couches or something. I've never liked eating alone."

Oh. He nudged Dane's hand, nodding. All the wonderful things Dane had offered him, he would be happy to eat together.

"Thank you, Tyg." Dane beamed at him and rubbed his head.

He moved into the kitchen, unsure whether he was

supposed to help, to watch.

"You want to help?" Dane asked him. "I'm not sure how much... undoggy stuff you want to do."

"I. Yves made the decisions. I can help."

"Well, if that's what you want, I suppose we can do it that way, but I would be more comfortable supporting your choices."

"I..." He shrugged, uncomfortable, nervous. "I never had choices."

"A bit overwhelming, is it?"

He nodded. "Yes. Scary."

"Well, I think you should get used to it. I'm not a domineering man. Now, I like dogs. I love dogs, so I'm very happy to have you as my pup, but if you want me to order you around and make you do things you don't want to..." Dane shook his head. "I don't think I can do that."

He nodded again. Okay. Okay. He would get used to it or at least pretend he was. He stood up, like a man, swaying a little. "What do I do?"

"You don't have to stand if you don't want to — you can be a dog, Tyg, but even most dogs get to do what they want." Dane sighed. "I just want you to be happy, Tyg."

He faded a little, suddenly tired in his bones. "Bed." Tyg headed back down the hall, sliding back into the bed, under his blanket.

Dane's hands were warm on him, petting him. "Tyg?"

He nodded, looking over at Dane, curious.

"Are you okay?"

He shrugged, then nodded. He wasn't dying, wasn't being beaten. He was clean.

Dane sighed. "Poor pup." The man lay down behind him, curling against his back, hand stroking along his side. "It's okay, Tyg, it'll all work out."

He nodded, tears sliding from his eyes, surprising him. He'd been Yves' forever, tried so hard, then he was no one's and now...

Now he wasn't sure what he was.

"Okay, Tyg, okay." Dane just kept petting him, murmuring soothing words.

He sobbed, the dam inside him unable to hold back his emotions.

His pain. His fear. His hope.

Dane held him, rocked him, petted him.

He whined, reaching out for Dane, holding on.

"Right here, Tyg. I'm not going anywhere. I've got you." The words were accompanied by more soft touches.

Dane had him. Had him.

He pushed closer, cuddling. Snuggling.

"Mmmm, sweet puppy."

Tyg blushed dark, but nuzzled in, groaning. Dane made a soft noise and held him close.

Oh, it felt good. Warm. Right.

Dane held him and stroked him and slowly fell asleep wrapped around him. He relaxed, eyes closing, nose nudging against Dane's arm, inhaling deep.

Dane murmured and pulled him closer, petting him absently.

Yes. Good dog.

Good dog.

Tyg and Dane Discover Pleasure Together

Dane woke several hours later, Tyg still sleeping hard, curled up under the blue blanket, snuggled up to him. He petted Tyg gently. Poor pup. For all Tyg was actually a human being, the abuse had affected him much as it would a real dog, except that Tyg was much smarter than a dog and no doubt less likely to trust again. It was criminal, what had been done to Tyg. Which reminded him, he needed to check with Mal, see if charges had been pressed against the man who'd done this. He would have recommended it even if Tyg had not been human.

He petted Tyg again and got up carefully, sliding out of the bed so he wouldn't wake the pup.

A short visit to the bathroom and then he was in the kitchen, going through the fridge. He needed to put a food order in. Fresh milk daily — a quart to start with — meats, breads, light on the vegetables, eggs, bacon, and a request for two slices of dessert to be delivered, something different each day from whatever the kitchen had available. If Tyg turned out not to have a sweet tooth, he'd... well, he'd have to indulge alone. Sweets were one of his favorites.

He took care of the order, using the comm to send it to food services, and found an orange to snack on. Once it was peeled, he settled in an armchair in the sitting room, slowly eating the sections as he went through some of the files on animal play that Andy had forwarded to him.

He heard the bed creak, heard Tyg padding about, the water running for a while in the bathroom, the cooler opening and closing, the thirsty gulps. Maybe a gallon of milk would have been better...

Then Tyg wandered in, blinking slowly, licking his lips before settling on the sofa with a soft sigh.

Dane shut down his handheld and finished his last section of orange, then stretched and licked the juice from his fingers. "Hey, Tyg. How are you feeling?"

The pup's nose looked terrible, both eyes black and swollen, but Tyg gave him a smile, a nod. "Better. E... empty? But better. Smells good."

"Empty? Oh, you're hungry. I thought we could order a couple of steaks from the kitchen, as we've nothing in the pantry right now. We'll start making our own tomorrow."

"Steak..." He could hear Tyg's stomach growl, see those eyes light up.

"How do you like it done, Tyg? Rare?" He'd order salads as well, find out if Tyg had given vegetables up altogether or if he still ate that kind of thing, without having to ask more questions, which seemed to make the pup nervous.

"Medium rare. N... no pepper, please."

"Sounds good." He placed their orders with the kitchen and went to sit with Tyg. "May I join you?"

Tyg nodded, shifting to give him room.

He sat, hand going to Tyg's head, petting the shorn head. "Are you going to let this grow out now? If not, we should shave it again soon."

Tyg leaned toward his touch, breath tickling his arm. "Do you care?"

"Yes, I do. I care that you're happy."

"I don't like having my hair pulled." The words were firm, sure.

Poor pup. "I don't blame you — I don't like it much, myself. If you decide to grow it again, I can promise you

I won't intentionally pull it."

Tyg nodded, nuzzled his hand with soft lips. "Thank you."

"You're welcome."

It made him furious. That such common decency would have to be asked for, begged for perhaps, even. He took a deep breath, keeping himself calm — he didn't want Tyg to believe he was angry with the pup.

Tyg slowly relaxed, carefully resting the shorn head in his lap. He relaxed as well, petting Tyg, enjoying the peace between them. He'd always found something soothing in having a pet, caring for it. Having another human being to care for was that much better.

He nearly jumped out of his skin when the discreet knock sounded at the door.

Tyg leapt up, a warning growl filling the air, the pup's teeth bared.

He stroked his hand down along Tyg's back. "It's all right, Tyg. It should just be our steaks."

He gave Tyg another reassuring stroke and went to the door. Sure enough, there was a boy with a rolling table, two covered plates on it.

The boy stepped in, eyes going wide at the sight of Tyg. "Oh. Wow. He's... uh... free."

"It's fine, he won't hurt you." He gave the boy a reassuring smile and took the end of the table, pulling it over to the couch. "Do I just leave this outside the door when we're done?"

"Yeah. Yeah." The boy nodded, eyes on Tyg. "I... I'm glad you got free. I hated seeing you in that cage. Honest."

"It was awful, wasn't it?" He smiled again at the boy, a little warmer this time.

The boy nodded. "Yeah. He looked... sad. I'm glad he's out. Maybe he'll get to come out and meet all of us, yeah?"

"One day. When he's comfortable. I think that would be wonderful."

If Tyg were a real dog, he'd be looking for someone like this boy to take him in when he'd finished sorting Tyg out. But he didn't think that would be happening this time. Tyg didn't need to be passed around, and he himself was already more than a little fond.

"Yeah. Me, too. Enjoy your supper." The boy waved, gave Tyg a smile and left, humming. Tyg looked a little confused, disconcerted.

He smiled and petted Tyg. "A nice boy. Maybe he'll be a friend one day like Richard."

Tyg shivered, almost whimpered. "He saw me, before."

"Yes, and he thought it was a shame to see a pup locked up in a cage like that."

Tyg nodded, growled. "No one came."

He petted Tyg again. "I know. I'm sorry."

"Yes. I am, too." Tyg nodded, eyes meeting his. "It makes me angry."

"It should. It makes me angry, too. It was a wrong thing to do."

"Yes." Tyg looked surprised, head tilting. "Yes, it was. I was not bad."

"That's right, Tyg. You weren't bad. He was a bad man to do that to you." Poor pup.

Tyg nodded, an ever-present tension seeming to shimmer around those massive shoulders. "I want to hurt him back."

"I don't blame you. But when they find him? He will be locked in a cage of his own."

Another nod, then Tyg's eyes flashed to the food. "Eat now?"

"Yes. Let's eat now." He petted Tyg's head and settled

39

on the couch, lifting the covers off the food dishes.

Tyg settled beside him, low hungry sounds filling the air, the strong hands awkward and trembling over the flatware.

"You can use your hands if you like."

"Could... would you cut it?" Those expressive eyes dropped, a flush covering Tyg's cheeks.

"Of course." He cut Tyg's meat into bite-sized chunks, then handed the fork to Tyg and went back to eating his own.

Tyg ate slowly at first, and then faster once he'd gotten the taste. Dane enjoyed his steak at his own pace. He hadn't had one this good since... well, since never. The quality of the meat was high, the chef obviously excellent. The salad was no less excellent. He couldn't wait for dessert, and if Tyg didn't like sweets? He was eating both.

Tyg ate the lettuce but avoided the dressing, devoured the bread and the potato, ignored the peas altogether.

He offered Tyg most of his own bread as he was beginning to get full. Tyg gave a soft purr of thanks, eating it all and then almost cuddling into him. He put his arm around the pup, petting and stroking. Such a good dog. He couldn't understand why anyone would want to hurt Tyg, would abandon him like that. Of course he never understood it, no matter how often he saw it.

"There's dessert." He took the cover off the last tray, which had two plates with berry trifle on them.

Tyg's nostrils flared, the pup licking his lips. "Oh..."

Dane chuckled. That answered that question.

He put one of the plates in front of Tyg along with a spoon. "Enjoy."

Tyg scooped up a fingerful of cream, licking at it, moaning low. Dane dug into his dessert eagerly and wound up moaning himself. Oh, it was exquisite. Just wonderful.

Tyg ate about half, and then a bite was offered to him, spoon held in trembling fingers.

He bent and took the mouthful, moaning again. "Thank you, Tyg. It's very good, isn't it?"

Tyg nodded. "Like."

"Yeah, me, too." He offered a spoonful from his.

Tyg's tongue slid out, licked the spoon clean.

He was struck suddenly by how intimate it was, sharing their spoons. Their desserts were the same, yet they were offering each other tastes. He kind of liked it.

He offered Tyg another spoonful. Tyg lapped the spoon clean, then moved to lick at his fingers. It was a perfectly natural doggy thing to do. But Tyg wasn't a dog, and heat slid through Dane's belly at the touches.

Those eyes kept hold of his, tongue sliding over his palm. He gasped as the heat blossomed.

Tyg stilled, eyes fastened on him, questioning.

He smiled, curled his fingers to stroke Tyg's cheek. "It's all right. Good dog."

Tyg leaned into the touch, a low vibration filling the air.

According to all the documentation he'd read from Mal, most 'dog'... owners had sex with their 'puppies'. He hadn't expected... well, he wasn't even sure if Tyg was offering, but he was aroused and he cared for Tyg and if that's what Tyg wanted, he was prepared to go there.

Of course, he was also prepared for poor Tyg to panic again. Or perhaps the poor pup was merely reaching for comfort.

Dane was going to play it by ear. And at the moment his ear was telling him that Tyg was enjoying his attentions and he was enjoying Tyg's.

Dane kept stroking, murmuring softly, telling Tyg how lovely he was, how good. Tyg was obviously aroused, trying to hide the thick cock between the muscled thighs.

Which was a shame because it was a beautiful cock, especially erect. Large and dark; he liked them large.

"It's okay, Tyg. I'm aroused as well."

Tyg growled, shifting closer, then pulling away as if caught between aggression and submission.

"We're learning each other, finding our way. You won't be punished for what you do, Tyg. Follow your instincts."

That huge head pushed back into his hands, Tyg's face rubbing into his belly.

"Oh." He dropped his hands to Tyg's head, rubbing and petting. "There, see. We're both feeling good."

Tyg nodded, cheek sliding against him, breath hot against him. "Dane."

He made a soft sound of pleasure, trying very hard not to push up against Tyg. Heat brushed against him, Tyg licking, lapping, nuzzling against his buttons, searching for skin.

He unbuttoned his shirt and shrugged out of it, giving Tyg access, moaning at the first touch of Tyg's tongue against him. Tyg was making hungry, needy sounds, licking his nipples, his ribs, his belly. He arched and jerked beneath Tyg's tongue, cock stiff as a board in his pants.

He pushed a hand between them, sliding it along Tyg's chest, finding one of the pup's nipples and stroking. Tyg rippled, hips rocking, almost fucking the air, mouth traveling down to nuzzle his cock.

He stopped what he was doing long enough to undo his pants, his cock pushing out as he freed it, his breath noisy and gasping. Tyg made a hungry, needy sound, lips dropping over him, taking him in a single motion.

"Oh!" He cried out, hands dropping to Tyg's head, fingers trembling as he stroked, encouraged. "Tyg. Good. Oh. Oh." Pleasure was shooting through him, so unexpected, so good.

Head bobbing, mouth and lips and tongue working furiously, Tyg drove him to pleasure with a single-minded intensity.

His hips started moving, pushing up into Tyg's mouth. "Tyg! Coming. Oh!" Hips snapping, he came, pleasure like an electric shock through his body.

Tyg drank him down, then licked him clean, tongue so hot, so soft.

"Oh. Oh, Tyg. Thank you. Thank you." He stroked Tyg's head and shoulders, every now and then a shiver going through him, lovely aftershocks.

"Now, what about you?"

Tyg shivered, nuzzling his cock and balls, lapping them gently. He tugged gently, trying to pull Tyg up so he could reach the large prick. Tyg shifted, sliding up his body, eyes fastened on his own.

"I would like very much to kiss you."

Tyg's eyes went wide, the look surprised and wanting and pleased all at once. "Really?"

He nodded and pressed their mouths together, lips moving over Tyg's. Tyg tasted like cream and him and berries. The kiss felt inexpert, clumsy, as if Tyg wasn't sure what to do, what to think.

He slid his tongue between Tyg's lips, hands moving down over the long back. Tyg was warm, strong, muscles rippling. He hummed softly, one hand going down to caress Tyg's ass, the other sliding around and finding the long, hard cock. A soft cry pressed past his lips, strong hips rocking.

Yes, Tyg, good dog. He circled Tyg's cock, hand sliding on the hot flesh. It felt good. It felt even better knowing it was pleasuring Tyg. Shudders rocked Tyg, the lovely eyes closed, breath coming sharp and fast. He licked and nibbled at Tyg's lips, free hand moving to find Tyg's nipples, fingers sliding across them.

"Please. I can't. It's been so long..." The words were whimpered.

"Come, Tyg. Let go. Enjoy."

Those eyes searched his own, full of raw disbelief. "I can?"

Oh.

Oh, Tyg was going to make him cry. Or scream and rage. Perhaps both.

"Yes." He closed his mouth on Tyg's again, kissing fiercely, hand working Tyg's prick, finger sliding across the slit.

Tyg jerked, hips moving furiously, slapping against his palm until heat spread between them, the scent strong, heady. He hummed happily into Tyg's mouth, kiss gentling, hand still moving, bringing Tyg down. The soft, low sounds pushed in, tongue sliding against his.

He wrapped his arms around Tyg, stroking and touching, loving on Tyg. Tyg pushed against him, cuddling, responding so well.

"Good, Tyg. So good. Thank you."

"G... good." Tyg ended, head in his lap, tears flowing. "Thank you."

He wiped the tears away as they flowed, figuring they were healing tears, necessary. "That was lovely. You're lovely."

"Want to stay with you. Don't want to go back."

He didn't answer straight away, gave Tyg's words the proper thought. He had no wish to lose Tyg to another or to send him back to the kennels. He wanted Tyg for himself. As a pup, as a lover, as whatever Tyg wanted, needed.

He nodded. "Yes, Tyg. You can stay with me. I won't send you back, I won't send you anywhere."

Tyg didn't speak, simply nodded and relaxed, the huge body going limp and heavy in his lap, Tyg trusting him.

It felt good, sitting with Tyg, loving with Tyg, feeling the trust between them.

An almost-there kiss brushed his thigh, a soft, satisfied sigh sounding.

"Good Tyg. So good," he murmured, smiling.

"Good." Tyg's eyes closed and the soft snores started. His comm buzzed, Andy's face appearing

"Yes, Andy?" he asked quietly.

"Dane? Is everything okay? One of the little workerbees told Mal that Tyg looked like he'd been beaten in the face. Are you okay? Did he try to hurt you?"

He probably should have expected this call, but he'd been so focused on Tyg. "Not me — he threw himself at the window, broke his nose. And he was too spooked to take to the doctor if he didn't need one, which he didn't. Broken noses look far worse than they are. It's going well, Andy. I'm fairly confident there won't be any more incidents like that one. I think Tyg finally believes he won't be caged or sent away."

"Oh, poor pup." Andy visibly relaxed, then looked at him, eyes sharp. "I'll be a monkey. You've claimed him as yours? Already? Our aggressive, growly pup? Congratulations!"

Dane blushed, but he was smiling. "Not so aggressive and growly when he's treated right. And thank you. And the best part is he's safe now. Have you heard any news on where his former... owner is? Have they brought him to justice yet?"

Andy shook his head. "I'm going to give you access to all the reports, the files, images of the man, in case he comes back to... Well, in case."

Tyg shifted, whimpering softly.

He petted Tyg gently, soothing his pup. "Make sure the front desk has those pictures, too. I don't want Tyg to even catch a glimpse of him."

Andy nodded. "I hear you. Tyg doesn't need that. Hopefully he's off-planet and never coming back."

"Hopefully he's dead." He spat the words out, letting the poisonous thoughts out.

"That would be best, yes. Although, I would have him starved and beaten to pay for Tyg's pain."

"Oh, that's how I'd like him to have died." He forced himself to breathe again, petting Tyg gently. "Was there anything else, Andy?"

"No. No, I was just checking on you and the pup. Thought you'd rather it be me on the comm than Mal banging at your door."

"Goodness, yes, Mal would have scared Tyg to death. Thank you. As soon as Tyg's up to it, I'll bring him down to see the doctor. And if he wants, we'll visit you and the other pups. But it has to be if he wants."

Andy nodded. "It might take a while. He needs his privacy, his own space. Maybe we can have a little pool party in a few weeks. Enjoy your pup. Oh! If you need... accoutrements? Collar, tail, muzzle — I order those items custom."

"If he wants that we know who to see. A pool party sounds fun. Tyg loves the water. Say, some of the pools are private, aren't they?"

Andy nodded. "Yeah, you just reserve them and they're all yours."

"Wonderful. Thank you, Andy. I'll keep you apprised of Tyg's progress." Within reason. Tyg deserved his privacy.

He signed off and put the comm down, curling up on the couch with Tyg.

Tyg nuzzled right into him, arms and legs curling around him, lips brushing his skin. Oh. Oh, sweet pup. Such a lover hiding behind that growl. He kept stroking Tyg, enjoying their closeness, the bond that was growing between them.

He closed his eyes and relaxed into the comfort.

Tyg is Dane's

He was happy. Warm. Safe. Loved. Well-fed. Given milk every day.

Bored.

Really bored.

He watched Dane closely, watched the pen in one hand, the commpad in the other. When he knew he could get away with it, Tyg grabbed the commpad and ran, chuffing with laughter.

"Tyg!" Dane sounded shocked, or at least like he was trying to sound shocked, the laughter kind of gave him away. And then the chase was on.

Tyg feinted toward the spare room before heading into their bedroom and ducking beside the bed, hind quarters almost wagging with pleasure. Dane came barreling in a moment later, going to the closet and pulling covers off the bed before he was seen.

"There you are!"

He barked and pounced, laughing good and hard.

He and Dane went down together on the bed, Dane laughing with him, hands sliding over his skin. He wriggled under the touch, nuzzling the soft belly, searching for more laughing sounds. They came easily, Dane laughing and writhing.

He pounced on Dane, then bounced off to the other side of the bed, crouching low, wiggling, waiting. Still laughing, Dane pounced on him.

Tyg barked again, happy, laughing hard, rolling and rubbing as they moved. This time it was Dane who tickled him, hands finding his ribs and digging in. He laughed harder and harder, arching to get away, cock beginning to fill.

Dane finally stopped tickling, lying on top of him and panting, eyes twinkling. "Oh, Tyg, that was fun. I can't remember when I last laughed so much."

He hugged Dane, the happiness so big it was almost frightening.

Dane kept smiling, slowly putting their mouths together. Oh. He was getting used to this, to the kisses. Dane was generous with them, offering them over and over in their day — breakfast, bathing, sleeping, waking.

Dane's tongue danced into his mouth and then out again, playing tag. He played along, chasing Dane's tongue, tasting the happiness, the pleasure. Dane hummed, the growing, familiar sound making their mouths vibrate.

He pressed closer, snuggling, hands rubbing Dane's belly. Dane touched him, too, fingers sliding along his sides and then over his nipples. Those touches made low, rough sounds pour out of him, made him hungry.

"Oh, Tyg, you're so warm and good to touch." Dane's mouth slid along his jaw, to his ear, nibbling.

"Like touching. Like this. You. Us."

"Yes, we're good together, aren't we?" Dane's tongue slid on his neck.

"Oh..." He shivered, chin lifting.

Dane hummed, licking, teeth scraping very gently. Tyg shivered again, pressing closer. So sensitive. No one had touched him like that there.

"Mmm, you like that." Dane licked and then scraped and then licked again.

"Y... I'm yours. Like that." The words were soft, whispered.

"Oh..." A shiver went through Dane. "Would you like me to mark you, Tyg?"

He whimpered, rubbing closer. "Oh. Would be yours.

Yes. Yes."

Dane rubbed against him. "You're mine anyway, Tyg, but I would be pleased if you wore my collar or a tattoo to show you are mine." Dane licked his neck again. "For right now I'll mark you with my mouth."

He was rubbing, humping shamelessly against Dane's body, caught by Dane's words. Dane hummed and then scraped his neck hard, lips wrapping around the spot and sucking. His head slammed back, hips moving furiously, honored and aroused beyond belief. Dane continued sucking, teeth sliding now and then against his skin. One of Dane's hands reached down and cupped his balls.

"Dane. Need. Need. Please." The room was spinning, his heart pounding.

"Yes, Tyg, please come." Dane licked at the place he'd been leaving a mark.

"Thank you. Thank you. Th..." He howled, body shuddering violently as pleasure poured out of him, sprayed against Dane.

Dane moaned, bringing their lips together, licking inside his mouth. Tyg moaned, pushing into the kiss, so happy, so needy. Dane hummed some more, sucking in his tongue.

His fingers started pushing away clothes, looking for skin, wanting to touch. He had never been allowed this before — allowed to touch, to feel. He could use his tongue, that was all. And now Dane was showing him so much.

Dane whimpered, helping him with the clothing until they were touching skin on skin. Dane's cock was so hot against his belly. He started licking, heading down to taste, to lap, to suck.

"Oh... your mouth feels so good." Dane's hands slid over his head, rubbing against the short hair that was growing back in.

He nodded, tongue sliding. He worked hard to not hurt, to make it good, to not bite.

"Wait," murmured Dane. "Let's try this."

Dane shifted and turned and worked until they were both face to cock, Dane's tongue sliding on his prick.

"Dane!" He looked down, gasping, groaning. "Oh. Oh, You're. To me. I. Oh."

Dane looked up at him. "You'll like it, trust me."

"You..." He met those happy eyes, needing answers so badly. "You don't think it's dirty to do that to me? You don't think it's nasty?"

Dane leaned up on his elbow. "Do you think it's nasty? Doing it to me?"

"No. No, I like to taste. I like to feel you."

Dane smiled. "Me, too."

He smiled back. Every day something within him lightened, some long-held shame eased. Dane reached over and stroked his cheek, and then lay back down again and licked the tip of his cock.

"Oh..." He purred, lips parting to take Dane's cock in deep.

Dane shuddered and whimpered, licking and nibbling at his cock. It felt amazing, so hot, so good, and it made him hungry, head bobbing, eyes rolling as he sucked. Dane's lips closed around the tip of his prick, sucking gently, tongue sliding across the tip, pressing into his slit.

He made noises around Dane's cock, head moving faster. Dane started moving with him, pushing into his mouth as more of his cock was taken into the incredible heat of Dane's mouth. It was as if they were linked, both moving together, both needing. Both loving. Tyg groaned low, the love reverberating within him. Loving.

Dane's head began to bob like his, finding his rhythm, sharing it. He let himself simply feel — no thinking, no worrying, no fear. Dane was humming again, making his flesh vibrate. He buried his face in Dane's pubes, purring.

Dane jerked, sucking hard as come filled his mouth. He swallowed hard, hips moving, thrusting, rocking as his own orgasm took him, sent him flying. Dane swallowed him down, took him in.

He reached out, fingers trembling as he soared. Dane's hand found his, held onto him.

Resting his cheek on Dane's thigh, Tyg relaxed, moaned. "L...love."

"Oh, Tyg, yes. I love you, too."

He whimpered, squeezed Dane's hand. "Oh."

Dane shifted once more, moving around so they were face to face again. Soft kisses rained on his face. "My Tyg."

Oh. Oh. "Yours. Yes. Yours."

Dane nodded, finger sliding along the mark on his neck. "Yes."

He shivered, arching. "Yours."

And Yves could never have him back.

"So what do you want? A dog collar? A tattoo? A ring?"

"A tattoo is forever." And Dane could never take it off, take it away.

"A 'D' maybe? Where would you like it?" Dane rubbed the mark on his neck again. "Somewhere very visible."

He nodded, pressing Dane's hand to his throat. "Here?"

Dane nodded. "Yes. And I'll get a little 't' put in the hollow of my own throat."

His eyes went wide. "A t. For... for me?"

"Yes, Tyg, for you."

Tears filled his eyes and he nodded, blinking hard.

"Oh, Tyg. I can't wait for the day when treating you right is something you come to expect." Dane wiped away his tears with gentle fingers.

"Happy. Happy tears."

"I know." Dane kissed his cheeks. "I know."

He snuggled in, nuzzling. "Mine Dane."

Dane chuckled. "Yes, Tyg. Yours."

Oh, that laugh made him fly. "Yes." He stroked Dane's belly. "Love."

"Mmm... yes, love." Dane settled against him.

He held Dane close, hands stroking the strong spine.

"Such a good dog," Dane murmured. "My Tyg."

Tyg nodded. "Yes." He smiled wide. "Yes."

Dane's.

Tyg and Dane Leave Their Rooms

Dane was excited.

They were venturing out.

It was about six in the morning, almost guaranteeing them a quiet trip down the elevator to one of the private pools. They weren't expecting to run into anyone, which was how he'd planned it. But he knew Tyg was getting as stir-crazy as he was. Nice as their rooms were, they needed a change.

It was the first step to bringing Doc in to check Tyg out, and to bringing someone in to do the tattoos.

"Come on, Tyg, are you ready to go?"

Tyg was vibrating in place, eyes alight, panting, nodding.

"Good. Me, too."

He opened the door and checked the hall, nodding and stepping out when it proved to be empty. Tyg followed him, heat sure and close against his back. He could feel Tyg's quiet breath on the back of his neck.

He reached back and slid his hand along Tyg's arm. "Would you like to walk next to me?"

"Oh... Yes. Yes, please." Tyg moved up next to him, shivering.

He smiled at Tyg and took the big hand in his own. "There, that's better."

"Yes." He got a grin, a nuzzle of the big head. "Better."

It felt good, getting out, having Tyg beside him.

The lift arrived almost as soon as he pressed the button, which was reassuring — it looked like the place really was deserted this time in the morning. Tyg walked into the lift, watching everything, breathing quickly.

He squeezed Tyg's hand. "If you change your mind, I won't be mad."

"No. I want out. I want." Tyg smiled at him, held on.

"You're going to love the pool. Have you ever been to one?"

The lift wouldn't take long to bring them down to the pools, but he figured it wouldn't hurt to keep Tyg distracted.

"No. No. I saw them once, but wasn't allowed in."

He shook his head. "As much as you love the water? That's a shame. Oh, here we are."

The lift doors slid open. Those fingers tightened around his, squeezing, Tyg almost bouncing. He grinned and stepped out with Tyg. The corridor was deserted. Perfect.

The boy he'd reserved the pool with had told him it was the third door on the right once you exited the lifts, so that's where he headed, looking for " Pool Room Three." He found it, palmed opened the door to a beautiful pool, gently lit, water perfect and clean.

"Oh, how wonderful! Look, Tyg!" He drew Tyg in, closing the door behind them.

Tyg blinked, stepping forward. "Oh, Dane. We can swim and swim."

He chuckled and rubbed Tyg's back. "Yes, Tyg. Go on. I'll just take off my clothes and join you."

His pup ran for the edge, climbing in eagerly. He stopped for a moment, watching Tyg's joy. It made him feel so good. Tyg moved through the water, unafraid, graceful.

Tyg was beautiful.

He got undressed and slipped into the water, swimming lazily. Tyg moved up against him, legs brushing against his before Tyg slipped away. He loved that Tyg was comfortable enough with him to tease and play.

He turned onto his back and watched Tyg swim. Tyg luxuriated in the water, slipping and sliding and playing. It was amazing how much joy Tyg could find in little things.

Dane just couldn't understand why anyone would want to curb that enthusiasm, joy, and life.

Tyg scooted close again, nudging him. "Love."

He reached out and slid his hand along Tyg's chest. Tyg's skin was slick and cool from the water. "Love, Tyg."

He got a huge grin, a hug. "Yes!"

He laughed and wrapped his arms around Tyg's neck as they half sank. Tyg's hands circled his waist, legs moving restlessly. He wrapped his own arms around Tyg's waist, holding on, trusting.

Tyg watched him, one hand sliding through his hair. "My Dane."

He rubbed their noses together, body sliding against the warmth of Tyg's. "Yes. Yours. And you are mine."

Tyg nodded again, cock beginning to fill, hands petting him gently. "Yes. Only yours."

He hummed, his own cock rising to meet Tyg's, to rub against the muscled belly. His fingers stroked the fading mark on Tyg's neck. That got him a shudder, a stretch, a swallowed cry.

"The mark is going away," he told Tyg. "I'm going to give you another. Just until we can get your tattoo done."

"Yes. Your Tyg." Tyg's cock leapt, pushing against him.

He loved that he'd found something that brought Tyg such pleasure, something that he enjoyed as well, though he'd never imagined himself the possessive type.

He leaned in, licking at Tyg's neck, searching for a sensitive spot. When he found it, Tyg whimpered, swallowing, throat working under his tongue. He kept licking, threatening now and then with his teeth, drawing the sensations out, trusting Tyg to keep them afloat.

The sounds Tyg offered him were amazing, warm. Happy and honest and so fine. He closed his lips around Tyg's skin and started sucking, pulling up Tyg's blood to the surface. The hand on his hip tightened, their bodies beginning to rock together.

He hummed around Tyg's flesh, moving with Tyg, moving with the rhythm of his suction.

A little bark sounded, then his name, then love.

He scraped his teeth across his mark as he pulled off it, licking it before looking into Tyg's face. "Mine."

"Yes. Yours. Yours." Tyg leaned down, lips nuzzling his throat. "Will you take me now? Touch me inside?"

His cock throbbed and he rubbed against Tyg's belly. "Oh... Oh, Tyg, I would love to. Let's... There's mats by the side of the water – let's go there."

Tyg nodded, moving with him, cock nudging his thigh, his hip. They swam toward the edge, Tyg carrying him, kissing and licking, rubbing together as they moved through the water. The ease and pleasure in Tyg was heady, exciting, gratifying.

They got out of the pool and he kissed Tyg, humming into his pup's mouth. "How do you want it, Tyg? Hands and knees? Or on your back?"

"I..." Tyg gave him another confused look. "On my back?"

He reached out and stroked Tyg's face. Poor pup, abused in so many ways. "So we can face each other?"

"Oh." Tyg smiled, pushed into his touch. "I like to see you."

He beamed at Tyg. Such a sweet, wonderful man —

why would anyone want to hurt him?

"Then lie on your back, my own. I'm going to get some lube — I'm betting there's some in that supply cabinet."

Tyg stretched out, toes curling slowly, a sweet humming sound filling the air as his lover waited.

He found lube along with medical supplies and some rather interesting-looking items, not all of which he recognized, in the cupboard. He just took the lube and returned to settle between Tyg's spread legs.

"You're not going to make me hurt." It wasn't a question; Tyg's hips tilted, body offered freely.

"I'm going to make you fly, my Tyg." He bent and kissed Tyg, tongue sliding into the wet heat.

Tyg's hands circled his shoulders, fingers trailing over his skin and petting him. He hummed into Tyg's mouth and then began to tease one slick finger around Tyg's hole. Tyg tensed for a heartbeat, then relaxed, fingers holding him close.

He pushed his finger in, breaching the tight ring. A soft sound pressed into his lips, Tyg watching him, waiting. He pushed his finger all the way in and then pulled back, slowly fucking Tyg with it. Tyg's face relaxed, hips starting to respond with slow undulations. He licked at Tyg's lips, watching the lovely eyes as his finger moved inside Tyg.

"You're feeling me."

"Yes. And you're hot and soft and tight."

"Good?" Tyg's fingers brushed his face.

"Oh, yes. You're going to feel so good around my cock."

He teased a second finger in.

Tyg purred, lips coming open a little. "Yours. You..." Tyg leaned up, whispered in his ear. "When you are inside me, I will not remember him."

Oh.

He whimpered, pushing his fingers inside Tyg, curling

them to find that little gland.

"Dane!" Tyg jerked, moaning low, hips rocking.

"That's it, Tyg, feel it, feel the pleasure." He kept hitting the spot, mouth sliding over Tyg's face.

The words stopped, only surprised, unbelieving sounds poured out, Tyg flushed and moving, crying out in pure need. So beautiful in his need, so sad that Tyg had never felt this pleasure before. At the same time, he got a thrill, knowing he was the first to teach Tyg how good this could be.

He moved his mouth down to Tyg's chest, sucking one of the flat nipples into his mouth. Tyg's body rippled, then arched, hips moving in quick, furious jerks.

He hummed around Tyg's nipple, pushing in a third finger, fucking Tyg's hard. Tyg cried out, spunk spraying, hot and heady. He kept moving his fingers, encouraging Tyg to stay hard as he slid his mouth down to lick away the come from Tyg's belly.

The jerks became rolling undulations, Tyg panting and moaning.

He licked Tyg clean, kissed the tip of his pup's cock, and then let his fingers slide away, settling with his cock at Tyg's entrance. Tyg shifted, slick, hot body slipping over his prick, drawing him in. With a moan, Dane pushed in, Tyg's body so tight and hot.

"Dane..." Tyg's eyes were shining, fastened onto him, warm and happy.

He drove in Tyg's heat over and over again, finding a solid, pleasurable rhythm. "I love you, Tyg."

"Love. Love. Love." Tyg rocked, focused on him, on them.

"Yes, my Tyg. Love." He shifted until he again found Tyg's gland and his hand wrapped around Tyg's cock.

"Oh." Tyg's head left the mat, shoulders curling.

"That's it, Tyg. Feel how good it is. Show me. Come

for me."

"For you." The words were sobbed, Tyg's body gripping him tight, milking him.

He cried out as he came, filling Tyg deep inside.

Tyg's hands were on his face, his hair. "Love..."

It was perfect, warm, and he nuzzled Tyg's throat.

He never heard the approaching footsteps, didn't hear anything but Tyg's growl, and then everything went black.

Tyg is Lost and Tyg is Found

Malachi hit the med door running, Kestrel and Hercules right behind him. "Doc! Is he awake? Does he know what happened? Does he know where they went?"

Fuck.

Fuck.

Pool Room Three was a devastation, blood and hair splattered everywhere, tiles broken. The communication department was trying to isolate the vidfeed still; it had been so long that they weren't practiced.

How the *fuck* did that bastard get in? Whoever let Yves walk past was going to die.

Slowly.

On a spit.

"I said let me up! I don't care if you would rather I stay for observation, I have to find him!" Well, that answered the question of whether or not Dane was awake.

He came out of the back room, with an unhappy-looking Doc trailing him. Mal had never seen Dane so pale, mouth set in an angry line, eyes furious.

"You! How the hell did this happen?"

"Me? What the fuck? I run the training salle, I am not head of security. Back the fuck off." He met fire with ice, staring Dane down.

"No. I am head of security and I just found my Billy dead in a maintenance closet." Monk, the massive head of security, was grey as fog, the only color the red spots on his cheeks. "But, before the fucker killed him, Billy locked the Club down. He's got to be here. No one left."

"Oh, God." Dane looked for a moment as if he was going to faint, but then he recovered and pushed past them, shouting out Tyg's name at the top of his lungs as he went.

"Fuck. Herc? Do something!" He followed Dane, completely fucking not sure what to do.

"All right," snapped Hercules. "Everybody just stop."

Even Dane stopped at the sharp tone of command in Herc's voice.

"I want every room locked down. No one goes anywhere. Monk, I want teams of two searching every nook and cranny, every room — no matter who it belongs to — until they're found. Mal, Dane and I will search the places Dane thinks they might be."

That tone relaxed Mal immediately and he nodded, suddenly right back online. "Kes. You get those geeks in communications to start looking with the camera. I want the heat sensors to tell me if there's a body where there shouldn't be, and I want to see the vid from Pool Room Three." He stopped suddenly. "Somebody comm Andy and Bear. If there's a place that bastard can cause mass chaos, it's there."

"I bet he's in the rooms he had while he was here," said Dane, heading off for the lifts.

"And he plans to get into them, how?" Herc asked, staring after Dane's quickly disappearing back. "Does he even know which ones they are?"

"The man lived here abusing Tyg for five years, Boss, and not one of us ever noticed. I wouldn't put anything past him."

He stopped short at Herc's look. "Oh. Dane. Right. Sorry. How the fuck should I know? The man just got whacked in the head."

Dane turned back toward them as the lift doors

opened. "Well? Are you two coming? The longer you spend blathering on, the longer my pup is being tortured. And if I find him on my own, I will tear the man limb from limb and then let Tyg eat him."

"Wait!" Kestrel came flying out of the med unit, hair wild. "There's a disturbance in the kitchen. Moffat's hurt, two of the worker bees, too."

Fuck.

"Monk?"

Monk nodded and they started moving, Monk comming his little squad of bad-asses to join them.

They all piled into the elevator, Dane practically vibrating.

"Kes? Jim's going to kick your ass. You're as useful around blood as a washrag in a flood."

"Bitch."

"Flit."

Monk looked over, arched an eyebrow. "Is the doc here? Or are we taking people up?"

"I'm here. Being squished by your extremely large muscles, Mr. Monk."

"Damnit," growled Dane, hitting the button for the kitchen floor again.

"Relax," Hercules suggested. "You aren't going to be any use to him going off half-cocked."

The howls of fury could be heard as the lift opened, the sound bone-chilling and horrifying. They moved down the hall, meeting Moffat first, the man's arm and shoulder cut, holding closed a cut on an unconscious sub's head. The other worker bee was pacing, nose bleeding, sobbing.

Moffat gave them a look, then nodded to the kitchen. "They were both torn to hell. The blond one's got a cage-thing around the big one's head, got a taser. The blond one's bleeding bad, though."

Dane shouted Tyg's name and sprinted toward the noise.

"He's going to get himself killed," growled Hercules. "Monk!"

The huge man reached out, grabbed Dane with one massive hand, and shoved him back into Hercules' arms. Rog and Trevor came around the corner, stunners drawn, and Monk overrode the code keeping the kitchen door closed.

The scene that appeared was out of a vid — Yves, who Mal remembered as a sophisticated dandy, was flailing at Tyg with a steel-tipped whip, tearing the man's skin. Tyg's head was covered in a steel cage, the base digging into the thick neck. Every blow that landed on Tyg was answered, Tyg literally beating the man to a pulp.

Dane sobbed, struggling in Herc's arms. "Tyg! Oh, my God, someone help him!"

The entire room filled with a flash of light, the stunners sending both men to the floor with a thump.

One thing you could say about Monk — the man was thorough.

Hercules let Dane go, the man flying straight to Tyg's side, Doc right behind him.

Dane figured out the cage fairly quickly, unbuckling and opening it. "Oh, Tyg. Oh, my sweet pup, I'm sorry, I'm so sorry." Dane's hands fluttered over Tyg's body, trying to comfort.

"Let me get to work on him, Dane." Doc calmly but firmly pushed Dane up toward Tyg's head, the man finally settling with the big head in his lap as Doc went over his injuries.

Monk stood over Yves, watching the man bleed, slowly turn grey. Mal looked up at Monk. "Looks bad."

"Yep."

"Too bad the Doc's got other patients."

A short nod. "Yep."

Dane spared them a glance. "I have dibs if there's anything left of him."

Hercules looked down at the man dying at their feet. "Monk, call city security — make sure the report's done up right — I want him on the books for abandoning the pup in the first place, and for Billy. For Dane's head, the kitchen staff's injuries, and what's happened to Tyg tonight. If he's charged posthumously, Tyg and Billy's families will never want for anything."

Monk nodded, watching the man take one last breath. "Okay, boys? Let's vid everything and contact the feds."

"What will we do about breakfast?" Kes was fluttering, white as Doc's little Ghost.

Hercules nodded. "Good boy. You call up Chez Lafite's and get them to cater in enough for the usual crowd — talk to Moffat, find out what the usual is. Nobody needs to hear about this."

"Yes, sir. Shall I plan on having them for lunch and supper, so we can disinfect in here?"

Mal beamed at Kes. Attaboy, Kes.

"Let's get the worker bees and Moffat upstairs. Can we move Tyg, Doc? We need to get a cleaning crew in here."

"We can move him up to Dane's rooms. He'll be more comfortable there and I imagine the major damage is not to his body. I'm going to let Dane finish patching him up and take care of him, so I can look after the kitchen staff right away."

Hercules nodded at Kes. "I'll leave it in your hands, Kestrel. The meals, the disinfecting, getting a new chef if Moffat's unable to resume his duties right away. I'm going to stick with Monk and the feds."

"I'll find out who favors the worker bees, get them held and attended to." Mal tilted his head. "Don't open the doors until Billy's been taken care of."

Monk gave a soft sob and Mal looked at Hercules. "Boss, Billy was *Monk's* boy."

Hercules growled. "I wish that bastard was still alive so I could kill him all over again and then line up those he hurt and let them have their licks. Monk. I'm sorry, but I need you until this mess is over. Once everything's cleaned up, you can take some personal time. On the clock."

Monk nodded, eyes closing. "I'm here, Boss. I'll make sure everything's on the up and up."

Herc growled and gave Mal a heated look, a promise that they were going to work this out together once everything settled again.

Doc and Dane were getting Tyg onto a stretcher, strapping the big pup in, and then Dane was on his way out and up to his quarters.

"Better make sure to override the lock-down on his door," said Herc. "And send two security personnel with him to sweep their rooms. Just in case." Hercules glared at everyone. "Okay, people, let's get moving. Paying guests have been locked down for twenty minutes already, I want them released before the hour's up."

Mal nodded, the group of them working as a unit. They'd get this mess cleaned up.

And then they were reviewing the fucking security protocols.

Tyg and Dane After Yves

All was quiet in their rooms.

Normal.

Surreal.

The security detail had helped him get Tyg into bed after they'd cleared the rooms as safe, then they'd left, and he'd pushed a chair in front of the door.

And blocked off the door to the kitchen where the food delivery lifts were.

He wasn't taking any chances.

Then he'd taken a quick shower to wash off the blood and returned to the bedroom, curling up in bed next to Tyg.

That's when he'd started shaking.

He wound up popping a low-dose anti-anxiety pill so he could take care of the gashes in Tyg's body where the steel-tipped whip had cut away flesh. And the places where the steel cage — a steel cage! — had dug into Tyg's neck.

Doc had warned him that with all the taser hits Tyg had taken, he might be wonky when he woke. Doc had also warned that being confronted with Yves might have caused severe emotional trauma. As if Dane didn't know that.

He was extremely worried as to how far back this might have sent Tyg.

It was possible that having a chance to fight, to stand up for himself, had actually been a help, but Yves had attacked them while they'd been out of their rooms, and who knew what effect that would have on his sweet pup?

Dane shook his head; the possibilities buzzing around were endless. There was nothing he could do until Tyg woke up.

Tyg made a soft, pained noise, hand reaching out. "Dane."

"Oh, my love, my Tyg. I'm here." He took Tyg's hand in his, and petted Tyg's head.

"Still yours? Still?" Tyg's fingers moved slowly, squeezed his. "So sorry. Tried to fight. So hard."

"Oh, you did wonderfully, Tyg. You have nothing to apologize for. And yes. Yes, you are still mine. You will always be mine."

Tears started sliding down his pup's cheeks. "He came back."

"I know. And I'm so sorry. But he won't be hurting you again. He won't ever hurt anyone ever again." He bent and licked Tyg's tears away, taking them into himself.

"He hurt you. He hurt the others. He never stops and it's my fault..."

"No! Yes, he hurt people, but it isn't your fault. He was a terrible, awful man. There was something wrong with him — that's not because of you!" He shook his head. How could this gentle giant think this was his fault?"

"If I had died, he would never have come here again."

"No, but he would have done it to someone else. And now he is dead. And he won't ever hurt anyone again." He hugged Tyg tight. "I don't want you dead, Tyg. That would be awful."

"I... I bit him. I hit him over and over and it didn't matter." Tyg shook, paling suddenly, then he bolted, heading for the bathroom, the sounds of violent retching sounding.

He followed, softly stroking Tyg's back, getting a cloth

and wetting it with cold water and gently patting Tyg's forehead. "He was a terrible, horrible man, Tyg."

"He hated me. Why did he hate me so much?" Tyg pushed away from him, growling, head tossing.

"I think he hated everyone and just focused it on you."

"I need to... I need." The growls were darker, lower, Tyg pacing, shaking.

"What do you need, Tyg? Anything, my love." He just wanted his pup back, he wanted things back to the way they'd been.

"I don't know. I don't know." Tyg threw his head back, howling, muscles taut.

"Do you need to run? To swim? To scream? To fuck?"

"I... Run? Scream? Take a bath." Tyg blinked. "I want a bath. I want him off me."

"All right." He went over to the bath and started it running.

Tyg started pacing again, muttering, hands slapping against the wall, his body.

"Here, Tyg. Let's get you clean."

He got a growl, a nod, Tyg pushing into the hot water, fingers tearing at his skin.

"No. No. Let me do it."

He took Tyg's hands and laid them on the edge of the tub. Then he climbed into the tub and began to dab at Tyg's skin with a soapy sponge.

It took a while, but Tyg began to relax, to breathe easy.

He slid his hands through Tyg's hair, spreading shampoo that smelled like the two of them together.

"Dane." Tyg nuzzled into his touch.

"My dear, Tyg." He kissed Tyg's forehead, his nose, his chin, and then his lips.

"Your head okay?"

"I'm fine. The doctor patched me up. Are you okay?" He looked into Tyg's eyes.

Those pretty eyes filled with tears. "No. Not okay."

"Oh, my love." He hugged Tyg tight.

"Dane? Am... Are they going to come take me away?" The words were whispered, so low. "Be...because if they are? If they're going to put me in a cage forever? I just want you to go and let me..."

"Oh, no, Tyg. No. Nobody is taking you. You are mine. *Mine.*" He pushed Tyg's head back and sank his teeth into his pup's neck, marking Tyg, reminding Tyg.

"Oh!" Tyg arched, hands wrapping around his head. "Yours! Yes! Dane's Tyg."

He wrapped his lips around the bite mark and sucked hard. Tyg panted, groaned, nodding and rubbing against him. He slid his hand down Tyg's body, finding his pup's cock and pumping.

"Tell me again. Tell me, please."

"I love you. You are mine. No one is going to take you away from me."

"Ever. Promise me?" The water splashed, Tyg rocking beneath him.

"I promise, Tyg. I swear it. You are mine. *Mine.*"

"Yes. Yours." Tyg arched into his hand, sobbing, seed hot on his fingers.

He brought their mouths together, hand still on Tyg's cock. Tyg's kiss was aggressive, hungry, tongue pressing into his lips. Moaning, he rubbed against Tyg, his own fears and worries leaving behind adrenaline and need.

Those hands found his ass, squeezing, pulling him in closer. He shifted, straddling Tyg and rubbing against the firm belly, humming into their kiss.

Tyg held him, mouth on his shoulder, on his neck. "You have to love me again. You have to so he didn't ruin that. Because he was there. He watched."

Dane nodded. "Yes."

He shifted again, spreading Tyg's legs, hoping Tyg was ready enough for him, still loose from before.

Tyg lay back and spread for him, shivering, eyes desperate, depending on him.

He pushed right in, eyes on his Tyg as he spread that tight hole.

"Oh... Not his. Yours, Dane."

"Mine, Tyg."

He thrust over and over again, each push harder than the last. The water was slapping against the side of the tub, sloshing over the edges as he took Tyg.

Tyg kept nodding, caught up in what they were creating, what they were doing. He wrapped his hand around Tyg's cock, finding it hard again. Tugging, he pulled Tyg along with him as he raced toward his climax.

Tyg jerked, sobbing, body tight and rippling against him.

"Come with me, Tyg. Come with me, my own." He thrust as hard as he could, feeling it in his bones.

"Yours!" Tyg came again, milking his cock.

"Mine!" he shouted the word, heat pushing deep into Tyg's body.

He collapsed against Tyg, breathing hard. Tyg was silent, still, just floating, hands wrapped around his waist.

He nuzzled Tyg's neck, nose sliding across the lurid mark he'd left. "I love you, Tyg," he whispered.

"Love..." Tyg sighed, relaxing further.

He reached over to the taps, adding some more hot water, replacing the water they'd sloshed out.

"Rest, Tyg. I've got you."

"For always. You promise." Tyg cuddled, head resting against him.

"I promise for always, Tyg." He stroked Tyg's neck. "Tomorrow we'll have my tattoo put on you."

"And... and my tattoo on you."

"Yes. Yes, my Tyg. You on me as well." He settled against his pup. "We belong to each other."

He got a soft moan, a nod, then Tyg's eyes closed.

He kissed Tyg's shoulder and let his own eyes close, let his pup ease his heart.

Tyg and Dane Continue with Their Recovery

After they had spoken to the feds and seen Paul for their tattoos, Tyg went to bed. He spent a long time in their rooms, refusing to leave, refusing to see anyone, refusing to do anything but bathe and sleep and drink milk. Tyg wasn't scared, he wasn't, he just didn't want to think, to remember, to look at people and have them know.

He could still feel the electricity along his nerves, the weight of the cage, and Dane's touch was the only thing that helped that. He curled in on the sofa, head resting on his hands, pretending to watch a vid.

Dane came over, hands sliding on his skin, scratching his head and petting his spine. "What are you watching, Tyg?"

He stretched into the touch, eyes closing. "I don't know. Something funny."

"Richard has commed every day. He'd like to come see you."

"I know." He couldn't. Richard was so good, so decent. He... wasn't.

Dane bent over him, kissing his shoulder. "Tyg. Please. We were doing so well. We were so happy. Don't let him do this to you again."

"I..." He swallowed hard. "You're not happy?"

"How could I be when you aren't, Tyg?" Dane kissed his shoulder again, the soft petting continuing. "It breaks my heart to see you like this."

"I don't know what to do." He cuddled into Dane, needing the comfort.

"You have to let him go, Tyg. He's dead. He can't hurt you anymore." Dane pulled him closer, letting him sprawl over Dane's lap. Those hands were so soft, gentle, loving.

"I... I am. I try." He relaxed, breathing slowing, easing.

"Tell me what you're thinking. Tell me why you won't let Richard come see you."

"I... Richard is so good. So good and I..." He shook his head, swallowed hard. "I can't see him."

"Are you saying you don't think you're good?"

"I..." He shivered, shaking a little. "I wanted to be."

"But you are. You most definitely are."

"No. If I was, he would not have chosen me. He came back for me."

"Ah, Tyg. That was him. Not you. He was a very sick man. What he did to you to start with was wrong, and you didn't do anything to deserve it. And him coming back for you? Not your fault, not because you were bad. In fact, I imagine if you were bad, he wouldn't have bothered to come back, but something in him was broken and he couldn't stand to see you happy, see you being good."

"I was happy. I was happy here." He blinked hard, trying not to cry. "I was happy with you."

"I don't understand why you can't be happy with me now?"

"M... maybe I don't..." He took a deep breath, hid his face, shook his head.

He wasn't ready to think.

Dane sighed, those hands still petting, still stroking him. "It's okay, Tyg. You believed it before, you'll believe it again."

"I believed it and he came back. I believed I deserved you and you were hurt."

"But it wasn't you who hurt me, Tyg. You can only take responsibility for your own actions, not anyone else's."

"I'm scared." There it was, simple, devastating, true.

Dane's arms wrapped around him. "What scares you most, Tyg?"

"Being lost. Left."

"I'm not going to leave you behind, Tyg. Not ever. Not for anything."

"I don't know what to do anymore, Dane. I don't know who I am." He shifted down, rested his head in Dane's lap.

"Do you trust me, Tyg?"

He nodded. Yes. Yes, he trusted nothing else.

"Then trust me when I say that I will help you find out who you are. And that I will never leave you. I love you, Tyg. And that will never change."

"I love you, Dane." His hand wrapped around Dane's thigh and held on.

Dane purred softly, petting him.

Tyg just relaxed, let Dane hold him, protect his heart.

"Would you like to have some supper with me tonight, Tyg? I've sent down for some steaks. Rolls, salad, baked potatoes with the fixings, dessert, and lots and lots of milk."

His stomach growled, loud enough to hear, and he nodded as they both chuffed with laughter.

A soft knock came at the door and Dane chuckled. "Perfect timing, as usual."

He grinned and sat up, stretching tall, muscles creaking.

Dane gave him a smile, fingers stroking his belly before going to get the door and pulling in the rolling table with their food. The smells were fantastic, his mouth watering, soft little whimpers escaping him, and he'd be wagging if he had a tail.

Dane beamed over at him and pushed the table up to the sofa. The lids were removed and Dane moaned softly. "I do love a good steak. Shall I cut yours up for you, Tyg?"

Tyg nodded, pressing close, almost rubbing against Dane. Hungry. Oh. He was hungry.

Dane cut up his meat for him and then nodded at his plate. "Go ahead, Tyg. Eat."

He started eating, moaning as the flavor of the steak coated his tongue, the food spicy and juicy and perfect. Dane nodded and made a happy sound around his own mouthful.

They ate in silence, both of them intent on their food. Dane put some salad on his plate and cut up his potato, split and buttered a roll for him. Every time he drained his milk glass, it was filled again.

Dane sat back first, patting his belly and sighing. "Oh, that hit the spot."

He nodded, finishing one more glass of milk before curling into the cushions, so full. "Good."

Dane smiled and stroked his head. "Yeah. I bet you feel a little better now, too."

He nodded. He did. He felt real, full, warm.

"Excellent." Dane's hands slid over him, warm and petting, stroking.

"There's desserts. Quite a few, I had them send up a half dozen different ones. I thought maybe we could invite Richard to join us. Just for dessert. Then if you didn't want him to stay, he could go."

Oh. He looked over at Dane, waiting for the panic and sorrow to hit him. It didn't, though — Dane's hands felt good, and he was home and happy and relaxed. So he nodded. If it hurt to see Richard, Dane could let him go.

Dane beamed at him again and commed Richard,

settling next to him and petting as they waited.

It wasn't long at all before there was a soft knock at the door.

"Do you want to get it?" Dane asked him.

He shook his head, but stood and moved toward the door anyway, opening it with his heart pounding in his chest. Richard stood there with Jean standing silently behind him. Before he could even react, Richard flew into his arms, hugging him tightly.

He whimpered, sinking to the ground right there in the doorway, wrapping around his friend, his sweet friend. The soft sobs started before he could stop them, rocking them both, howling out his sorrow, his pain, his apologies.

Richard's tears joined his, quiet sobs as the small hands slid over him, petting him. He felt hands on them, shifting them into the rooms, the door closing.

"Thank you, Dane. He's been so worried. Noel and I have been beside ourselves." Jean's words were soft.

"He isn't the only one who's been worried. Tyg just... he needed some time to trust again before he could see Richard. I'm so glad he agreed today." Dane's hands patted him gently.

Richard just cuddled in, hand soft against his belly, head on his chest. He held Richard, rocking and swaying, something deep inside him easing. A tissue was pressed into Richard's hand and the boy cleaned both their faces, those blue eyes gazing up at him, full of love and trust. There was no revulsion in them at all.

He rubbed their cheeks together, their noses, rumbling soft and low. Richard beamed at him and rubbed back.

Dane chuckled softly. "Well, there we go, still friends. You see, Tyg, Richard still loves you."

Richard nodded enthusiastically, giving his cheek a kiss.

"Come on," suggested Dane. "Let's make a dent in this pile of desserts, and then we can sit and watch a vid together. Maybe you'll let Richard groom you, Tyg."

He nodded and stood, carrying Richard to the sofa, curling them together, body pressed close to Dane when his lover sat.

"Jean, you don't have to lurk in the corner, please join us. I had enough dessert sent up for more than four people. I wanted to make sure there was something here to tempt each of our palates." Dane nodded to the big chair. You could watch the vid feed from there as well as the couch.

Jean settled in the chair, massive and scarred. "Thank you, Dane. Have you both recovered?"

Dane's hand stroked along his arm. "We're getting there."

Richard reached out and grabbed one of the sweets, offering it to him with a warm smile.

He leaned over, ate it from Richard's fingers. "Mmm..." Chocolate. Richard giggled when his lips tickled the little fingers.

Dane grinned at them both, looking happy. He relaxed, Dane and Jean speaking, Richard petting him, loving him, easing him deep inside. His best friend.

Eventually a vid was put on, all of them relaxing into a silence that wasn't awkward or heavy. He shifted until he was in Dane's arms, Richard resting against his chest, hands in his hair.

So happy.

He hummed, lifted his face for Dane's kiss.

It was given so easily, no hesitation on Dane's part whatsoever, just the soft touch of Dane's lips against his own.

Oh. Oh, sweet. Tyg closed his eyes, melting, purring.

Home.

He hugged Richard.
Home.

Tyg and Dane Have a Good Day

Dane's eyes flew open as he woke, his body going tight for an instant before he realized he was in his own bed, the familiar, comforting weight of his Tyg next to him. It didn't happen every night, but sometimes he'd still wake up from a dream, unsure where he was, searching for Tyg in the few seconds it took to recognize his surroundings.

He took a deep breath, calming himself before turning and curling around Tyg's bulk. Tyg purred, drawing him closer, surrounding him with strength and heat. He snuggled in happily, loving his pup. Loving that Tyg was comfortable enough again to cuddle and press close while still mostly asleep.

One huge hand stroked his spine, Tyg trying to ease him, gentle him. He purred, the sound a pale imitation of Tyg's deep rumble, his own hands sliding over sleep-warm skin. Tyg's face buried against his throat, tongue coming out to lap and taste.

"Oh." He gasped softly, pushing against Tyg as his cock came awake at the gentle touches.

Tyg rumbled. "Dane. My Dane."

"Oh yes, my pup. Your Dane." He kept his hips moving, sliding against Tyg's muscles. Tyg licked and moaned, hands smoothing over his skin and driving him wild. "Oh Tyg, you make me want so much."

"Want you. Want you, Dane." Tyg's voice was a growl, harsh and husky.

He nodded and whimpered. "Oh, please, yes."

Tyg slid down, hands turning him, helping him get

to his hands and knees, breath on the small of his back. "This is good?"

He nodded, shivering at the sensation of Tyg's breath on his skin. "Very good, Tyg. Please." He pushed back toward Tyg, needing.

"Please..." Tyg's tongue slid down his crease, wetting his hole.

He shuddered, a cry breaking from his lips. "Tyg!"

Oh. He pushed back harder, wanting more. Tyg growled, licking faster, thumbs holding him open. He shook and rippled, Tyg's tongue driving him wild. Soft, gasping noises came from his throat, his cock hard enough it hurt, leaking and ready.

Tyg lifted his head, moaning. "Now, Dane? Now? I need..."

He nodded vigorously, voice gone, lost in the haze of pleasure that held him.

His pup's heavy cock pressed against him as that hot body covered his back, mouth fastening onto the back of his neck. It felt wonderful, safe and good, sexy, being totally surrounded by the big body. With a whimper, he pressed back, taking in Tyg's cock.

"Dane!" Tyg's bark was sharp, needy, prick pressing deep.

"Yes!" So good, the way the need vibrated between them. His body yearned for Tyg's touch, to be filled, taken, to let Tyg mark him inside and out. Tyg surged inside him, strong, powerful, unafraid, hands hard on his hip, his shoulder. "Yes." He repeated the word again and again, once for every time that Tyg pushed into him. It was hot and hard and glorious.

The pants and cries that filled the air just made it hotter, more desperate. His body began to shake with the force of Tyg's thrusts, pleasure shooting up his spine each time Tyg's large cock slid along his gland. He had to lock his elbows hard and just hold on, riding the thrusts.

"Love you." The words were snarled, low and husky. "Mine."

"Yes!" And just like that he came, come spraying his chest and the covers beneath him.

Tyg roared, jerking a few last times before heat filled him.

He collapsed onto the bed, groaning as Tyg's weight came down with him. Hot and solid, he didn't feel crushed, but safe and loved.

Tyg nuzzled his nape, purring. "Dane."

"Yes, my Tyg. My sweet pup. I love you." He reached back, petting awkwardly.

"Love you." Tyg shifted, pulling him back into those arms, nuzzling in. "Good."

He chuckled. "Oh yes. Very good. Thank you."

He felt his pup's smile, heard the pleased little grunt. He petted the big hand on his belly and then twined their fingers together. It was good, what they had together. It made him happy and, what was more, it made Tyg happy, too.

"What would you like to do today, my Tyg?"

Tyg tilted his head, thought. "I... I want to play in the water."

"Oh, what fun!" He dared to push, they'd been doing so well. "We can fill the tub, or... we could try the public pool." He didn't think either of them were ready for a private pool. Not on their own.

Tyg cuddled close, but he nodded. "You'll stay here?"

"I will, Tyg. And there will be others there, we will not be on our own. But not too many. I asked Kestrel — the pools are fairly quiet early in the day." He took a deep breath, turning to pet Tyg's belly, to look into the soft eyes. "If you wore a leash, you would know I was always near."

Tyg's eyes went wide, so dark, so big. Then Tyg pushed against him, lips against his ear. "I... I would wear your collar, your leash. I would wear a tail for you. Your pup, Dane."

"Oh, Tyg. Tyg." He slid his hands along Tyg's skin, petting and loving his pup. "My pup. My beautiful, brave, wonderful pup." Tyg snuggled, licking and kissing, moving lazily under his touch, so trusting, so loving.

He remembered his shock and surprise when he'd discovered the abused "puppy" he had come to take care of was actually a man, but now he couldn't imagine not having the big pup in his life. "I love you, Tyg."

Tyg nodded. "Love you. My Dane." Hands stroked his face, his lover happy, whole, close.

He nuzzled into the touches. "We'll go down to see Mouse after breakfast. I... well, after what happened, I went and commissioned a collar and leash for you. In case you would be willing to wear them for me. It was when I understood why you might want them and that I wanted you to wear them. Hopefully they'll be ready. We'll look at the tails for you, too. See if they have anything you like."

"Anything we like." Tyg kissed him.

He smiled, beaming at his pup. "Yes, Tyg. Anything *we* like."

It was shaping up to be a most excellent day.

Tyg and Dane are Home

They had eaten sausages and eggs and melons and berries and milk for breakfast, and then cleaned up before heading downstairs to see the collar. He was getting furry, his hair black and thick, soft, too.

They walked together to the lift, Dane holding his hand, helping him not be nervous. "Do you like me with hair?" Tyg asked.

Dane turned to him, looking carefully, considering. Then one hand reached up, petting gently as Dane smiled. "Yes, Tyg. I do."

He nuzzled in, pleased. Warm.

Oh, good.

Dane continued to pet him, hand moving from the top of his head down along his spine until the elevator made its soft noise as it stopped for them, the doors gliding open. He took a deep breath and stepped in, only trembling a little.

"These lifts are nice and quick, Tyg. We'll be down in no time, you'll see." Dane's fingers kept stroking his hair, gentle and soft.

He nodded, stayed close. They were safe now.

It wasn't long at all before the lift stopped and the doors opened. Dane took his hand and led him out.

They came across Bear and Zim, the big handler carrying a shiny new saddle, the pup bouncing beside his master. "Hello, there! How are you both today?"

"Hi, Bear, hello, Zim." Dane laughed as Zim's tail wagged eagerly, the little pup looking up at Bear and whining softly before looking at him.

Tyg smiled at the little pup, arms opening as Bear nodded. "Go say hello, puppy."

Zim barked sharply, bounding into his arms, licking and petting, wriggling for all he was worth. Dane beamed at him, petting Zim. It felt good to rub their cheeks together, to not be scared. To feel like he belonged.

Zim rubbed their noses together, eyes shining at him. "I'm *so* happy to see you!"

"I am, too. How are you? How are the other puppies?"

"Good! Zeb will be sorry he missed you." Zim's tail wagged madly. "Everyone asks about you — it'll be so good to tell them I saw you and that you look happy!"

"I am. I am happy." He chuckled, laughing at the hyper pup. "We are going to get my collar."

He could feel Dane beaming proudly beside him as Zim's eyes got wide. "Oh, Tyg! That's wonderful!"

Zim ran back to Bear's side. "Did you hear? Did you hear, Bear? Tyg's going to wear a collar again." Then the puppy came back to him, rubbing against his legs.

Bear smiled at him, nodded. "Congratulations, pup. Maybe you and Dane could come to supper in a few days? Visit with me and Andy and the puppies?"

He looked over at Dane, tilted his head.

"If you would like to, Tyg, it would be my pleasure as well."

Zim vibrated, tail wagging. "Say you'll come, Tyg, say you'll come."

He nodded. "Yes. Thank you." It was scary, but good. So good.

Zim ran into his arms again, hugging and rubbing and licking his cheek. "I'm so pleased! Just wait until I tell Zeb!"

Dane chuckled. "We'll look forward to your call," Dane told Bear. "Come along, Tyg, we have a man to see about a collar."

"Yes, Dane." He kissed Zim's nose. "I'll see you soon."

Zim bounced and licked his cheek again and then returned to Bear's side, eager and happy, his tail wagging from side to side as they headed down the hall.

Dane chuckled again. "Now, there's an eager puppy."

Tyg nodded. "Very."

He leaned down, rested against Dane a moment, centering himself. "Love you."

Dane's hands slid over his head, along his arms. "I love you, Tyg. And I'm so proud of you."

He smiled, purred. "Yours."

"Yes. Mine."

Dane petted him a moment longer and then took his hand and led him to the leatherwork shop. A small bell sounded as they went in, and they were assailed by the scent of leather as soon as they crossed the threshold.

He sniffed, looking around, curious. It smelled warm. Good. Exciting.

A huge man — one big enough that he felt small — came out. "Mr. Dane. Hello. Is this your pup?"

"Yes, this is my Tyg." The way Dane said that sounded as if he were the most wonderful pup in the world.

Mouse smiled at him. "Nice to meet you, Tyg. I'm Mouse."

He nodded, almost panting, excited, wanting to see everything.

"I know we didn't set a time frame, Mouse, but I was hoping you might have the collar and leash that I ordered ready."

"In fact, I do. Little One? Love? Can you get Mr. Dane's order, please? It's in one of the white boxes."

There was movement from the corner of the room, and the littlest boy Tyg had ever seen, smaller even than the pup Zim, with dark hair and big eyes, nodded his head and hurried into the back.

"That's wonderful! Thank you, Mouse." Dane shook the big man's hand. "Now, we'd also like to see your tails. Something to compliment my Tyg."

Mouse gave him a long look, then tilted his head. "Not something long and fluffy, I don't think. Maybe something heavy and bobbed, something that draws attention to his strength?"

Dane beamed. "Oh, I can see we're definitely at the right place. What do you think, Tyg?"

He nodded. "I don't want fluffy." He didn't want to look silly.

Mouse nodded. "I agree. You're a beautiful pup, Tyg. Nothing should detract from that."

"Yes, exactly," agreed Dane. "Have you got something in the same color as his natural hair?"

The wee one came out then with a small white box. "I found them, Mouse. For Mr. Dane and his big puppy."

"I do." Mouse bent and kissed the little one, long and deep, making the boy's eyes sparkle. "Show the collar and leash to Mr. Dane while I find the tails."

"Okay, Mouse." The little one looked up at him. "You're almost as big as Mouse."

"Almost. You're even tinier than Zim."

"The little puppy? He and Zeb are so cute. Can I pet you?"

He looked over at Dane, not as much for permission as for a signal it was safe, good.

"If you wish it, Tyg."

He scooted closer to Dane, then nodded, kneeling down so the little one could reach.

Small hands touched his head, sliding over his hair and then petting his shoulders. "You seem like a very nice puppy."

He relaxed, eyes closing. He was. A good dog. A very good dog.

"Yes," said Dane, warm hand joining the little one's in the petting. "My Tyg is a very good dog."

Dane let the petting go on a little longer. "Could we see the collar and leash now, little one?"

"My name is Peep."

"Very well, Peep, could we see the collar and leash?"

Peep nodded, opening the box. Inside was a simple black collar and leash. It wasn't until it was brought closer that he realized there were designs carved into the leather.

He reached out, stroked them softly. "Oh... Oh, Dane."

"Do you like them?" Dane's hand slid along his back.

"So pretty..." He was shivering, so honored, so pleased.

"Mouse did a wonderful job. It's just what I asked for."

Dane picked them up and opened the collar. "The buckle is black onyx, so it would blend in. I wanted you to be able to take it off whenever you needed to."

He lifted his chin, vibrating, wanting to feel Dane's collar.

Dane's hands stroked his skin softly and then the buttersoft leather slid around his neck. Dane fastened it closed, loose enough he didn't feel as though he were choking, but tight enough he knew he was wearing it.

He turned his head, swallowed. "Pretty?"

Dane shook his head, no. "Magnificent."

Oh, he was so proud, fingers stroking his collar. He pushed into Dane's arms, holding tight.

Dane's arms wrapped around his middle, proud eyes smiling at him. "My Tyg."

"Yes. Yours. Your pup." He nuzzled in, happy, warm.

"Oh, it looks fine." Mouse came in with three tails on a tray — two were short, thick, the other longer and thin like a whip. "The one on the far left can be filled — warm water, beads, vibrating eggs, whatever you'd like."

"Wow. That's." Dane looked at him and smiled. "What do you think, Tyg?"

"I don't like the long one, Dane."

"Take it away please, Mouse."

Dane's hand was warm, sliding on his arm, soothing. "And the other two. Both or just the... simple one?"

"Do..." He leaned in, whispering. "Would you like to play with me? With the fillable one?"

Dane shivered. "I never have done anything like that before, but..." he heard Dane's breath quicken, could smell his Dane's sudden musk. "I am intrigued."

He groaned, pressing closer, wanting to rub. "Both. Please, Dane. Both."

Dane's fingers slid along his jaw and down to his collar. "Yes, Tyg. We'll take both."

"Mouse? Should we show them the change room where they can try them on in private?"

Mouse nodded and smiled. "Yes, Peep. There is a room with a bed, a sink, anything you could need."

He blushed and nuzzled into Dane's throat.

"Thank you, Mouse."

Little Peep led the way, carrying the tray with the two tails for them, closing the door behind them once they were in the room.

He pushed into Dane's arms, panting. "Thank you. Love. My collar."

"Yes, Tyg." Dane's fingers traced it as if drawn, their mouths meeting in a fierce kiss.

He rubbed against his Dane, his lover, his heart, so hungry, so hard.

"Will you wear one of the tails while you take me,

Tyg?" Dane asked, rubbing back, cock like a brand against him.

He groaned, nodding, tongue sliding on Dane's skin, passion pushing him, riding him.

Dane's fingers were trembling as he reached for one of the tails and the small tube next to it. "We need to hurry, I want you." His Dane's eyes raised to meet his, so dark and needy.

"Yes. I need. Please." He was growling, hips shifting, cock full as he draped himself over Dane's lap.

Two slick fingers pressed into him, stretching him hard and fast. He could hear Dane panting, the sounds harsh, desperate. He bucked up into the touch, eager, needing, spread wide. It was just a quick stretch and then Dane was pushing the tail into him, the end solid and hard, familiar despite how long it had been since he last wore a tail.

He arched, barking, panting, the stretch familiar and good.

"Oh, Tyg, you look magnificent." Dane's fingers rubbed the small of his back and then Dane pointed to the mirror along one wall.

The tail was short, heavy, accentuating his muscles. "Oh..."

Dane moaned, fingers stroking the short hairs, and then in the mirror he watched as Dane went to his hands and knees. "I want to watch us, Tyg, watch you with your tail as you take me."

He whimpered, pounced, tongue moving to wet his lover, his heart, his Dane.

Dane cried out as his tongue touched the hot hole, eyes watching him in the mirror. He pushed his tongue in, hips rocking in time, entire focus on their need.

"Oh, Tyg, please. Hurry. Hurry." Dane rocked back on his tongue, wanting, eager.

He nodded, sitting up, tugging Dane into his lap, onto his cock. Dane's back slid against his chest, body gripping his cock, holding him tight. He jerked, pushing up, ass clenching around his tail.

Dane moaned, fingers finding his thigh, digging in. "More."

He growled, nodded, moving faster, harder, needing.

Dane watched them in the mirror. "Look at you. So strong and beautiful."

"I... for you. For you." His teeth scraped Dane's shoulder.

Dane cried out, body rippling around his cock. His hand was taken, drawn around to Dane's hardness.

"Dane..." He groaned, hand pumping furiously, the collar warm and heavy on his throat.

"Tyg! My own!"

Dane went stiff, body so tight around him as heat splashed over his hand. His eyes went wide, hips pushing up and up and up, his howl ringing as his pleasure poured from him.

Dane slumped against him, hand stroking his thigh. "Oh, my love."

"Yours. Your pup." He nodded, licking Dane's skin, panting.

"Yes. My pup." Dane turned, bringing their lips together, kissing him. "My beautiful pup. So strong. So brave. So mine."

Tyg nodded, fingers brushing the ink on his own throat, the collar. "Yours. For always."

Dane nodded, fingers following his, soft on his neck, sliding along the collar. "Yes. For always."

He was given a tight hug and a quick kiss. "Shall we put on your leash and go swimming, my Tyg?"

He nodded, nuzzled, a soft bark leaving him. "Yes."

Dane petted his head and down along his back, fingers

sliding to tweak his tail. "It makes me happy to see you so happy, Tyg."

"I haven't ever been. Not ever before."

"Oh, Tyg." Dane held him tight, looking him in the eye. "I'm so sorry for what happened to you before you came to me. But you're mine now, and if you are ever unhappy you have to tell me so we can change that."

He nodded, smiled, nuzzling into Dane. "Yes."

"Good."

Dane patted him and then stood, finding his clothes and putting them back on. "You'll keep the tail in?"

He nodded. "If it's good for you."

Dane gave him a smile that was very sexy. "It is, Tyg. You look... magnificent."

His cheeks heated, cock leaping. "Thank you."

Dane's hand slid along his belly and down to pet his cock.

"Oh..." He purred, stepping closer, cheek nuzzling against Dane.

Dane purred softly, hand wrapping around his cock. "We may never leave this room."

"Okay." He licked Dane's ear, jaw.

Dane laughed. "Okay."

Then his Dane's mouth closed over his, tongue sliding into his mouth as Dane's hand slid on his cock. He rocked, body hyper-aware of the tail inside him, shifting. Dane's other hand stroked his belly, pushed down to cup his balls and slid around him to play with his tail.

He barked, hips pushing harder, faster, cock beginning to leak. Dane moaned and slowly slid down, kissing his chest, his belly, the tip of his cock. Tyg braced himself, watching and panting.

Dane's hands settled on his hips, mouth wrapping around the tip of his prick, suction starting along with Dane's tongue pushing into his slit.

"Dane. Dane. Dane." He moaned and growled and panted, hips rocking.

One of Dane's hands slid around to his rear again, playing with his tail as Dane's mouth took him in deeper. He arched, body jerking, eyes going wide. Dane's eyes gazed up at him, looking into him as Dane sucked harder, tugged a little on his tail.

His world shorted out, seed pouring out of him, entire room spinning. Dane took him all in, swallowing around his cock and then licking him clean.

Groaning, he slumped against the wall, panting. "Dane..."

His tail was stroked, seated properly again and then Dane petted his thighs.

"Love you." His eyes closed and he couldn't stop smiling.

"I love you, too, Tyg." Dane kissed his cock and his belly and then stood.

"Come. Let's go pay for our purchases and go swimming." Dane put the leash on his collar, but took his hand as well.

He nodded, following easily, happily, his heart whole.

Velvet Glove, Volume IV

Anything for a Byline
Prologue

Okay.

Okay, I can do this.

Four years of journalism school, two years of mailroom work, two years of obits and fuck, I need a break in the worst way.

So when the old-queen photographer — Al, his name was — suggested to me that there might be a way to break into features, or if not features, then at least the lifestyles page? I said yes. Sure. Anything. Please.

Of course, I was thinking I'd interview drug dealers, puppy smugglers, people who thought they were vampires, maybe. I never thought that I'd be interviewing for a job at a... God. These BDSM club things weren't real, were they?

I wiggle a little as I wait for the service door to open; the big building looks so huge, so cold, so... unnerving in the pale moonlight. I'm in a pair of leather pants two sizes too small, a mesh shirt that my pale skin just glows milk white in, and I look like a dork.

Al promised me a job interview, though. A chance to look around, to see, and I couldn't say no.

Even if the *Herald* doesn't take it, one of those jerk-off magazines might, and a byline is a byline.

When the door opens, I blink up.

And up.

And up.

Christ, the dude is tall. "Hey. I... I'm Nathaniel. I have an appointment. Albert set it up for me."

The guy looks me over from head to toe, one eyebrow going up in a way that clearly says "oh, really?"

"Follow me," is what he actually says, though, and the tall dude turns and walks me past security and through a back room. I can't get a really good look at anything, though, as we're moving pretty quickly.

Dude. Leather pants? Squeak.

A lot.

And hot?

Damn.

On the other hand, Mr. Tall and Quiet doesn't seem to be having the same problem with his leather pants. Maybe it's the laces up the sides.

We go up an elevator, my... guide not saying a word, and then we're through a door into an office that has more light and a big desk. The guy pulls one of the chairs out for me and goes around to sit behind the wooden desk. There's a stationary comm unit on it, a couple of smaller comms, a large coffee cup, and a bunch of... well, sex toys. A fat purple dildo and a silver plug and a whip, and a few things I'm not exactly sure I can identify.

I swallow. I can do this. I can.

The guy looks me up and down again. "Are you sure

you're in the right place? I mean, you *know* what a BDSM club is, what the Velvet Glove is, right?"

"Of course." I'd *read*, hadn't I? Researched. Looked on the web. I think the clubs are fake, but I know what it's all about.

"All right. You just don't exactly look hard core."

I'm handed a comm with a datapen. "There's a permission form on top for your interview scene and a list for you to tick yes or no to on each item. I'll call Richmond, get him down here so you can start as soon as you've filled that all out."

"Oh, cool. Okay." I pull the datapen out of the clip and start reading, start, uh... worrying.

The contract is for a "scene," which will be my interview. The Dom — with a capital D — will choose things from the list that I've marked yes to. I absolve the club of any responsibility for damages, physical or mental.

The list... is long.

Dude. Maybe I can just get out of here with the list. There's no way I'm going to let someone do half. No, three-quarters. No. Fifteen-sixteenths of this shit to me. I'm just here for the story.

The story I'll never get if I fucking walk out now.

Still...

No one said I'd have to *do* anything but look around and talk.

"Richmond's on his way down." Tall dude's voice is sharp and short, startling me. "You about done?"

"I... Yeah, almost." Fuck. I start clicking randomly, adding my thumbprint and standing. I'll meet this Richmond guy, talk for a few minutes and bail. That way I'll have my story and Al won't tease me for being a chickenshit.

The guy takes the form from me, checking to make

sure I've signed it. He raises another eyebrow when he glances through the list, but doesn't say anything.

"Okay, follow me."

"Sure." What's that saying about God looking out for fools and angels? He leads me back through the whitest halls with doors that all look alike. "How do you find your way around in here?"

"I know where everything is."

I'm led through a door into a simple room with medium lighting coming from a hidden source. A mirror along one wall, two padded benches, and a chest-high table are the only furniture, aside from a large, wardrobe-type cupboard.

"This will be your interview. You do well, we'll take you on as a for-pay sub."

I swallow hard, nod. Whatever it is, I can deal. I can deal with anything for fifteen minutes, even half an hour. Christ, is unnerving future employees part of the deal?

I force myself to relax, to focus on what everything looks like, smells like. That's the secret of a good story — remembering that the benches were blue, not black, that the cupboard looked classy, older, a little scarred up.

The door opens again, a slightly older man coming in. Taller than me but shorter than the guy I'd been... interviewing with, this guy has on a pair of leather pants and nothing else, big muscles that seem to gleam in the light and long brown hair pulled back into a ponytail.

"Mal! You've got work for me tonight."

Tall dude — Mal — grins and shakes the man's hand. "Richmond. Yeah. This guy's here for an interview." Mal hands over the comm.

"Hi, there. You got a safeword?"

"Hey." This, at least, I've read about, and this man doesn't look as... terrifying as Mal. And what the fuck kind of name is Mal, anyway? "Penguin."

"Penguin it is. You get that, Mal?"

"Got it. Have fun."

Richmond grins wickedly. "I will."

I run one hand through my hair, wincing at the dull ache the pull of my wiry copper curls causes. I'm getting one hell of a tension headache and just want all this *over*.

"So, uh... How long has this place been around?"

Richmond closes the door behind Mal as the tall guy leaves, and smiles at me. "I ask the questions around here, Nat. You answer. And you can call me sir."

"Oh. Sir. Okay." I nod, filing away the phrase to quote it later, bouncing idly on the balls of my feet, trying to dilute my nerves.

"This your first time?" Richmond asks, walking slowly around me.

I almost lie, but hell, surely the guy would know and there isn't any harm in this truth. "Yeah. Yeah, it is."

"This something you always wanted to do, or a whim?"

Richmond stops behind me, big hands landing on my shoulders, stroking out from my neck and down along my arms.

I jump a little, squeak. "Sorry. You... I'm nervous. I..." The best thing is the truth, or a close approximation. "Someone I work with suggested I come. I didn't even think stuff like this was real."

"You came for a job interview to a place you didn't believe even existed?" Richmond snorts. "I think you're about to find out it's very real, Nat. I mean, you were the one who filled out this form, right? You signed the scene contract?"

"Yeah. Yeah, I did. You want me to go? My friend Al said I should come, said it would be a good move."

"No, I don't want you to go. You want a job here, I'm

not going to discourage you. Good subs, especially ones with some of the kinks you ticked off, are always a good find."

Richmond turns me. "I'll try to make this as good for you as I can. I'm very good at what I do."

My mouth is taken, the kiss starting out slow and growing teeth.

Kinks I ticked off... Fuck. Fuck, what had I... I keep getting distracted, the demand of Richmond's mouth sending a jolt of electricity to my cock, surprising me.

"That's right," murmurs Richmond. "Forget it's an interview and just enjoy yourself — you're more likely to get hired that way." The big hands land on my ass, pulling me close to Richmond's heat.

I swallow my moan, eyes going wide for a second, then closing. Shit. Shit, this is way more up close and personal than I expected. One of Richmond's hands stays on my ass, holding me firmly; the other hand pushes up under my mesh shirt, stroking my back as the kiss gets deeper again, Richmond bending me back.

I'm stiff for a second, breath catching as my body screams about falling, but it doesn't matter, does it? Richmond has the height and the balance and I'm going to fucking bend anyway, might as well relax and go. I can catch myself, if I need to.

The kiss goes on for a long time, making me breathless, and then Richmond pulls away, dark eyes intense, staring into my own as I'm led over to the table. "Take off your clothes and then bend over, holding onto the table."

Every muscle in my body tightens, but I get the shirt off without freaking out. My fingers are trembling badly, getting tangled and caught in the fucking laces and...

Okay, so I'm not going to get naked without wigging.

Richmond moves over to the cupboard and opens it up and I can glimpse paddles and dildos and plugs and stuff

I'm not even sure what it all is. After pulling out a few items, Richmond comes over to me. The air is electrified, every step sounds loud.

"When I tell you to do something, I expect it done or you will be punished, Nat."

"I'm sorry. Fucking laces." I step away from Richmond, tugging at the damned things. Nobody's given me a fucking time limit, have they?

"If you need help, you are to ask for it. If you get hired, you'll choose to wear something you can get out of easily. If I was paying you for your time I'd be really pissed off right now." Richmond's voice is calm, even, but I have no doubt I'm being told off.

I blush dark, unaccountably embarrassed. "Man, if grace is part of the equation, I'm in the wrong place."

I manage to get undressed, put my clothes aside, cock limp and quiescent, which sort of makes me feel better, makes me feel less like a freak.

"Obedience is far more important a quality than grace in a sub. Besides, you'll learn grace. Lean over the table."

Three items are put on the table. A silver butt plug with a wide base, a pile of leather straps, and a tube of lube.

My asshole clenches tight. Okay. Okay, breathe. I did a little bit of assplay in college, nothing serious, but I'm not a virgin-virgin. I can deal. I can.

Think features page. Features.

Bylines.

Career.

I lean over the table, gasping at the chill.

"The cold making your titties hard?" Richmond asks, hands sliding over my ass.

"I..." I blush again, ass tensing. Titties? Girls have those. I have... pink little vestigial bumps that don't like the cold. "Yeah, I think so."

"You think so? You need to learn your body, Nat."

Richmond's hands spread my ass cheeks, thumbs sliding along my crack and pressing against my hole.

"I... I'm usually busy." My breath catches, asshole clenching.

Richmond leans over me, thumbs sliding away to be replaced by a single slick finger that pushes in, Richmond not seeming to even notice my resistance.

"Sex is about more than just your cock. Much, much more." The words are spoken quietly, almost whispered into my ear. "There isn't a single place on your body that can't be an erogenous zone."

I shiver, toes curling, eyes closing as I fight the wave of heat inside me. Work. This was...

Work.

"So many people get stuck on the obvious ones."

One finger becomes two, Richmond stretching me, making my ass burn with it. My thighs part a little more as I try to spread myself wider. Richmond's fingers curl and spark something deep inside me.

"Oh!" I rise up on my toes, hips jerking involuntarily.

Richmond hums, the sound vibrating along my neck for a moment before my skin is licked, the jolt of pleasure inside me sparking again.

I shiver, eyes going wide. "I... I... that... Oh..."

"Yes, 'oh.'" Richmond's chuckle vibrates deep inside me and his big fingers find that spot again. My hips start moving, pushing toward the touch, cock getting hot, heavy, stiff. A third finger pushes more lube into me, the gel cool, almost shocking.

"Full..." My breath comes faster, heart pounding.

"Not as full as you will be." The fingers stretch me several moments longer before the warm fingers disappear.

I rest my head on my arms, trying to catch my breath. Fuck. Fuck, I feel...

Fuck.

More cool slick stuff is pushed into me and the plug is placed against my hole, the tip pressing in. "Push back against it. Bring it in, Nat."

I shiver, pressing back tentatively, feeling the hardness spread me.

"That's it. Keep going." One of Richmond's hands slides around my hip, squeezing me but not forcing. It stretches, making me lift up on my toes, my body trying to escape, my cock wanting more. Richmond's hand moves me for the last bit, forcing me to take it all, and I swear I can hear my ass snap around the base.

A sharp cry escapes me, pleasure and burn curling in my belly. "Oh. Oh, fuck."

"Not yet, Nat."

Richmond chuckles and slowly straightens me, turns me. "And now we'll do something about this." Richmond's hand drops to my cock, pumping firmly. "Because coming is also something you won't do yet."

I whimper, hips thrusting like I have no control, like I'm a slut, which I'm not. Richmond's purr slides along my lips, followed by his tongue. Before it can become a kiss, Richmond steps back and picks up the leather strips, which now that they're being stretched out are obviously a cock ring. The leather slips around my cock and balls, tightening until they almost hurt and then snapping closed.

The black leather is obscene against my white skin and bright red pubes, pushing my cock and balls forward, making them seem huge. I reach down, touching the leather, shivering. I can feel Richmond's eyes on me as I touch the cock ring. "It's obscene. So... dark."

Richmond's large fingers slide over my prick, meeting

mine on the leather. "It stands out well against your skin."

I blush, take a deep breath, cock swelling.

"Very pretty skin. It'll mark well." The words are murmured against my lips and then Richmond's tongue presses into my mouth, hand exploring my cock, my balls, and the leather that binds them.

I gasp, shaking hard, lips parting and accepting Richmond. My head is swimming, need riding me.

"Take off my pants," Richmond murmurs into my mouth. My fingers slide around Richmond's waistband, looking for a button, a snap. Something. One of Richmond's hands takes mine and brings it to the laces in the back of leather pants.

"Oh..." I close my eyes, focusing, making my fingers work. Obedient, not graceful.

The laces open as my thought surprises me. Scares me.

"That's it, Pet."

Something plastic is slipped between my lips. "Put this on with your mouth once the pants are off. We're all clean at the club, inoculated, but we don't know you yet and we're careful."

My eyes go wide. Oh. Oh, God. I've never. And how?

I can see myself in Richmond's eyes, my look panicked. Richmond's doesn't blink, just looks at me, waiting for me to obey.

I push the leather down, slowly dropping to my knees, coming face-to-face with Richmond's heavy, hard prick. God, it's... dark. Wide. Smells sexy, though. I try to press the rubber on, pressing the latex against the tip with my tongue, and I wince as it shoots across the room.

"Oh, shit. I'm sorry. I haven't ever..."

"Ever what? Put a condom on another man?"

I nod, swallowing. There's probably a lot I haven't

done.

Okay. Definitely.

For sure.

Richmond reaches down for the leather pants and produces another condom package. "You can put it on with your hands." I can't tell if the man is upset or not.

I nod, embarrassed, ashamed. I just need to get through the interview and go. Focus. I slide the condom on Richmond's cock after one more false start.

"Now suck me."

I nod; this I've done before. I wrap my lips around the tip and start taking the hot flesh in. Richmond's hand slides through my hair, holding on and guiding my mouth. Oh. Okay. I can do this. I relax, moving with Richmond's hands, feeling my worry slip away. Richmond groans, moving me faster, cock pushing into my mouth.

Oh.

Oh, fuck.

I look up, the sight of the man burning into my eyelids. Richmond is watching me, heat in the dark eyes. I groan, cock throbbing, stomach muscles rippling, balls aching.

Faster and faster Richmond fucks my mouth, the fat prick spreading my lips and hitting the back of my throat. I try not to gag, not to tighten up. Try to just keep breathing. Just when I think I won't be able to finish it, Richmond comes, prick jerking in my mouth.

I gasp for breath, jaw aching, heart pounding. Richmond holds my head a moment longer and then releases me, removing and disposing of the condom.

I catch my breath, look around, unsure what to do, what to say. What to *think*.

Richmond is back at the cupboard. "So which do you prefer, the paddle or the whip?"

I blink, shake my head to clear it. "I... paddle. Whips are... They cut."

Fuck. This was the longest fucking interview ever.

"So that's why you like them?" Richmond asks, pulling a whip out of the cupboard.

I shake my head, confused. "No."

Richmond comes over, sliding the whip over my chest. "Why do you like whips, then?"

"I don't know. They scare me." I shiver, arms wrapping around myself, ass clenching around the plug. "Are we almost finished with the interview?"

"We're done when I say we're done. That's the way it works. Lean back over the table." I whimper, holding myself tighter, brain zipping ninety miles a minute as I stumble to my feet. "You keep making me repeat my orders and you will *not* get the job, Nat."

"I'm doing what you said." I don't want the fucking job. I don't. I...

Fuck, I need to get out of here.

Once I'm leaning over the table, Richmond's hand slides down along my back, warm, solid, almost gentle. Then the whip hits me.

I jerk, crying out, the cut like a flame. I buck up, pushing myself off the table, intending to run. "No."

That big hand pushes me back down and the whip falls again. I panic, fighting Richmond's hold, eyes rolling in my sockets as the whip keeps hitting and hitting. My back, my ass, the tops of my thighs, all get hit.

Finally the whipping stops, but before I can catch my breath the plug inside me is jostled and pulled out, a hot, fat prick slamming in to replace it. Something inside me goes quiet, still and shocked and...

Quiet.

Richmond's cock is huge and hot and hard and filling me over and over again, sliding across my gland. The big hands are wrapped around my hips, fingers digging into already abused skin.

I keep my eyes closed, keep breathing. The leather around my cock and balls is released, one big hand wrapping around my cock, working me in time with the thrusts.

"Oh..." I sob, rocking between cock and hand, tears spilling from my eyes, pre-come pouring from my cock.

"Come on my cock, Nat. Let me feel how good it is for you." I groan, rising up on my toes, sobbing as I squeeze, balls going tight. "That's it, Nat. Give it to me. Give it to me now."

The room spins as I shoot, a low scream sounding, cock throbbing and sore.

Richmond growls long and low, fucking my ass a few more times before collapsing against me.

I shudder, eyes closed, tears flowing freely, my entire body shaking hard. Richmond kisses the back of my neck, purring as that fat prick slides out of me.

I'm straightened, turned, held against the sweaty, muscled chest as Richmond pets me, hums. "Oh, you pulled that off in the end, Nat. You really surprised me. I'm going to recommend Mal hire you. So well done."

I find myself leaning into Richmond's arms, soaking up the praise, the sensation. "Thank you, sir."

"Thank you, Nat." My face is turned up, a gentle kiss sliding across my lips. "Beautiful."

I open to the kiss, our breath mingling. I don't think about what this means, about what is happening. I don't. I can't.

Richmond keeps the kisses light, tongue sliding on my lips, breath dancing against my teeth. The burn on my back, in my ass, the dull ache in my balls — they all mingle into something almost sweet. Oh. Oh, sweet lord in heaven. I can do this. I can learn to need this.

I can.

Chapter One

I t's been a long month and I've been a growly bastard for most of it. I didn't even notice it at first.

It was when I realized the subs were giving me the big wary eyes they usually reserved for Mal and that the biggest pain sluts were signing up for time with me that I figured it out.

I hate waiting and someone is making me wait. That's what it boils down to.

It's been just over a month since the innocent, green-eyed kid walked in asking for an interview. Mal pegged him as a reporter right away, got the kid to sign an interview consent form, which automatically protected the club — there was an airtight non-disclosure clause on that puppy — and called me in to give the kid as intense a scene as I could.

Which I did.

I'm fucking good at my job. By the end of the scene he was in tears and clinging to me, thanking me, something deep inside him opened to the light.

Of course, him being so affected doesn't explain why I've been dreaming of black leather around a pale-skinned cock dark with blood and framed by bright, fiery curls.

The thing is... when a sub opens to you like that, especially a newly discovered sub? It touches you, too.

You can't pull that kind of emotion out of someone without putting your own emotion in.

As I held him that day, something inside me slipped.

My objectivity.

I have never become emotionally involved with a sub before. It's one of the reasons I'll have sex with them. It never crosses the line.

It crossed the line that night.

I don't even know why, except that he touched me, perhaps as much as I touched him. Perhaps more, since I am still affected by him and it has been over a month, while he has gone on with his life.

I lace up my leather pants and braid my hair, going shirtless as is my custom. I haven't had a holiday in a number of years — enjoying my job here at the Glove to the fullest and not needing or wanting one. I think, though, I need to take some time. To find my center and control. I have made each of the subs I worked with this week safeword.

The lift carries me quietly and efficiently down to the training salle where I have a brief appointment with Mal. The salle's dead quiet, Mal sitting on the edge of the main desk, leg swinging. "You're late. The boss wants me. Now. So, what's your problem? You've been evil."

I chuckle. "Oh, I don't know about evil. But I haven't been myself, I'll grant you that. I was thinking a week off might do me some good. Help me find my center again."

One white eyebrow goes up. "A whole week? Hmmm... I could possibly arrange that. Assuming, of course, that you deal with the worker bee waiting in the back. Herc needs me, and he's more your type than mine."

I frown. "A worker bee? If he's not a client, he can just wait until a top wants him. I don't want to frighten any more worker bees this week, Mal."

"It's not negotiable, Rich. He's new and I'm not

convinced he belongs on the main floor and Herc's waiting. You want a week off? It starts in the morning."

I sigh. I can't refuse. I just hope I can keep from pushing the worker bee too far. "All right, Mal, I'll do it. And I'll try not to push him into safewording."

I take a deep breath, trying to get my head into a good place.

Mal reaches out, pats my cheek. "Good. Thank you. Have fun. He's waiting in the red room. Comm me in the morning."

Then? Poof. The son of a bitch is out the door.

I check my hair and take a few more deep breaths, pushing Nat from my mind. This new boy needs me, needs my attention to be full, my focus to be him. I head for the red room. Mal's got the kid naked, bound against the wall, shivering and limp and pale and...

Pale.

White pale.

With red hair and green eyes and a happy little cry as I walk in.

I swallow my own cry with an effort.

He came back.

"Well, well, look who came back."

The light fades a little in those pretty eyes as they drop to the floor, but he doesn't pull away; if anything, he's arched toward me, trying to reach me.

"Congratulations on getting the job." I walk right up to him and let one hand touch, sliding along his stretched side, warming the cool skin.

"Th...thank you. I... Thank you." He leans into the touch, shivering a little, those pretty nipples going tight.

I hold back my purr, needing to start slow, needing to keep myself from forgetting that he's here to learn, I'm here to teach him. He's not mine to fuck blind. Not yet, anyway. I don't even know if he wants...

"What do you want?"

Those eyes slowly lift up to mine, scared and shy. "I... I can't stop thinking about you."

I do purr this time, a reward for his honesty. He's lovely, his innocence still shining despite what we have done.

"What do you think about me?" I ask, fingers no longer able to stay away from the tight little nubs that are just begging for my touch.

"Y...your kisses. How... How I felt after... after you..." The words are gasped, broken by my fingers pulling those nipples. "I wore your marks."

"How did you feel after, wearing my marks?" I will leave more, cover him with my need.

"Special." Nat shakes his head, eyes closing. "I'm sorry. I'm sorry. I know it's a job. I just. I didn't think. I didn't know. I had to come back."

"You had no guarantee it would be me again." I slide my hand down, wrap it around his hard cock, pumping gently, thumb brushing across the tip, rewarding him again for his honesty.

"I had to take the chance. I dream about you." Nat arches for me, offering me everything, and it's addictive, arousing.

I slide my hand down lower, cupping the balls that have been tightly bound. A flare of jealousy goes through me, that Mal has touched him, fingers stroking his sweet prick to hardness to bind it up tight.

"Tell me your dream." I could make it come true.

"Oh... Oh, I..." Those eyes squeeze shut, face going bright red. "I was yours and you touched me everywhere, knew me everywhere. M... marked me."

I lean in, lips close to his ear as I whisper, "And you came here, looking for me, wanting me to mark you, to know you inside and out."

A soft sob sounds, Nat nodding, heat pouring from him. "Yes."

"So brave, Nat." I lick at his earlobe. "Penguin, right?"

"Yes, sir. P... penguin." Nat shivers, head tilting for me.

"Use it if you have to." I nibble at his jaw, teeth threatening, trying to decide where I will mark him first.

"I... Okay. Yes. Okay." Nat's breath comes quick, heart pounding against me.

"Good boy." I decide on the place where his jaw and neck meet, just by his ear. I lick it first and then suck gently before letting my teeth sink into his skin.

"Oh..." The low cry is sweet, Nat arching for me. I run my hands down his back, letting my fingernails slide against his skin. So responsive. So scared. So needy.

All mine.

My hands cup his ass and lift him from his feet as I drag my teeth down along his neck to his shoulder.

"Oh..." Another cry, another leap from that hard cock and Nat's hands twist in the bonds.

"Did he fill you?" I ask, another surge of jealousy going through me at the thought. No other will touch him again. Not without my permission.

"No. No. He... he said he'd leave that g... gift for you." Nat looks over at me, eyes needy, desperate.

"And you want to be filled, don't you, Nat? Need it, even."

"I..." Oh, that blush is amazing, I feel it in my balls.

"Answer the question, Nat." Before I flip you around and nail you to the wall.

"I..." Nat swallows hard, nods. "Yes."

I lick his lips and then reluctantly step away, heading for the cupboard where the toys are. Those green eyes watch me, watch every single step, Nat panting for me, cock hard and throbbing for me. My own cock is hard, pushing at my leathers. I want him. Forty years old and I want this pup. More than anything I've ever wanted before.

He's so pretty, hanging there, black leather making that pale skin glow. All mine.

I find a string of beads, the first ones small, each one that follows larger than the last.

Perfect.

I loop them around my neck and grab a tube of slick, eyes on my beauty as I return to him. Nat flushes, eyes on the beads, on my chest, down to my cock.

"I'm going to take you down from the wall and bend you over the table. Fill you with the beads and then let you service me." I wait until I'm right in front of him and smile. "What do you think about that?"

"I... I don't want to think. I just want to feel."

"Mmm. Such a smart boy." I take his mouth with mine, pushing my tongue in. Oh, yes. Open, wanton, needing. The kiss is sharp, sweet, hungry. I unhook his hands from the wall as we kiss, leaving them cuffed together. I slowly back us up toward the table, tugging him along by his joined hands. I can't wait to spread him open, fill him up. He's warm against me, almost hot as he follows, cock tapping against my belly.

It makes my own throb, and as we get to the table I force him to his knees. I unlace my pants, letting my prick push out toward his lips. "Me first."

"Oh. Yes." Those pretty lips wrap around my cock and, fuck, he's eager for it, sucking hard, eyes shining. I know he's inoculated now that he's working for the club, know Mal will have explained I am, too. We don't use condoms if we don't have to.

I purr, hand sliding into those bright curls. I remember this, remember the eager, inexpert way he sucks. I let him have his head to start with, let him do as he will. His tongue slides over the tip, pressing, sending a little jolt along my spine. He's learned a thing or two since he was last here and I wonder if he did that for me and how he did it — did he just research it on the global net, or did he get hands-on experience? I know which one I want it to be, and my own need to have him pure, untouched, mine alone surprises me, excites me.

My hand tightens on his head, my hips starting to move. He moans for me, eyes closing, wrists twisting in the bonds.

"That's it. Feel me. Suck me." I move faster, sliding the tip of my cock to the back of his throat.

He gags a little, jerking, trying to take it all, trying to take me. I pull out and slide back in more slowly, giving him time to adjust. He's doing so well, I want to encourage him. He's going to be so good at this one day.

"Oh, that's it. That's a good lad. Relax for me, moan for me." The sound settles in my balls and I move a little faster, push a little harder, letting him take me in deep. Those pretty eyes open for me, watching, fucking clinging to me. Needing me.

My free hand strokes his cheek. "Nat..." I murmur his name as I speed my thrusts, expanding my pleasure, taking his mouth.

It's the hum, the happy little purr that travels up my cock that sends me flying. I force my eyes to stay open, watching him as my seed fills his mouth. He swallows hard, a bit escaping, sliding down his face.

Humming low, I wipe the come from his chin and bring it to my mouth, tasting what he's tasting as I let my prick slide from his mouth. Nat whimpers, licking those swollen lips, eyes wide. "That was nice — you've been practicing or something..."

Those eyes go wide. "I... I... No. Not with a person.

With a ratoa tuber. I... I didn't want you to send me away."

"A tuber? Oh, Nat..." I rumble, the sound vibrating inside me, pleasure going through me. "You've done very well. Time for your reward." I pull him up, bring our mouths together in a quick, hard kiss, and then I bend him over the table, bound hands up over his head. "You're going to love the beads."

"Beads?" That pretty ass isn't carrying any of my marks.

"You saw them, didn't you?" I draw the string of ebony beads over his ass, up his back, and slide them slowly over his shoulder to parade them in front of his eyes. The first one is small, like the tip of my little finger. The last one is not quite as thick as my cock.

"I... Yes. Yeah. I... They go in... inside?"

"Yes. One at a time. Filling you." I'm going to mark his ass first. A bite, or maybe one from my hand.

"Oh." Nat shivered, tongue sliding out, licking those lips.

I lean forward over him and lick at his ear. "My mouth or my hand?" I ask, letting him choose, but not letting him know what he's choosing.

"I...Your... your mouth."

"As you wish." I let my mouth slide down along his back and sink my teeth into the meaty globe of one ass cheek.

"Oh!" Nat jerks, body pulling away, shaking. Yes. Yes, just so. I lick at the bite mark, the shape of my mouth on his skin.

"You were naked," I tell him. "Now you're not."

A soft, sweet moan filled the air, Nat's legs parting. "Oh. Oh, gods."

"I usually go by sir, but if you want to call me god..." I tease him as I slick my fingers up and work the lube around the first few beads.

That gets me a giggle, a sweet laugh that's surprisingly sexy, hot. My cock is hard again. Between my mark on his ass, his honest emotions, and the string of beads, ready now to start filling his ass, I'm on fire.

"We begin." I push the first bead into him. There's resistance for a moment, and then he relaxes and it slides right into him. Nat gives a soft gasp, ass muscles clenching, hole tightening around the string.

"We've only just begun," I tell him softly, eager to feed each one into him, to feel and hear his reaction.

"Oh..." He likes that sound. Nat's body ripples, hips tilted and offered to me, and I don't think he knows how fine he is. I bend to kiss the small of his back, unable to keep from touching his skin with my tongue. Salt and musk fill me, make my balls ache. I rub my cock against the backs of his thighs, his balls, and then feed in the next bead. The mixture of nerves and curiosity and need is heady and he wriggles, trying to close his thighs, trying to hide.

"No. No hiding, Nat. You are mine; I will do with you as I want." I push another bead in, moaning at the sight of the pretty little ass with my mark on it, beads hanging from the tiny hole.

"Y...yours?" A faint blush starts up, sliding up Nat's spine.

"Mine." I growl the word this time and push the next bead in. I don't care what I have to do, what I have to offer Malachi, no one else will touch this one without my permission.

Nat nods, head bobbing, bright red curls bouncing. "Yes. Yes. Okay. Yes."

"Yes." I agree. My free hand is on the small of his back, not that I think that he'll try to get away, but because I want to touch him. I feed the next bead in. One more and

I should be able to let the string of them hang on their own. I'll give it a swing and let them tug at the beads inside Nat. It should be most delicious. For both of us.

The skin under my hand is so soft — untouched, unmarked, virginal. Nat is going to be so much fun to teach, to mark, to push. I push in the next bead and slowly let the string slide from my fingers. I watch it swing between Nat's legs, the black beads dark against his pale skin. "How does that feel?"

"Oh. Oh. Oh, it... It pulls. Inside me. Like a weight."

I nod, even though he can't see me. "It's good, isn't it?" I ask, pushing in the next two beads and setting the string to swinging again.

His flush darkens, pretty ass pushed toward me. "Yes."

"I told you you were a natural, did I not? That first day? I was so right." I lean again, lick my mark, press my tongue against the broken flesh as I push another bead in. They've gotten bigger — wider than my finger now.

"Yes. Please. So full. So full." His hole is pink, slick with lube, the string holding the beads stretching it slightly.

"Not that full yet, Nat. You've got over a dozen beads yet to go. The last one is almost as wide as my cock." I push the next several in before he has a chance to take a breath.

His legs spread, trying to make room, to open. I can see him in my mind's eye, hole snapped tight around my wrist, my arm. I rub my cock against his thighs again, so hard, wanting him so badly. This is for him, I remind myself, and push another bead in, nice and slow. Letting him feel the stretch. His cry fills the air, like a bird, lips open, panting. I push another one into him, eager for more noises. He gives them to me, one after another, like the beads push them out of him.

"Just three left now," I tell him. The thick ones. The ones that will stretch him like my cock would, forcing the smaller beads deeper into his body.

"I don't think they'll fit. I... So *full*."

"They'll fit." I lean forward and whisper in his ear as I push the next one in. "This is the least I'm going to make fit inside you."

He arches, moans low. "Oh... Oh, how..."

"You stretch, Nat. And you'll stretch as far as I demand." I force the next one in, knowing I'm filling him deeper now than he's ever been filled, and nearly as wide as my cock filled him last time we were together.

"Yes. Yes, for you." He's panting now, body covered in a fine sheen of sweat.

"Yes, for me." Fuck, he's amazing. Beautiful as he writhes on the beads.

"Only one more."

I begin to push it in, letting it stretch him wide, hold his body open. He's all flush and shivers, voice gone, sinking into that sweet silence, that acceptance we found before. So slowly, I push it the rest of the way in, knowing it's making the rest of the beads roll forward, sliding across his gland. Hovering on the edge, he just waits for me, waits for me to control him, to push him over.

My own cock is throbbing, watching the beads as I pull them out of him, hearing the cries I know will come, I know that will be enough to pull my own pleasure from me. Another time I might leave them in him, force him to walk with them, spend the day with them. Another time I might whip him, mark him while he holds the beads deep inside. But not today. Today I'm just going to undo the bindings on his cock and bid him come as I pull the beads from his body.

My hands fondle his heated, stretched flesh, sliding across the leaking tip as I undo the snap that binds his cock. His eyes fasten to mine, clinging, shining. His lips are bitten and swollen and parted. "Please. Yours. All I am."

"Then come." I take hold of the rope that hangs from him and pull it with one smooth, continuous motion. The beads pop from his body, one at a time, first stretching his hole from the inside. It closes up behind each one before stretching again for the next and the next.

His come sprays over the table, hot and heady, those green eyes rolling back as he slumps. The last bead pulls from his body, his hole seeming to cling to it, to try to hold it in, and then gravity takes over, the beads falling to the ground. I let the other end go and step forward, rubbing my aching cock against his ass, thumb tracing my bite mark. With a groan I come, my pleasure like a shock of electricity passing through my body, shooting from my cock.

Nat pants softly, body hot and pliant beneath me. I turn his face, licking at his lips and then make it a kiss, my mouth sinking against his, tongue pushing in to taste the hint of my seed that still lingers there and the unique, fascinating taste that is Nat himself.

He opens up, lets me right in, returns the kiss with a tentative touch. While we kiss I remove the cuffs, hands sliding over his wrists, massaging. Standing, I pull him into my arms, holding him against me. He leans against me, chin lifting silently for a kiss.

I grant it.

I would, I think, grant him whatever he wishes.

Our mouths come together, my hands sliding over his skin. A peace I haven't felt in a month settles over me.

"Can I stay? Please? Please, sir."

I nod. He'll stay. With me.

"What did you sign?" What am I going to have to pay to get him out of it?

119

"Sign?" He blinks up, frowning. "The man said that you would take care of everything. That you'd know what to do."

Oh, that sneak.

That bastard.

That sneaky, beautiful bastard.

I owe Mal and one day he's going to come collect. I'll do whatever he asks and happily.

I smile down at Nat. "I do. Come and see your new home."

I don't remember much about last night after Richmond brought me upstairs. I remember we bathed, I remember I cried a little like a moron, but I was so tired, so relieved, so overwhelmed and Richmond didn't fuss, just pulled me into the bed and wrapped around me and I slept. Hard.

I wouldn't have come back, but...

I needed to. I needed to know, to see. To feel. I need him.

It's morning now, though, morning and I'm awake and he's still holding me and I don't know what to do next.

Piss, I guess.

Yeah. Bathroom. Good plan.

Richmond grumbles and his arm tightens around me.

Oh.

Okay.

Wow.

I try to get up again, sort of more to see what Richmond does, more than to really go.

One eye cracks open. "Stay."

"I... Okay." I still, watching Richmond close, my morning hard-on fading.

He grumbles again and brings our mouths together,

the kiss soft, but growing deeper. Oh. Oh, morning kisses. It steals my breath, makes me hard — a real hard, not a morning hard.

Richmond's tongue pushes into my mouth, sweeping through it like he owns it. Like he owns me. I can't breathe. I can't see. I can't. I'm just feeling and rubbing and this isn't *like* me. It isn't.

One of his big hands slide around to my ass, rubbing our groins together. I'm not the only one who's hard and he's so big when he's hard. Fuck, hot. Hot. Hard.

I lean back, trying to catch my breath, clear my head. His other hand slides behind my head and brings our mouths back together, making me breathless again before I even have a chance to catch my breath.

It's so...

Hot.

Scary.

Sexy.

Good.

Fine.

Fuck.

He rolls me onto my back, sliding our cocks together. He's everywhere around me, tongue inside me. I wrap my lips around his tongue, sucking, pulling, trying to get some control, some handle on things. He purrs, hips moving harder against me, knees spreading my legs.

Oh. Okay. I'm stretched and aching from last night, I dreamed that he'd kept me filled, but my legs still spread, still open for him. His fingers are slick and cool as they slide inside me, but only for a minute before they're warm, hot, pushing, insisting and spreading. I hiss, not sure whether I like the burn, whether it should make me so hard.

He nips at my lips with his teeth, a third finger pushing insistently into me. "I'm going to keep you filled from now on. Always ready for me."

"Oh." Oh, gods. Filled. Filled. "Always?"

"Always." His voice is low and growly, fingers sliding across my gland and then doing it again.

"I... Oh..." God. Please. I need. Yes. I... "Again?"

He does it again and then he does it again and again. "I have a plug. It has a remote. To make it expand, vibrate. I could drive you mad." I shake my head, gasping, balls and nipples and cock aching. "You're going to love it."

His hands disappear and then his cock is pushing into me. So hot. So hard.

"Richmond!" My back bows, a scream tearing from me as I ride the burn.

"You're going to make me like mornings, Nat." He doesn't give me a chance to get used to it, just starts to fuck me. I just ride it, ride the burn and love it and go with it.

"God, you're tight. And hot. So fucking good, Nat. Want to do this forever." And he's fucking me like he is going to do it forever.

Okay. Yes. Forever. I can handle forever. Just...

Just don't make me go.

His eyes bore into mine, his hands framing my face as he pounds into me over and over again.

Oh. Oh, yes.

I nod, I can't help it. I don't want to help it.

He reaches down and grabs my cock, pumping me in time with each hard thrust. "Come for me, Nat. Show me."

"I... You..." I jerk, heels slamming into the mattress as I come.

"Yes!" Richmond roars, slamming into me and filling me deep with heat. It's like drowning, not being able to breathe, to think clear thoughts, to do anything but need. He collapses onto me, still hot and hard inside me. He feels good as I reach up to hold him, to touch him. He purrs for me. "My Nat."

I like the way that sounds. "I didn't have nightmares last night."

"You usually do? Or just since our first scene?"

"I... I've dreamed about you since the scene. Dreamed I was looking for you. Dreamed I was lost." I'd never dreamed like that before, never woke up scared and lonely and shaking.

His fingers are gentle, soothing as he strokes my cheek, making a soft sound. "You aren't looking for me anymore — I'm right here. That's why you didn't have any nightmares." He kisses me. "You won't dream anymore unless I allow it. You won't do anything anymore unless I allow it."

"I..." I don't know what to say, how to say anything. "You're talking about the impossible."

"Before you came here, you thought the idea of this club was impossible, didn't you? And after that first time you dreamed of me every night. Nothing is impossible."

"I... Yes. Yes, I did. I thought... I don't know. I don't know what to do."

"You are mine, Nat. You don't need to know what to do." He kisses me again, tongue sliding into my mouth. I know I should argue, should complain.

Should fight.

But...

I hear myself groan, feel myself squeeze the flesh still inside me. Richmond moans, the sound fed into my mouth. He likes that. I squeeze again. And again.

And again.

He nuzzles me, growling a little. "You keep that up and I won't be responsible, Nat."

"Won't be responsible? For what?" I can't think when he's making that noise.

"Fucking you through the mattress again." He makes his point by pulling almost all the way out and thrusting back in.

"Oh." I take my chances and squeeze again.

He growls again, thrusts again, demands more. "Again."

I squeeze hard, not sure when this moved from me doing something to doing what he asks. The growl and thrust and demand come again, just like before. His eyes are hot on mine, dark with passion.

"I... You. Yes. Yes." I squeeze and arch, toes curling.

"Again," he orders, thrusts coming now without my squeezing preceding them. He's just fucking me, pushing into me over and over, expecting me to keep up, to add to our rutting. My heart's pounding, my ass is burning, and my cock got hard without me ever noticing — hard and hot, throbbing. He's watching me with those dark eyes, watching my soul as he fucks me, takes me flying again. And I just give it up. All of it. Everything. Because he wants it and I want to, and it feels good. Damned good.

Even when I think I've given it all to him he demands more and proves I have more to give. I don't understand, don't begin to. Can't. All I can do is feel.

His hand is back around my cock, pulling the pleasure right out of me, demanding it as well as everything else.

The room goes quiet and still and grey as I come, the whole world spinning. I can feel his heat as he comes, filling me, pushing deep inside me, branding me from the inside out.

"Richmond..." I have to close my eyes, so vulnerable, so exposed.

He slides out of me then, pushing something inside, keeping me full of his seed, keeping me stretched. I'm wrapped in his big arms and pulled close. "I have you, Nat."

My ass keeps clenching against the hard intrusion inside, and I snuggle in, letting the scent and warmth comfort me. "Have me."

His chest rumbles against my cheek. "Mine."

"Yours."

Chapter Two

I'd like to stay in bed and make love to Nat all day. Or drag him down to one of the playrooms and explore with him. But I've got an appointment with Mal and I want that time off more than ever. Though now it's to play with Nat instead of retreating to lick my wounds. "I have to see Mal this morning. You'd better come with me. We'll make sure you haven't signed anything and then set up something between us, get the paperwork taken care of."

Still dazed green eyes blink up to me and Nat nods, so off-balance, fucked and found and filled, looking to me for where to go. "I... Okay."

"We have to find a better plug for you first. Something simple to start off with, I think."

I pull out a box from under my bed and start rummaging through the toys there.

"A... Good? What makes one good? And I'll wear it when...when we go?"

"You're to be filled all the time. With me as often as possible." I smile at Nat, stroke his cheek. "And what makes it a good one will change. For now, it needs to be something not too heavy or too big — that will come later. You aren't ready to walk around with the one you're wearing right now. I want you to feel it, to know it's there always, but it shouldn't hinder you. Oh, here we go." I pull out a thin plug, not much wider than one of my own fingers, and only a few inches long. It won't stretch Nat very much, but he will be aware of it. In fact, it should tease him mercilessly. I like the thought of him begging me to fill him with something else, something more. Me. Nat's breath is quick, light against my skin, those eyes searching my box of tricks.

"Do you see anything that interests you?" I'm curious; I'd like to know his honest wants and needs. His choices on his intake form had been so erratic, almost if he had checked stuff off at random.

"It's all so new." He pinks, swallowed. "So exciting, like a dream, a fantasy."

"It's real, though. After we see Mal, we'll go through the kink list together, sit down and discuss everything. We can go through some of the toys available for play then, too." I smile and shrug. "Mal doesn't like being kept waiting, so we need to get moving. Not to mention he's lost several tops and subs to exclusivity as it is, he isn't going to be feeling charitable toward this news."

"I... Okay. What do you want me to do?" Nat gives me a smile and I just want to kiss it. Hard. "I'm a little lost."

I take out the lube and slick up one of his fingers. "Lie back and take out the plug you've already got in."

I grab the slick stuff and make the little plug I've got nice and slippery. I won't make him put it in. Not this time.

"Oh. Okay." Oh, man. The squeak is hot. Mal's going to regret giving him to me.

Nat reaches behind those tight balls, tugging at the plug, cheeks bright red. I slide my hand up his thigh, stroking, soothing, and arousing at the same time. At least that's my plan. I let my fingers stroke his, attention split between his ass and his face. He moans, the plug sliding free, still wet from my seed, hole pink and stretched and needing to be filled again. Groaning, I lean forward and blow against his hole. Nat offers me a desperate little cry, that hole winking at me. I blow again and then push the little plug in, his hole swallowing it up hungrily. His body tightens around, looking for more, needing more.

I almost change my mind, almost choose something bigger, but he will be desperate for me by the end of our conversation with Mal and I want to see that in his eyes. He looks beautiful, flushed and needy, well fucked. Wanton.

Oh yes, this is how I want to lead him through the halls. Preferably naked, bound to my will, cock highlighted by a dark cock-ring. I think, though, I might save that for another day. He is not quite ready yet.

I pet his ass, pet his cock and help him up. "How's that?"

"Okay. It... it's okay." He offers me a kiss, soft and sweet.

"Okay will do. Many times you'll wear nothing at all, but I think we'll start you out slowly. You may wear the leather pants you came in with, but nothing on top, and you don't need socks or shoes, or a hat or anything else." I won't truss his cock up today, either. Mostly because I wonder if I can make him come without touching him, with only a look or a word.

It's sweet, watching him dress and trying not to jostle the plug or get hard.

I put on my own leathers, the ones that I have to use powder with to slide on, they're that tight. I make no effort to hide my own hardness — he affects me and I will not hide that from him. With my leathers I put on a silver mesh top, a mate almost to the one Nat wore for his interview, and I slide my feet into plain leather boots.

I brush my teeth and hair, wash my face, and am ready to go face Mal, my Nat at my side.

Mal's waiting for me, eyes twinkling and wicked. "Things went well, then?"

Bastard.

Smug, know-it-all bastard.

"You could say that."

"So, tell me. What kind of contract is he signing?" Wicked, evil, smarmy bastard.

"He's signing a contract with me and we haven't discussed the details yet." I resist the urge to cross my arms over my chest. I've been a top and a fucking good one all my life, but Mal is something else and even us big tough guys have been known to feel his heat.

"Exclusive? You're not sharing? You realize there's a list of tops aching to break in a pale little ass?"

I growl, rising to the fucking bait even though I know he's doing it just to get my goat. "Nathaniel? Are you interested in a list of tops aching to break in your pale little ass?"

"No! No, sir." I can feel those eyes, begging, pleading with me.

Mal just grins, like a big bastard shark.

"It looks like I'm not sharing." I go and stand behind Nat, hands dropping to his shoulders. "He's mine, Mal. Exclusive. We'll do shows, once he's ready, but he's mine."

"Shows and training classes — no one has to touch, but you can explore our more... intense methods with him so the new tops can learn."

Nat leans back against me, trusting.

I nod. That's not only acceptable, but arousing. It's not going to take long for him to be ready — he's a natural, taking to it like he's been doing it all his life — and I can't wait to show him off.

"Done. Nat will be employed by the training staff as you are." Mal meets Nat's eyes for a moment. "The pay is atrocious, but knowing Richmond, you won't be needing spending money."

Nat nods. "Okay. Yes. Anything to stay."

Mal winks, laughs. "You, sweet boy, are about to no longer be in the position to offer anything to anyone but your Richmond."

I curl my hand over his shoulder. "Mal's about to give you papers to sign, Nat. The shortest contract for training staff is five years. This is your last chance to change your mind until that time is up." He's not going to change his mind, I know it. Still my heart beats, waiting for his answer. I need this. I need him. Tough, a cool customer, one of the best training tops the club has and I'm sunk, as needy as any sub.

"I won't change my mind. I left everything behind — all of it — to come here to you."

I growl softy, pleased beyond belief with his answer. "We'll sign the papers now, Mal."

"Excellent." Mal types quickly. "Any special terms?"

"No. He's exclusive to me. We do shows and training sessions once I say he's ready. Otherwise I think the standard contract works."

"Done. Come here, Nat, I need your thumbprint."

Nat looks up at me and I nod, such a fast learner. Thumbprints here and there and he's mine. Signed, sealed, delivered.

I feel like pouncing. Mine now. All mine. "Good boy."

I turn to Mal. "Do you need anything else? I have a boy to train."

"He's all yours. You need a room reserved or are you keeping him upstairs for the week?"

I can feel Nat, vibrating beside me, nerves firing now

that things are done.

"I'm keeping him upstairs for the duration, Mal. He's mine now." I'm talking to Mal, but my eyes are on Nat.

"Excellent. Enjoy your vacation and congratulations, Richmond."

Nat's eyes are fastened to mine, wide, watching.

"Two weeks off, right?" I'll take anything I can get. Anything and everything.

Mal's chuckle is low. "I'll schedule a public showing of your new boy, then. If there's a problem, comm me."

"I will." Nat's eyes are still glued to mine and it's all I can do not to throw him onto Mal's desk and fuck him through it.

"Go home, Richmond. Train your boy. You're pouring off enough energy to set off every sub in the salle."

"Yes, boss." I grab Nat's arm and drag him out of Mal's office and to the lifts. I don't look at him, not for a second. If I do, I'm going to take him right where we are.

Nat stumbles along beside me, breathing hard, skin cool in my hand. The lift only has to go a few floors, but it's never seemed so long a trip before. "Come on, come on," I growl.

"Did I do something wrong?" Those huge eyes are so bright, so big.

"No, Nat. We just aren't ready to do this in public yet."

"Oh. Oh, yeah. Okay." He gives me a smile, a nod. "I'm yours now."

I nod, growl. "Mine, Nat. Yes."

The lift finally stops, the doors open, and I drag him down the hall, into my — our — rooms. As soon as the door closes behind us, I shove him up against the wall, kissing him hard. Those pretty little lips open right up for me, arms around my neck, moans sounding. I hump against him, cursing my decision to go with the leathers. Naked would have worked. Nat's rubbing makes me think he'd agree with me, fingers tangling in my hair.

Fuck, the leather's gonna be hell to take off with everything all sticky, but I can't find it in me to give a shit and I rub harder against him, fingers finding his nipples, tugging on them. Low, desperate sounds fill his mouth, Nat's motions more desperate, needier.

I reach down to grab Nat's ass, fingers pushing hard to jostle the little plug. Nat screams, going stiff, body shuddering as he comes. The smell is strong, good and enough. I come as well, the relief only enough to let me drag him to the bed and attack his pants.

I'll take a knife to them if I have to. He helps me, shoving his pants down, moving into my hands, whimpering softly, still hard for me. Mine aren't going to be as easy, but I'm not going to have to worry about that, they're going to be his job. I pump his cock a few times and then back off. "Undress me."

"Yes." His hands are shaking, unlacing, fingertips brushing my cock as the fly's worked open. "You... you smell good."

"Taste me." My voice is rough — he makes me need. His pink tongue peeks out, laps at my prick, my slit, fingers still trying to work my pants off. I groan, cock jerking. "How does the plug feel, Nat?"

"Teases. I... It's not you. Not you."

"Get my pants off, take out the plug, and it will be."

"Yes..." It takes him a bit, but he manages to slide the pants off my legs. Then he hides his face against my belly, fingers sliding the plug out.

Oh fuck, he's beautiful, amazing. Mine. "On your back, legs up."

He nods, leans back on the bed, legs bent, spread wide. "Like this?"

"Yes, just like that." I lean over him, put his feet over my shoulders and start to push in. Fuck, he's tight, hot, perfect.

"Oh. Oh. You. It's you." He's sweet, body gripping me, pulling me in.

"It's me." I keep pushing until I'm all the way in and then I bend and take his mouth, folding him like a pretzel. He opens right up, gasping and moaning into my lips.

Perfect. I start to fuck him with long, hard strokes. Fuck, it's sweet. Nat whimpers, taking me deep, ass rippling and squeezing my cock. I just keep pounding into him, watching his eyes.

"Yours." His eyes go sharp, focused, so bright.

"Yes. Mine." God, he's a fast learner. Sexy. Hot. Tight. Fucking mine. Harder and harder, I thrust. I'm going to send him to the fucking sky. His entire body shakes with each thrust, eyes rolling, flush covering the pale body. I grab his cock with one hand, pumping hard, determined to pull him over the edge with me. It takes two tugs and he's coming, ass milking my cock, pulling the spunk right out of me.

I keep pounding into him until my cock is screaming with sensation overload and then I collapse onto him with a groan. He's shivering, shaking a little, but quiet, holding on tight. I nuzzle into his neck, groaning as I feel my prick slowly slip out of his body.

He needs a plug, needs to be kept filled and wanting. I lean over and grab one of the medium sized ones out of the toy box, quickly lubing it and sliding it in. He shifts, whimpering softly, legs shifting on the bed.

"Sh. Sh." I pet him and lie back, pulling him against my chest. I help him slide his top leg over one of mine; the plug should be more comfortable for him this way. He sighs softly, body relaxing as he cuddles into me, eyes blinking so slowly. "Go ahead and sleep, Nat. When you wake we'll go over the kink list."

"'Kay..." My poor overwrought sub's asleep, resting, just like that.

I stroke his back, letting his breathing and the warmth of his skin soothe me.

It's going to be a most fascinating two weeks.

Chapter Three

The first thing I notice when I wake up is that I'm warm. The second comes right after, when I move and bend.

Oh.

Full.

Sore.

Stretched.

Oh.

Damn.

I reach back to... hell, I don't know *what*, really. Touch it, take it out, something.

My hand is taken in Richmond's. "You don't touch yourself unless I've given you permission."

Oh. I bite back my moan, teeth sinking into my bottom lip. "I... It aches. I didn't think..."

"Didn't think what?" He's still holding my wrist in his hand.

"About not touching." I twist my hand, not fighting, more testing to see how tight his grip is.

"No touching, no bringing yourself pleasure — or pain — unless I allow it. You are mine now." The grip on my wrist never falters. A shiver shoots right through me and oh, oh, my body knows what I need, what I want, even as my brain's running in panicked little circles. He chuckles softly and whispers into my ear, breath hot on my skin. "Stop thinking about it and just go with it."

"I... Okay. Okay." I'm rubbing, wiggling, caught between his skin and the plug filling me.

"Hmm... I think I'm going to have to bind you, keep you still while we discuss the big list."

"Bind me?" My cock is so hot, so heavy. Leaking.

"Yes. To keep you still." I'm let go and he crouches by the big box next to the bed, taking out leather and rope. I stretch, moaning as the plug in me moves, my hands sliding over my belly, easing the ache.

He tsks and my hand is slapped lightly. "Didn't I just say not to touch yourself?"

"I didn't. I mean, I did, but I wasn't going to touch down there. Just my belly."

"Is your belly not a part of yourself?" Richmond grabs hold of my prick and pumps lightly.

"Yeah. Yeah, I didn't know you meant..." Oh, yeah. Good.

"No touching means no touching at all." Leather slides along my thigh and around my balls, loose and cool, slowly warming. Slowly becoming tighter as Richmond tugs the ends together. I can feel my heart beating in my cock, in my balls, and my legs spread wide, just like a slut, trying to make room for all the sensation.

"Beautiful." Richmond's voice is gravelly, his hands hot on my skin as the leather tightens almost painfully around my balls and then wraps around my cock, holding me so tight.

I look down, fingers twitching, wanting to touch, to feel the so-black leather on my skin. I don't have long to try to resist the temptation, though, because Richmond is gently tugging my hands behind my back and tying them together. I don't know if I like this, like being trussed up and helpless. Richmond disappears for a moment and then comes back with a familiar-looking clipboard.

"I'm starting us out with a new survey." He sits on the bed, casually leaning back against the pillows, unconcerned about us being naked, and pulls me up close against him, my head on his shoulder. Oh. Yeah. Survey. I hadn't even read it before, just sort of ticked and chose, too scared and worried to read. "You don't mind, do you? That I'm discounting the original one you filled out?"

"No." I blush, cheeks going all hot. "I didn't read the one before. I was... I was scared and just trying to figure out how to get out of it."

Richmond raises an eyebrow. "All right. Before we take another step. What's your safeword?"

"Penguin." That was the part I'd been sure of, even then.

"And you know what it's for? How to use it?"

"Yes. It's for if I need you to stop, need you to stop everything, right then."

"Good. I don't ever want to hear you say again that you were scared and were trying to figure out how to get out of something. Because all you have to say is that word." He looks so serious, almost angry.

"Okay. Okay, I will. It's different now. I... It's not about a job. It's about you." My heart's pounding like a jackhammer, just thrumming.

"That makes it more important than ever that you use your safeword if you need to."

I nod, sort of cuddle in. I will. I will. Honest. Richmond growls a little, the sound sexy.

"All right. Favorite toys and favorite kinks. To date — we can revisit this later."

"I... I liked the beads. The plug is... So much." I shrug, unsure what to say. "Do you count as a kink?"

Richmond writes down anal beads next to favorite toys. "A kink is anything you like, that turns you on. It can be as simple as kisses or hickeys or as complicated as a detailed, far out scene."

"Oh. Kisses. Your voice. M... marks." It was the marks that haunted me, brought me back. The marks and that odd silence.

Richmond purrs a little and writes down kisses, voice, marks under favorite kinks. "Next come the specifics. Willing to try or already tried... anal sex, anal plugs, small and large, anal plugs in public. Well, that's an 'already tried' for all of those. Animal roles."

"Animal roles?" What the fuck?

"Pretending to be an animal. Barking like a dog, wearing a harness and tail like a pony. That kind of thing. Willing to try?" Richmond says it so matter-of-factly, like it's all the most natural, normal thing.

"You're not serious. People do that? On purpose?"

He chuckles, hand sliding down my back to jostle the plug inside me. "They do indeed. Would you like to give it a try, or are you at least willing to do so?"

Oh! Oh... I jump, wrists pulling against the bonds. "I... If you wanted, I'd try. I'd laugh, though. I'm bad about that, laughing."

"Well I could always gag you." Richmond winks at me and puts a check mark beside that one. "Auctioned for charity. I think not." An x is placed beside that one without my having said a word.

I snuggle in. His. I'm his. Yeah. There's a kink.

"Oh, ball stretching."

"Ow?"

"Are you asking me or is that your opinion?"

"Yes. I mean, that's not sexy, is it?" Old man saggy balls... Scary.

"It can be quite intense, but this is your survey." Richmond puts an x by that one and then purrs. "Beatings. Soft and hard are listed, but there's more to it than that, isn't there?" He purrs again and puts a check mark beside both.

"Yes." I push closer, lips trailing over his skin. His cock is starting to harden up, our conversation affecting him.

"Blindfolds." He winks at me. "For you."

I nod, laugh. Yes, that's okay. Not scary.

He puts a check mark by it. "Being serviced. Sexually." Another grin and another check mark without consulting me. "Being bitten." There's that sexy growl again and he puts down another check mark, turning to look at me with heat in his eyes. I can't stop my moan, my jerk, the way I rub against him. Oh. He licks his lips and his teeth and growls for me again. The check mark is darkened.

"Boot worship."

"Like licking them?" At his nod, I shrug. "I would do it for you."

He kisses the top of my head and puts a check mark by it. "Oh, another good one. Bondage. Light, heavy, multi-day and public."

"Uh... This is light? And public is sort of my job, right?" This is easier than I had expected, almost fun.

Richmond nods, smiling at me approvingly as the check marks were placed. "Branding. And yes, it's what it sounds like."

Oh. No. No. I shake my head, hips rocking against him, cock so hard.

"Is that a yes or a no?" Richmond asks.

"I... No?"

Richmond looks at me. "Your mouth is saying maybe, your body is saying oh fuck me yes."

"My body is not being sensible." Nope — not sensible. Hard? Yes. Aching? Yes. Rubbing? Yes.

Richmond laughs and writes maybe down on the sheet. "We'll talk about it again at a later date."

"When they make it painless, maybe." I wink at him, admiring his eyes, his jaw. God, he's sexy. Really.

"It's not painless when I bite you." The remark is offhand, casual. "Next up, breath play."

"That's... blowing in your ear?"

Richmond puts his head back and laughs, fingers finding the plug inside me and jostling it again and then again. "No, Nat. It's controlling the sub's breath during sex. Either using your hand over their mouth and nose or a rope around their neck."

I swear with some of these I think Richmond's just testing me, seeing how gullible I can be. "Right. Because suffocating? Is sexy." My voice is all raw, rough, my hips wiggling. "It's hard to sound sarcastic when you're doing that."

Richmond does it again, jostling the plug hard this time. "I have seen it done several times. It was... the most intense and beautiful demonstration of trust I have ever seen. I came without touching myself anywhere when the sub did."

He's serious — it's more than my brain can fathom, but he's serious. Fuck. Fuck. I'm burning up here and we're on the b's.

"I... You... That scares me. It scares me that I would do it for you." I hide my face in his shoulder, gasping.

He groans, the sound sort of vibrating me, hand stroking up and down my back. "Thank you, Nat." I can hear him put a check mark by that one. "Bruises. I think I can safely put a check beside that one. Cages, as in being locked inside them."

"I'd try." It doesn't sound fun, but it doesn't sound terrifying either, more... uncomfortable.

He nods and puts a check mark. "Just because we're putting check marks beside stuff doesn't mean we're going to run out and do them all as soon as we've finished filling out the form. Caning is next."

"Caning, that's like the whipping?" I nod, I can't believe I'm nodding. I'd dreamed about the whipping for days.

"Excellent." Yet another check mark. Oh, God, I'm such a slut. "Castration fantasy."

"Not even at my weirdest."

Richmond chuckles, but doesn't try to talk me into this one. "Catheterization."

"Like at the medunit? Why?"

Richmond nods. "Because it can feel good. There's a thing called a sound. It can be slipped into your urethra, stretches it a little, makes it impossible for you to come until it's pulled out." Richmond purrs. "I enjoyed it when Mal did me."

"You did? What did it feel like?" I scoot closer, drinking in the feeling of his skin.

"It burned. But it was a good burn. Like this." He jolts the plug inside me again. "When he pulled it out and I came, I almost passed out."

"Oh..." My cock throbs, balls feeling so heavy. "Oh, Richmond... Okay. Yeah."

"Good." Another check mark. "Cattle prods, tazers, electric shock toys."

"No. That's too... police and scary, you know?"

"Fair enough. Being locked in cells and closets."

"That's a kink? Really?" God, people are weird. "I mean, I'm not scared of closets, but I'd probably just nap. I used to build a fort in mine at home when I was a little boy."

Richmond chuckles. "I imagine the people who have diapers and baby rattles as kinks might also check off being locked in closets. It could be a possible area for punishment — as could any of the ones we don't check off." Richmond puts an x down. "Chains." Richmond tapped the clipboard with the pen. "And I'm going to split this into, beaten with and bound with."

"B...beaten with?" Man, that could break something. "I... You don't mean *injuring*, right? I mean, hurting and harming are real different things."

"I'd have to be very careful. Some people are into being injured or causing injury, but not at this club. That crosses a line."

Yeah. Yeah. I nod, feeling more at ease. "Then yeah, I guess so to both, but only you. I wouldn't trust anybody else."

"Nobody else is touching you." The words are said matter-of-factly, but there's a core of steel in them, too. Richmond puts in the check marks and continues. "Chastity belts — short term and multi-day."

I roll a little, looking at him. "That's one of those things that I'd do for you, right?"

Richmond laughs. "I think that's one of those things you'll do when I think you're forgetting your place and or in need of a lesson in control." He writes "punishment" beside them and continues on. "Chores — domestic service."

"Well, I know how to do dishes. Again, necessary more than erotic."

"It isn't always about eroticism. It's about control, servitude and punishment. Some Dom/sub pairings live a master/slave relationship every moment of every day."

"What will we do? Oh, and I don't hate cleaning. I mean, it's a chore, not hell."

"I've never felt the need to be in a master/slave relationship with anyone, though I'd not be against it if it's what you want. I do expect your obedience at all times."

"I'm not sure I get the difference." I manage to sit up, stretch a little, trying not to jostle the plug any more than

I have to. "Is the master and slave deal where the sub is brainless or something?"

Richmond chuckles, eyes dancing. "Not at all. But the slave is expected to wait on the master hand and foot, his opinion is never sought, the master makes decisions unilaterally. The dynamic is somewhat different. I mean, I expect you to obey, but you may speak, ask me questions, do your own thing if we're not... busy."

"Oh." Okay, so the master/slave thing? Not for me. Not at all. "I get you." I can't even imagine; I mean, I don't even do sit-still-for-a-long-time things well, much less... waiting-hand-and-foot things.

"I like a clean house and I can be anal about it." He winks at me. "But we'll share the chores. Next are clothespins. And not to hang up clothes, but to attach to your skin." Richmond reaches over and pinches my arm and then one of my nipples. "Like that, only they'd stay on."

I shiver, nod. Okay. Yeah. Tingly. Damn. Another check mark. Wow, we've hardly left anything with an x.

"Cock rings, straps. Check." I get a wink from Richmond and then he purrs. "Oh, one of my favorites. Cock worship."

"Cock worship? As in making love to?" I can handle that. God, I'm a slut.

"As in you worshipping my cock with lips and tongue and hands and ass and everything you can think of." His voice has gone all growly rough and the cock he's talking about is really hard now, the tip leaking a little, making it shiny.

"Oh." I lick my lips, eyes on his prick. "Yeah. Yeah. That's a check."

"Thank god." He winks at me and makes the check mark nice and heavy. "Collars. Worn in private and in public."

Another nod. I could handle that. It wasn't like people wouldn't *know* I was his.

He checks it and gives me a hot look.

"Competitions. Like with other subs." He tilts his head. "I'm not sure the Glove approves of these."

"I'm not interested." What would I be competing for? I already have Richmond.

He just puts the x beside it without saying anything else. Technically, we're filling out a list of my do's and don'ts, but I'm finding out about what he wants and likes, too as we do it.

"Corsets and cross-dressing."

"That'll get you beat up. Besides, I'm not pretty."

Richmond snorts and puts punishment down beside the words.

"Cuffs. Leather, metal."

"Okay, sure." I peak at the list, my eyes going wide at the next item. "Cutting goes with branding."

He writes down maybe. "Dildos." He puts a check mark next to that.

I chuckle. "Electricity, enemas, enforced chastity. Well, there's a trio of unpleasant things."

"Have you never had an enema you've enjoyed? Cleansing can be quite wonderful for bringing you together with your top."

"I've never... Not for any reason."

Richmond put an x beside everything but the enema, which he put a check mark beside. "Erotic dancing. Are you a dancer, Nat?"

"Me?" I shake my head. God, no. "I've got the grace of a drugged bull."

"Oh, that isn't true, Nat. I've seen you move under my whip." He puts "explore" next to erotic dancing. "You'll have an examination with Doc, but it hardly merits its own category. And exhibitionism is, as you've said, part of the job description." More checks. "Eye contact restrictions."

"As in don't look at you? I can, I guess, but..." I blush dark, duck my head. "I like looking at you."

That earns me a bit of a purr. "A punishment, then. What about with other people?"

"I don't follow. Not being able to look at other people? They wouldn't think I was being an ass?"

"Here? They would know."

"It would be hard. I'm..." I meet his eyes, grin sheepishly. "I'm a reporter, or I was. I'm curious."

"So, still a punishment. Good to know. Face slapping."

Oh, that's odd. "I... It shouldn't matter because I said yes to the caning and chains and stuff but... Does it feel different to you?"

Richmond nods. "Yeah, it's different. Humiliation over pain."

"I don't want that." I want to know he wants me here, likes me. Cares.

He puts an x by it without comment. "Fantasy abandonment, fantasy rape and fantasy gang rape."

"No." I shiver, press closer. "No."

He raises an eyebrow but doesn't say anything, just puts the x next to the items. "Fear. Being scared. As in deliberately going into dangerous situations for the rush."

That tickles me. "Given how we met? I don't know how to answer that."

He gives me a grin and puts a check mark next to it. "How about fisting?"

"Fisting." No fucking way. That's a myth. I know it. "We talked about pain versus injury already."

Richmond arches that fucking eyebrow again. "Fisting has nothing to do with injury. And very little to do with

145

pain unless it's done wrong."

"Really?" I blink, trying to wrap my head around that. "You're serious?"

"I am." He puts a check mark next to it. "You've the makings of a size queen, the way you take to that plug. You're going to love it."

"A size queen?" My cheeks heat again. "God, I look like such a slut."

"You say that like it's a bad thing."

"Well, yeah." I roll my eyes, grin. "It's not a positive character trait."

Richmond snorts. "It is to me."

He goes back to his list. "Flame play."

"What is it with this list and the burning?"

"There's been a lot of burning?"

"Branding and flames and... oh, that was cutting, wasn't it? Well, you probably have to get the blade hot to clean it..."

Richmond chuckles and puts in maybe. I notice he's not taking a whole lot of outright nos. "Following orders. Yes. Food play?"

I can't help but notice that I didn't get to choose on the following orders one. "Food play? Is that like whipped cream and stuff?"

"Anything, everything. Whipped cream, honey, cucumbers..."

"Ew. One of those things is not like the others." My nose wrinkles up, but we're chuckling, laughing together, and it's good.

"I think we'll do cold plugs at some point — with ice water." He waggles his eyes at me. "Foot worship."

"Suck my toes, baby?" I'm giggling hard now, belly shaking. "If it turns you on."

He just grins at me and puts the check mark beside it. "Forced masturbation, forced nudity - private and public."

Like he'd have to force me. I'm the jerk-off king. I don't tell him that, I just nod.

He checkmarks them, free hand sliding slowly down my back again. I know it's coming, but it still makes me jump when he gets to my ass and twists the plug. "We've already covered forced servitude, really. Full head hoods."

"I..." God, he makes my toes curl. "Okay, I guess. Sure."

He gives me a look and puts the check mark there. "Gags, cloth through rubber, ball and phallic."

"If I said no, would it matter?" I don't know. I don't think I'd hate them, although I imagine whatever made him decide to use them? That, I'd hate.

"It would depend on why you said no."

"I don't know. I don't know what I think about them."

"So we'll try them out." He puts a plus sign beside it. "Gates of hell. Do you know what that is?"

"Nope, but it sounds unpleasant."

"It's a type of cock-ring. A bunch of rings like a ladder. We'll work you up to it." He puts the check mark next to it. "Now this one I can't figure out why it's in here — genital sex." He writes on the check mark. "I'm not even asking you, we're having sex involving our genitals."

"Oh. Yes. I approve." Over and over and over.

And over.

Daily.

"Given away to another Dom temporarily and permanently." He snorts and crosses them off the list.

"How about hairbrush spankings?"

I nod, blush, look down. "Yeah."

He purrs and slaps my butt. "Hair pulling."

"Yours or mine?"

"Yours."

"Oh." I shake my head. "I don't think so..."

"Hand jobs, giving and receiving." He's already put in a check mark, looking at me for confirmation.

"Yep." I peek over. "No harems, though. Harnessing sounds okay, but I'm a picky eater." People let other people choose their food? Weird.

He puts in the check marks and the x marks. "What about choosing clothes? Provided I let you wear them."

I'm too busy blushing to pay attention to the fact I'm nodding.

"Head — covered under cock-worshiping. Homage with tongue — covered under boot-licking. Hoods, also covered. Hot oils! On genitals."

"We're heading into that burny place again." I haven't laughed so hard *ever*.

He snorts. "I'm putting a check on this one. There's some interesting oils."

"Interesting. Okay." I look again, leg sliding along Richmond's. "Boys don't hot wax. We've gone over housework and human puppies and humiliation. Hypnotism? For real?"

Richmond shrugs. "This covers everything."

"Okay. No hypnotizing. I'll just be good. Mostly."

"Ice cubes?"

"They're nice and cold."

"And they make excellent plugs, even if they do melt." He puts a check mark by it. "Immobilization."

"That's different than heavy bondage? Or the one underneath it? The intricate rope bondage?" This stuff is complicated.

"No, we can throw it all together and I'll just put a yes on anything to do with bondage." Richmond chuckles and puts a check on the next one. "Interrogations. Like this one. Oh, kidnapping. Would you like to be kidnapped and have me rescue you?"

If I laugh any harder, I'm going to hurt myself. "My hero!"

"I would, you know. If it happened." He puts a check mark there, his look daring me to protest. "Kneeling." He hums, the sound just luscious. "On your knees, boy."

Oh. "I love that sound."

He puts a check mark there, his look beginning to smolder. "Knife play can fit under cutting. Leather clothing, I think that's a given. Leather restraints we've already covered. Oh! Lectures for misbehavior!"

"You'll do that anyway and I'm going to be good."

He laughs and jostles my plug again. "Licking — non-sexual. Now, where's the fun in that?"

My moan is loud, my ass clenching around the plug. "N... none. No lingerie — it's silly. Massage is good. I like touching."

"Medical scenes, modeling, mouth bits and mummification." He winks. "One of these things is not like the others..."

I shake my head. "Who thinks this stuff up?"

"Yes for the pictures, no for everything else? And don't make fun."

"Sorry, it's just so different than I thought." I have to swallow the urge to say "yes, sir." It seems too easy, scary-easy.

"What did you think it would be like?"

"I don't know that I did, really. I didn't know there were so many choices, that there was so much."

"There are as many things as there are people to think them up. Who knows, maybe before we're done you and I will have added to this list."

That makes me smile, dare to dip my head and take one of his nipples in my mouth, licking at it.

He purrs for me. "That's not new."

"Sometimes the tried and true is the best." I nip a little, take the hard bit of flesh in my teeth and tug.

He groans, hand coming up to hold my head in place. "I didn't say you could do that."

No. No, he didn't. I do it again, ending the bite with good, hard suction, hoping I'm doing it right. His fingers dig into my scalp, a low moan coming from him. "I think it's time to explore that cock worship thing..."

Oh. Okay. Yeah. God, I want. I rub up against him, purring around his nipple, wrists twisting in their bonds. He lets my head go and stretches his own hands up above his head, like he's offering his body to me. I manage to shift until I'm straddling him, lips moving over his skin, licking and nipping and tasting. Teasing.

"Mmm, that's right, Nat. Show me what you can do."

He's sort of seen all of my repertoire, but I hadn't been at the top of my class for nothing and I've researched and it's easier now, less overwhelming, more equal.

He's still got his hands up over his head, body stretched for me. I explore his arms, his neck, his chest, lingering at the places that make him moan. My belly is rubbing his cock, so hot, so hard. I hope he likes it because I can't figure out how to get my head down there without impaling myself or giving myself a black eye.

He seems to have figured that out, though, because he grabs me around the waist and moves me down so my head is resting on his belly, the scent of the drops on his cock strong, male. I moan and the noise sounds so raw, so slutty, obscene, but I make it anyway, tongue sliding out to lick and lap. Oh. Oh, yeah.

"Oh, fuck. Yes." His hips push up, taking me with them, and his hands drop to my head, fingers wrapping in my hair. I groan, legs curling under me, plugged ass in the air. My hips are moving with his, in time with the pressure in my mouth.

He's growling, moving, pushing into my mouth. "Sexy slut," he mutters, and I can hear the pleasure in his words.

I blush, whimper around his cock, but I don't argue. I can't. I want it. I came to him and begged for this, begged to be his. His cock is huge in my mouth and he's moving faster now, more insistently, thick head bumping the back of my throat. My thighs are spread, ass clenching around the plug as I try to swallow, fight the urge to gag and pull away.

He flips us suddenly and my cuffed hands are under me, forcing my back to arch as he fucks my mouth. My hips slam back into the mattress, rubbing hard, jostling the plug over and over as he pushes deep into my throat, feeding his cock to me, taking me. Over and over he pushes into my mouth, like he's never going to stop.

He does, though. With a shout, he forces himself deep and his come pours down my throat, burning me, owning me. I swallow him down, sucking and sobbing and rocking, needing to come so bad, needing the pressure in my ass and balls to ease.

He pulls out slowly and lies on his side, dragging me up into his arms. His hands pet me, soothingly, his lips pressing kisses over my face. "Sh. Sh. Relax, Nat. Rest easy."

My heart is pounding, so hard, so fast, but his hands ease me, relax me.

"Not yet, Nat. We have the list to finish before you get your reward for being so good."

I hear my whimper — there's another of those slutty sounds, begging for it. "Yes... yes, sir."

"Oh, very good. Very good indeed."

He kisses me, long and slow. A promise.

***

I spend a long time just kissing Nat. We have to finish going through the list — and how pleased am I that he is refusing very little? I am very pleased. And then I will tease him some more, make him beg to come, make him think he's going to explode if I don't let him come. It'll be so good for him.

I take his cock in my hand. Even the leather that surrounds it is burning up and his balls... fuck, they're hotter than anything except maybe his ass.

At length I lie back again, tugging him against me and picking up the clipboard.

"Name change. Scene and permanent." My voice is all rough and husky and that's because of him.

"Hmm? Why would you want to change my name?" He rubs against me like a kitten full of cream.

I shrug. "It's important to some people, like a rebirth, coming into a new life."

It's not important to me, though, so I put an x by them and go on. Oh, the next batch are all fun. "Nipples are next, Nat." I pinch his lightly. "Clamps, rings, play/torture and weights."

"Oh... Rings? Like piercings?" He's rocking again, nipples going tight and hard. So pretty.

"Yeah. There's a whole range of piercings we can play with." I tug on his nipples again and then palm them, rubbing my hands over the little points. Nat whimpers, eyes sliding shut, so responsive. "That's a yes."

I put a check mark next to each one. "Oral/anal play — also known as rimming. Oh, I think that's a yes, don't you, Nat?" I've already put the check mark in.

"Oh... okay. Yeah." He's so hot now that he's forgetting to be embarrassed and teasing.

"Over the knee spanking."

He blushes, but nods, looking down at the list. "If you want to. Orgasm denial and control. If I say no to those, can I come now?"

I laugh, but he doesn't succeed in distracting me. All the times spanking has come up, it's excited him, and I'm more pleased that he's admitted it than that he wants it. He has no idea how transparent he can be, which makes it all the sweeter when I give him what he really wants.

"You don't want to come now." I put a check next to the spanking and the orgasm ones. "You want to come when I say you can."

"I don't? I mean, I do? I mean..." He shakes his head, licking his lips. "I can't think, you've got me all jumbled."

"You don't need to think, you only need to feel." I lean in and lick his lips, too, before settling back and continuing. "Outdoor scenes and sex. I think we can file these under public and mark them yes."

I do that, smiling at the next entries. "Pain. Mild, medium and severe." I can't keep from purring. He's beautiful when I hurt him.

"Severe? Severe sounds... severe."

"The whipping our first day was... a little more than medium, but not as severe as it gets." I wait, letting him figure out for himself that he wants it, needs it.

"I..." He buries his face in my chest, shuddering, gasping, his need fighting his upbringing.

"You agreed to the cane," I remind him, my hands sliding over his skin. "And my marks show so well on your pale skin..."

He nods, moaning low, twisting under my touch. "For you. For you."

I bite my lips to keep my chuckles quiet. For me. Right. Not that I won't enjoy it, not that I don't love the way his skin marked up for me, but that's not why he's agreeing.

"Persona training in scene and permanent personality changes. I think we can safely cross this out. You know to obey and yes sir during a scene, that's good enough for me. Which brings us to piercings, temporary and permanent, though really, none of them are permanent like a tattoo or a brand would be."

"I... I guess. I don't know. I've never tried."

"Wonderful." I put a check mark next to those. "Pony slave." I manage to say it with a straight face and I can't wait for his reaction. This is such fun — this shouldn't be this much fun, but it is.

"Pony..." He gives me a look. "I couldn't carry you. Ever. No. That's... No."

I throw my head back and laugh. Oh, such fun.

"Public exposure." I put a check mark next to it and move on. "Punishment scene."

"What's that?" He rolls his shoulders, shifting down as my hand reaches for the plug again.

I jostle the plug, leaving my finger on it and rolling it inside him. "It means instead of just assigning something or doing something as punishment, we turn it into a scene."

"Oh. Oh, Richmond... I can't think when you do that!"

"Say it with me, Nat. No thinking, just feeling."

"Just feeling... I need to come... So bad." He's mine, would do anything for me.

"You want me to checkmark the rest of them? Because you don't get to come until we're done." His need makes me hard.

"No. No, I'll wait. Scenes are... are okay."

Clever boy.

"All you have to do to avoid them is make sure you don't need punishment." I kiss him hard and play with the plug some more, making sure he stays high, needy.

"Riding crops, yes. Religious rituals."

He wrinkles his nose. "Not sexy."

"What about non-religious rituals?"

"I guess. I don't really know, but I'd try."

"I won't put no. We can see what develops for us. Restrictive rules on behavior."

"Is that like you saying I can't touch myself?"

I grin and put a check mark next to it. He has a point. "Yes. Rubber/latex clothing."

"Sure. It's sort of hot, though." He's relaxing again, focusing.

"So what kind of clothing do you find sexy?" I reach down and pump his cock a few times.

"Uh... to look at or wear? You looked good in the leather." The leather holding him is wet from the drops leaking from him.

"Thank you," I hum. I like wearing leather. I like the way it clings to me. Makes me feel sexy, which gives my walk a predator's roll. "And to wear?"

"I like soft stuff. I like the leather, too, but it squeaks and seems silly."

"Even if seeing you in it makes me hot?"

He pinks and gives me a grin. "That's not silly."

"No, it isn't at all." I put a check mark by the rubber/latex clothing. "Rope body harness."

He nods. "Okay. I can do that."

"I knew you could. Scarification has really been covered by markings in general and branding. It's just a different way of doing it. Scratching: giving and receiving."

"Like 'I itch? Scratch my back?'" He nods, enthusiastic. "That's a wonderful feeling."

I laugh again. "No, I think they mean like this." I scratch my fingernails lightly over his nipples.

"Oh..." He arches, toes curling.

Oh, that's a yes. Purring, I put in the check mark. I

scratch his nipples again, a little harder this time. "Sensory deprivation."

Nat shakes his head, gasping, tongue licking at his lips. "Want to *feel*, Richmond, remember?"

"Ah, but you know how much better it feels to come after you've been refused that release? Sensory deprivation works the same way." Though just because I enjoyed it with another top I could trust, doesn't mean Nat has to.

"I'd try it, I guess. See how it was."

"Excellent." I give him a hard kiss as his reward. He purrs, lips wrapping around my tongue, sucking, hips rocking into me. He's so ready, he's going to go off like a rocket the minute I loosen his cock. I'll have to make sure I have his ass first.

"Serving's next. In general, as art, as furniture, orally — it's checked off already, Nat — other Doms — already marked no."

"Art? Me?" He grins, nose wrinkling. "I could, I guess. I'd try."

Chuckling, I go ahead and mark yes through them. "I think you'd make a lovely table..."

"Table?" He giggles, rubs his cheeks against my chest. "Okay."

Grinning, I jostle that plug again. Is there anything he won't try for me? I think not, and I don't know if the idea thrills or scares me more.

"Sexual deprivation — I don't see the point aside from how it factors into sensory deprivation. Shaving! Body, genitals, head."

"Oh. I don't know..." He shivers, cuddles in that way that I'm learning means I'm pushing his comfort level.

I put a check mark next to it and play with his plug some more. "Skinny dipping, yes — the club has some wonderful pools. Sleep deprivation."

"I don't think you could, Richmond. I'm unbearable,

all my uni dormmates said so. I get... fluttery."

"Oh, that sounds interesting. We might do it once, just to see, yes?" I put down a check mark without waiting for his answer. As long as he's not safewording, I'm figuring I'm pretty safe.

"Sleepsack, slutty clothing." I snort — it's not the clothing that makes a man slutty and he's sleeping with me. They both get an x. "Spandex clothing's been covered. Ah, spanking, general."

I know it's been covered, but I like the way talking about it makes him react.

Those cheeks are going to have a permanent blush and his ass-muscles are going to be tender tomorrow, from squeezing the plug. "H... haven't we already said yes to that?"

"More or less." I stroke his back. "Speech restrictions."

"Only if you want me to screw up."

"Oh, a challenge. I like those." I put a check mark by it and move on to the next item. "Not much longer, Nat. I know you're eager to be done." I tap the plug in his ass, just to make sure he remembers why. "Speculums, anal, this was covered in medical — you'll only get it if Doc needs to examine things. Spreader bars."

He nods, eyes wide, hungry. "Spreader bars? To hold me open?"

God, he's a slut. How could I have gotten so lucky? Mal could have chosen any one of a dozen of us to do his initial "interview."

"That's right. They keep your arms or legs open a certain amount." I put a check mark there, purring at the look in his eyes.

He's mine.

"Standing in a corner."

He snorts, shakes his head. "Like a bad little boy?"

"Yes, exactly. And if you prefer the punishment scenes, that's not a problem for me." I cross it out and read off the next two. "Stocks and straitjackets."

"What's a stock and straitjackets are for crazy people."

I cross them both out, since stocks need to be custom made and aren't that much different from spreaders. "You must know what stocks are, what with having researched things — you know, old-fashioned from long, long time ago punishment. Head and hands in wood that you have to wear for a certain amount of time."

"Oh! No. Yuck." He looks at the list again. "Strapping and suspension and then we're done with the S's. So long as we're sticking in the pain-not-injury field, that's cool."

I checkmark them off. "We're going to have such fun, you and I. Tattooing will be at my discretion, teasing goes without saying and we've covered tasers. Thumb cuffs are ridiculous and I've yet to see a top who could make them look sexy. Oh, tickling. I think that one goes without saying as well."

We're speeding through this now. It's one thing to make him wait, but I'm starting to need again, wanting him tight and needy around my cock.

"Urethral sound we've already covered. Uniforms — you'll wear one if I want you to, but on the whole? They're ugly. Including others."

He shakes his head, sure. "No. I want you."

I nod, I can deal with that. Hell, yes, I can. "They can watch, but they can't touch." I'm interested in his reaction to this next one and pay attention to his body language as much as his words — most folks can't admit they want this. "Verbal humiliation."

His head tilts and he thinks, cock rubbing my thigh. "I... I don't know. I mean, you called me your slut and that's embarrassing, but sexy and stuff. But if you were mean? That's not."

"My calling you a slut was a compliment, not verbal humiliation. That would be more along the lines of my telling you you were a worthless piece of shit while we were in the dining room or on display in a training salle."

"Well, then it's not only mean, it's a lie. If I was worthless you wouldn't want me."

Laughing, I cross it out and then move the plug inside him, pushing it in hard so it rubs over his gland. "Vibrator on genitals. Never mind, it's a yes."

He chuckles, then nods to the next item. "Electricity is burny."

"Oh, but a violet wand is special. You remember the sound? Now add voltage." I put a check next to it. We'll work our way up to it.

"Voyeurism. Watching others, watching me with others."

He shakes his head. "Not really my thing. I mean, it's okay, but not a *thing*. Oh and the next one? Vids? They're okay if you have to jack off, but sexy? No. So... joyless?"

"What about a recording of us?"

"That's getting into the 'it's sort of the job' thing. It'd be weird, but not horrible. What's water torture? And the torture part? Not confidence-inspiring."

"Long and boring. I saw one Dom/sub pair do it and nearly fell asleep. It's this one drop of water at a time thing, supposed to really sensitize the sub or something. Waxing — we could do that. Wearing jewelry — the only thing symbolic I can think of is a collar, and you've already agreed to that. Weight gain/loss, nope, you look good the way you are. Oooo, whipping."

"Oh." That's a sweet little peep. "We've already done

159

that."

"We have, indeed." I happily checkmark it and the paddles. "So many fun ways to hit you." I wink at him. "Last one. Wrestling."

"You're not serious. You'd kick my ass." He is rubbing harder now, eyes shining, excited.

"Sounds perfect, that's a yes. And we're done." I put down the pen and the clipboard and lie back, hands under my head. "Whatever shall we do now?"

He growls — and damn, it's cute. "Me? I need, Richmond."

I nod. I imagine he does. Pretty fucking badly. "Take out the plug and ride me, Nat. Show me how bad you need me."

He whimpers, then turns, offers me his bound hands, wrists red and chafed.

I tsk. "You shouldn't fight them, Nat."

I undo the restraints, rubbing the abused flesh.

"Oh. Oh, ow. Burns." He bucks, shoulders rolling. "Didn't mean to. Honest."

"We'll spray them later. I want you to ride me."

Nat nods, reaches back and pulls out the plug, his body fighting it, trying to keep it in. He wriggles, struggles, and it's sexy as fuck, the cry he makes as it comes free. "Oh! Oh, fuck. Please!"

I'm growling, wanting. "Come on, Nat. Fill yourself." My hands land on his waist, but I don't help him — he was told to do it himself.

His hand wraps around my cock, trembling as he slides himself down. He's hot, swollen, tight and slick, and I know he's got to be sore, but I also know he doesn't care. It's all good, all hot. His ass squeezes my cock as he lowers himself down and it's fucking sweet, fucking perfect.

"That's it, Nat. Take what you need."

His hands land on my chest and he starts moving, starts fucking himself hard and fast, head ducked, eyes closed, ass working me like a fist. Fuck, it's good, really good. I let him keep going at it until I'm ready to pop and then I undo the bindings holding his cock and balls.

Nat screams, really screams, head snapping back, spunk spraying as he slams down on my cock. His ass milks my cock, pulls my orgasm from me and I pump my hips up, filling him with my seed. He slowly collapses, shaking as he settles on my chest. I slide my hands down along his spine, soothing. "Such a good boy."

His ass squeezes my cock, body rippling. "Thank you."

"You're welcome, Nat."

His eyes close, breath slowing, ass slowly letting my prick go.

I reach down and open my toy box, find a smallish plug and slide it into him. He shivers, whimpers, but doesn't wake up, just rubs against me. Sweet boy.

My sweet boy.

I reach again and get the lamp turned off, the covers up over us.

My boy.

Chapter Four

It's my stomach that wakes me up this time, disoriented, confused, and starving to death.

I roll off Richmond's chest, moaning as the plug shifts, and get my bearings. Okay. Bedroom. Door. Hallway. Kitchen.

Oh, yay. I was sort of worried that there wouldn't be one, that there was some fucked up employee cafe or something. I find some milk in the cooler, along with some butter and bread slices and cheese. Sandwiches. I could grill cheese sandwiches.

I go and find my pants first — because really, burned cock? Ow — and then find a little pan and get to work, making one for me and two for Richmond.

I'm about done when I hear a noise and there's Richmond in the doorway, absolutely naked and watching me with heat in his eyes.

"Oh! Hey! You hungry? I made us cheese sandwiches." I'm feeling odd and overdressed, sort of goofy and nervous.

"I thought you weren't interested in servitude." He's grinning at me, but it doesn't feel mean.

"I'm interested in not starving. You said we'd share the chore-y type stuff, anyway." I grin back, hand him a plate. See? I was listening.

He takes the plate in one hand and my arm in the other. "The sitting room has comfy-er chairs."

Oh. Good idea. My ass is all about comfy chairs.

I follow him, managing to walk without making the leather creak. I'm getting better at it. He sits in a big, comfy-looking chair and puts his plate down. "Come here."

My pants are pulled down and off and then I'm pulled down into his lap. Oh. Okay. He's warm and comfortable and I'm way too used to feeling our skin together already. Way too.

He gives me a shit-eating grin. "Feed me."

"Bossy." I grin and tear off a bite of sandwich, holding it to his lips, feeding myself with the other hand.

"It's in the job description."

I laugh, feed him another bite and another, feeling good, relaxed, at ease.

"How's your ass?" He doesn't just ask, his fingers slide under me, thumb finding the plug and tapping it.

"Oh!" The oddest mix of pain and pleasure and need shoots through me and I jerk, cock filling. "S... sore."

He purrs. "You like it."

"I..." I offer him another bite, cheeks pinking.

"I don't know which I like better, that you like it or that you don't like admitting it."

My face is going to catch on fire and I duck, trying to find my balance. He chuckles and taps against the plug again.

I groan, I can't help it. I'm aching for him. "A... another bite?"

"Thank you, Nat. It's very good." He's smiling at me, almost purring.

"Thank you." I feed him his sandwiches, my cock rubbing against his belly.

"Make sure you get enough, you're going to need your

energy."

"I... Okay. Energy? Why?" I eat another bite, finish my sandwich.

He snorts and knocks the plug again. "Why do you think?"

That's going to drive me out of my mind. I arch, heart pounding, hard and wanting.

"Yes, exactly, Nat. You're going to be a very busy boy."

"I do busy really well. Always have."

"Excellent." He brings our mouths together, tongue slipping into mine.

"Oh..." My hands find his hair, holding on, stroking, my lips wrapping around to suck his tongue. He hums, hands roaming over my body, occasionally stroking my ass, jostling the plug. Okay. Okay, wow. Good. Yeah. Good. My heart's pounding, head swimming.

Richmond ends the kiss. "Well, my dear Nat, where do we start?"

"Start? Where are we going?" He's got me confused.

"To the sky."

"Oh... Okay. Yeah."

"Yeah." He slides his hand down along my spine, headed toward the plug again. I wriggle, shift, trying to avoid the jostle and burn I know is coming.

"Relax, Nat. You're not going anywhere." His fingers tap the plug, just gently and then hard enough to push it in further.

My cock jerks, nipples going tight-tight. "Fuck."

"Oh, yes, eventually." He leans in, mouth closing over my shoulder, sucking, teeth threatening. I can't catch my breath, can't focus, can't think. His teeth sink in, biting me. Hard.

My whole body goes stiff and I jerk, trying to pull away, head snapping back. He growls around my skin, the hand at my ass pushing the plug again. I'm babbling, begging, I'm not even sure whether I'm making sense. I'm pretty sure I don't care.

His other hand finds my cock, barely touching. I push up toward the touch, needing more. The biting eases, his tongue sliding over the bite mark as his hand moves down to cup my balls.

"Oh. Oh. Richmond." How does he do this? Make me go from want to need in seconds?

"I'm going to let you come, and then we're going to clean you. Inside and out." His hand slides up and wraps around my cock, pumping firmly.

"Oh. Oh, yes. Okay. Yes. I need. Thank you." I'm just talking, needing, fucking Richmond's fist like a man possessed. He growls, one hand around my cock, the other on my ass, torturing me with that plug. It's no time before I'm coming, sobbing, giving it all up for him.

He's still pumping my cock, even as he's pulling me against him, free hand sliding up and down my back, soothing. I cuddle close, resting against him, panting.

"Lovely." Richmond stands, setting me on my feet and taking my hand. "Bathroom's this way."

"Hmm?" I follow without thought, mind still purring and humming with pleasure.

We walk into the bathroom and I get a chance to really look at it. It's huge. God, there's a shower and a Jacuzzi tub and this big, full-length mirror.

That's where he leads us, standing behind me and holding my arms out away from my body. "Look at that."

My eyes trail along Richmond's body, so tan, so strong in contrast to mine.

"You looking at yourself as well, Nat? Looking at all that lovely pale skin with my mark on your shoulder? Your skin just begs for my marks."

Oh.

Oh.

Goose bumps rise up all over me, my stupid prick trying to throb.

He chuckles, hands sliding over my skin. "So what do you think of pleasure 24/7 as a job?"

"So doesn't suck." I grin, shifting for him.

"Good." He jostles the fucking plug again. "You ready to lose this for awhile?"

I nod, bite my bottom lip at the burn. "Yeah. Yeah."

He bites my earlobe. "So take it out." And steps back, eyes on me.

"Oh. Oh, I... Okay." I reach back, ducking my head, moaning as my fingers brush the edge, brush my tender hole.

"Tell me how it feels."

"Tender. Achy, but tingly. Good." I pull, the plug stretching me.

He comes to stand at my back again, fingers sliding along my side and wrapping around my hips. I moan, lips parting as the plug comes free, knees buckling a little. He catches me, hot against my skin. "Easy, Nat. Easy."

Nodding, I let him hold me, support me. He backs me up into the shower and turns on the water, still holding me as the water sprays over us.

"Mmm..." Oh, yeah. That feels so good. Warm. Slick. Easy.

"Oh, a waterbaby... nice."

"Waterbaby?" I stretch, rocking, sliding against Richmond. "Oh. Oh, it feels so good."

"Yeah, you like the water. The shower and pool are excellent places to make love." His hands start to move over me, slick with soap, sliding like a breeze.

"Oh, yeah. Love the water." I reach over, run my hands over his arms, touching, feeling. He's strong and hot. "You feel so good."

"Soap up — you can wash me while I wash you." I nod, grabbing the soap and turning, lathering my hands. He doesn't stop touching me, fingers sliding over my nipples. They perk right up, hard as little rocks as I start washing him, fingers sliding over that hard belly.

"Oh, you are a slut, aren't you, Nat?" Damn, that makes my stomach flutter, makes my balls draw up. He purrs. "My slut. You hear me, Nat? Mine."

"Yes. Yes. Yours." I trace his hipbones, cup his sac. "You make me..."

Oh, gods and fishes, so hot.

"Make you what, Nat? You have to learn to finish your sentences." His voice has gone husky, telling me he's not immune to my touch.

"Hot. Need. Horny." I lean forward, lips wrapping around one nipple and sucking.

"Good. You can have my cock, Nat."

Oh... I'm on my knees before I ever knew I moved, lips open and pulling that hard cock in. I want it — want everything he'll give me. Maybe need it.

"So eager. I like that." His hands are on my head, thumbs sliding along my cheeks. I hum, eyes closed as the water pours around us, that cock sliding on my tongue.

"You're getting better at this," he murmurs, hand starting to guide me.

Oh. Oh, that feels good. Damned good. I pull, moaning softly. He moves my head up and down on his cock, hips helping, pushing his prick in. It's easier now, to relax, to give him control, to just relax with the water and hum, hips rocking. He purrs and growls above me, hips moving faster, pushing harder into my mouth. My hands are on his hips, holding on, moving with his thrusts.

"Mmm... yeah, Nat. Suck me."

There's nothing so sexy. Nothing.

"Soon, lovely. Soon."

He thinks I'm...

Oh...

I purr, swallow, needing him, so hot.

"Yes!" He shoves in deep, heat pouring down my throat. I drink down what I can, swallowing hard. "That hit the spot." He helps me up, licking at my lips. My lips are tingling, feel swollen, hot. His hands are on me again, sliding, teasing, fingertips pushing one after the other into my hole, as he nibbles at my lips. I lean into him, moaning a little, petting his belly. "So sensual. You're something else, Nat."

He backs away from me and lets the water hit me, clean the soap away. I rinse myself off, fingers pushing the soap off my skin. He gives me a quick kiss and steps out for a moment, coming back with tubing.

I know my eyes are about as big as saucers. "Richmond?"

"I did say we were going to clean you inside and out. This covers the inside part."

"Oh." I take a step back, worried. "Does it hurt?"

"It's not comfortable, but it doesn't hurt. And you need to be cleaned inside — you've had a plug in for two days straight."

"I *know*. You put it in!"

He chuckles, leans right back against the tile and laughs. The temptation to stick my tongue out at him is huge.

Huge.

Really.

"Sorry, lovely, it was just the outrage in your voice." He comes over and kisses my forehead. "I want you to lean against the tile and spread your legs."

Oh, there's that word again. Lovely.

Oh.

I meet his eyes, nodding. "Okay."

He helps me turn, his hands hot on my waist. "A little wider."

It feels so exposed, so wanton, so obscene. I'm trembling, not scared, but...

Worried.

His hands stroke down along my spine. "Relax, Nat. We're going to start with my fingers."

"Okay. Okay." He's warm and close and it makes it easier, makes me feel more protected. One finger pushes into me, warm and slick.

"Oh..." I lean against my arms, the contrast between finger and water sweet.

One finger becomes two, stretching slightly, making my sensitive skin ache. I'm gasping, hips moving a little. He purrs, lips sliding over my shoulder, tongue lapping at the water. "You'd give it up for me again, wouldn't you?"

I nod, riding those fingers, moaning, fingers sliding along the tile. "I would."

"Such a good boy." He keeps fucking me with his fingers, in and out, finding my gland and pegging it over and over, stretching and sliding. I'm spread wide, ass offered up, balls swinging, needing it. Needing him.

The finger fucking slows and he's whispering in my ear. "The tubing's in, lovely. I'm taking my fingers away now."

I lean toward him, whimpering as his fingers slide away. Oh. Oh, the things he makes me feel.

He kisses my shoulder. "I'm filling you now. It's just warm water and a touch of antiseptic. It shouldn't hurt, though as you get full it won't be particularly comfortable."

"Oh. Okay. Okay." I shiver, shift a little, gasping as warmth fills me.

His hand slides over my skin, distracting. "We will do this on a regular basis to ensure you don't pick up infections and to keep the swelling of being constantly filled down."

"You... Always? Really?" Oh, gods...

"Well, it won't always be me — even I can't keep it up all the time. But that's what the toys are for. Oh, there's the one that has a remote control — it vibrates." He purrs. "Oh, we're going to have *such* fun, Nat. I can't wait to spank you while you're wearing a plug."

"Richmond..." I'm thrumming, cock harder than stone, head swimming. "Oh..."

"Oh, yes, you like the idea of that. We'll play, experiment — the effects of different plugs and different spanking implements."

"I... Oh, I can't... I can't think when you say things like that." The water keeps filling and filling me.

"And I keep telling you that you aren't meant to think, lovely. Just feel." He's petting my stomach now, hands dropping now and then to stroke my cock. "All right, I'm going to take the tubing out, you must hold the water in as long as you can and then let it go when it becomes too much. I'll wash you again and we'll go play."

"Just... In front of you? Oh. Oh, Richmond, I... Oh..." My whole body's burning, eyes rolling.

"In front of me, Nat. There is nowhere you can hide from me. Nowhere."

The tubing feels strange, cool and impersonal, as it slowly slides out of me.

"I... I don't..." Oh. Oh. I don't know if I can. I don't know if I can. "So full..."

He chuckles and ducks under my arms, back against the tiles in front of me. He takes a long, slow kiss. "Hold it as long as you like, Nathaniel."

My heart's pounding, arms and legs shaking, pressure

huge. "Richmond. I. Oh."

"Yes, lovely?" He's nuzzling my face, lips sliding over my cheeks and my eyes, my nose, my lips and jaw.

"I... I..." I'm following his lips, fighting my body desperately. It doesn't matter, though, because I can't hold it. I can't. I just hide my face, sobbing softly in overwhelmed embarrassment as the water rushes out of me.

Richmond just keeps touching me, stroking my back, fingers sliding on my nipples and my cock, my balls as the shower rinses my legs, rinses away what was inside me. I'm never going to be able to breathe again. Ever.

"So lovely. My Nat." He never stops touching me.

"Y... yours." I lean in, resting against him.

"Yes." He moves around me, leaning me against the tiles as he soaps up his hands and begins to wash my ass, my legs. The touches make me ache, make me hide my face. So exposed. He keeps seeing me. "You can't hide from me, lovely."

He leans in and kisses my ass, my thighs.

The moan that leaves me is from deep inside. "Richmond."

He kneels behind me, hands holding me open. The water from the shower rinses the soap away and his tongue slides along my crease, pushes against my hole.

"Oh!" My cry echoes, cock slapping against the tile as I jerk forward.

He doesn't let up, just moves with me, pushes his tongue right into me.

"Richmond! Oh! Oh, I..." My nails are scraping along the tile, hips pushing back towards him. He just purrs and starts fucking me with his tongue. The whole world goes bright and I'm just pushing and pushing and screaming out his name and begging and flying. His hand wraps around my cock, tugging in time with each thrust of his tongue. Everything stops as I shoot and all I am is cock and ass and his. All his.

When the world stops spinning, I'm curled in his arms, being carried out of the shower. He grabs a towel and we continue down the hall to a new room.

I'd ask where we're going, but that would assume my mouth and brain are still connected. Which? No.

"This is the play room. It should have everything we need."

"Need?"

"All manner of toys, tools and restraints, several tables... you name it, we've got it."

I've never worked so hard in my whole life.

He sets me down on a table and dries me off before drying himself off, giving me a look at his muscled body.

"So fine..." I'm swaying, loose and relaxed and dazed.

He smiles at me and goes over to the wall, pressing something to reveal a cupboard. He comes back with another plug, something that looks like little paper clips and what is definitely a paddle. I draw my legs up, giving my chin something to rest on, eyes wide. "These are nipple clamps. This is a medium size plug. And this is a paddle. It's spanking time."

Spanking time. I grin, giggle softly as I shift. "Is it going to be a daily activity?"

"Would you like it to be?"

"I..." Normal people wouldn't even hesitate, they'd just say no. No. NO!

"I'll note that you'd like it to be, but I make no promises."

"Wh... what do you promise, Richmond?" I let my legs ease down, lean towards him a little.

"To keep you close. To use you well. To push your boundaries, but never break you, never damage you."

"Oh..." Goose bumps break out over my skin and I moan as I nod, willing to do almost anything for him.

He leans in and kisses me, something cold and smooth rubbing on my skin, slowly warming. It's the plug.

I wrap my arms around his neck, fingers sliding in his hair, trying to just trust. He opens my mouth wide, tongue sweeping through it, owning it, owning me. Never. I never thought I could feel so much, need so much. I let him in, let him have everything he wants.

He kisses me until I'm breathless and the plug is at my ass, sliding along my crease, teasing my hole, lifting my balls.

"Oh. Richmond. I... You make me feel so much."

"Yes, that's the idea, isn't it?" The plug disappears for a moment and then comes back, cool and slick, pressing against me, asking to be let in. I gasp against Richmond's lips, thighs parting a little, bearing down just enough to let the tip slip inside. "Oh, lovely — such a good boy."

He's kissing me hard again, like he owns me. I'm moving against the plug, fucking myself on it, pushing down until it burns and then sliding up again.

"Fuck, that's something else." He breaks the kiss so he can look, his eyes hot as he watches me slowly take it in, watches me fuck myself with it. I close my eyes and let myself move, expose my need for him. It's like dancing, fucking myself to the rhythm of his breaths. He growls and purrs, hands sliding over the rest of my skin, tweaking my nipples and stroking my belly, the insides of my thighs, my cock.

I'm his — open and hungry and relaxed and...

His.

"So lovely."

Once the plug slides all the way in, my body snaps closed around it, keeping it where it is, my body holding it tight, refusing to relinquish it again.

"Oh, yes. Is it long enough?" he asks, fingers moving the base.

"L... long enough?" The tip nudges my gland, bumps it hard and I jerk, crying out.

"Ah, yes, perfect." He's smiling at me, eyes hot, proud and happy.

"Oh." My head rolls back, moaning low. "Oh, wow."

"Yes, wow." He nudges the plug again, purring as I react.

"Richmond!" My cock and nipples and belly muscles are so hard.

So hard.

"Lovely." There's that word again, whispered against my neck this time.

"Nipples now." He takes one of the hard little points between his fingers and tugs. I whimper, chest arching to ease the pressure. He chuckles and then puts the... clamp? pinchers?... fucking painful torture device on. It grips my nipple between its sharp, little teeth.

"Ah! Richmond!" I jerk, hands going to touch, breath coming hard and fast.

His hands take mine, pull them away. "Touching it will only make it ache harder. See?" With that he flicks the clamp with a single finger.

"Oh! I...I... Richmond!" My hands twist in his hands, my hips rocking.

"Yes." He leans forward and takes my other nipple in his mouth, licking and tugging with his lips, biting lightly with his teeth.

"Oh. Oh. Oh. Richmond. Please. Please. I." Babbling. Again. Fuck.

"Yes, I'll do the other one, Nat." He's smiling at me, eyes full of mischief, and then he sticks the other clamp on my other nipple, eyes going even hotter.

Oh. Fuck.

Fuck.

I'm jerking, gasping and shivering for him. "Richmond. I. Oh. They burn."

He nods. "Yes." He flicks them again, one and then the other. My cry is hungry, even to my own ears, and I tug at his grip. "You ready for the main event already?"

"Huh?" The ache eases, turns to a dull throbbing, and I start to catch my breath.

"The paddling." He winks and sits up on the table, patting his legs.

"I..." Oh. Oh. I'm dying, burning and aching inside. I shouldn't want this. No sane person wants to be... But I do. I want.

"Lie over my lap, lovely. Let me have that fine ass of yours."

I'm moving before I realize what I'm doing, cock sliding over Richmond's thighs, rubbing. He's purring, the sound approving, aroused. His hand is warm and soft on my ass, rubbing gently, nudging the plug.

"I'm... I shouldn't want this. Why do I want this?" I'm moaning, rocking for him.

"Why shouldn't you want it, lovely?"

"Be... because it hurts and I'm... I'm over your knee, Richmond."

"Yes, so sexy, and eventually you will learn to accept that pain and pleasure are intertwined and one not better or worse than the other."

"I... I couldn't stop thinking about you." It hurts to say it, admit it like that. "I came back for you."

"You are so brave, Nat. Do you realize that?"

"Me?" I blink, twist to look at him. "Me?"

He strokes my cheek, his smile soft, the look in his eyes completely serious. "Yes, lovely. You."

"Oh." Tears fill my eyes and I nuzzle into his touch.

"No one's ever thought that about me."

"They don't know you like I do." He kisses me softly. "You don't know you like I do."

"No one knows me like you do."

"True." He gives me one more kiss, hand sliding around to flick at the clamps on my nipples. "Now, lie back down and let me paddle your pretty little ass like we both want."

I've never felt so weird, bending over for a spanking while I'm laughing. My laughter stops as the paddle lands square on my ass, jolting the plug. I don't scream or anything, because it isn't horrible — there's a heat, a sting, a throb, and it's fucking sexy.

He finds a rhythm, hitting me again and again. My ass is on fire, each spank driving the plug into my gland again and again. He's murmuring, doing that sexy purr thing and telling me how lovely I am, how much it turns him on to see me spread out on his lap, ass going red.

"Oh. Oh, love that. The things you say. Burns. Richmond. Please. Oh."

He shifts me with his legs and suddenly my cock is trapped between his thighs, sliding in that tunnel of skin every time the paddle hits my ass. Oh, sweet fuck. Yes. I'm humping his thighs, moaning with every blow, thrusting into him over and over.

"You'll come for me while I'm paddling you." His voice is husky now, his cock pressing against me, leaking.

"Yes. Yes, please. Richmond. Yes." I'm nodding, gasping, rocking, so close.

His free hand reaches around and touches the clamps, first my left and then my right nipple teased, pinched harder for a second. The rhythm of the paddling never falters.

I can't hold it. I can't. I need this. Need to come. Need to. "Richmond!"

I come hard, world spinning wildly.

He hits me a few more times, keeping everything spinning, keeping me shuddering and then he comes, his spunk splashing against my skin. He stops paddling me, hand sliding over my ass instead, the touch gentle, my ass on fire.

I whimper, thighs parting. "Hot."

"Burning up," he murmurs, fingers sliding toward my nipples again.

"Oh. Oh, careful. Please. They ache so."

"I know, lovely, I'm going to take the clamps off — they shouldn't be left on too long." His hand moves quickly, taking off one and then the other.

My shoulders lift up, shaking as my nipples catch flame, free hand rubbing them hard.

"Oh you're lovely. Just lovely." He leans down and kisses me.

I push up into the kiss, pressing hard. Moaning. He turns me over, my ass sliding against his legs. Tingles. Burns. Hot. Damn. I can feel every fucking hair on his thigh. He's rubbing his come into my skin, fingers hot on my belly. I moan into his mouth, one hand in his hair, fucking melting. He keeps kissing me, leaving me breathless and lightheaded.

"You..." He's got the most fascinating eyes.

He purrs. "What, Nat?"

"I... Your eyes. They make me... burn... inside."

"Oh... good." Richmond nuzzles me. "My eyes burn you inside, my hands make you burn outside."

"Yeah." I take a kiss. "Thank you. Thank you, Richmond."

"It was my pleasure, lovely."

I shiver, gasp. "Oh. That's... I love that."

"What's that?"

My cheeks flame and I duck my head. "That you call

me that."

"What, lovely? But you are."

"I'm not like you, though. So fine."

He purrs. "I'm glad you like what you see."

"Who wouldn't?" I sound as shocked as I feel.

"Believe it or not, lovely, I'm not everyone's type. There are some who don't like muscles. Who don't like to be dominated." He's nibbling along my jaw, my neck, teeth threatening but never biting. Not yet.

"You're my type. I didn't even know you were my type."

"And you, lovely, are very much my type. But I knew that the moment I saw you. I knew I needed to push you, knew I risked pushing you away, but I had to take the chance, had to let you see the least of what you are capable of."

He makes me shake, makes me close my eyes and breathe.

"Mmmm, I think a massage. And then perhaps a trip to the shops. See what Peter and Paul suggest, visit Mouse and order some custom stuff."

"Peter and Paul?" My lips slide along his skin, mapping him.

"Yes, they run the body modification shop. Tattoos, piercings... Mouse makes magic with leather."

Body modi... Oh, okay. Maybe a long massage.

Really long.

Chapter Five

D espite the fact that it was my suggestion, I'm reluctant to take Nat up to the shops so soon. Or maybe, if I'm being honest, time has nothing to do with it. The truth is, he's mine and I don't want to share. Not even to let anyone else see him. Which is unfortunate, given that we are to be putting on shows in two weeks. Which means now we have to go because I have to prove to myself that I can let other people look at him.

I make him keep the plug in and I let him wear his leather pants, but nothing else, not even shoes.

"Ready to go?" I ask as I do up my shirt buttons.

"I... Yes?" His hands brush through his mass of curls, trying to tame them.

"You'll have to talk to the twins about your hair. They're rather good at fussing with it."

I turn to him, catching my breath. He doesn't look any different than he did earlier, still in the leather pants and nothing else. No, not different at all. As long as you didn't count the myriad bite marks.

"Okay." He gives me a nervous little grin, slides his hand into mine and squeezes.

I squeeze back and then let go of his hand in favor of leaving my hand, sitting heavily, in the small of his back as I lead him out to the lifts. He's shivering, walking with careful steps that slowly smooth out. "You'll get used to the plug. It'll make you graceful."

I get him onto the lift and press the floor for the shops, excited to show him off now that we're on our way. Yes, contradictory, but honest. "We'll go see Peter and Paul first. Have you ever considered any body modifications before?"

"Body..." He stumbles a little, shakes his head, curls bobbing. "No. No, I haven't."

"We'll have to see what appeals. Get the boys to show you theirs. One's got a guiche, the other a Prince Albert." I wonder how far he's taken his research. Will he know what those are?

"A guiche?" He tilts his head. "I know what the other is — ow, but a guiche?"

"You've heard of the other — ask the twins, I doubt ow is the appropriate response, not once it has healed." Although perhaps something that causes an ow reaction is more appropriate for Nat — he likes the heavy beat of pain. "A guiche is a piercing in the flesh between your balls and your hole."

"Oh. Ow. Really ow." His hand reaches down to his crotch, holding it. "People do that on purpose?"

I laugh. Oh, I don't mean to laugh at him, really, but he's such a delight, genuine and sweet. Mine. "They do indeed, Nat, along with many other far more drastic things. Scrotal ladders and wands. Rings big enough to hold leashes."

"Wands? Like magic wands? Ladders?" He is curious, I can tell, those eyes bright and wide.

"Wands like sounds — the thin metal rods that go into your slit. We talked about them when we went through the kink list. They can be made permanent, holding orgasm and even the bladder under strict control. A ladder in this case means a series of piercings that climb along the penis — really does look like a ladder, too. Mostly." I look at Nat out of the corner of my eye, eager for his initial reaction.

Another stumble, those pretty eyes staring up at me. "I... I... I didn't say yes to those, did I?"

"I believe you said yes to just about everything, lovely. Including piercing."

"I... I did?" He blushes dark and presses close to me. "Oh."

"You don't remember? For almost every item you said you'd do it for me." I groan, as turned on by the memory of it as I had been by the event itself.

He nods, face hidden. "I remember."

"Here we are." I lead him out of the lift and toward the body mods shop. A part of me hopes that Peter and Paul are in full argument. My boy needs more experience with such things.

Of course, when we walk into the shop? They're kissing, rubbing together, almost a matched set. Nat squeaks and Paul — or is it Peter — looks up. "Richmond! Hello!"

Ah. Paul.

"Hello boys. I'd like you to meet Nat. He's mine." It isn't quite how I'd meant to put it, but that's how it comes out and it's accurate enough.

"H...h...h...h..."

"Hi, Nat. I'm Paul, this is my tongue-tied twin." Paul shakes Nat's hand, grins. "What're we doing for you?"

Nat blinks, backs up. "Doing?"

I chuckle. "I'm just showing Nat around today. I'm sure you'll show him all sorts of shocking things he'll shake his head at and then we'll be back within a week to do them all."

"Excellent! Ink or piercings!" Paul bounces and Peter giggles, drawing Nat into the shop, showing off photos

181

and jewelry.

"Everything, boys. Absolutely everything." And not just to shock Nat; I'm learning that he really does want to know everything. It's funny, how Nat goes from panicky to curious, my boy almost relaxing with the twins. "I told him you boys might model some of the piercings for him."

"O...o...oh, sure. H...here." Peter opens his pants, completely uninhibited, exposing the long, thin cock, topped with a thick ring. Nat's eyes go wide and he blinks.

"Ow."

"N...not anymore."

"Yeah? Because..." His hands cup his cock. "Ow."

I have to bite my lip to keep from chuckling. "How long did it hurt for, Peter?"

"W... w... well, only the piercing p... part. I p... put a... a... anesthetic on it because P... Paulie wanted to play."

"You see, Nat? It hurt for all of twenty seconds or so, he sprayed anesthetic on it, and was ready to go right away." I let my eyes drop and stay focused on his crotch. If I was closer I'd jostle his plug and test the strength of his erection.

Nat gives Peter a curious look. "You must be brave."

Peter laughs, but it's Paul who nods. "My Peter's very brave, but that's not about the piercings. Those are just for sex and being pretty."

"Speaking of pretty — you have a nipple ring as well, don't you, Peter? In fact, I'm guessing you're aware of that one more than you are the PA — am I right?" I know it's shocking Nat, that we're speaking about sex and piercings and such so casually, but we work here at the club, sex is casual until we make it something more. Like what's between Nat and myself.

"O... oh yes. The n... nipples are m... much more

sensitive." Peter lifts his shirt, pretty little nipples pierced with some glowing material.

I do walk over then and touch them gently, my eyes on Nat.

Peter grins and those nipples go hard, tight. Nat looks partially jealous, a little curious, more aroused.

As he's without a top, I can clearly see the way his nipples harden up and I reach over, pinch them. "What do you think? Just like the plug inside you, they'd leave you constantly stimulated."

"I..." He turns a deep, dark red, face hiding in my arm as Paul chuckles and Peter smiles.

"Oh, we like the idea of that," I murmur, letting my hand drift down his back, just barely nudging the plug inside him. "You want one or both done, Nat?"

Peter grins and holds up a set of barbells, a chain between them. "Th... these are pr... pretty and c... come with a m... matching sound and plug with m... matching ch... chains."

Nat whimpers, eyes wide.

"Oh, they're lovely. Order us a set — we'll have it later, once Nat's had a little more experience. For now I'm just thinking a ring I can tug on, twist, something to keep these sweet little nipples hard." I pinch Nat's nipples again. "If you don't give me an answer, lovely, I'm going to have them both done."

"I..." He swallows, eyes fastening to mine, the mixture of fear and need and want addictive.

Mind you, I don't actually have a preference — one will let him feel the difference, remind him of the difference, and there's something appealing to the idea of him begging me to get the other one done so they match in sensitivity, but both to start with would be just plain fun. I'll even let him wear shirts just because the material will rub the sensitive little nubs and drive him crazy.

"Both? Just the left? Just the right? I'll even let you pick out the piece of jewelry you want. "

"Just... I mean... I don't know... I..." He shakes his head. "The left one, I guess. I mean, both would hurt twice as bad."

"Are you sure you don't mean twice as good?" I ask him, jostling the plug yet again.

Oh, that color is beautiful, the way he twists and bites his lips and wants it. "No..."

"We'll get the left one done," I tell Peter, fingers playing with the nipple in question. "What would you like, Nat? A barbell? A ring? With something in it perhaps?"

"What do you think is best?"

Peter makes a soft purring sound. "Such a g... good boy."

"Yes, he is, isn't he?" I kiss the top of Nat's head. "A straight ring. And some chains with weights on it we can add when we're playing."

My thumb stays at his hole, playing with the plug as a reward.

Nat melts against me, eyes focused, clear. Mine. I wasn't lying when I said the boy is a natural. I bring our mouths together, work harder on the plug. He's going to have to get used to an audience sooner or later and Peter and Paul are a good start, used to all sorts of things happening in their chairs.

He whimpers, opening for me, shaking hard. Those hands push against my shoulder for a second, then curl around me, holding on. Purring, I give his nipple another pinch and then slide my fingers down along his chest, pushing into his pants. The piercing won't hurt as much if he's already high on the endorphins.

"Oh... Richmond..." Nat's hard, so eager. Good boy. So good.

I lick the inside of his mouth, working the plug hard as

my hand circles his cock. It's a tight fit inside his leather pants, but leather stretches some and I'm not going to give up my prize, not until he's spent again.

Peter and Paul are moving about, getting things set up, sliding around us as Nat's thighs spread, hips moving in tiny jerks. Yeah, that's it, Nat — he's forgotten about them, totally focused on the sensations pouring through his body, totally focused on me.

I could ask anything of him right now, and he'd do it. For me.

There are days when I will take advantage of that. Today, I just want his pleasure and the rush of endorphins and relaxation his climax will bring. I break our kiss, meeting his eyes. "Come," I whisper, thumb sliding across his slit, fingers squeezing the heat of his prick.

He gasps, jerks, lips open in a perfect O as heat sprays over my fingers. "Such a good boy."

I lick his lips and then help him down into Peter's chair, nodding at the slightly smaller twin. We'll do this before Nat can think about it and start tensing up.

He's not watching Peter, he's watching me, eyes soft and dazed, blinking slow. Peter is a pro, cleaning the little nipple and grabbing it with forceps before Nat knows what he's doing. "D... d... deep breath, Nat."

"Remember, you're doing this for me," I tell him, keeping his focus.

"F... for you." Nat takes a deep, deep breath, eyes so wide.

"G... good boy. Now l... let it out." As Nat exhales, Peter slides the needle in, the motion smooth and easy, Nat giving a sharp cry.

Purring, I stroke his belly. "That's it, lovely, feel the pain, make it yours."

Nat's breath comes faster, my boy riding it, scared and maybe a little ashamed, but soaring on the pain.

"Oh..." Peter slides the ring in, fastening it. "H... he's f... feeling it."

"He is, indeed. I'm so proud of you, Nat. Once he's done I'm going to clear the room and fuck you hard. Make you scream."

A quick swipe of antiseptic and Peter meets my eyes. "A... a... a... anesthetic?"

I shake my head. "No, he wants to feel it, don't you, Nat?"

Nat's eyes drop, but he nods, so embarrassed, so overwhelmed. "Yes."

"Thank you, Peter," I murmur. "Lock the door for me, please."

I don't bother waiting for an acknowledgement, I just take his mouth, one hand hard on his belly. Nat cries into my mouth, pressing into me. Mine. He's mine and so willing, so eager. Peter and Paul have disappeared, leaving us alone. I open his pants and push them down, working them off as I plunder his mouth. When I break away from the kiss and work his pants the rest of the way off he's flushed and breathless. "Tell me how it feels, lovely."

"It burns. I can feel it, under my skin."

"And your other nipple?" I take his unadorned nipple in between my fingers and pinch and tug.

"Mmm... I think it's scared." He grins even as he moans and presses into my touch.

I laugh, tugging harder, my other hand sliding over his hard cock, down along his balls and back to tease the plug inside him.

"Oh. Oh." His legs raise and spread, ass pressing into my hands.

"You want me, Nat? Undress me. Get me ready to take you." My thumbs tease and then press at his hole, making the plug shift, move.

"Oh..." Those little fingers work my buttons open,

trembling, adrenaline making him buzz and jitter.

"That's it, lovely. Just ride it."

He hasn't got a clue how fucking sexy he looks. He's wide-eyed and alive, hard and flushed and wet-lipped, tugging my clothes from me, lips surrounding my nipple as it is exposed. I slide my hands over his skin, leaving the nipple be for now, saving it for while I'm fucking him. He slides down, works my pants down, then remembers my boots.

"Do you want to lick them first?" I ask him. I know we went through this with the list, but it's one thing when you're in bed with your lover and quite another when face-to-face with your Dom's boots, pain and adrenaline making you need.

"Do... do you want me to?" His breath is panting against my knee, hot and quick.

"I do. I want you to want to." Very much so. He looks the consummate sub, naked and flushed, desperate and wanting at my feet. I want him to do it, to crave doing it, just because I desire it. He whimpers, eyes closing, as he bends, lips parted. His hips sway as his tongue slides over the leather, the plug filling him deep. I let him hear my pleasure, growling at the sight of him. He would do anything for me. Absolutely anything. "Take them off me. I need."

He nods, sliding the boots off, then my pants. He's clumsy, still, awkward, but willing, so willing. I step out of my pants, my cock hard and wet-tipped, throbbing with the need to be buried inside his lovely body.

"Lie back on the chair. Spread. Get rid of the plug." I'm barking out the orders, need driving me.

"Okay, oh. Yes." He moves quickly, legs splayed over the arms of the chair, exposing his hole, fingers pulling at the base of the plug, cheeks flaming.

His eagerness spurs mine and I'm on him, pushing my

cock into his hole almost before the plug is gone. His body pulls me in, grasping hungrily at my cock. He's crying out, fingers white-knuckled on the chair arms, body riding me, almost fucking himself on my prick. I start to slam into him, filling him again and again with my need, my passion. He's beautiful like this, spread and speared and hard, knowing nothing but my will. I call all my control to bear, holding on so I can fuck him for as long as possible.

"Richmond!" He arches for me, thighs straining and spread, full cock slapping his belly.

I reach out and slip my little finger through the ring in his nipple, turning my hand to twist the new piercing as my cock hits his gland. Nat screams for me, muscles going taut, body a fist around my prick as he shoots, come spraying over the flat belly.

I let his orgasm pull me into mine, shooting deep inside him. His body milks my cock, makes my pleasure last and last until I collapse against him, hand flat against his ringed nipple, the heat of the metal against my palm.

He moans, hands shaking as they hold me tight.

"Very good, Nat. You're doing so well. You're such a natural sub. It's beautiful — you're beautiful." I slide out of him with a sigh and bend to kiss his ringed nipple. We'll leave it to heal without anesthetic. I know he'll remember this reaming every time he moves and it aches.

"Th... thank you." He looks debauched with his dark nipple, hole swollen and wet with my spunk.

I purr and pick up the plug, using Peter's antiseptic to clean it and then a familiar golden tube to lube it back up. I tease his hole with my thumb first, pressing against it, gasping as he opens for me.

He whimpers for me, lips parting. "A... aches. So sensitive."

I nod and slide the plug back in. "So beautiful. I love

knowing that you are always ready for my cock. Anytime, anywhere."

"A... always." His groan is sweet, husky.

"Yes." I flick my finger across his ringed nipple and then step back and get dressed.

"Come along — I'd like you to see the pictures Peter and Paul have of the other piercings, talk to them about tattoos. And there's still Mouse's leather shop."

"Talk?" He gives me a dazed grin. "You melted me."

"Well, they can talk — you can pretend to listen." I bring our mouths together, kissing him deep.

He's mine. All mine.

And we both know it.

I've never slept so long, so hard, body loved and touched and pushed into exhaustion from one new lesson after another. I ache — nipple and ass and balls — and it feels so good. So amazing.

I vaguely remember the tattoo discussion, sort of, Paul laughing hard and making a bunch of suggestions that made my head swim. Then we hit the leather store — collars and bonds and whips and chaps and...

Fuck, the place smelled like sex. We ended up with all sorts of things — sheaths and straps and harnesses and things I am so not ready to learn about.

By the time we got back, I crashed, just shattered, and I sort of remember Richmond popping my ass and shoving me between the covers, and now?

Now I think I'm staying here for a month.

Maybe two.

The bed bounces and Richmond, at least I hope it's Richmond, strokes my ass. "Rise and shine, lovely."

I keep my eyes closed just for another second.

"Already?"

He laughs, the sound rich and good. "You've been asleep for twenty hours, Nat."

I look over, blinking slow. "You melted my brains."

His eyes twinkle. "I don't think that's what I melted."

My chuckle surprises even me, but it also wakes me up enough for my body to figure out twenty hours is a long time not to pee. "Gotta. You know. Be right back."

I start to hop up, wincing as certain newly stretched muscles talk back.

He growls a little, hands warm on my skin as he helps me up.

I walk to the bedroom all bow-legged like an old-time cowboy, but man, it feels good to take care of business, then wash my face.

Ooh.

Shower.

"Brush your teeth and come back out, Nat. I need you."

"No time for showering, huh? Okay. I'll be right there." Oh, damn. I grab the toothbrush and scrub, the water making my dry mouth wake right up.

"We'll shower after." His voice has that don't be long edge to it I'm coming to recognize. I hurry it up, moving easier now, eager for Richmond's hands, to see those eyes. He's waiting on the bed for me, naked, hard, slowly pumping his cock. His eyes are hot.

"Oh..." I stop in the doorway, watching. "Oh, Richmond... So fine."

He grins. "And all for you. Come and get it, lovely."

My words just get lost and I nod, crawling up between his legs, almost drooling. He spreads wider, hand pushing his prick down toward me. I make this noise that can't possibly be coming out of my mouth, tongue sliding over the tip to taste. He purrs and fuck, that's a sexy sound.

"Lovely..."

Oh, that makes me hot, makes a ball of need settle in my belly, and I take him in, hips swaying as I bob. His hand drops to my head, fingers sliding through my hair. "Pull out your plug, lovely. I want to fuck that perfect ass."

Oh.

Oh, is it ever going to not make fire shoot down my spine when he tells me what he wants?

The base of the plug is warm and my body doesn't want to let go of it.

"Oh, good idea, lovely. Fuck yourself with it first."

My head lifts, my eyes wide enough they pull at the corners. "Fuck..."

He slides his fingers along my lips. "And suck me while you do it — such a pretty sight from here."

I kiss his fingers, wiggling, shivering. "I... I... Oh... Okay."

"Less talk and more do, lovely. I've been patient for hours."

Hours? He's complaining about hours? My ass is never going to recover.

I take the tip of his cock in again, trying to manage sucking and feeling and moving and taking out the plug all at once.

"Take your time, enjoy it. I want to feel the pleasure in your ass through your mouth." The things he makes me feel... I whimper around his prick, jerking whenever my pierced nipple touches his leg, my arm. "Yes. Nat, feel it all. Now the plug, move it."

I shift the plug, the tugging ache causing my prick to jerk and bob.

"So lovely. Such passion. Such pleasure." He spreads his legs and starts to thrust into my mouth. His cock is so thick, so long, pushing over my tongue, bumping against the back of my throat. Purrs and moans come from him, his hand holding my head where it is. My hands land on his thighs, my throat trying to relax, to take him in. He settles back onto the bed, prick sliding from my mouth. "Is the plug out?"

I sort of blink for a second, tongue still moving, searching for his flavor.

Then it hits me, what he said, and I reach back, whining as I yank the plug free. He growls and pulls me forward, hands grabbing onto my hips and guiding me insistently.

"So hungry..." I stop trying to help, just doing what his hands ask.

He gets me where I need to be and just like that his prick slides into me. He doesn't move me, just stays buried balls deep, me straddling him. His hands are hard on my hips — I might be on top but he's the one in control.

"Oh. Oh, Richmond. You. So deep..." I'm squeezing, needing, panting as the sensations fill me.

"You ready, lovely? Ready for it hard and good?"

"Ready. Richmond. Please. Yours." The words just fall out of my mouth. His hands are tight on my waist, digging into my hip bones as he lifts me up and pulls me down again, nice and smooth and hard. "Oh!" Lightning shoots up my spine. "Richmond!"

"Yeah?" He does it again.

"Good. More. Please." Again, Richmond. Again.

"Slut," he accuses. Or maybe it's a compliment. But he does it again. And again. And again.

Yes. Yes. Oh, it feels good. Right. Perfect. Over and over Richmond raises me and brings me down, prick sliding against my gland.

I throw my head back, shuddering, needing, so close. "Gonna..."

"Wait for my command, lovely." Oh, fuck. He wants the impossible. He does. "Wait, Nat." He brings me up and drops me twice more.

"Richmond..." I arch, back bowing. "Please."

"Only on my order." Up and down. Again. The room spins and I reach down to squeeze the base of my cock. "One day you'll be able to do it without having to touch yourself."

Those eyes are so hot on me as he lifts me up again.

"Come." The word is quiet, insistent, his hands driving me down onto his cock.

"Yes!" It takes a single pump and I'm shooting, balls aching I'm coming so hard.

"Yes." I'm still coming as he flips me over, putting my feet over his shoulders. He rolls me up onto my shoulders, pounding into me.

My breath whooshes out of me, forcible pants and I can't stop shaking, like every nerve in my body is coming over and over. I don't know how long it lasts, but it seems like forever and yet it isn't enough and he's coming, shouting out my name as heat fills me in strong pulses.

He's stunning — so male, so hot, so strong.

He gazes down at me, holding us locked together at cock and ass and eyes, and then slowly lets my legs down, slides out of me and lies down next to me, panting.

I just sort of relax, one hand sliding along his side, listening to his breath slow. He slides away a moment, coming back with a little plug that he slicks up and feeds into my ass just like that. I whimper, legs spreading as a sweet jolt of sensation fills me. Richmond chuckles and slaps my ass.

"Are you more hungry or tired?"

My stomach growls, loud enough to make us both laugh. "Oh. Food."

"Fair enough. Put on your new leathers and we'll go down to the dining room. Show off the new ring and that fresh-fucked face."

My face turns bright red — I can feel the heat — but I nod, slowly slip out of bed.

He strokes my ass as I go, not hard, not jostling the plug, just... possessively.

It makes me hum, makes me pleased.

Makes me wonder how far I've lost myself to him.

Chapter Six

I almost put the leash on Nat, but I don't think he's quite ready for it. Not in public. Besides, the one I want to use attaches to one of the new cock rings, and I know for sure he isn't ready to be paraded around naked.

One day, though. And sooner than I had imagined. He's so responsive to everything.

I take his hand instead, standing proudly at the elevator. He looks lovely in his tight leather pants, little ring in his nipple shining, catching the light. There is no mistaking the look on his face, in his eyes — he's been fucked good and hard — satisfaction practically oozes from him. I would have matched him, worn my leather pants and nothing else, but he needs to get used to being more naked in public than others, so I wear a silver mesh long-sleeved shirt over my leathers. It moves with me, feels good.

The elevator lets us off and I head into the dining area. It's busy this time of day — it's week's end and everyone is indulging in the best food on the planet.

Nat squeezes my fingers, hanging back in my shadow. "It's busy."

"Yes, it is — I told you I wanted to show you off."

Someone would find a table for me, but I decide to step

in, look around, see if there's someone fun to eat with. Noel and Richard are eating in one corner, their huge, scarred lover hulking, silent, between them. Interesting. I didn't think he'd come out onto the floor. Des and Hawk are at Des' table, heads together, looking over some paperwork, their subs chattering happily.

Mal and Kestrel are sitting together, Mal quiet as Kestrel chatters. I head for them, bringing Nat along with me. I have to admit, I want to show Nat off to Mal.

"Good afternoon, Kestrel, Mal."

"Richmond! Hello!" Kestrel gives me a wide smile, eyes shining from under the fall of rainbow-colored hair. "I do love that shirt on you. I hear you've got two weeks off? So lucky. Now, introduce me to your... friend? Trainee?"

Mal just rolls his eyes, winks at me.

"This is Nathaniel. Nat is... Mine. Nat, this is Kestrel — you've already met Mal."

Nat holds out one hand to Kestrel, nods. "It's very nice to meet you, Kestrel."

"Oh, look at those sweet curls! Now, when you say mine, are you saying he doesn't do scenes? We have a new guest who's looking for a specific body-type..."

I growled a little, stepping in front of Nat. "He's mine."

I don't know why I'm surprised, I knew I felt this way about him, but I'm all but ready to tear Kestrel's head off his neck and it was just an innocent question. I take a breath and pull a chair out for Nat, helping him into it before taking my own. "We'll do show scenes. And I'm still working here. But Nat is mine alone."

Kestrel nods, completely at ease. "Show scenes would be lovely. If you need anything, Nathaniel, dear, just let me know."

"Thank you." Nat looks over at me, eyes warm.

"Richmond gives me what I need."

I purr, warmth going through me. Is there any question why I'm so possessive? "He's such a good boy," I murmur, admiring how the lights pick up the marks on him and make his nipple ring shine.

Mal chuckles. "You're hooked, Rich, through the balls."

And just like that Mal pinpoints the truth of it, the truth of the Dom/sub relationship that I don't think had occurred to Nat before. I am indeed hooked.

He has the power.

"Very happily so, Mal. And Kestrel, I understand congratulations are in order. So that just leaves you, Mal."

Mal shakes his head. "I don't see that in my future. I'm bound to the club herself."

Kestrel makes a soft, unhappy noise. "You need a lover, Mal-love."

"Too bad you're taken." I give Kes a wink. I've never seen anyone get along with Mal like Kestrel does.

"Mal and I weren't good lovers. I'm too flighty and sensitive and he's too good a friend."

Mal leans over, kisses Kes on the forehead. "In other words, Kes bruises too easy."

Bruises. That makes me purr and give Nat a hot look. "Nat bruises. They're lovely."

Oh, that is a sweet shade of pink my pet turns, too.

Mal purrs, nods. "I can't wait to see you in action. He's got that reluctant slut thing going for him."

I laugh. Oh, Mal is good at his job. He had Nat pegged the moment he walked in the first time. Not to mention he had me pegged as the top for Nat. "He does, indeed. I can't wait for everyone to see him in action. It's terribly sexy."

Mal's smile is wicked. "What will he do first, do you

think?"

"Nat? What's your favorite thing we've done?"

Nat turns dark red, eyes wide, tongue wetting those swollen lips. "I... I... The... The..."

"Yes, lovely?" I'm not going to let him off the hook — talking about it in front of Mal and Kes? The least of what I'm going to make him do.

Nat ducks his head, curls bobbing. "The fucking af... after you spanked me..."

"Oh, he's a love, Richmond." Kes is almost bouncing.

"Yeah, he is." I beam over at Nat, fingers stroking his belly. "And there is your answer Mal. We shall do a spanking scene."

"Excellent. You let me know when he's ready and I'll set something up."

Nat is glowing, vibrating beside me.

"You think there'll be a lot of interest in the scene?" I throw the question out, really just looking to stroke Nat's ego.

Mal arches an eyebrow. "You'll have a slew of wannabes watching technique and a bunch of strokers wishing they were you and watching that skin turn colors."

Nat peeps beside me.

"Indeed." I smile and stroke Nat some more. "You're going to be a star, lovely. Our public scenes will come to be greatly anticipated."

Nat leans into me, cuddling, shivering as the waiter came by with drinks and plates, a selection for us to choose from.

I pick for both of us. I'll let him feed himself today — he's probably wigged out enough — and after we eat, I'll pamper him. He's been so good, taken everything I've thrown at him and begged for more.

"I imagine we'll be ready in a week or so, Mal. Maybe

you could put us on the schedule."

"Excellent. I'll arrange a select group, those who'll appreciate a first look."

Kestrel nibbles, picks at a bowl of fruit. "Des and Connor, perhaps?"

"And Hawk with his new boy — I haven't had a chance to meet him yet, but I hear he's a sweetheart. He and Nat would get along well, I imagine. Connor, too. Outsiders to the life."

"Oh, maybe Rivan and Kytan and their boys?" Kestrel stole a berry off Mal's plate.

"Excellent. Would you plan a little party for after, Kestrel? So my lovely Nat can meet some of the other subs."

"Of course. In the same room, so you can plan some down time alone between?"

"Excellent, Kes. I shall leave the details all to you."

Mal's chuckle is familiar, warm, fond, eyes on Nat. "That's what everyone does, leaves the details to Kes."

Nat grins, eating his sandwich with neat bites.

"That's because he's so good at it. If you're busy, Kes, I can move the date."

"Oh, no. That's perfect. I'll arrange it." Kes has the warmest, friendliest smile.

"Thank you, Kes. I hope you'll bring your new man, too." I like Kestrel. Before Nat came along I had fantasies of topping him.

"I wouldn't miss it." Kestrel steals another berry, grinning as Mal whacks his hand.

"Excellent. Well, lovely, have you eaten your fill? We have an afternoon planned."

Those stunning eyes meet mine, all bright and warm and happy and setting off a ball of heat in my belly. "Yes."

"Good. Mal, Kes, it was a pleasure."

I have an afternoon of pampering planned, but I'm not sure I can keep my hands, or my cock, to myself. Perhaps the pampering will include another lesson.

Nat stands with me, shaking Kes and Mal's hands, then sliding his hand into mine. So trusting.

All mine.

I lead him back to the elevators, walking slowly, letting everyone see my boy.

"Did you get enough food, Richmond?" I look down and can see that little pierced nipple, hard and stretched and red.

"I did, though I'm hungry for you more than anything else." I reach out and touch his nipple and he gasps, the flesh drawing up, wrinkling.

Purring, I push him into the lift as the doors open, shoving him against the wall and taking his mouth in a hard kiss. Those arms wrap around my neck, lips open and needy, parted for me. He makes me so hard, makes my control fade to nothing and I want him. Hard and fast and constantly. I rub against him, fingers sliding up his chest to tug at the nipple ring.

"Oh!" There it is. That sharp, shocked sound that means he's never and he can't and yes, please. I keep working at it, tugging and twisting, my free hand rubbing against his cock through the leather.

"Oh. Oh, you'll make me... I'll..." His eyes. Fuck. They shine.

"That's the point, lovely. I want to see your pleasure. Come for me." Those eyes go wide, lips open and wet, body jerking under my touch. He's so beautiful, so responsive. All mine. I tug harder, tongue pushing into his mouth. He cries out, jerking for me, coming for me. "So lovely. You're going to make people so hot next week when they watch you."

"I've never... not in front of anyone."

"I know. But you will because I ask it of you."

He nods for me, swallowing hard. "I will."

"I know." I kiss him, almost gently and then notice we're on our floor. "Come along. I've got plans for you."

His hand is warm, fingers sliding on mine. "Yes."

Oh, yes, such plans.

I lead him back to our rooms. "How does the hot tub sound?"

I get a quiet, playful giggle. "Bubbly?"

I pop his ass. "Cheeky!"

It isn't a complaint.

He laughs again, takes off running, teasing me, playing.

"That ass is mine when I catch you!"

It's a promise, a note of intention, and it slows me down, the thought of him tight around me. He crows, zipping through the rooms, doors slamming behind him. Laughing, I follow more slowly, letting the anticipation build, letting him lead me to the bathroom with its hot tub. He's waiting for me, eyes shining, bouncing by the edge of the tub.

I purr. "Get naked, lovely. I'm going to have that ass."

"Okay." He starts stripping, bending as he does, and I can see the hint of the plug filling him, keeping him spread. I groan, all but undone by him — by how beautiful he looks, how sexy. He straightens, gives me a surprised look. "Are you okay?"

I nod. "Just hurry, Nat. Get naked and get rid of the plug. Now."

"Oh. Yeah. Okay." He steps out of the pants, then bends, leans against the side of the tub, fingers working the plug out of that hot little hole. I don't give him any more time than it takes for him to pull it out, no warning either, then I'm inside him, buried to the hilt in his amazing, tight heat. He cries out, head jerking back, calling my name.

"Yes." I grab one hip and his shoulder and start a quick, hard rhythm, slamming into him over and over.

He opens to me, gives me everything, gives me all of it. It's that response as much as the heat and tightness of him that turns me on, makes me frantic and lacking control. I just keep plowing into him. I can see his face in the mirror, see the bliss, the surrender, the eager need.

"Pump yourself," I order, watching him closely.

"Oh..." His hand works hard, fast, pumping the long cock furiously, almost brutally.

I thrust harder, faster, spurred on by the way he's touching himself. I wait a moment and then whisper the word. "Come."

Nat jerks, goes stiff, eyes unbelieving as spunk sprays from him, ass milking my cock. I growl happily, cock emptying, filling his ass.

"Oh, lovely, you are inspiring."

"For you. Only."

I kiss his back, drawn by the knobby spine. "For me only to touch, but I assure you, starting next week, others will be inspired by you."

That sweet body tightens, ripples. "Me?"

"Oh, yes, Nat. You're beautiful. You glow. Everyone who sees you will want you. But you are mine." I push my cock deeper for a moment and then let it slip from Nat's body. "Come now, a soak in the tub, a bit of a massage, and then we'll replug you and get back to our lessons."

"Okay." He shivers, slides into the tub with a low moan. I follow him in and draw him into my arms. Sometimes it's good to pamper your sub, find pleasure in the simple things.

Just to balance out the other ninety percent of the time.

Chapter Seven

My days and nights are all confused. Hell, I don't even know what day it is, what season it is. All I know is that my nipple aches, that my ass is full, and that my cock is hard.

Again.

Richmond is asleep, snoring in his chair. I decide it's time to do some personal maintenance. Wash and shave, clean the nipple ring. Normal stuff.

I almost laugh out loud as I head toward the bathroom. Normal.

It didn't take long at all for weird and scary to become normal. Maybe coming here wasn't so out of character after all. I fill the sink with hot water, start cleaning and soaping, enjoying it.

I realize suddenly I'm not alone. Richmond's standing in the doorway, absolutely naked, gloriously hard, just watching me. His eyes are so hot and I can't help responding to them.

"Hey. I was just…" I wave the razor, point to my cheeks.

Richmond nods and grins, coming slowly toward me. "I noticed." He's looking into my eyes in the mirror and he obviously likes what he sees. His hands land on my shoulders and slowly slide down my back.

My hands are a little jittery as I start shaving, my focus on Richmond's heat, Richmond's touch.

"Don't cut yourself, Nat. That's my job." As he says it, his hand slides right down to my ass, going for the plug, pushing and twisting it.

"I can't concentrate when you do that..."

"No? How about when I do this?" He takes the plug partway out and then pushes it back in. Hard.

I drop the razor, only part-shaved, hands bracing on the sink. "No."

"No? It seems to me you're concentrating *very* well." God, his voice is like a tiger growling. "On your ass, anyway."

He picks up the razor and leans me against him, tilts my head and starts to pick up where I'd left off. I swallow, the act less scary than... intimate. One more thing that Richmond's making his.

Oh.

I can feel his cock, hard and hot and wet as he rubs it against my ass, almost idly. His eyes meet mine in the mirror again and he smiles.

"How's your concentration now, Nat?"

"F... fine. You like clean shaven?" My skin is so alive, nerves buzzing.

He purrs, the sound vibrating his chest where it presses against my back. "I do. In fact..." One of his hands slides around me, pumps my cock and hefts my balls, and then his fingers are carding through my curls. I relax, the touch easing me, gentling me. Those hands are addictive. "I'd like to see you bare all over. Don't get me wrong. I love these red curls, but you'd look stunning naked." He purrs again. "Not to mention the waxing has a delightful sting."

"Waxing?" Oh. Ow. My cock throbs, aching now, just from the touch and the purr and *Richmond*.

"Oh, yes. I think we'll go down for breakfast this morning and then visit the salon on our way back up. Let them wax you. You need your physical, too, before we get into serious playing..." Richmond frowns, growling a little.

I blink up, worried. "What's wrong?"

"He's going to have to touch you." Richmond gives me a rueful smile. "I'm a bit possessive where you're concerned, Nat. I don't want anyone touching you, even clinically."

"You'll stay with me?" Not that I'm nervous, it's just that...

"Oh, yes. I'll be right at your side for both procedures." He sounds very sure of that. Very sure.

"Thank you." I offer my mouth for a kiss, for reassurance, for the heat that no one but Richmond gives me.

He chuckles. "Pushy, pushy."

His lips brush mine though, and then they press harder, his tongue invading my mouth.

Oh. Oh, yes. I arch, the plug inside me making me twist and jerk, making me ache. The razor drops from his hand as the kiss deepens and he's devouring me, eating me right up. Anything. Everything. All of me. I open up, arching until my muscles complain.

He's purring again, one hand playing with the plug, making me ache and push against him like the slut it seems I am. His other hand finds the nipple ring and just twists it, making electricity shoot through me. I push a cry into his lips, going up on my toes, body burning.

He licks at my lips and backs off, eyes dragging over me, so hot, burning. "Oh yes, just like that. You can wear light linen pants. I think I have some with a drawstring you can borrow."

He's panting, cock hard and leaking, obviously

wanting. He's so beautiful. I need him. I need to be his. I lick my lips, eyes on his prick. His eyes go hotter. "You may pleasure me, but you're not allowed to come."

I whimper, drop to my knees even though I know it'll make the ache in my balls worse. His hands go into my hair right away, like they belong there, and he's guiding my mouth. The noises he makes are loud, echoing against the tiles. I dreamed about this — after the first time. Dreamed about his taste, his cock spreading my mouth open. Pushing into me.

Oh, fuck. Fuck, I'm going to.

Think rats. Roaches. Dead bunnies.

He's not helping, making those noises, pushing his cock over my tongue and deep into my mouth again and again. The fingers in my hair tighten on my scalp, and I can tell he's getting close, I'm making him need to come. My hips are fucking the air, throat swallowing around the tip of his cock.

"Don't come, Nat." He groans the words, slamming into my mouth again and coming down my throat.

I obey, but just barely, my prick leaking, dripping copiously as I swallow Richmond down. He sounds pleased, satisfied, and he helps me up, hand wrapping around my cock and stroking, spreading the liquid down over my skin. "I think a ring's in order."

He must keep them stashed all over the place, because his hand disappears for a moment and then reappears with a simple band of leather that he wraps around my cock, my balls, and snaps closed. "Oh, that's stunning."

It's obscene. Pure slut. Pure need. I can't help whimpering, body begging without me saying a word.

He touches the tip of my cock, spreading more of the leaking pre-come around. "Patience, Nat. The waiting will make it better."

He grins at me and grabs a cloth, cleaning my face.

Then I'm led, plug in my ass, cock hard and red and leaking, so needy, back into the bedroom, where he finds clothes for us. The customary pair of leathers for him and the softest, loose linen pants I've ever felt for me.

The touch of the cloth makes me shudder and I'm going to stain them. "Richmond. I'll leave a spot."

"You'd prefer to go naked?" He sounds surprised.

"No. No. I just don't want to ruin them." I reach down, push the tip of my cock under the drawstring, leaving the folded material to catch the clear drops.

He pouts, but his eyes are twinkling at me. "Come on, lovely. Let's go eat."

I just nod, step carefully, each motion making me harder, making goose bumps rise. Richmond isn't content to let that be enough, either; his hand slides over my ass, the inevitable jostle coming to the plug inside me. By the time we reach the lift, I'm panting, nipples hard and aching, legs weak.

"What kind of breakfast food do you like?" Richmond asks the question like it's perfectly normal to be walking in just thin linen pants, cock bound, ass full, needing so badly.

I can see his cock, though, see that he's hard already again in those sexy black leather pants. I did that. I made him hard like that.

"I like fruit. Rice. Pancakes." Richmond.

"Oh, a bowl of fresh fruit would do well. I can feed you. You can feed me." He even makes that sound sexy, like it'll be something special.

I'm never going to survive it.

Never.

We're back down in the dining room in no time. It's not as busy as it was the last time we were here and it's quieter. There's a lot more skin, though, too. Naked or near naked... subs. Guys like me. The ones like Richmond are all more or less dressed. I don't know where to look. There is one with an elaborate chastity device, another with a glowing red ass, another kneeling under the table, head bobbing.

"Ah, there's Hawk with his Jester. I have yet to meet the boy." Richmond leads me to a table with a man who's imposing, but in a quiet way. The guy with him looks... sweet and innocent. "Hawk. I'd like to introduce you to my Nat."

"Hello." I don't know whether to offer my hand, or not.

The fierce man smiles at me, holds one hand out to Richmond. "Richmond. This is my Jester. Be gentle. He's sensitive."

Richmond nods at Jester. "Congratulations, Hawk. Can we join you?"

The guy called Jester gives me a tentative smile.

"Absolutely. Jester and I were just about to order." Hawk sits, drawing the little man into his lap.

And Jester just kind of melts against the strong body, almost oblivious as Richmond sits next to Hawk and pulls me down onto the chair next to him. "Nat is new. Isn't he lovely?"

Hawk looks at me — looks through me and into me like the tall guy I met when I first came here did, almost like Richmond does. "He needs beautifully, Richmond. Congratulations."

Richmond beams. "He does. Thank you. We'll be performing our first scene at the end of next week. I would be honored if you and Jester would come. Kestrel's taking care of the details."

Jester's looking at me, watching me and Richmond from the safety of Hawk's lap.

"We'll be there. Jester always learns so much at these performances." Hawk smiles, tilts Jester's face up for a kiss.

Jester just melts into it, opening right up to Hawk as if we aren't even here, as if nobody else exists but Hawk. So maybe I'm not the biggest slut ever after all. Richmond purrs and slides his hand into my lap, stroking me. I whimper, try to fight the urge to push up, fuck that beautiful hand.

The waiter is unobtrusive, but both Hawk and Richmond stop and order. Both get the fresh fruit, and neither of them let me or Jester order anything. Jester doesn't even seem to notice, to care. It's unnerving watching how focused the man is.

Richmond seems to know where my thoughts are, and he chuckles. "Jester's focus is good. He's been here a little longer than you have, though. You'll learn, I'm sure."

It's like I can't hide from him. Like he sees everything. "Everyone's been here longer than me."

"At the moment. That will change." He leans in and nips at my earlobe. "They'll all be watching you no matter how long you're here. You glow. They'll all want to be me."

Oh.

Richmond's eyes are. Oh. Oh, I'm meant to be his.

He grins then and reaches to jostle the plug, laughing softly as I jerk. "Such pleasure."

"I want you more than anything." The words just sort of tumble out with my breath.

Richmond's eyes go hot. "How do you want me?"

"I... I want you to touch me. Make me feel. I want you inside me."

"Then shed the pants and come sit in my lap like Jester." He's looking right into my eyes, right into *me*.

My hands are working open the drawstring before I even know what I'm doing. Right here. At the breakfast table. In front of Hawk and Jester and all the other patrons spread out through the room.

And Richmond's eyes are just getting hotter and hotter. "Open my pants and then take out the plug."

My heart's pounding, so hard, so desperate. "Y... yes. Yes, Richmond."

I don't look at anyone, just Richmond, focusing as the plug slips out, leaving me almost painfully empty.

"Now come sit on my cock, Nat. Take what you need." That voice is like a caress, like a drug.

"Oh." I straddle Richmond, his hands helping me, that cock filling me up. "Yes... Yes."

He growls a little, hands on my hips, guiding me as I start bouncing in his lap. There's a moan from Jester, low and wanton, and it looks like I'm not the only one getting fucked.

"Richmond." I'm flying, so fucking hot, so full. My bound cock's slapping his belly, the tip dragging against his skin.

"Just like that, Nat." He groans, hands hard on my hips, pulling me down harder and harder. Then his hand begins to stroke me, sliding on my cock, which is so wet now.

"Oh. Oh, I. I won't. I'll. Richmond. I." I can't think, I can't talk. I just need.

He nods. "I know. But you won't until I say you can."

Then he keeps stroking me, finding a rhythm to match the way his cock is fucking me. Everything goes away, everything but cock and hand and ass. Everything but Richmond.

When he finally unsnaps the leather holding me so tight, I know I'm going to explode and he's barely whispered "come" before I am, shooting so hard I see stars.

Anything.

I would do anything for him.

The thought, mixed with the orgasm, completely undoes me and I slump forward, almost sobbing. His arms are around me, his voice soft, whispering nonsense to me, soothing me. His heat is inside me still, keeping full, keeping me anchored to him.

"Thank you." I kiss Richmond's throat, floating there.

He purrs. "It was my pleasure as well as yours, Nat."

He's doing something, cleaning the plug, I think, because the next thing he does is lift me off and put it in me. Next he starts playing with my nipple ring, forcing my cock back to life. I wriggle, sliding on those leather-clad thighs, ass clenching around the plug inside me.

"That's it, Nat. Let's get you nice and hard again so we can slip the ring back on."

Oh. Oh, vicious bastard. Wonderful bastard.

Hawk's voice sounds, husky and low. "He's a natural, friend."

Richmond chuckles. "He is. And he's all mine."

The food's been delivered, too, while I was... losing my mind, and once I'm back in my seat again, plugged and bound, Richmond begins to feed me with his fingers. I lick and lap at Richmond's fingers, pushing a little, playing now that I'm all melted and sated and mmm. Richmond's trying to be polite, to make conversation with Hawk, but he's distracted by what I'm doing. It feels good, knowing Richmond wants and needs, knowing I make him hard.

He feeds me until we're both full and then he offers Hawk and Jester our apologies. "You'll have to forgive us. It's so new."

Hawk nods, looking more than a little distracted himself. "Go. Explore. We... have plans." Jester is blushing, burying his face in Hawk's chest.

Richmond chuckles. "He's beautiful, Hawk. Have fun. I know we will. And we'll see you at the scene."

We stand and I reach for the soft pants, which are still on the floor in a pale puddle.

"Leave them," Richmond orders. And then he turns to go, expecting me to obey, just like that.

I hurry behind him, naked and exposed. He walks like he owns the place, like he belongs here. Like he knows I'm following him. I don't know where we're going, what's next. What to do except don't think. Just walk.

We stop at the lifts and he leans against the wall as we wait, looking casual. Except for his eyes. They're hot, burning me up where I stand. I don't know where to put my hands, where to look, what to do.

"Just feel, Nat." Richmond chuckles. "Feel your pubes because they're about to disappear."

My eyes go wide, hands covering my cock, fingers stroking my curls.

The lift comes and Richmond puts his arm around me, tugs me in, and presses the button for the second floor. "The waxing, remember?"

"Waxing before doctors, then?" Waxing sounds... ow.

He nods. "I'm going to need you when he's done."

"Need me?" What does that mean?

"I'm going to have to let another man touch you everywhere, including inside, and I'm going to need to prove who you belong to when he's done." Richmond's growling again, glowering.

Oh. I move closer, needing Richmond's presence, needing Richmond right there. He takes a deep breath and puts an arm around me. "Many would consider it a fault, to need you so much."

"Do you?"

"It might be wrong, but I wouldn't change it. You belong to me and that is what matters."

Okay. Yes.

The lift opens and we go in, heading down a floor, heading back to the service areas. My crotch is starting to throb, to ache, the hair follicles seeming to pick up every breeze.

"Are you ready?" he asks as we stop in front of a door that proclaims this to be the "hair emporium."

"I don't know. I... I don't know."

The door opens, a bright-eyed boy appearing, all smiles. "Good morning, Richmond! Is this your Nat? Paul was right, his hair is amazing! Come in!"

"Thank you, Bino. I trust Thomas is here?" Richmond's hand is on my back, urging me in.

"Yes. Mister Thomas and Bryant are both in today." Bino turns, showing us a brightly spanked ass, eyes warm and happy. "And in wonderful moods."

Richmond laughs and ushers me into the room proper.

"Richmond. The boys said you'd taken on a sub. Welcome, welcome." The man who comes to us is wearing beige pants topped by a white top. He's rather unremarkable, except for his smile, which makes his whole face light up.

"Thanks, Thomas. This is my Nat."

Thomas bows to me. "So nice to meet you."

"Thank you. Good to meet you."

I just stop speaking when a muscled man with an air of power and strength steps in, standing at Thomas' side, staring at me with still black eyes. "Oh, you will transform him, Richmond."

"I already have," Richmond notes. I can hear the pride in his voice. Pride for me.

"What will you require, Master, and I will arrange equipment." The boy smiles, just glowing.

"Hair removal. Everything but what's on his head. I want him bare, smooth, hyperaware of his whole body."

As if I'm not already.

Thomas nods. "We'll need the wax ready, Bino. In the back room, I think, the soft table. Will he require something to dull the pain?"

Richmond shakes his head. "No, that's part of the experience."

"Excellent!"

"Might I suggest the vibrating plug, the one that expands? It will heighten everything." The man with the black eyes looks unflappable, but somehow amused.

Richmond nods. "Yes, please." Then his attention is on me. "Are you ready?"

"I. Oh. Okay..." I'm not sure if I am. If I want to be naked, bare, exposed.

Richmond takes my arm and we walk into the back room, which is intimate, cozy. The three guys from the salon come with us. The man with the longer hair digs out a large plug, a cord coming from the base. "Do you want him bound, Rich?"

"No, he'll stay still. And I'll put that in." Richmond reaches for the plug and smiles at me. "Take the one you're wearing out, lovely."

The men are heating pots of wax and laying out strips of cloth and I'm going to freak out if I think. So I don't. I just watch Richmond's eyes and pull the plug out, blushing dark as I realize it's wet with Richmond's spunk. It makes him smile, though, his eyes going hot. I hand it over, hands shaking a little.

"Back or front first, Rich? And do you want his throat and chin done?" So casual.

"Yes, everything but the hair on top of his head." Richmond isn't quite as casual, the heat in his eyes is incredible.

"Eyebrows and lashes? Impressive. On your belly, please, Nat, and spread for your master."

Oh.

Oh, fuck.

Oh, I don't know if I.

Oh.

Richmond seconds the order. "Do as you're told, Nat."

I try to move, I even want to move, but I simply can't figure out how.

The dark-haired man smiles, the look almost gentle. "Vapor lock. Should I assist him?"

"No, I will. Give us a few minutes, please." Richmond waits until we're alone and then he strokes my cheeks. "Nat?"

I look up, heart pounding. "I'm sorry. I couldn't. It's. It's big."

"The people or the waxing?"

"The people? So many strangers watching me do this and I... What if you think I'm ugly? What if I can't be still? What if..." Now that I've started talking, I can't stop and it feels good, to just give my fears, my heart to Richmond.

"I could never think you were ugly, Nat, not if you were bald all over. And you can be still — you will be. For me. Just like you'll do it even though there are strangers watching. For me." Richmond kisses me, hard, tongue pushing into my mouth. "You'll do it for me, Nat, and I'll make you fly."

I press closer, panic easing some, finally able to move, to press against Richmond. He slips the new plug into me while we're kissing, the act so familiar now I almost don't notice it. I moan into his lips, hips rocking a little, clinging. His hand slides on my cock, pressing into the slit and then teasing around the leather band that holds me so tight. Then he steps away.

"After the doctor, Nat."

"Yeah. Okay. You'll stay?"

"Oh, I'm not going anywhere, Nat. I'm not going anywhere at all." He knocks on the door and the three of them come back, the one called Thomas handing Richmond a little remote control. He grins and presses a button, the plug inside me starting to vibrate.

"Oh!" I step toward him, shivering, but those warm hands lead me to the table, help me stretch out.

"My only regret, Nat, is that I can't do this myself. But I'll be right with you the entire time, for every rip, every tear."

"It'll be mostly warm and uncomfortable, okay? Almost a sting. The worst bits will be around your hole, between your legs." The low voice is somehow soothing. Sort of. Oh, what am I into? "Rich, would you like a stool to sit on?"

"Thank you, Bryant. You're going to be lovely nude, Nat. Just lovely." Richmond sits next to me and he fiddles with the remote control, making the plug grow inside me.

"I... I'll look like a freak, with no eyelashes."

Oh, the wax is warm, the stretch and sting on my leg making me wince.

"Ah, I knew you'd eventually tell me what was really at the root of your worry. What do you think, Bryant, Bino, Thomas? Will he look like a freak with no eyelashes?"

"You will look exotic, otherworldly." Another strip is laid down, another pulled away.

Thomas adds his agreement. "Yes, Bryant is quite right. It will be quite special. I would even go as far as to suggest you be balded everywhere."

Richmond shakes his head, thank the gods and little fishes. "No, Thomas. I'm rather fond of the mess of curls."

My legs are done quickly, then the back of my arms,

the small of my back. The burn makes me shift, moan.

A soft hand lands on my ass. "Still now, little one."

The vibrating inside me increases and Richmond purrs. "This one's going to hurt, Nat. Focus on the pleasure of the plug, and on the pain. Feel it."

The sting on my hole makes me cry out, every muscle going tight. "Burns. Richmond!"

"And you love it," he tells me, voice low, purring. The next three pulls have me undone, shivering. Richmond's still making those sounds, and his breath is coming more quickly. "Beautiful. Such a good boy, Nat."

"We're ready for the front."

I shake my head, gasping. "I don't know if I can, Richmond."

"Of course you can." Richmond's mouth is at my ear. "For me."

"F... for you. Only for you." I turn over, shaking badly, eyes squeezed shut.

Nat's on the table, shaking like a leaf, cock hard, bound, and I swear I can see his heartbeat along the big vein, tripping along as he starts to freak out. I put my hand on his belly and stroke gently, leaning in to bring his focus back around to me as my other hand works the remote on the plug he's got in. I make it bigger, make him take notice of it. "You're doing just great," I tell him. "You look amazing already."

Bryant comes over, whispers softly. "Thomas will trim the lashes close. Plucking them will cause the eyes to swell. He will not know the difference."

I nod, pleased with the compromise. If I were stronger, less enamored, I would agree to have him made completely bald. But his red curls are a part of his charm, and I won't part with them.

"You ready, lovely?" I ask Nat as the wax is spread over his balls.

"Trying to be." Those pale cheeks are dark red, hot, wet with the first trace of tears.

I lick them away and nod to Bryant. "You will be so beautiful, all smooth and hairless, but more than that, you will be so sensitive."

Nat's cries sound against my cheek, almost like that first night when I took him, made him mine.

"Yes. Beautiful. Oh, Nat, so beautiful." I reach down and slide my fingers along his bare balls. So soft, so smooth now that the tiny hairs have been removed.

Those pretty balls draw up into stones, so hard, so tight. Bryant gives me a soothing cream to smooth on as Thomas and Bino work on Nat's legs.

I smooth it in, anticipating Nat's reaction when the rest of his pubes are dealt with, anticipating how he'll look, feel.

It's not long before Bryant's lips are at my ear again. "What's last? Face or pubes?"

I nod toward his pubes; the wait will do us both good.

They do Nat's belly, the few hairs around his nipples. The rip as the red hair under Nat's arms comes off is stunning, Nat's cry ringing out.

I groan audibly, my cock so hard it aches, as do my balls. "You're doing so well, Nat. So well."

"Almost done?" He's panting, lips parted.

"Bino will do your arms and I'll do your face, just close your eyes." Thomas has the little curved clippers, eyes gentle, but firm.

"Do as he says, Nat." My voice is gentle but firm as well, and he's already so attuned to me that he does as he's told. So eager to please, such a natural. All mine. I must have been a very good boy in my former life.

Bryant gets Nat's eyebrows waxed as Thomas gets in position, then, in unison, they do one side and then the other. It's a beautiful thing how they work together and I purr — Nat and I will move like that when we do our public scenes, so in tune.

"Almost done," I tell Nat. "Just the pubes — I had them save the best for last."

The tears are falling now, Nat overwhelmed and shaken. Thomas motions with the ointment.

"Before he sees," Bryant mouths. Ah. Yes. No bumps. No burning. Nat will be able to see his beauty.

I spread the ointment on him, slowly working it in everywhere, letting the soothing be sensual. I lap at his tears, tasting his pain, his fears. "You are stunning," I tell him as Bryant gets ready to spread the wax on his pubes.

"N... not ugly?"

"Not in the least, and when they're done here, there's a mirror — I'll show you." One day he'll believe he's beautiful without my having to tell him, to convince him.

Thomas buzzes off the pretty red curls to a long stubble, then starts removing them, my Nat completely bare to me.

Oh, he is beautiful bare, I knew he would be. Not that the pretty cock rising out of the nest of fiery curls isn't lovely, but this is nice, too, and I know it's going to feel amazing, so sensitive.

I'm a top, experienced, tough, but here I am, squirming on the stool like a barefaced virgin. I use the ointment on the newly bared skin around his cock. "How's it feel, Nat?"

"Hot. It's hot." Nat shifts, breath catching.

"Would you like some time alone, Rich?"

"First I'd like Nat to stand and turn for you, and you

can let me know what you think of my lovely sub."

I help Nat up off the table. He needs to get used to this, used to being shown off, looked at, the center of attention. I hit the remote as he stands, making the plug as large as it goes and setting the vibrations to high. Nat stands, eyes screwed shut, hands fisted. He looks like he's a breath away from crying and screaming and coming, all at once.

"He's beautiful, master." Bino nods, gives me a smile. "Can I get you both some juice, please?"

"That would be lovely, thank you." Bino is such a pleasant lad, always trying to please. I look over to Bryant and Thomas — Nat needs to hear it from them as well. Next time I'll make him open his eyes and accept the looks, take them in.

Thomas nods, smiling. "He is beautiful. Your touch makes him glow, Rich, it's a lovely thing to see."

Bryant's voice joins in. "Magical. He'll soar whenever you touch him."

A bottle of oil is handed to me, the label reading, "To retard the growth of new hair for up to two cycles."

"Thank you, gentlemen. And now if we could have that moment?" They close the door and I move Nat so he's standing directly in front of the full-length mirror that adorns the back of it. I stand behind him, letting him feel the warmth of my body, my strength. I have not left him alone in this. "Open your eyes, Nat. Look at how beautiful you are."

Nat leans back into me, shaking. Those eyes open slowly flicking over his reflection, skin flushing deep rose.

I purr, letting him feel the vibrations of my pleasure. "What do you think, lovely?"

"I... I look alien. Odd. N... naked."

"Exotic," I tell him, running one hand across his

nipples. "Beautifully bare," I say next, my hand dropping to play along the bared skin where his pubes had been. "You make me hard." I rub myself against his ass, wishing I wasn't wearing the leathers, though it's probably a good thing. We still have to see Trip.

He whimpers, rubs back against me, stretching up with a little cry.

"So what do you think now?" I ask.

"For you. I'll be bare for you." Those eyes just beg me to hold him, take him home, comfort him. One more visit, little one. One.

I tilt his head back and take his mouth, let my fingers slide across the leaking tip of his cock, one pressing into the slit. "I'm very proud of you."

"Th... thank you. Thank you." Nat pushes up toward my touch, begging.

I let my hands slide on his body. "You can't come yet, lovely."

Another desperate whimper, almost a complaint. "Need you, Richmond."

"I know. And you'll get me. After the Doc has his look-see." I step back and away. "Bend over the table, Nat. I'll take out the plug."

He bends slowly, as if his skin doesn't quite fit him, offering me that pretty pink hole. I stop the vibrations and then bend and lick at the skin stretched around the base of the plug. He's entirely smooth down here now and so unbelievably hot. Those bird-like cries fill the air, the sounds settling in my balls. I have to force myself to stop or I'll be fucking him, and Doc needs to make his exam. I tug on the end of the plug, his body releasing it reluctantly.

Nat pants, hole winking at me. "Oh. Empty."

Groaning, I lean in and push my tongue into him. How can I not? He needs it, needs to be filled.

"Richmond!" Nat pushes back, so smooth, so bare.

I hum, letting the vibrations fill him; I fuck him with my tongue for a moment and then reluctantly pull back, stand. "Come, lovely. A quick visit to the doctor and I'll fill you like you need."

Nat stands, shaking. "Oh. Okay. Yeah. Okay."

I put my arm around him and lead him out.

We go through the salon, Thomas working on a beautiful sub's blue hair, Bryant painting a henna tattoo on the man's skin.

"Thank you," I call to them.

Trip's office is close, little Ghost meeting us at the door, looking at Nat with wide eyes. "Hello."

"Hi, Ghost. This is Nat. We have an appointment." And then we need to get home so I can fuck my boy through the mattress. Or the floor. Or the wall. I'm not feeling particularly picky about the where part.

Ghost nods. "Trip says to please come into the examination room."

"Thank you, Ghost." I guide Nat in and help him get up onto the table. "I'm not sure he'll let you keep on the cock ring. If it comes off, you're still not allowed to come."

"That's so not fair." Nat winks, playing. "Is any of it going to hurt?"

"Have you never had a complete exam before?" I ask, surprised.

"Well, just the normal stuff. Look in your ears, look in your throat. Listen to your heart. Do a scan. Here's some cold pills. Next, please."

"I'm surprised you've never had an employer who insisted on a full physical."

"Oh, Richmond, give the poor boy a break and reassure him that the full med exam is relatively painless. And if you've kept him open and stretched, I imagine the only thing that can cause a little pain won't."

I turn and smile at Doctor Trip. "Who's been telling tales?"

He laughs. "Your reputation, Rich."

Ghost is at Trip's side, eyes warm as they land on Nat. "It will all be okay. I promise."

Nat smiles, nods. "Thanks."

"He's mine full time, Trip. And you know how I play."

Trip nods. "I do. I'll make sure he's healthy, can handle what you're going to put his body through."

The exam is fast, but thorough, Trip touching every inch of my Nat. "Looks good. Make sure he eats iron-heavy meats and dark greens, minimum two meals a day. He's a touch low. Besides that? He looks great."

"Does that mean no activity that might cause bleeding until his iron levels are back up?" I hope not. I need to whip him again. Or cane him. Something heavy after our day of others touching him.

"Oh, no. This is minor. Most pale redheads need a touch more than most. He'll just need to learn to like spinach and steak." Trip winks.

I chuckle and hold out my hand, shaking Trip's. "Thank you, Doc. Nothing personal, but hopefully we won't have to see you again any time soon."

"Once a year, besides that? You'll keep him well-lubed."

Nat's vibrating visibly, needing for this all to come to an end. Needing me.

"I will. Thanks again, Doc."

I grab Nat's hand and try not to run out of there, but Nat's need fuels my own and I know Trip can see it, know Ghost can feel it. They won't begrudge us a little hurrying.

"Home now?" Nat's cheeks are streaked with tears,

the pure adrenaline fueling them.

I nod. "Home. Where I'm going to fuck you until you can't see straight. And then when you've come so hard you're an empty shell, I'm going to beat you. Whip, flogger, cane. I haven't decided yet how much you need." The fucking will tell me.

"I'm empty." The lift gets us upstairs and it's a few steps to our rooms. Only a few steps.

"Not for long, lovely." Not for long at all.

As soon as we're through the door, I push him up against the wall, my body pressed hard against his as I kiss him, no, as I take his mouth like I own it. Nat sobs, arms wrapped around me, holding on tight, thin body driving against me.

I lift his legs, get them around my waist so I can drive my cock into his needy, hot hole.

"Please! Please, Richmond! I need you." He pushes himself down, fucking himself on me for a few strokes before I grab his ass and take control.

I pound into him, just let him have it, bringing his ass down onto my cock again and again. It's wild and hot and my hands are holding his ass tight enough I'm going to leave beautiful bruises on his bared skin. I bend my head and get that little nipple ring between my teeth, tug on it.

Nat's shaking violently, eyes rolling, feeling nothing at all but me. I'm not going to let him come yet, he needs to feel me inside him a little longer, needs to bend to my will until he just can't take it anymore.

"Oh! Richmond!" Nat arches, ass clenching around me. "So full."

Yeah, yeah, that's it, lovely, don't you worry, you're never going to be empty again. I fuck him over and over and over again and, finally, I get a hand between us and I let his dripping, red cock free, unsnapping the leather

225

ring.

"I want you to hold it off as long as you can, Nat." I want to see how far he can control his body for me. He just sobs, head tossing, teeth sinking into those full lips as he fights the urge to come. "That's it, hold on as long as you can. For me. I know you can do it."

I wrap my hand around his prick and stroke him off, while I fuck him, then I add back in tugging on the nipple ring, giving him as much sensation as I possibly can.

"Master! Master, *please*." Oh. Oh, the honorific hits me hard, the word in Nat's voice huge.

"Yes! Come for me, Nat. Come." Because I'm going to, any second now, just from the power and the beauty of his devotion. Nat goes tight as a fist, seed spraying between us as Nat collapses, eyes rolling.

I thrust twice more, coming deep inside him and holding him up between me and the wall, trying to catch my breath. I can feel Nat's heart, beating like a little trapped bird in the thin chest.

I kiss his heart, kiss his neck, drag my tongue up along his jaw.

"Y... yours." The words are mere breaths.

"Yes, Nat. Mine. You know it. I know it. Everyone we meet knows it." I straighten and head for the bedroom, carrying him with me. "We need to plug you again. And a short nap, a good meal, and then we play hard."

Nat just purrs low, limp and quiet against me. I chuckle. I've exhausted him. It won't be the last time.

Chapter Eight

The club has a series of pools, and every other day Richmond and I come in the late night to stretch and swim and relax. I love it. It's quiet and easy and the water touches me everywhere.

Well, everywhere but inside, because there's a wide, thick plug inside me tonight, easily as big at its widest point as Richmond's cock. Maybe bigger.

Richmond's long strokes carry him by me, one hand sliding along my skin as he swims.

That's another reason I love it here, he's as naked as I am and he's got the most amazing body.

He's taught me so much in just a few days — how to accept his will, how to accept pleasure and pain. Sometimes I think there's nothing else to learn.

Richmond gets out and sits on the edge of the pool, watching me. I can *feel* his eyes. I keep swimming and moving, letting him see everything. He lets me, watching and watching, and I'm almost ready to quit when he bangs on the side of the pool, my signal to come out. I slide out, stretching, the pull of the plug drawing me short.

Richmond chuckles, hand sliding along my leg. Sliding up my leg. Toward the plug. He can't seem to keep his hands away from my ass.

"It's so big. Bigger than anything."

"That's why you're here. That's why we're all here."
His hand keeps sliding up, touches the base of the plug
inside me.

I go up on my toes, keeping the pressure off. The
bastard laughs and pushes his hand up higher so the
plug pushes into me. I make a soft, low sound, the plug
stretching me. "Oh..."

"Yes, oh." He tugs me down and kisses me, hard. His
hand stays on my ass, squeezing.

Every squeeze makes that plug feel bigger. "Richmond.
I'm so full."

"Yes, yes, you are. I think we need to reinforce that."
He pats his lap.

"Hmm?" Reinforce what? "You... you want me to
sit?"

He shakes his head. "No, Nat, I want you to lie across
my lap."

"Oh." My belly goes tight and hard, focus clenching
down to Richmond, heart just fluttering. "Oh. Okay."

"You know what's coming, Nat." His voice just drags
over my skin, kind of like the hand that's rubbing my
ass.

"Uh-huh..." I shouldn't want this. I shouldn't. I do,
though.

"My lovely, lovely boy."

I don't get a warning. One minute he's rubbing my
ass, the next he's spanking me, making the plug rock,
making my skin sting. My entire ass starts to feel swollen,
hot, burning, my hips rocking with Richmond's rhythm.
Richmond's hands are large, they cover a lot of territory,
and he moves them around, hitting the bottom of my ass,
the top of my thighs, every part. I start wiggling, the burn
overwhelming, pushing.

"No moving."

"Richmond!" I have to move. I need to.

"Right here, Nat. Not changing my mind." He keeps spanking me, making me burn.

My toes curl, my fingers clench, a soft cry filling the room. "I have to move, please." I don't move, though, do I?

"No, you don't have to do anything but what I tell you."

I moan, muscles tense. My ass is afire, burning, hurting. I'm so hard, needing so badly.

"Good job, Nat. Excellent." I can feel each finger as he spanks me, I can almost feel his fingerprints.

Oh. Oh, Richmond knows how that affects me, how I feed on it. Need it.

"You make me so proud." He leans over and kisses my ass. "And now you can come."

Oh. Oh...

I hump against his thighs, once, twice, three times and I'm shooting.

"Oh yes. Lovely." His hand keeps sliding in circles over my ass, making sure I remember exactly where I am. Like I'm in danger of forgetting.

"Burns. Richmond." My ass is working the plug, moving it.

"I know." He tilts my face up, takes a kiss. "And you're beautiful."

Then I'm shifted, moved so my head is in his lap. "I need, lovely."

I make this obscene sound, hungry for his prick, for his pleasure.

"All yours, Nat. I'm yours. Take it." Oh, the need in his voice is high praise.

"Yes..." I suck him down, swallowing and begging, fingers stroking Richmond's balls.

Richmond pushes his hips up into my mouth, sliding his cock over my tongue again and again. I take him in deep, head bobbing. His hands drop to my head, fingers tangling in my hair. Each moan, each groan he makes is the sweetest praise. This is the best part of everything, the hunger I have for him, the way he feeds me.

"Soon," he tells me. "Suck me harder."

I bury my nose in his pubes, pulling with all I have, trying to make Richmond feel it.

"Nat!" he shouts, hips snapping, come pouring down my throat, hot and salty and good. I swallow it all, proud that I can, now that I can take him. He pets my head, my back, making sexy purring sounds and telling me how good I am. I hum, rocking just a little, ass swaying. Happy, Richmond makes me happy.

His hand slides on my ass, not hard, just touching, my skin aching. It makes me moan, that touch, makes the heat on my ass unavoidable. "I've been thinking about your debut, lovely."

I rest my cheek on his knee. Listening.

He pets me, fingers always stroking, touching. "I've been trying to decide whether we should go with the cat o' nine tails or the flogger. Something like the cane would be intense, but we haven't done that between us yet and I want your first public showing to be comfortable, familiar."

I nod, the tension less than I thought it would be. I don't like the pain, but I know I need it, know that wearing Richmond's marks is amazing. He smiles. "It doesn't really matter what we do, everyone will see you shine, see you take my marks and be entranced, enthralled. Excited."

"What happens after?"

"There's a reception. Kestrel is arranging it so that we have some time alone together between the scene and the reception. Everyone will want to meet you."

"Can I stay beside you?" I don't know why it's

important, but it is.

"That's the only place you'll be allowed."

"Thank you." I kiss Richmond's knee, nodding.

He purrs and lifts my chin, bending to kiss me. Richmond's lips give me just what I need and I know he can taste himself on mine. His hands find my arms and wrap around them, holding hard enough to bruise, to leave his marks on me. I moan into his mouth, body gripping the plug again.

"Needy. I like that." He stands, though, tugs me up with him. "There's a vid night tonight. For the staff. Would you like to go?"

"What kinds of vids?" I can't help but be curious.

"I'm not sure. I think tonight is action night." He laughs softly. "It's not porn, lovely."

"I knew that, Richmond." Harley, Harvey, Hardy — somebody, caught me in the hallway yesterday, jabbering about it.

"We can go. Eat popcorn. Sit and neck in the dark."

"Can I sit on your lap?" It sounds perfect.

"My lap or at my knees. There won't be a chair there for you."

"No? They don't bring enough chairs for everyone?"

He laughs, sounding delighted. "Of course they do, Nat. Still, there won't be one for you there."

"Oh." Okay, I'm a big dork.

"It'll be second nature soon enough, lovely. You're a natural."

I kiss his shoulder in thanks before standing up on surprisingly unsteady legs. Damned plug.

He doesn't help, either, his hand sliding to my ass and jostling it. He grins as I try to push my ass out of his reach. "We could swap it out for a different one before going to the vid-room."

"Different? Different how?" Not that I don't trust

him, but...

He chuckles and kisses my nose. "Just different, Nat. I thought you might like something other than the stretch of that one."

I nod. I do want another or more lube on this one or something different. A different pressure. "It's... this one is harder to get used to. Like it almost doesn't fit."

"It's wider than any we've used. I felt you'd gotten to the point, though, where you hardly noticed the plugs anymore. And we can't have that."

Richmond winks and goes to the wall, opening the cupboard there and looking through the available plugs. There's some interesting-looking dildos in there on the same shelf, some slightly scary-looking ones as well. All the rooms seem to have cupboards like this, full of anything you could possibly want, all clean and ready to go. Not to mention the gold tubes full of lube that are simply everywhere. He pulls out two plugs and puts them on a table in front of me. One is fairly slender, but it's got a little antenna sticking from the end, which I know means it has a remote and either vibrates or grows, or possibly both. The other one is medium-sized, with a large round head on it that's covered in little triangular bumps. There's bumps on the length of it as well, all different sizes and shapes.

"You've been so good, Nat. Your choice."

I look, then meet Richmond's eyes. "Can I sit on your lap with both of them?" That's really what I'm looking forward to, being in Richmond's arms.

His eyes go dark and he swallows, nods. "Yes, Nat."

I moan, then touch the remote control plug. "I'm yours, Richmond."

"Yes, you are, Nat." He puts the other one away and pockets the little remote control device.

"Lie over the table. Spread your legs and push out the

plug."

My eyes go wide. "Without using my hands?"

"That's right." He gives me a smile and guides me to the table. "Come on, Nat. Do as you're told," he tells me as he settles in behind me, no doubt getting a clear view of my plugged ass.

"I don't..." I don't know if I can, my thighs shaking now. He pushes me places I don't know I can go.

"Don't make me tell you again." His voice has that dangerous edge to it. The one that reminds me he's in charge. Totally and utterly in charge.

It's so big and my body doesn't want to let it go. "I'm trying, Richmond."

He leans over me, kisses the top of my spine. "Try harder."

Then his hands grab my hips, thumbs massaging the small of my back. I arch, panting, wanting to do this for Richmond. The plug starts to move, slowly, but surely.

He purrs. Fuck, I'd do pretty much anything for that sound. "That's it, lovely. Don't stop now."

"F... for you." I grunt as it comes free, just slumping to the table, hole twitching and empty.

"Oh, yes. Always and only for me." His hands are heavy on my ass, thumbs teasing into me and then disappearing, coming back cool and slick, pushing lube into me. I can relax now, spread and let Richmond touch me deep, stretch me. His thumbs disappear again and this time it's three fingers, pushing more of the cool lube in and working inside me.

"Mmm..." It feels so good and I push back against the touch.

The pattern repeats, fingers disappearing, coming back as more; this time two from each hand. It stretches, but it's a good feeling, the slight burn echoing in the still-heated skin of my ass. I almost don't notice when he slips another finger inside me. Almost.

A soft little sound leaves me, but it doesn't hurt, just stretches a little farther, my body accepting what Richmond wants me to have. He purrs, that sound just sliding through me. And then he adds another finger, three from each hand.

It stretches me wider than his cock.

Wider than anything.

"Oh." My chest lifts off the table, ass lifting as I go up on my toes. "Master."

"That's right, Nat. I'm your Master." The words are growled, possessive. His cock rubs against my balls, pushing at them.

He doesn't back off on the fingers in me though; he's fucking me with them, pushing them deep.

I can't think. Breathe. Anything.

Just feel.

Oh.

Oh, fuck.

He keeps bumping against my balls with his cock, almost like he's fucking them, making them swing, making them push up against my own cock. He does something with my ass, and instead of all those fingers, I've got his hand inside me. His whole fucking hand, moving, pushing, knuckles brushing over my gland.

My head slams back, sounds just pouring out of me. In. His hand. Richmond's. Oh. Oh, please.

He makes a fist inside me, cock still fucking between my legs, making sounds of his own. "Nat. Lovely. Mine. Oh. Mine."

"Yours. Master. In me. So much. So full." Tears start pouring and I can't stop them, there's just no room for them inside me.

"Yes. Yes, Nat." His hand is moving now, passing over my gland over and over again.

Everything tightens down to the pressure inside me, the ache of my cock and balls and the slide of Richmond's cock. I don't know how long it goes on for, time has no meaning here, nothing matters but this. It only ends, only changes when he grinds out the word, "Come."

My hands scrabble on the table, entire body bucking violently as my balls and cock obey.

The pressure is huge, enormous as his hand slides out of me as soon as I've come. I'm not empty for long, though, because his cock fills me, pounds into me. I just whisper my pleasure, over and over again, offering Richmond all of me.

He takes me with abandon, just plowing into me, telling me how hot I am, how perfect. How I'm his.

His.

Only his.

I nod. Yes. Yes. His.

Sweat's pouring off me, dripping onto the table.

"Yes!" he shouts, and slams into me, filling me with his heat before collapsing over my back.

I don't move.

I can't.

I'm just going to enjoy Richmond. Now.

Chapter Nine

It's our public debut tomorrow.

Well, his. But this will be my first time showing him off in front of a large group. My first time sharing him, though I've tried to get us both used to others seeing, watching, being there.

He's nervous and, frankly, so am I. So we need to play. We need to do something new that won't take away from tomorrow's flogging, but that will blow both our minds tonight.

There's really only one choice — the sound. We haven't touched it yet. It's time to give him something new to love.

He's in the bathroom, cleaning himself inside and out, as I asked him to earlier.

"Nat? Lovely? Are you ready yet?" The enemas still bother him, I can tell, still make him feel invaded, but he obeys.

"Yes. Yes, Richmond. I'm just drying off."

"Meet me in the playroom in two minutes."

I head there myself, prepare the cuffs that hang from the ceiling, the ones on the floor. I'm going to spread eagle him. Then I take out the sound, give it an antiseptic wash and lay it on a tray on the table. I find a plug as well. It's not thick but it's long, and it'll echo the sound in his cock.

Nat's about fifteen seconds early, so beautiful, bare and clean, eyes huge and beautiful. My marks are standing out on his shoulders, his chest.

My cock throbs. "Undress me, lovely."

Nat nods, smiles at me, unfastening the leather straps of my harness. "Do you want your hair left in its braid?"

"I don't mind one way or the other — take it down if you want." I know he likes it down, but I usually don't give him much in the way of choices.

He kisses my shoulder in thanks, carefully loosening the heavy braid, face in the mass as it's freed.

"It's such a pain to take care of, I'm thinking of cutting." I can't resist teasing.

"Cutting it?" Nat's voice is pure horror. "I'll take care of it, Richmond. I will. Please. It's so beautiful, smells so good..."

I chuckle. "It's a pain, Nat. You'll need to wash it, dry it, brush it..."

"Okay. Please, Richmond. It smells like you."

"If you take care of it without complaint, I'll keep it."

"I won't complain." I smile. Nat doesn't really complain about anything, just blinks and then adjusts. He's a wonder, my beautiful boy. "Then you can start by brushing it now. After you get me naked."

I let him distract us both with my hair and now my cock is pressing against the zip, making me ache. Nat is careful not to catch my cock, stripping me down, hand sliding over my skin. I purr for him, every touch so good. He's so good at this, at being mine.

He nuzzles my cock, cheek so smooth, so soft.

"Careful, now," I warn him. "I didn't say you could do that."

Those pretty eyes flash up at me, confused. "I was just

loving on you."

"I said get me naked and do my hair, Nat. Come on, now, you've done so well, you *know* how this works." He's relaxing, getting used to this, to us. It's a good thing, but not without its little problems.

Those eyes drop, Nat flushing dark and stripping me down quickly, not even touching my skin as my boots and pants come off. "I'll go put these up and get the brush."

I stop him, wrapping my hand around his arm and tilting his chin up so he has to look at me. "Don't pout."

There's a spark in those eyes, a hint of real anger. "I wasn't. I'm trying to do as you asked, Richmond."

I slide my hand through his curls, kiss him softly. "I'm sorry, lovely. I didn't mean to snap."

Just like that, Nat eases, that anger disappearing. "I guess I'm a little buzzy about tomorrow, too, huh? Let me grab a brush."

I nod. "You can do my hair and then I have something special planned. Something to help you find your center and sleep."

Nat nods, disappearing, ass wiggling back and forth. He's empty and feeling it. It makes him sexy. I take myself in hand, stroking idly, thinking of him in the few moments he's not with me.

Nat hurries back, brush in hand, curls bobbing.

I purr. "I'm looking forward to this."

"I'll be careful. Promise." Nat bounces behind me, the brush moving through my hair, so gentle.

My sounds get louder, it feels so good to be cared for like this. Nat hums and brushes, the act warm and happy, normal.

"This will be your task every evening, Nat." It will be a gift to both of us.

"Yes, Richmond." Nat sighs, the sound peaceful, happy.

I let it go on until we're both lazy with pleasure. "It's time, Nat."

"Yes, Richmond. Thank you. It looks beautiful."

"Thank you." I draw Nat around and kiss him. "Now, go and get me the lube and that plug out on the table. It's time for a little fun."

Nat nods, eager and wanton, trusting me so much more now than just two weeks ago.

He gets me the lube, the plug, and I have him bend over for me, his body supple and flexible. "Nice." I'm purring again — he just brings it out in me. And I'm using two slick fingers to spread the lube inside him, get him ready for the plug.

"This one is thin, but possibly longer than you've had inside you before."

"Oh. Okay. Okay." Nat spreads for me, body clean and smooth, hole eager to be filled.

I lube up the plug and slide it into his body. "How does it feel?"

Nat wriggles, stands. "It's deep. Different."

"So is the sound." I take his hand and lead him to the cuffs hanging in the middle of the room. He's blinking, mind working, and it's easy to cuff him, get his hands settled before he remembers what that means.

I do his ankles next and he's all spread for me, cock hard even though he's remembered. Or, more likely, because he has.

"Is it going to hurt?" Nat's eyes won't leave me, not unless they have to.

"No. It won't be comfortable. But it won't be entirely unpleasant, either." I smile. My little pain slut is going to love it.

"Okay." Nat's shivering a little, offering me a weak smile.

"Relax, Nat. Just feel. Feel me. Feel the plug inside

you. Feel the way your body is stretched for me." I run my hands over his limbs, his torso, not necessarily trying to arouse him, but wanting to remind him that I'm here, that he's mine and I've got him. I've got him.

I can feel Nat relaxing, eyes closing as he listens to my voice.

"This is going to be good, lovely. You're going to enjoy it." I let my hands focus on his belly, his hips, the base of his cock. "I'm not going to tie your cock up tonight because the sound will keep you from coming until I take it out."

"Will it stay in on its own?" So curious, my Nat.

I nod. "It will as long as you stay hard." I grin and lean close to nip at his collarbone. "You'll stay hard."

Nat chuckles and gasps. "You make me hard. All the time. You taught me about needing." Then Nat's mouth snaps shut, cheeks going pink.

I purr and reward him for that with a kiss, long and deep, giving him as much of myself as I can in a kiss. Nat's melted and mine, lips swollen and cock hard as glass. He's ready. Very ready.

I back off, licking at his lips as I go, and then get the sound. I'm using a thin one to start with. If he likes it, we'll build to something bigger. We may do so even if he doesn't like it — if I do.

"Here it is," I tell him, wanting him to see. "You need to watch as I put it in."

"I do?" Nat tilts his head, that curiosity back in force. "Why?"

I chuckle. "Because I want you to. Because I don't think you can *not* watch."

"Oh." Nat chuckles, nods. "Right. I thought you meant..." I get another smile, this one a little nervous. "No thinking, right?"

"That's right, lovely. Thinking is bad for you." I wink

and grab the lube, take hold of his cock and stroke it a few times. Then I start pushing in lube. Just lube, but lots of it. Nat wiggles, hips shifting, cock trying to pull away from my hand.

"You're not going anywhere, lovely, just relax and enjoy it." I give him a wink and squeeze his cock to make the slit round and as open as possible and push some more lube in.

"I'm trying. It... I've never. I." If I've got him babbling now, he's going to be mindless when the sound's in.

"I know you've never. I'm going to go slowly and carefully. The sound itself now, yeah?" I smile and kiss his lips quickly, then the tip of his cock, and then I grab the sound, lubing it up and placing it at the slit of his cock, holding it there, letting him see.

There's a hint of panic in his eyes. "Richmond."

I shake my head. "I've got you, Nat, and I'm not going to let anything bad happen to you."

I squeeze his cock again and let the tip of the sound slide in.

Nat's eyes are wide, breath caught. There is still worry, apprehension, but the panic is gone, the real fear given up. Because of my words. Because he trusts me. Fuck. My cock throbs, hard and eager, and it almost gets in the way — it does touch his briefly, and it's in that moment that I switch my hold to the base of his cock and let the sound go, let gravity pull it right in.

Nat cries out, surprised and startled like a bird.

I stroke his belly, purring softly. "Look at that. Isn't it beautiful?"

I let his cock go, the hardness of it keeping it reaching up for Nat's belly, keeping the sound in place.

"I. Richmond. I feel. Oh. Oh." Nat's eyes are wild, that pretty belly taut as a drum.

"Good, lovely, that's the idea, isn't it?" I lean in and

take one of his nipples in my mouth, looking down while I'm sucking so I can see that pretty cock in all its filled glory.

Nat's head falls back, the hard prick red and dark, harder than I've seen it since the waxing. My fingers find his other nipple, flicking across it, squeezing and pinching it, even though I half wonder if he can feel anything other than the metal filling his cock.

His ass is working the plug, little slut, trying to get more and more. I reach around and push on the base, making it slide deeper for a moment, wiggling it. Then I reach down and do the same to the sound, only with a more delicate touch.

"Master!" Nat shudders, tugging hard on the bonds, head tossing.

"Yes, just like that." I love it when he calls me Master like that. I've never asked him to do it — I've never had to.

Nat's head tosses, curls wild as they swing. So beautiful, so wanton, and all mine. I growl, let him hear the noise, so turned on by him.

I step back and start stroking my cock, eyes traveling over him. "You make me so hard, Nat."

"Oh. Oh, you... Want you. Always." Nat's eyes shoot from my cock to his.

I step closer, sliding my cock along his, reaching down with my free hand to cup and tug on his balls. Nat bucks, whimpers as the ball at the end of the sound rubs my belly.

Groaning, I lick at his lips, pumping my cock faster. I'm not going to last long, not with the way the need that's pouring over him smells.

"Yours. Smell you. So good. So good." Nat's eyes roll, hips bucking.

"All mine, lovely. All mine." With a possessive growl I

come, seed spraying over his cock, his belly.

Nat jerks hard, body a hard arc, demanding that he climax and physically unable to. Oh, fuck, that's incredible, and I moan, my cock jerking, trying to fill again immediately.

"Tell me what you feel," I demand.

"It burns a little, aches. Need to come, need to, but it won't."

"No, you won't until the sound comes out. Do you like it?" As I ask the question, I touch the ball on top of the sound again, making it move even as I reach behind him and make the plug move as well.

Another sharp cry, Nat rocking between my hands. "Please."

"Please what, lovely?" I want him to beg, I want to hear him plead to come.

The chains rattle as Nat's feet shift, hips fucking the air, trying to reach me. "I need."

"Yeah? Want me? Want this?" I stroked my hardening cock — I'm going to fuck him, fill him with my seed before I take out the sound.

"Yes. Yes, please. In me, I need more, to be full."

"Such a good boy." I move behind him, tugging eagerly on the end of the plug. He lets it go easily. Sweet slut, he likes the burn, the stretch, needs to be full now, heavy and plugged and mine.

I nudge at his hole with my prick, teasing us both. Nat arches, trying to take me in, trying to tempt me. "Want me, lovely? Need me desperately?"

"Yes. Yes, need. In me. Please, please."

I close my eyes, trying to hold on, just barely penetrating him before pulling back again.

"Oh. Master. I need you. Yours." Nat arches, trembling, hands fisted around the chains.

"I know." I push into him, my low moan betraying my

own need. Nat's burning inside, gripping me, squeezing. I start to thrust, loathe to leave that heat, eager to push back in.

"Yes." Nat nods, body not yet figuring out it won't be able to come yet.

I purr and agree. "Yes. Yes, Nat."

In and out and in and out. I move faster and harder, pushing us both. Nat's babbling, working my prick, crying out every time his prick bobs back and hits his belly. My hands slide along his chest, fingers flicking at his nipples, sliding over his abdomen. Everything about Nat is hard and hot and needy. Perfect.

"Soon, lovely," I promise him. "Soon."

"Soon..." Nat leans back, beautiful eyes huge. "Your own."

"Oh, yes. Mine. All the way through." I keep looking into his eyes, watching as my fingers find the little ball on top of the sound. Carefully, very carefully, I pull it from him, my lips forming the word "come." Nat groans, heat pouring over my fingers. His ass squeezes me so hard I almost scream, coming deep inside his body.

Nat slumps, rocking and sliding against me, just panting.

"That was beautiful. Stunning." I moan and push into him, thrusting a few times.

"Mmmm..." He rocks back, nodding. "Good."

I nod and keep moving, nice and slow and deep. Nat gives me a purr, moving with me, all sweet, melted slut. My cock is still hard, and I want. I want him so much. We just keep moving together like we're going to do it all night. Maybe we will.

Chapter Ten

I'm pretty sure I don't want to do the display. Or really, I want to do it and have done well and have Richmond happy.

I woke up early — way earlier than Richmond — and have been pacing.

Watching vids.

Going for walks.

Fretting.

Wandering.

Worrying a little about freaking out.

Normal stuff.

I'm pacing the hallway when I hear him wake up, growling a little. Probably because I'm not there.

"Nat?"

"Yeah. Yeah, Richmond."

I head in to see him. I'm already dressed, because I've been out, but he's naked. Naked and fine.

He purrs when he sees me, just like he always does, like it makes him happy just to have me in the room with him. "Someone's dressed."

I nod, smiling as I look at him. Need him. "I went for a walk. I brought pastries up from downstairs."

"You haven't eaten, I hope. No eating for you until after the scene." He sits and smiles at me, cups my cheek.

"Although you can have some protein if you're in the mood."

"I didn't eat." I press close to Richmond with a moan. "And I am."

He taps his cock, already hard and eager, tip glistening with wetness. "I'm all yours, Nat."

"So pretty..." I should be ashamed, to want this so bad, to need to give this to him. I should be.

My lips wrap around his cock and I moan, head starting to bob. He lies back, hips rocking slightly, but letting me set the place, letting me do him however I want. "Oh yeah, like that, lovely."

I don't hurry, because I want to hold onto this, I want to have this heat and happiness in me for the rest of the day.

One of his hands comes down to play with my hair, sliding through the curls, getting tangled in them. "Mouth's so hot."

It makes me hum, the praise, makes me suck harder.

"Yes! Gonna make me come, Nat, make me feel so good." I reach down, stroke Richmond's balls, moaning as they draw up. "Soon, lovely. Gonna fill you with me."

It should be cheesy and silly, but it's the truth, so it isn't. I take him all in, in deep, so hungry, needing him, his heat.

He cries out, hips bucking, the head of his cock hitting the back of my throat and then exploding with heat. It's easier now, swallowing him down, not missing a drop. Easy and good and right.

He purrs, hands sliding down the back of my shirt. "That's a great way to wake up. Makes me feel ready to face the day. What about you, Nat? You ready to face today?"

"I'm nervous, but I'm trying to be ready."

"You're going to do great, Nat. You're going to make me so proud." He sits up and starts to undress me, fingers warm as they slide against my skin.

"I want to, more than anything." His hands feel so good, so solid.

"You will. It doesn't matter if we are alone, with one or two others, or in a room full of people all watching us, what really matters is what's going on between you and me."

I nod. "Yeah. I don't think... I mean, you make me only see you."

He chuckles. "No, you do that, Nat. You have incredible focus, once you know what you need."

He takes off my shirt and starts working on my pants. "You, of course, will be naked. What do you think I should wear? A suit? A caftan?"

"Leather." I'm hard and throbbing, needing him. "Definitely leather."

He chuckles and nods. "Yes, so I match the leather you'll be wearing."

His hand slides down my belly and wraps around my cock, stroking me.

"Mmm... you're binding me?"

"Yes. No coming until I let you."

"Not... not even now?" I'm already rocking, already needing it.

He shakes his head. "No. I want all your focus on the scene. No food until after, no clothes, and definitely no coming until during the scene."

He stops stroking me, fingers gripping my balls hard.

I twist, whimpering low. "Oh. Oh, okay."

"Go on, go to the chest and bring me something to bind you with and the plug you want to wear for the scene." He's watching me, he wants to see what I'll pick.

I look, biting my lip. I want something big enough

to feel, big enough to stay, and leather bindings. I find a comfortable figure-eight cock ring, one where the leather won't cut into me, won't chafe. The plug I find is my favorite, wide as Richmond's cock, filled with a liquid inside that's warm and sloshes.

He purrs, obviously pleased with my choices. The hot look in his eyes as I go back to him confirms that. "Don't forget the lube, lovely."

I nod, get one of the gold tubes and hand it over. My cock bobs, hoping to convince Richmond that it should get one orgasm. He chuckles and strokes it again, then slips on the cock ring, not relenting at all.

"Mean, mean man." I'm not complaining, just playing, teasing, and Richmond knows it.

He laughs and strokes my cock, fondles my balls in their tight sac. "Turn around, lovely. Let me at your ass."

I moan low, turning and spreading, ass in the air as my elbows land on the bed. He purrs, oh, how I love that sound, and plays with the plug that's been in my ass overnight. It's a medium-sized one with little bumps, and when he slides it out the sensations are soft, but all over. Oh, it feels good and I arch, the sounds just slipping from me.

"Yeah, such a sweet, lovely slut." The emotion in Richmond's voice is huge and all mine.

"Love..." The word slips out of me and I bite my lip, groan.

"Yes, sweet Nat. Love." He purrs and kisses the top of my ass, tongue sliding down along my crack.

I spread wider, just begging shamelessly. I've learned to need this, crave it.

"Yeah, you're missing something now, aren't you, lovely?" He surprises me, his cock pushing into me instead of the plug.

"Yes!" I raise up onto my hands, welcoming him in — his girth, his need, his heat deep inside me.

"Yeah. I want you filled with my seed when we get out there." He starts pounding into me, pushing that heat into my ass over and over again.

Oh. Oh, fuck. I need to come. Need to. Want to, so bad. I'm not going to, though, because he's not teasing or taking his time, he's just pounding into me like he's going to drill me through the mattress, pushing toward his orgasm. I push back, squeeze, wanting to make him need me.

"Oh, fuck, Nat." He groans, hands squeezing my hips hard enough I'm sure he's going to leave bruises, more of his marks to decorate my skin.

"Yes. Master, please. I need you." I bear down, squeezing him as tight as I can.

He shouts, fingers so hard on my hips as his heat fills me inside in long pulses.

Oh. Oh, I want. My cock is throbbing, aching, and I need so badly. He just purrs and slides out, pushing the already lubed plug in, trapping his seed inside me.

"Uhn." I go up on my toes, hips rocking, cock fucking the air.

His fingers slide along my back, down my ass, and play with the base of the plug, my own motions driving it against his fingers. "Beautiful."

I am never going to survive until the scene.

Never.

He pulls me up so I'm leaning against him, his hands gentle on my skin. "Your need makes you glow, Nat. It increases your beauty. They'll all see that out there."

"For you. I need you." He's so warm.

"I know. It's your need that I feed off, that makes you special." He holds me tight for a moment and then kisses the top of my head. "Are you ready?"

I surprise myself by nodding. "Yes. Yes, Richmond. I am."

I am.

He nods and looks so pleased with me, happy. "As am I, lovely. Help me dress and choose the flogger and we'll go."

"Yes, Richmond."

It doesn't take any time before we're moving down the hall, me wearing nothing but the leather straps — trembling and hard and panting. His hand is against the small of my back and he's walking tall, proud. That's me he's proud of, making him strut.

"Are there any rules I don't know about yet?"

"No. You do as I say and you use your safeword if you need to. Same as always. The only difference is people are going to be watching."

"Okay." I tilt my head, suddenly curious. "Should I have used it? My safeword? I mean, do people use it?"

He chuckles. "Oh, lovely. You use your safeword if I push you beyond endurance. If the pain is no longer good." He shrugs. "You'll know if you ever need to use it."

"Do you have one?" It makes sense that he should, really. A way to tell me he needs things to change.

Richmond shakes his head. "I control the scenes, our relationship."

"I think you should have one. Just in case. So I know it's not a scene. So I know if you need... me."

"I have never done anything with you that I did not need *you* for, Nathaniel. Even when we've been in scenes, it hasn't been an act. However, if you'd like me to have a safeword, I suppose we could do that." He's stopped me in the hall, our faces close together as we speak.

I meet his eyes, nod. "I'd like that. Just... It doesn't seem fair that you can't let yourself be... vulnerable, if you need to."

He kisses my forehead. "You are a pure treasure, lovely. Will you help me choose?"

I nod, stroking Richmond's belly. "Something weird that you won't use."

"That leaves out enema, ball-stretcher, and guiche..." He winks, hand stroking the small of my back.

Evil bastard. I love him. "How about... pickle? Or... egret?"

"Well, pickle won't do. I mean, what if I'm in a mood and tell you to suck my pickle?" His eyes are just dancing.

My laughter just rings out. "Obelisk?"

"That just might work. As long as we don't find any toys that shape." He kisses me. "Obelisk, then. Thank you, Nat."

"Thank you." It just feels right. Fair. Good.

He smiled and heads us off again and suddenly we're there, in the room.

There are people, lots of people, watching and talking and looking. I'm nervous, but Richmond is right there, hand on my back. The tall guy is there, with the white hair — Mal — looking smug. Beside him is Kestrel, the pretty, bird-like one. And Hawk and Jester, the little guy clinging to Hawk.

"Focus on me, Nat. And the stage where our scene will be."

"Yes, Richmond." That I can do. I'm shivering, eyes focused on Richmond and Richmond alone.

"I think you're going to enjoy the flogging, lovely. It'll help you focus."

"You always help me find where I am."

"It's my job." He kisses me again. "And my pleasure."

He leads me to the stage and the place grows quiet, the

chairs quickly filling. I don't know what to do, where to stand, so I just stay still and wait, trusting in Richmond to show me.

Richmond begins to cuff me, back to the audience. I guess so they can see him flogging me. I'm cold and burning up all at once, the soft chatter starting up again enough that I hear it.

"This is our life, lovely. Put on display as payment for living here, loving here, being able to do anything we want."

I nod, holding Richmond's eyes. "I can do this, to be with you."

"I know, Nat. You'll do anything to be with me. I know because I feel the same way."

I know, too, that that's not the only reason we're here. I know that I won't hate this, that I was made to do this. "Yes. Yours."

Richmond purrs and nods. "Mine."

Before I know it I'm in the cuffs, arms above me, stretched almost to my tiptoes. Richmond's hands move on me, stroking my back with a gentle touch. I close my eyes, just focusing on that touch, on my lover, my Master.

He touches me all over, long sweeps of his hands, sensitizing my skin. It's amazing, perfect, and the room fades away, Richmond my only thought.

He's telling me how beautiful I am, how hot and sexy I am. "I'm going to flog you now, Nat. I want you to focus on the pain, on the fact I'm the one flogging you."

"Yes, Richmond." For him. Just like the first night. Only for him.

The first hit is a shock, the flogger is heavy and the thud is loud. It takes a moment before my nerves translate the sensation as pain. I can't remember whether he wanted me silent, if he wanted me still. What he wanted from me.

"Let us hear you, lovely."

The next thud falls harder across my shoulders. A low groan escapes me, hands tugging at the bonds. Oh. I ache.

The hits start to come often, with a rhythm that's like he's fucking me with the thick leather. Soon I'm simply a part of the rhythm, my cries, my heartbeat, my motions. I'm just another part of Richmond's arm. It goes on and on, pulling each cry from me, pulling tears from me, pulling my need from me.

"Master..." I'm shaking, chewing my lips, beginning to slip into desperation.

"Right here, Nat." He moves around and the next two hits fall on my chest, one hitting my nipple. I try to pull away — physically, mentally, all of me trying to hide, to protect myself.

"One more, Nat, and then I'll let you come. You can do one more for me, I know you can." He sounds so sure, so convinced.

"F... f... for you."

Only for him.

"I know."

The flogger falls just above my navel, heavy and thick, wrapping around my ribs on one side. But then Richmond's fingers are on the leather cock ring, releasing my cock and my balls, his voice the only sound in the room. "Come for me."

I didn't even think I was hard, much less ready to orgasm, but my body responds, even as I sob out his name.

"Yes. Yes, Nat. That's right, lovely." His hand cups my cheek, holds my head still for his kiss. He fills me with his breath. I lean into him, crying, breath hitching.

"Good, Nat. So very good. I'm so proud of you." I can

hear it in his voice, that pride. It gives a fierceness to his words.

He begins to undo me and that's when I realize that there's applause. I shiver, push closer to him. I'm not ready to remember the audience. I need some time.

He gets me undone and then turns us both to face the audience, guides me through a bow. "Thank you for coming, my friends."

I can't make out faces through my tears, but it's Mal's voice that gets people moving. "Okay. Out. Kes has arranged some food next door. Come on. Out."

Richmond turns me to him, holds onto me, fingers sliding lightly along my back, along the welts that burn on my back.

"Master." The word is whispered and I don't want him to let go of me. Ever.

He tugs me closer, humming, purring. "So proud of you, Nat. You did beautifully. Can you feel my marks on your skin? Each welt is there to remind you of our connection."

Yes. Yes, I can feel each and every one. I nod, heart pounding, just sort of lost in Richmond's arms.

I hold Nat until the room clears and then I pull him closer, purring, telling him how wonderful he is, how beautiful, how proud I am of him.

I'm surprised by how shattered *I* am by what we did.

The flogging was intense; to do it in front of an audience had brought it into such sharp focus.

And so I hold him, as much for my own benefit as his.

"I love you," I finally tell him as my store of words runs out.

"Love." Nat nods, clinging to me, heart finally slowing, cheeks drying.

I sit down, my feet hanging over the edge of the stage, holding him in my lap. "Yeah. Yeah, love."

Nat sighs, leaning in, one hand petting my belly, trying to soothe.

"You okay, lovely?"

"Yeah. A little shaky. Feeling like I need to stay in your arms forever, but okay."

"Oh, I'm thinking that's not a bad plan." I chuckle and hold him tight, unmindful of the welts on his back and front that have to be hurting. I need this, maybe more than he does. "That was... intense."

Nat nods. "At the end, I was almost scared."

I kiss him hard at the admission. I've not pushed him anywhere near his limits before, I'd almost forgotten what it was like to really push a sub.

Nat opens for me, moaning low and begging for me. My tongue pushes in hard, taking his mouth, making it mine all over again. Oh, he's burning up, marked and filled and needing and mine.

I look around without breaking the kiss, looking for a bed, sure that Kes wouldn't have failed to take our need into consideration. There, a button on the wall. I get up, bringing him with me, and the button yields to my touch, a bed coming up through the floor of the stage.

Nat's hard again, whimpering as I lay him down on the soft bed. He'll sleep on his belly tonight, maybe sleep draped over me.

I take his mouth again, working my leathers off with one hand. So hungry, he fucks my lips, almost aggressive. Oh, it feels good, and I let him take my weight, lying on him. His cry pushes into my mouth, his body so hot against me.

We're both on fire and I rock against him, feeling hard

cock meeting mine.

"Yes. Master, please. In me. Please. Yours."

"Yes. Yes." I reach between his legs and pull out the plug. There's no need for stretching, he's already open for me, slick with my own seed. I push in, eyes rolling at the heat of his body around my cock. Nat's almost fucking himself on my cock. Oh, yes. My lovely slut, look at him, spread and needing. He was born for this life.

Bending, I take one of his nipples into my mouth, licking and tugging on the abused flesh as I wrap a hand around his prick. Those sweet cries ring out, fill the air. He doesn't come, though. He's learned. He waits. I make him wait until I'm there, I'm ready and unable to hold back a moment longer because I want us to come together. "Now, Nat. Now. Come."

Nat bucks, ass gripping me tight, heat just spraying. My own heat fills him, spraying from me like a geyser, the pleasure huge, just enormous.

I collapse down onto him, panting, spent. Nat cuddles in, breath slowing, undone and sated and quiet. I slide out and push the plug back in before lying beside him and pulling him to me.

It feels so good just to hold him.

It's no time before he's asleep, worn through. Mal comes in, smiling, voice pitched low. "He's going to be a hit."

I give Nat a gentle stroke and sit, to smile back at my old friend. "He is." I don't need anyone to tell me that. Still it's nice to hear.

"I've told the observers that they can stay and party, but that Nat needs privacy. He looked close to the edge."

"Thank you, Mal. It was... bigger than we were both expecting. It would have been even without the audience."

Mal nodded. "I think you should stay with smaller,

private showings for a while. I don't want the random tops thinking they can expect the same response from any boy."

I shake my head. "No, something like this comes only with a deep connection." I laugh, I know I'm beaming. "We had it from the start. Do you know how rare that is, Mal?"

Mal smiles. "I do. Congratulations, my friend."

"Thank you."

I couldn't be happier if... if... well, I can't think of anything that could be better than this.

Than Nat.

"You can stay here as long as you'd like. I'll have a light meal sent." Mal looks at Nat, covered in bruises. "He's going to be sore tomorrow."

"And he's going to get hard every time he feels the ache." I stroke my hand over his skin. "He's a natural, Mal. Utterly amazing."

Nat murmurs in his sleep, arching under my hand. I purr, almost forgetting Mal's still in the room as I curl around him, my focus shifting back to him.

"Both of you have a long soak in the hot tub, Richmond. Boss' orders." Mal heads out, grinning from ear to ear.

I stick my tongue out at him and then chuckle.

He's a smug bastard. A good man, but a smug bastard all the same.

I turn back to Nat, lying with him, touching wherever I can.

He curls back into me, mine.

Chapter Eleven

Two weeks of shows. Four weeks of spankings and fucking and I? Have a day off.

Richmond's friend Bowie invited him to go to some weird Dom training thing — like Richmond needs training — and Paul and Peter and I have gone to play. I had forgotten how weird it was to wear clothes, to wander the streets. To play.

We eat at street vendors, shop, run from security, goof off, miss the good transport and bum a ride from one of the twins' friends.

By the time we tumble into the main lobby, we're filthy, starved, and laughing.

And Richmond and Bowie are standing by the front desk, looking... well, Bowie looks kind of resigned, like he's used to it. Richmond doesn't look like he's used to it, though. Not at all.

Paul and Peter bounce over to show Bowie all the bits and bobs they've bought, and I head over to Richmond. "Did you like your training?"

"I did. It finished over three hours ago and I couldn't find you. You didn't leave a message. The last transport in from downtown came and went."

"We missed it. Some... guy gave us a ride." Oh, fuck. Don't be pissy.

"You should have called, Nat. I didn't know if you'd been killed, jailed, hurt, or were just ignoring your curfew." He turns and heads for the lifts.

Curfew? What the fuck? "I'm an adult, Richmond. I lived out there for my whole life."

Man, he's got long legs.

He turns and gives me a shocked look. "You're mine now, Nat. You'll do as I say. And when I say I'll see you at seven, then I sure as hell expect to see you at seven. Not ten minutes past, not an hour past and most certainly not almost four hours past!"

"I'm sorry. I didn't have any creds on me; I couldn't call."

"And the boys didn't have any creds? Why weren't you on the transport? Damnit, Nat, I was worried sick about you!"

"I'm sorry, Richmond. I hurried." The twins swore to me that Bowie would know, would explain to Richmond.

I follow him into the lift, watch him jab at the button for our floor. "Bowie told me this kind of thing happens all the time with his boys, but I assured him that *my* boy wasn't like that. That *my* boy would call. Obviously, I was wrong."

If there's something I learned from getting bawled out by bosses, editors? It's to just stand and take it. It was my day off. I was late.

"I can't remember the last time I was this disappointed."

"What do you want me to do?" I'm tired, I'm hungry and I have blisters on my feet. Somehow I've gone from trustworthy adult to getting chewed out in a lift.

"Get a good night's sleep. Tomorrow we'll talk about your punishment."

Right, like I'm going to sleep. Ever.

"I'm sorry I worried you, Richmond. I didn't mean to. You said I had a day off; I honestly didn't know it would upset you so much."

He closes his eyes and takes several deep breaths. "It is my fault, I should have made sure you understood the rules before you left. I should have told you to stay at the club."

The lift arrives at our floor and he walks to our rooms, back stiff.

"I'm going to go take a shower." And sit. For, like, hours.

"No. You're going to go into the playroom and wait for me. I trust you are at least still wearing my plug."

"No, I had a moment of complete insanity and threw it off a building. Of course I have it in. I wasn't trying to hurt you." Jackass.

"Careful, Nat. You're on very thin ice as it is."

"Well, you're acting like I did something vicious, something shameful. I didn't. I made a mistake."

"I've already said this is my fault, Nat. You'll have to excuse me if I'm not used to this kind of behavior in a sub. Most subs who act the way you have are looking for a punishment. I realize that isn't why you did it. Now, go to the playroom and wait for me. I will not ask again."

"Okay. Okay." I head to the playroom, shaking with frustration, pacing and running my fingers through my curls.

Richmond comes in a few moments later, wearing only his leather pants, looking damned hot. "Strip."

I nod, feeling more than a little queasy, more than a touch off-balance. My toe and heel are bleeding from the stupid shoes and I'm dusty, sweaty. Tired.

He gets the cuffs ready, testing the chains hanging from the ceiling. I can't help but wonder what he's going to do to me. I don't want to wonder, but I can't help it. Once

I'm naked he puts me in the cuffs, spread eagle, doing my ankles as well.

"I'll be right back," he tells me before going.

I turn my face, hide my eyes and try to just... Just...

Not freak out.

He comes back a moment later with a small bowl of what looks like water. He sets it down next to me and takes a cloth, begins to clean me, starting with my back. It makes me shudder, makes goose bumps rise up all over. Once my neck and shoulders are clean, he kisses the top of my spine.

It surprises a sob out of me. "Love you. I do."

"I know." He continues with the careful cleaning, the cloth touching me everywhere. I'm shaking hard by the time he's done, not even sure why I'm so undone. He saves the plug for last, taking it out, cloth pushing inside me as he cleans me.

"Oh." My belly goes tight, hard, the act intimate, still hard to accept.

"Sh. Sh." He whispers it against my neck and then suddenly it's his cock that's pushing into me, filling me with heat, with him.

Oh, yes. Yes. I need this, need to know I'm his, I'm wanted. Loved. Taken. His head rests on my shoulder, breath warm against my neck. His arms are around me, fingers stroking my belly as he fucks me. I just move with him, needing him to know that I want him, that nothing's changed.

His moans fill me as much as his cock does, one hand dropping to stroke my cock. I moan, too, turning to kiss his jaw, his cheek. He growls a little and nips at my lips. "Pushy."

Then he's kissing me, tongue pushing into my mouth, and it's so good.

Yes. Yes, Richmond. Love.

He fucks me hard and deep, with cock and tongue, hand tugging on my prick. He fills me, surrounds me, owns me.

I'm going to come, desperate for it, but I hold it back. Hold it until he gives me leave. He's making me wait, making me work for it, but I know it won't be long; his thrusts have become wild, desperate. Finally he groans the word, giving me permission to come.

I cry out for him, hips bucking as I shoot, room just spinning. His heat fills me, so hot, so good. His mouth opens on my shoulder, not quite biting, definitely leaving a mark.

His. All his.

I hold onto Richmond's cock, keeping him inside me. He keeps kissing me, giving me all of himself. And I respond, giving him all I am. Eventually the kisses end, his cock sliding from me. He puts a plug into me, one of the bumpy ones that make walking... interesting.

Then he comes around, begins to undo me. I'm shivering a little, eyes fastened to him, loving him.

He gets me free and then takes me into his arms, holding me, kissing me, keeping me close to his heart.

"I'm sorry I worried you. I swear." I kiss his chest, snuggling into his heat.

He nods and holds me tighter. "Next time you have a day off I'll make sure you understand what I'm expecting of you."

"Okay. That's fair. I wouldn't have upset you on purpose. I love you." And the whole wanting someone to be angry at you? Weird.

"Well, that's because you're not used to the games a lot of the subs play. I need to remember that." He kisses me and puts an arm around me, guiding me to the bedroom. "It's late. Let's get some sleep."

"Games?" I yawn, get settled around him, suddenly

exhausted, almost immediately asleep.

His chuckles follow me into my dreams.

I let Nat sleep in, and then I fucked him hard and left him plugged and bound.

He's had his breakfast and he's waiting to hear what we'll be doing today. I put on my leathers, leaving him naked, and lead him from our rooms.

"Are you ready for what the day will bring?" I ask him.

"I guess I'll have to be, won't I?" The words aren't sarcastic, more resigned, nervous.

"Yes, you will." I'm not going to tell him what we're doing until we're there. The tiniest of punishments for his worrying me yesterday.

"Well, then. I'm ready." He offers me a half-smile, those eyes still warm for me.

I purr and smile, unable to do anything but respond to him. It's almost scary, the power he holds over me.

We take the lift down to the body modification studio and I watch him as we go in. The only sense of worry I get is when he cuddles against me. I knew he'd wonder why were here to see Peter and Paul after yesterday.

"Hello, boys. We're here to get Nat a tattoo. I trust you can fit us in?"

One twin is gagged, bare ass red and glowing, eyes just shining. The other has his cock bound, ass filled with a plug. "Y... y... y... y... yes. Y... y... yes, s... sir."

I purr. They're lovely, but such a handful. Of course Bowie has quite the hands. I look at Nat, to see what effect it has on him. Nat looks confused. Utterly, completely confused. "Something troubling you, lovely?"

"I..." He pushes up, whispering in my ear. "They got

in trouble, but they — especially Paul — look happy."

I nod and answer him in my regular voice. "Paul needs to push his boundaries, needs to have Bowie reel him back in. Isn't that right, Paul?"

Paul nods, eyes just happy and peaceful, entire body at one with the world. The only time Paul is settled like this is after Bowie's focused on him.

I stroke Nat's belly. He needs the same focus from me, but arrives at it in a far different manner. "Do you understand, Nat?"

"In theory, if not in fact, yeah?" Nat kisses Paul and Peter's cheeks. "I don't want to be in trouble, though. Okay?"

"O... o.. .o... o... o... o..." The stuttering goes on and Paul rolls his eyes, elbowing Peter. "Kay!"

I nod as well. "Okay. And you aren't. This is a reward, a gift for us." Richmond turns back to the twins. "I'm thinking something for his belly. To take up his whole abdomen."

Paul's eyes light up and he takes the gag off. "Don't worry. Bowie says I can for work. Do you have a pattern? A design?"

Nat is humming, warm and rubbing against my side.

"I was thinking a flying dragon — wings spread, head above his navel, tail maybe stopping alongside his cock?" I draw my fingers along Nat's belly.

Paul nods, grabbing a pad and pencil, suddenly businesslike and focused. "Colors?"

"This dragon will represent me, my ownership of your body, my watching over you always, with you always. The color will be your contribution, Nat."

"Red. My red dragon." He doesn't even hesitate.

I purr, still petting his belly, pleased with his choice. "Red like blood."

"Red like passion." He smiles, nods.

"My mark. Permanent. For everyone to see." I grin and give him a quick kiss. "Not that you won't still wear plenty of my less permanent marks..."

"Promise?" Nat smiles, eyes dancing. "Yours. Always."

I purr and bring him to me, kissing him hard. "Always, Nat. I promise."

"P... p... p... p... pretty."

Nat blushes, cock tapping my belly, leaving kisses.

I chuckle and give it a stroke, thumb sliding across the wet tip. "Ready for the tattoo, lovely?"

He nods, gasping softly, hips pushing up toward me.

"Does he need shaving, Richmond? Or is he smooth?"

"Oh, he's still smooth." I chuckle. "We saw Thomas and Bryant a few weeks ago, and I've been using the retardant to keep his hair from growing back." I slide my hand down to Nat's ass, pinching lightly.

Nat squeaks for me and Paul laughs, spreading him out on the bed. "Okay, then. We'll get started..."

Bowie's voice sounds suddenly. "Put the gag back in, Paul. Only for work."

"I am working!"

Bowie comes over and he's giving Paul a hard look. "Make sure that you keep it to work."

Nat and I are given a warm smile and Bowie gives me a wink. "I hope my boys are taking care of you."

"You know they are, Bowie."

He nods and goes to give Peter a kiss and to smack Paul on the ass. Both twins are just glowing, Paul's face turning, begging his own kiss. My Nat is wide-eyed. Bowie's big hands land on Paul's ass and grab it, mouth taking Paul's in a long, deep kiss, and they're just beautiful together.

I purr and stroke Nat's ass, which is currently unadorned, not even a little bruise on it, though his hips hold the marks of my fingers. Paul melts, responding beautifully, the need he has for Bowie obvious. Peter's watching, smiling, his own happiness evident.

It's good for Nat to see that need, to know that the things that we do that are kinky and perhaps still strange to him are not confined to just the two of us. Here, we are similar to everyone in our need for something more than just the everyday or "normal."

By the end of the kiss, Paul is quiet again, almost kitten-like as he rubs and thanks Bowie. Bowie gives him one last kiss and then offers another to Peter before beaming at me and Nat again and heading off. The benefit of working beside his boys is being able to see them easily.

Paul smiles at Nat and pulls out some antiseptic. "It stings a little, but it's not bad. Just breathe and try to relax."

Nat nods, hand reaching out for me. I take his hand and sit at his side, near his head. I have an excellent view, though. "Would you like me to hold his cock out of the way?" I ask. Nat's prick is bound, hard and reaching up over his belly where the dragon will go.

"Please. Do you want the tail to trail onto his sac?" Paul leans in close. "Just breathe, Nat. I think you'll like it."

"Yes, yes, Paul, I think that would be lovely." I reach for Nat's cock and hold it toward his thigh, keeping it out of Paul's way. It's hot in my hand, silky.

Nat's eyes are huge for the first few strokes, then his body begins to respond, sweat making him shine, eyelids drooping.

Peter comes up with a notepad, a picture of Nat spread drawn for me, five little rings added in — three on the smooth ballsac, two behind. Underneath Peter had written. "I could make it so he doesn't even feel them going in, heal them completely so you could play." So wicked, to look so innocent.

I like the way he thinks, though, and I smile and nod. Yes. He can do it, and I'll surprise Nat later when we're alone.

He brings out rings of different colors and shapes and sizes, offering them to me. I turn so Nat can't see what we're doing. I figure Paul's got him pretty well occupied as it is. I like the little bronze ones that shine. They look warm and will look lovely against his pale skin. I choose three of the bronze ones for his ballsac and two black ones for behind.

I can just imagine his face the first time I play with them and he finds out they're there. Peter truly has a wicked, wicked mind. Bowie is a lucky man. Peter smiles and hurries off, walking carefully because of the plug.

I turn back to Nat, smiling. Oh, we're going to have fun tonight.

"You... you look happy." He's flying, the endorphins hot and sweet and rushing through him.

"So do you, lovely." I lean in and kiss Nat. "It's better than a drug, that."

Nat kisses me, moaning low.

"Careful, now. No moving." Paul's voice is sure, stern.

"Sorry," I murmur, grinning down at Nat. "We mustn't be naughty," I tell him, winking.

"No?" Nat licked his lips. "Is it neat? The tattoo?"

It's beautiful — deep red wings raised up, head curved around Nat's navel. Peter is sitting between Nat's legs, working silently.

I nod, reaching out to feel the heat of it just above Nat's skin. "It's stunning. Like you."

The job lasts for hours, Nat trembling and shaking by the end, just from the sensations pouring through him. Peter puts in the rings while Paul works, Nat completely oblivious to the extra small pains.

"Do you need something for the pain, Nat?" I ask him. It's up to him, and if he wants it, no, if he *needs* the pain, I want him to admit it.

"No. No, Richmond. It's... I'm good."

Paul smiles knowingly, mouthing, "this is going to feel good," as he picks up a spray bottle.

I smile and turn my attention back to Nat. "Good boy. I'm very proud of you. Paul's got a reward for you now."

Nat opens his mouth to ask what when Paul sprays the cold cleanser on his skin. Nat almost screams, hips bucking, pushing his cock into my hand.

"Take off the ring," I tell Paul, my hand working Nat's cock with hard, quick jerks. Paul does and I hold my breath for a count of ten and then lean in. "Come for me."

"Master." Heat sprays over my hand and Paul cleans us up, quickly and gently, smoothing a cream and nu-skin over the tattoo.

I give Paul a smile of thanks and lean in to kiss Nat, tongue pressing into his mouth. He's so beautiful and I'm so proud of him, so in love with him. Nat opens, taking me in, murmuring soft little words into my lips. I smile down at him, so hard inside my leathers I'm in pain, but he's just so inspiring, so lovely. Now more so than ever.

The twins clean up quickly, but I barely notice. I only see Nat's eyes.

"You make me need, lovely." I tell him. Because he should know.

The words make him glow. "Can we go home now?"

"Oh, yes. I need you." I help him up, admiring the way the dragon moves on his belly.

He looks down, takes a step and tilts his head, feeling the rings move. I continue to watch him, not saying a word. His hand reaches down to move his cock, then those eyes flash up at me, looking for permission.

Oh, good boy. I'm so proud of him. "No, lovely. Let's go home. I need your mouth and then we can play."

Nat nods, presses against me. "Thank you, Paul. It's beautiful."

Paul just grins, nods. "'Course it is."

Peter picks up the gag. "T... time for this, Pauley. Open up."

I'm grinning as we go, arm around Nat — such a handful, those two, but delightful. And talented. I'm extremely pleased with both modifications and can't wait to play with Nat's new jewelry.

And I can't wait to show my boy off.

"Richmond?" There's something wrong. Something tugging between my legs as we walk to our rooms.

The tattoo — the fucking amazing tattoo — didn't go down there.

"Yes, lovely?" He's smiling at me, looking happy and horny and he's only got eyes for me, even though there's people passing us as we wait for the lift.

"There's something wrong. Under my balls."

He chuckles, actually chuckles. "There's nothing wrong with your balls, lovely."

"No, you don't understand, there's something behind them."

"Oh, I do understand, lovely. I do."

He does? "Oh. Okay..."

Every step is weirder and weirder.

"Just trust me, Nat." He's smiling, happy, it can't be bad.

"Yes. Okay." It's easier than it sounds, to trust that

voice, those eyes.

"Can you see the way everyone is looking at you, enchanted?"

"Everyone?" Richmond is right, people are watching, staring. Looking at me.

"Yes, lovely. You draw the eye." Richmond's fingers are stroking around the tattoo, outlining it with fire.

Oh. Hot. So good. I arch and rock my hips, then stop suddenly, the odd pulling coming again. The look on his face is wicked and he tugs me into the lift that's just come, mouth on mine, tongue pushing in as he pulls me close. I reach up, hold on and press close, just gasping.

He ends the kiss and pushes me to my knees. "I need, lovely."

"Is there time?" I'm already opening his leathers.

"I won't be long." His voice is rough and I believe him, his cock springing from his pants, dark red and so hard.

I swallow him down, thanking him for my tattoo, for my orgasm earlier, for loving me. He's right, he doesn't take long, his hips pushing his cock deep in my throat and heat shooting into me.

Oh. Oh, hot. He makes my head swim.

The lift has stopped, the doors opening, waiting on us to notice, to care. His hand is warm on my cheek as he pulls gently out. "Tuck me back in, lovely."

I get him put back together, struggle to my feet, that weird... something bothering me again. He takes my hand and strides to our rooms, not giving me any time to worry about it. But it's there.

It *is*.

It's maddening.

He's still grinning, looking like that cat who swallowed the canary, and as soon as we're in our room he's got me on the bed, my legs spread, and he's tugging. Oh fuck, he's tugging something in my balls, behind them, and the sensation goes straight to my cock.

"Richmond?" My toes curl up, body twisting to avoid the sensations until I can understand them.

"Give me your hand." He takes it and brings it down so I can feel.

I squeak and scramble up, pushing my cock out of the way to stare. Rings. RINGS!

Richmond chuckles. "You look shocked."

Then he bends and takes one in his mouth, sliding his tongue through it and tugging on it with his teeth.

"How? I. Oh." My eyes roll, toes curling as my head shakes.

"While Paul was doing the tattoo. A surprise for you." He takes the ones behind my balls into his mouth and tugs on them.

"Oh. Oh. Th... thank you." I can't breathe, the sensation beyond anything I understand.

He keeps playing with them, his lips and tongue so hot on my skin, his breath a tickle of pleasure.

"How many? How many are there?" Oh, I can feel them, in my skin.

"Count." He takes them into his mouth one by one and tugs.

"One. T... two. Three. Oh. Oh." I moan and twist. "Four. F... five."

"Oh, I need to work harder if you're coherent enough to count." He laughs and takes out the plug, filling me with his own cock.

And I can feel the rings every time his body pushes against me.

"Yours." I look down and see ink and rings and heat and his cock. "Yours."

"Yes. Mine." He nods and plunges into me, making it true.

"Master!" I grab my knees, pull them up and back.

"Yes. Yes."

Harder and harder he pushes into me, his eyes boring into mine. Oh, he's got me, I'm so his. I lose myself in his motions, his eyes, the things he finds in me. His hand wraps around my cock, urging me to come with him as his eyes widen and he fills me with his pleasure. Things go a little hazy, the last two days huge and strange and stressful and all I want to know is Richmond above me.

"Love you," he whispers into my ear, lying solid and heavy on me.

"Love. Yours."

"Mine. All mine." Richmond pets me. "All mine."

I nod, dizzy and breathless.

He pulls out, leaving me empty only for the time it takes for him to get a new plug, slick it up, and push it in.

I still shiver when he does it, but it's sweet, right.

Richmond lies on the bed next to me, fingers tracing the tattoo on my belly. "Do you like it?"

"It's beautiful."

"And the rings? Do you like your surprise?"

"They're... huge. It's amazing." I can't believe they didn't hurt.

"Good." I'm given a kiss. "You'd better sleep, Nat. I'm planning to have lots of fun with those rings."

I smile. "Loving you requires a lot of rest."

Richmond chuckles. "You're not complaining that I work you too hard, are you?"

"Not even a little." I settle in and yawn, hand curled around his waist.

"Good." He kisses me, and presses close. "Good."

"Mmhmm." It is.

Good.

Chapter Twelve

It's been weeks — hell, it's been months — and we're settling into a nice routine of work and play, Nat growing more and more comfortable with the small scenes we're doing.

It's not that it's any less intense between us, but we know more how to handle it now, we're expecting it and can usually deal with our audience instead of needing them to be rushed out so we can have some private time. We still need it, but it's almost as if the interaction has been incorporated and is now a part of the scene.

It works for us.

In fact, everything is working for us like a dream. Nine weeks and the closest I've had to come to punishing him is that one time he stayed out late and worried me.

I'm waiting for the other shoe to drop.

I'm thinking today might be the day, though. Nat woke up growling and frowning, searching for meds in the bathroom. If he'd just say he had a headache, that would be one thing, but no, he's going to rumble and stalk and snap.

I told him to make us breakfast and that I want it served in bed. I'm going the whole Master routine today — he's going to feed me, then he's going to massage my feet and whatever else I can think up until he's willing to admit he's not feeling great.

I hear something glass shatter and a violent curse snaps out, the autovac sounding. I bite my lip and wait. It won't be long before he does it in front of me. I mentally go through our list, putting the punishment kinks on the table.

It takes a while, but the breakfast comes out. Eggs and toast and juice, Nat just vibrating with frustration.

"Ah, lovely." I sit on the bed, tugging the sheet up to protect my genitals. "You can put the tray in my lap if you wish. And then you may feed me."

"Oh." He gives me a vaguely confused look, but nods. "Okay. Do you want your eggs on the toast or separate?"

"Separate, but in the same mouthful. No bacon or sausage, though? That's a bit disappointing." I know I'm pushing him, but he needs to learn to express himself, to tell me when something's wrong instead of just moping and sulking and stomping about.

"I didn't know you wanted bacon." He tears off a bit of toast and spears it, then some egg. "Open up."

I let one eyebrow go up. "Elegant," I note, leaning forward and opening my mouth. This could be a sensual exercise, if he lets it be.

"I was thinking more ingenious. One bite. No touching." I almost get a smile. He's trying.

I smile at him and lean in, close my lips around the fork. Humming, I pull the food off, eyes on him the entire time.

"Are the eggs okay?" He gets another bite ready, so careful.

"They're not bad." I open my mouth, but don't lean in this time, waiting for him to bring the food to me.

His lips tighten and I get the next bite without a word.

"Problem?" I ask.

"I didn't say anything."

"Not with words, no."

Those lips tighten even more. "Would you like some juice?"

"I don't know, what kind is it?"

"Dina fruit."

I wrinkle my nose. "Is it fresh? Have you tasted it to make sure it's good enough for me?"

"What?"

"Do I really need to repeat myself?"

Nat takes a deep drink of the juice, then offers me the glass. "It tastes good."

"I want to drink it from your mouth." I'm pushing him, I know that, but he needs pushing today. Besides, mouth-to-mouth is the sexiest way to drink.

Nat looks at me, cheeks flushing. "I don't like dina fruit, Richmond. You do."

"I'm not asking you to drink it, Nat. I'm asking you to act as my glass."

Nat sighs softly, forehead wrinkling as he takes a sip, leans forward to offer it to me. I purr, impressed that he hasn't lost it yet. I take his chin in my hand and tilt his head slightly, keeping our eyes locked as I place my mouth over his. Nat opens for me, feeds me the juice. Fresh and sharp and with a hint of my lovely boy added. I really couldn't ask for more. I lick his lips after swallowing the last bit, humming my pleasure.

That gets me a soft sound, a happy sigh.

"Another mouthful, please, lovely." If he can feed me more of the juice he dislikes? I'm going to spank his beautiful ass. With my hairbrush.

After he's groomed me.

Nat nods, kisses me before leaning up and reaching for the glass. As he moves, the tray starts to slide, the entire

275

breakfast landing in his lap.

"Damn it straight to the lower bowels of Hell!" With that he snaps and screams, the tray flying through the air with a crash as he stands and makes a beeline for the bathroom. The door slams shut behind him and I arch an eyebrow. Well, if that's the other shoe, I can handle it.

I get up and step over the mess, pulling on my leather pants and then strolling through to the bathroom. Stillness and silence are called for, I believe. And if he succeeds at that, we'll see about that spanking.

I let myself in.

He's in the shower, head on his knees, grumbling and fussing.

"You usually don't have a problem telling me what's on your mind, Nat."

"My head hurts and I dropped a plate and I had a nightmare and you wanted bacon and I can't fucking read your mind!"

And there it is, buried amidst the rest of the petty problems. "What was the nightmare about, lovely?"

"You fell outside, past the transports, and I couldn't find you, couldn't reach you, but I heard you calling me." The words are almost ashamed, sort of angry.

Interesting. "It was just a nightmare, Nat. Why is it affecting you so strongly? Do you think I'm going to leave you?"

"It's not. It was just a stupid nightmare."

"Then why is it still bothering you?"

"Who said it was bothering me?"

"Oh, come on, Nat, you've been stompy and sulky all morning. And you're sitting in the shower curled up in a ball." My voice fades away as I remember a promise I made to him, about his not having nightmares anymore. I'm not sure I'd even meant it literally, but I did say it. I crouch down next to him, watching the water slide on his skin. "Lovely. It doesn't mean anything. It has no power over you."

"I know. I know. I just. I know."

I lean over and turn off the shower, grab a towel and tug him to me. "I think what you need is to be reminded what does have power over you."

"Do you want me to clean up the bedroom and fix you more breakfast?" Those eyes are begging me to make it right.

"No." I reach over to the counter and manage to snag my hairbrush. "I want you to turn over, cock between my legs."

He blinks, body moving before his brain catches up. That's right. Good boy. Don't think.

I lean against the tiled wall, feeling it heat up beneath my skin. I don't give him any extra time to prepare; as soon as his cock is seated, hot, not hard yet but thinking about it, between my legs, I let my arm fly, bringing the back of my brush down hard against his ass.

"Richmond!" Nat's cry is sharp, ass tilting up for another blow.

I nod. "Right here, Nat. Right here. With you."

I give him that second blow and then a third, feeling his cock harden, expanding and heating to fire between my thighs. He loves it — loves the pain and the sound, the vulnerability and the power. Loves that it's me, my hand, my arm. And he's beautiful with it, the sounds he makes, the way he moves, the smell of it on him. I keep hitting him with the brush, watching his ass turn red all over, the tops of his thighs, too, as I bring the brush down on them. He starts to shift, rocking against me, sounds going deep and needy, raw.

"That's it, lovely, feel it. Feel me." I continue to let the brush fall, the color of Nat's ass going dark, welts forming.

"Master." Nat's sobbing for me, cock hard and burning between my thighs.

"Hold on, lovely. Just a few more." I'm going to push him as far as I can, as far as he can last. Nat nods, twists, entire body shaking, ass moving in my rhythm. Two more hits, three, four. He takes it so beautifully, wants it and I give it to him. My own cock is hard, pressing against his side, and I can't take much more myself.

"Come," I tell him, letting the brush hit once more, this time low, near his balls.

His scream echoes and echoes, his come pouring against my thighs like liquid fire. My own come explodes from me, the pleasure intense, beautiful. I drop my hand to his ass, sliding over the heat, moaning. Nat groans, rocking so slow, panting.

"Here we are, Nat. Here we are. Just you and me." And this pleasure between us.

"Yes..." I can feel him relax, feel him trust in me to keep him.

I purr, fingers dancing on his skin, only hard enough for him to feel, not to hurt. He hums in return, "Master" and "love" and "thank you" whispered out. I nod and continue touching, holding us together.

It's not long before he's asleep and boneless, red ass burning under my hand. I lean my head against the wall and close my eyes. Let sleep take me with him.

To guard his dreams.

I wake, ass hot and in the air, snuggled on the bed in the playroom.

Oh.

Man.

What a morning.

There are pillows under my belly, keeping me comfortable, and my hands are tied together, as are my legs, from elbows to wrists and from knees to ankles. I'm plugged, of course, and I can feel my heartbeat in my cock and balls, which are tightly bound.

Oh, man. What a day.

I shift, try to stretch a little, the bonds comforting, settling.

There's a purr from beside me. Richmond. He leans in and I can feel his heat, feel his hand as it slides on the burning skin of my ass, sending sparks off in the darkness.

Oh.

Oh, I'm blindfolded, the material soft and furry, warm on my skin.

I take a deep breath, relaxing. "Richmond."

"Yes, lovely." A soft kiss slides on my ass, Richmond's breath making the burn hotter.

"Mmm... Master." I don't know whether to apologize or say thank you or what.

He purrs louder at the word, like some huge, happy cat. "Tell me what you feel, Nat."

"Held. Settled. I wanted to thank you, but I didn't know if that was right."

Richmond's lips press against mine this time, the kiss soft, warm. "You're welcome, lovely. And you're comfortable as you are?"

"Yes. Yes, I am." More comfortable than I thought I would be.

"Good, good." His hand slides over my ass again and then begins to wander, touching me all over, not lightly, either. He's not exactly massaging me, just... pushing himself into me. Some touches push out deep sounds, some cause me to shift, some to sink deeper into the pillows.

It's like we're connecting on some deep, pre-verbal level that my skin and blood and bone and muscles recognize. He's inside me. Not in my ass fucking me, but inside my cells, my brain, my soul.

"My lovely Nat," he whispers, shouts, I don't know, I can't trust my senses anymore, he's everywhere. His. Inside and out. All of me. Every inch.

Richmond's fingers eventually make their way to my ass, playing with the plug inside me, making it twist and push. Moans start flowing out of me, rough and surprisingly wanton.

"I'm going to change the plug now," he murmurs against my ear, soft kisses making their way down along my spine.

I nod. Anything. I can take anything for him. I want anything he needs me to have.

"Such a good boy." He sounds proud, turned on. His kisses arrive at my ass, sparing the abused flesh no quarter, kissing just as hard on the tender skin. It burns, aches, feels so good and I need it, need him. He licks around my hole, tongue sliding on the stretched skin. Oh. Yes. Yes. It feels so sweet, makes me shift and gasp. He hums and licks some more and then his fingers have the base and he's slowly, so very slowly, teasing the plug out of me.

Another moan escapes me as he pulls, my toes curling. So stretched.

My body seems to snap closed as the plug pulls completely out and he purrs again, two fingers sliding into me, curling inside me until they hit my gland.

"Oh!" I shift, arms jerking. "Yours."

"Oh, yes, lovely, you are." Those fingers hit my gland again. "I'm just going to clean you, Nat."

I nod, not even willing to lose my peace to tense up. "Anything."

"I'm using a syringe with an antiseptic wash. Just to make sure you don't get an infection." He strokes my ass and then inserts the tip of the syringe into me, the plastic thick as a couple of his fingers. "You'll need to hold it in like a regular enema, but there won't be as much liquid. And I've got a bowl here to catch it when you release, so there's nothing to worry about, lovely."

"Okay, Richmond." I nod, let myself relax, let myself trust him completely.

"That's my boy," he murmurs, kissing my ass.

The liquid is cool as it slowly pushes into me, warming with the heat of my body. One of his hands rubs slow circles on one ass cheek.

"Mmm." I stretch slightly, making room inside me, sighing. "Yours."

"Yes, lovely. All through." The syringe is removed and his hand comes around to massage my belly, his skin sliding against my cock. "Just hold it for a moment or two, lovely, let the antiseptic work."

I nod, moaning low. I can't believe I'm at peace with this, allowing Richmond control over even this. "Yes."

"Excellent." He continues to rub my belly and puts a kiss on my ass, telling me wordlessly that he isn't disgusted by this, it doesn't bother him. "All right, lovely. I've a bowl in place, let it go."

This is harder, always harder, but I offer it to him, offer him my obedience, my trust, the water rushing from me.

"Yes, lovely. Very good." I can hear the water going into the bowl, but Richmond isn't embarrassed, isn't offended. The bowl is removed and a soft cloth cleans my ass, the top of my thighs. He's so careful, so gentle.

"Th... thank you." I take a deep breath, the darkness, the blindfold such a comfort.

He knows me so well. A soft purr sounds and he kisses my hole and then begins to push a cool lube into me. Oh, yes. So good. I just focus on the feelings inside me, the pleasure, the touches.

"This is one of the plugs you consistently don't choose," Richmond tells me. "The big one with the round top and all the funny-shaped bumps on it." He runs it up my thigh.

I shiver, moan. That one is unforgettable, intense, thick.

"You're going to take it today. And you're going to love it." He kisses my ass again and then the large, round top of the plug is at my hole, pushing, opening me up wide. I try to spread my thighs, but I can't. I can't move. I can only accept it, accept Richmond. "It's a hefty plug, I know. But you're going to love it. All the bumps and ridges — they're going to feel amazing when I rotate it inside you and later, when you walk with it in."

"W... walk." His fingers rub my hole, slick and cool with lube, encouraging my body to spread.

"Yes, lovely." He chuckles. "I think we'll have supper in the dining room tonight. You'll glow for me. Like you are now." He places a soft kiss on my stretched skin and pushes the plug in a bit deeper.

"Will we feed each other?" It's so sensual, so intimate, to sit with Richmond, eat.

He purrs. "Oh, yes, my lovely. I would like that very much." The sound of his voice is a distraction and he pushes the plug in a little further.

I ripple, inside and out. "So much, Master. It is."

"You can take it, Nat. It's made especially for you."

"For me?" I rub my cheek against the sheets, little sounds escaping my throat.

"Yes. After your 'interview' I went to Sallut and told him what I wanted. If you had never come back, I would have never used it."

"You knew, even then." It makes me whimper, makes

me push back on the plug.

"I did. I knew from the moment the whip first hit your back."

"I was so scared. So terribly frightened. And then I went home and looked in the mirror and made myself come over and over."

He purrs for me and the plug slides in further, slides in all the way, I can feel my body closing tightly over the base. I pant, waiting for my body to adjust, accept it. His hands aren't still, petting me, sliding over my skin, my thighs and my heated ass. I can feel every touch, every breath.

He blows on my ass and then licks the base of the plug.

"Master!" Oh, fuck. Fuck!

"Right here, Nat." He licks again, tongue sliding on my skin, on the plug, jostling it a little.

"Yes. Here. So big." My head tosses, cock throbbing in its sheath.

"Yes." He grabs the end of the plug and turns it slowly, the protrusions bumping along the inside of my ass.

"Richmond. Richmond. Oh." My hands fist, hips starting to rock.

He purrs. "Feels good, lovely, doesn't it?"

I nod, I can't not. It's so good, so much.

"You'll need to come, I think. Before we go anywhere with it like this." He undoes the leather around my prick and balls, hand sliding on it as he continues to jostle and rotate the plug.

"Oh..." I move as best I can, fucking Richmond's hand, needing so badly. He leans in somehow, so that as I fuck his hand, my ass hits his shoulder every time I pull back. "Burns." It isn't a complaint, just the truth. "Master."

"Ride through it, lovely." His hand squeezes my cock a little harder.

"Okay. Okay." I just keep agreeing over and over, soaring, feeling.

"So beautiful, Nat." His hand keeps sliding along my cock, squeezing randomly.

"Yours. Love. Your own."

"Yes, mine. You may come, my lovely boy." His breath slides across my sensitive ass.

Seed just pours from me, the pleasure crashing over in waves.

"Nice. Nice. Beautiful." He purrs, rubbing his cheek against my ass, and I can feel every whisker.

I just sort of fight to breathe, to focus. He doesn't bind my cock again; instead, he's slowly undoing the ropes from my legs, hands working my muscles, massaging as he goes.

"So good..." Heaven. Maybe better than.

Eventually I'm free, the blindfold the last thing to come off.

"Are you ready? I have the lights turned down low."

"I am. The blindfold is... peaceful. I was surprised." The dim lights make me blink, make my eyes water a little.

He strokes my face, fingers so gentle. "You're learning." He kisses me. "Are you hungry? I hear Moffat is making a curry feast this evening."

"Mmm... I'm starving. Can I sit in your lap while we eat?" I press close, humming and happy.

"Oh, yes, I'd like that. You can feed me. I'll feed you back." He purrs and licks at my lips. "And then we'll come back here and I'll eat you."

"All of me." I can't help chuckling. Laughing softly and loving him.

"Oh, yes, I'll eat you all up, from your toes to your nose." He looks happy, eyes shining at me.

"Nathaniel Dessert."

"Sh. Everyone will want one."
Our laughter rings out, full and right. Happy.

Chapter Thirteen

Weeks have become months have become nearly a year and I can't remember a time when I didn't have Nat with me. We've explored and loved and pushed boundaries. Nat has done more than he ever could have imagined and I've done more than I ever thought I would, pushed further, loved further.

If it wasn't so good it would be scary.

Today was a day off and I spent it with Mouse, working on Nat's collar, finishing it up. He doesn't know it's coming; it'll be a surprise. It's quite thick, over an inch high, and the leather has been stained a dark, dark purple. It'll look like a bruise on his skin — a perfect match to the real ones he wears so beautifully.

I glance at the clock and see it's not even six yet and he's not due back until eight. I'm a little eager to give him his gift...

I finally wind up leaving him a note, in case he comes home early, and going down to the training room to work off some of the excess energy on the weight machines. I catch sight of him, head-to-head with one of the little house subs, Nat scribbling furiously on one of his little dat-pads, a look on his face unfamiliar and odd. It's the look on his face as much as anything that has me heading toward him. Well, that, and I haven't seen him all day and that feels like a lot longer than it probably was.

The little sub sees me coming and scrambles, Nat blinking and confused for a second.

Well, now I'm really curious. I let my hand slide on Nat's shoulders, happy that he's topless, even if he is wearing leather pants. Not that he doesn't look good in them, but I'm more used to having total access. "Hey, lovely."

"Hey." The dat-pad is slipped away and I get a smile, Nat pushing into my arms.

I purr, arms looping around him, hands finding his ass as our mouths meet. "Missed you," I tell him, fingers pushing, aiming to jostle the plug inside him, despite his armor of leather.

He moans, presses closer, pierced nipples hard and tight against me, chain between them leading down to the gold band circling cock and balls. So pretty.

I stroke the dragon tattoo, fingers finding the warm ridges of his abdomen, my other hand still on his ass, teasing at that plug. It's been too long a day without his body to hold and touch and send soaring.

I would have thought a year would have found the passion abated, less ready to burst into flame at the smallest touch, but I would have been wrong. I love the little sounds he feeds me, rich and hungry, loving. I take a step backward, leaning against the wall as I rub our bodies together, our leather creaking in harmony.

"Mmm... you smell so good." Nat pushes closer, pretty eyes just focused, wanting.

"You smell pretty good yourself. Like home and need and good things." I grin at him — he makes me sappy. Of course, he also makes me want to whip him and mark him and fill his body with elaborate plugs and sounds, so it evens out.

"Where were you going?" Curious boy, always

looking, questioning.

"To the training room to kill time until you got back."
I look at my watch. "And you still have some time — I
didn't mean to send your friend scurrying off. Some of
the little worker bees are so skittish." Surely I'm not *that*
scary. I'm not Mal, after all.

"Oh, he's just..." Nat shrugs. "Got stuff on his mind.
No biggie."

"Yeah?" I remember the look on Nat's face. "You
sure?"

Nat actually looks away. "I think so, yeah."

I frown. "Nat?"

"Hmm?" He reaches up, touches my forehead,
distracted. I shake my head and let it go. If he felt I needed
to know, he would tell me.

"I have something for you," I tell him.

"Yeah? What?" There was that curiosity again, sharp
and fierce and unmistakable.

"Something special that a Master can give his sub so
everyone knows the sub belongs to him."

Nat searches my eyes and I know he knows, my lovely's
too sharp not to.

"I made it myself, lovely. Under Mouse's supervision."
It's in my pocket and I want to give it to him, but I wanted
it to be special, not just handed over in the corridor.

"Oh." His eyes light up and I get a long, deep kiss,
Nat's hands in my hair.

I turn it into a second kiss, hand sliding down along
his back, purring. His spine is such a lovely trail. "Where
do you want it?"

"Wherever pleases you. It won't matter; it'll be...
yours."

"Let's go home. Then it'll be ours."

Nat nods, fingers twining with mine. "Do we have
many shows this week?"

"One on Tuesday. Another Friday."

I lead us back up to our rooms, but I don't make it any further than our hall before I stop him and take it out of my pocket. "This is for you."

"Oh... It's beautiful, Richmond." Nat stops and looks, eyes shining and bright and happy. So happy.

"Let me put it on. It'll look beautiful on you." Another permanent mark on my beautiful boy.

Nat nods, chin lifting, so proud. "Yes, okay."

I put it on him, snap it in place. "We'll go tomorrow. Have it soldered on permanently." He looks magnificent. He looks like mine.

"Is it good? Do you like it?" He moves his head, getting used to its weight.

"It's stunning. Just like the man who wears it." Nat's cheeks go pink, Nat so pleased.

"We should do something to celebrate, to mark the occasion. And I think it should be your choice, Nat. Because it's your night."

Nat grins, eyes lit up, and I know what he wants. "Let's go dancing, Richmond. Let's go dancing and let everybody see."

"Yes, lovely. They need to see what's mine." I look at him and walk around him. "I'm not sure about the leather pants, though," I tell him, tugging on the chain. "It hides half the loveliness."

"No naked dancing, Richmond." Those eyes laugh for me, love me.

"No?" I pout. "Things would bounce so nicely."

"No. I'll wear silk and chains for you, line my eyes."

I purr, the vision so enticing I don't even mind that he's telling me what he's going to do instead of asking. "I'll wear my hair down for you."

He moans, presses closer. "You'll be the most beautiful man there."

"Nobody will even see me, lovely. All eyes will be on you." I kiss him, hold him close, feeling the need deep in my belly.

"I don't care about anyone's eyes but yours."

He's perfect — how could I ask for anything more? "And I will have no eyes for anyone but you."

"I want you. Please. I need."

"Yes." I close our mouths together and walk him backward toward our room as we kiss. He's melted against me, moaning and close, groaning. Hard.

By the time we're in our room, his leather pants are undone and halfway down his legs, baring that beautiful cock for me. Hard and full, Nat's dark cock throbbing, aching. I'm suddenly struck with the need to give him another gift and I go to my knees, looking up to see if he sees the significance.

Nat's eyes go wide, fingers so soft in my hair. "Master."

"I want to taste you." I turn my attention back to his cock, leaning in to lick at the tip. He whimpers, nods, hips rocking in tiny jerks. "No coming," I warn. "I just want a taste."

"Yes. Yes, Richmond." He shivers, eyes focused on my mouth.

I take the heat into my mouth, sucking until the hot, bitter drops slide on my tongue. Then I take the whole thing in and feel it in my mouth, the heat, the silk of his skin, the bumps of the glans and veins. I bob my head a few times, feeling the need building in him.

"Master..." He knows not to come; he knows the consequences.

I can't stop myself from bobbing some more, sucking and licking the length of him. I'm not trying to tease him, though that is no doubt how it's coming across.

"You're beautiful," I tell him, when I finally pull off.

He's panting, sweating, wanton. "Th... thank you. Thank you."

I stand, fingers releasing the ring that binds his cock. "You may come when I do." I put my hand on his shoulder, pushing him down.

His fingers are sure, pulling my cock free, lips dropping over it and sucking hard enough to make me jerk.

I groan, my hands dropping into his bright red curls. He's gotten so good at this, enthusiasm, talent, love. It takes all my control not to come right away. He wants it, wants me, and he's making me fight for my control. It's heady, amazing.

I finally give in as his throat swallows around the tip of my cock, let him have my pleasure, my seed, my cry of pure need. His seed splashes on my calf, hips fucking the air as he swallows. I can smell him, smell myself, and it makes me groan. We're fucking good together. The best.

He rests his head on my hip, panting. "Oh. Wow."

I purr and stroke his face. "Yes, lovely. It just gets better and better every time."

"Yeah. It's... it's just right, Richmond."

I reach for his collar, fingers sliding around the leather that's already warm from his skin. "It is, lovely. You are."

Nat just beams, eyes warm, happy. "Thank you."

"What plug are you wearing, lovely?"

"The little heavy one."

"I don't know if that's the best one for dancing." I help him up and head toward the big cupboard in the playroom, my arm around his waist.

It won't take us long at all to get ready and then I'll take my boy dancing, let him enjoy himself, let everyone see how lucky I am.

Chapter Fourteen

I hate not sleeping, but I can't.

Not after all the things Pix told me.

So I'm sitting and researching, drinking caff and trying to be silent as a mouse.

Pix says one of the paying tops is bringing in Risque, shooting bound boys up and getting them hooked. The question is, why? Well, the first question is whether Pix is telling the truth. I think he was, though. He looked scared. Scared and screwed.

Damn.

Pix just remembers his last name — Georix — and I'm damned if I can find it anywhere in the databases.

"Lovely? There can't be anything more fascinating than me on that comm." Richmond is standing in the doorway, hair coming out of its braid, looking amazing in all his naked glory.

Damn it. I close down the account, unable to stop my smile. "That's the truth. I didn't mean to wake you."

"Then you should have stayed next to me." He winks and holds out his arms for me.

I nod, moving across the room and into those arms eagerly, their strength and warmth my finest addiction. He purrs for me, hands landing on my ass, one of them inevitably going to play with the base of the plug I'm wearing. It makes me twist, cock flaring to life, rubbing against his belly, his hip.

"If you're having trouble sleeping, you should let me know, lovely. I know just how to tire you out so you sleep good and hard." His voice makes me such promises.

"I just had something on my mind."

"Oh?" He kisses my nose but is obviously waiting.

"It's nothing. Just something I'm researching for a friend. Reporter's instinct, you know?"

He chuckles. "Just make sure it doesn't get you into trouble. After all, isn't that how you ended up here?"

"Yes. Best instinct I ever had."

"Oh, you're a sweet talker tonight, lovely." He kisses me, hard, mouth pressing against mine, tongue filling my mouth.

I just melt, moaning into his lips, forgetting everything else. All else. Just sinking into him. He walks me backward toward our room. Our bodies rub, his cock already leaking against my belly, so hard and hot. I love how much he wants me.

I'm aching, each piercing throbbing, the dragon on my belly burning. "Love."

Richmond groans and nods. "Yes. Love. Need. Pain. Pleasure. Love."

"Yes. Please." I crawl up his body, legs sliding around his hips.

His hands settle on my ass, supporting me as he leans against the wall, our bodies rubbing together. His fingers push and push, knocking the plug, making me ache inside, making me need. I'm close already, cock hard as crystal and pulsing.

He purrs, one hand raking down my spine, fingernails digging in along the way, leaving trails of fire behind them.

Everything in me ripples. His marks. Yes. His.

"Master."

"Yes, your Master. Come for me, Nat, show me how much you want me."

I just nod, heat spraying between us, my body tuned to hear him. He groans, his fingers pulling out the plug, shifting me, pushing inside me in a smooth, hard motion. We're working together, grunts and groans filling the air, just like his cock's filling me. He manages to get one hand between us, tugging on one ring and then the other, insisting I get hard again.

The ring in the tip of my cock aches, the pleasurepain just perfect.

Once I'm hard his hands settle on my hips, keeping me in place as his hips snap, pushing that thick cock into me over and over again. I throw my head back, hands squeezing his shoulders, and just fly.

He growls, the sound sliding through me, heat pushing deep inside me as he comes. I moan, the heat sweet and right, making me ache deep inside. He walks us the rest of the way to the bedroom, still buried inside me. He's so strong, sexy.

"So good." I squeeze him, working his cock with my body.

He groans, fingers squeezing my ass. "So beautiful, Nat."

We're in the bedroom now and he's sliding out of me, groaning again. It makes me shiver, the feeling of him, the loss of him.

He purrs. "When was the last time I left your ass red, lovely?"

I whimper, cling to him. "Twelve days."

Twelve days.

"No. No way." He growls. "Get on the bed, lovely. We've got some time to make up for."

I moan, moving toward the bed, body empty, except

for his seed. Needing him.

"Pick your plug from the box first, lovely." He knows. He always knows exactly what I need. I pick my favorite, the one he had made for me, the one that drives me to hysterics and tears and pure bliss.

He purrs, taking it from me. "Excellent choice. You won't be unable to sleep when I'm done with you tonight."

He nods toward the bed. "Bend over, hands on the bed, legs spread for me."

"I love you." I bend over, knowing my hole is wet, red, swollen from being used. Being filled. Being his.

He moans at the sight of me. Then he bends and kisses my hole, tongue dragging over my skin. It makes me moan, makes the whole room shift as my breath catches. He pushes his thumbs into me, testing how open I am.

I push back against the touch, unable to stop myself, unable to hide my need.

"Pushy boy." There's no heat in his words, though, and his thumbs disappear, replaced by three fingers.

"Yours." I move, riding the touch, thighs parted and shaking.

"So sexy. You need spectacularly." He slides in three fingers from his other hand as well, spreading me wide.

"Master!" I go up on my toes, panting, stretched so fucking far.

"Yes." He places another kiss on me and then his fingers disappear, leaving me empty again. Soft noises escape me, quiet little complaints as I wait for him, for his attention.

"Sh, sh. It's coming, lovely. I know you're empty and needing. I always know, don't I?"

"Always. Before I do." I arch my back, stretching, feeling every moment.

"Never forget it." Two fingers test me again, and then

the head of the plug slides against my hole.

"Never." I close my eyes, focus on relaxing, on taking the plug in.

He rolls the head against me and then pushes it in a little, twisting so I feel all the bumps and protrusions.

"Feel it. So... so deep. Richmond." I'm still, letting him give me what I need.

"Just right," he suggests, sliding it in all the way until I feel my ass close around the base.

I just nod, pant. Ache for him. "Uh-huh. Just. Just right."

He licks at the skin stretched around the base of the plug, and then he slaps my ass and I can feel each finger. I jump, cry out. I want to be over his lap, cock sliding between his thighs, aching for it.

He tsks and slaps my ass again. "Focus, lovely."

"I... Okay. Yes. Okay." Focus. Feel. Oh, fuck.

His hand comes down again, low enough his fingertips catch my balls, slamming against the rings. I actually shift forward, hips ducking, rolling away from the blow.

He growls. "Playroom. Now."

I flinch, nodding. I hate disappointing him. More than anything.

"This is my fault," he says as we go down the hall. "It's been far too long since we played hard. The shows are becoming easy for you. I haven't challenged you."

"I'm sorry, Richmond." My heart falls, eyes on the floor.

"Yes, so am I." He's still stiff, face tight as we get to the playroom and he silently leads me to the cuffs that hang from the ceiling. I'm shaking, limp, pleasure gone, only a dull, sick feeling in my belly.

He puts my hands in the cuffs, and tilts my face up. "Focus, lovely. Don't make the same mistake a second time."

I just nod, wishing I'd never woken him up.

He drops a hard, brief kiss on my lips and goes to the cupboard, pulling out a cat o' nine tails. I close my eyes, turn my face to my arm and just wait, trying to remember to breathe.

"Now," he says quietly, and the first lash of the tails fall hard against my back.

I don't move, I don't say a word, I just take it. Take my punishment for disappointing my lover. Again and again the tails hit me, leaving lines of fire behind. I start to shiver, trying to think of anything to keep still, keep from moving.

Anything at all.

"I want to hear you."

The next lash is the hardest yet.

I gasp, but I've been so focused on still and silence I can't make any noise.

The next blow comes over my ass, all nine tails biting in.

I whimper, the air pushing out of me. Please. Master.

The tops of my thighs get hit next, my back again, and then he comes around and hits me full on in the chest, some of the tails catching on the rings in my nipples. I won't look, I just sob, letting the chains hold me up. He hits my chest again, the tails digging in deep.

"Last one," he says, doing it again.

I'm lost, sorry, so sorry. This wasn't like a scene, wasn't like pain for pleasure. This was just pain and shame and disappointment.

He throws the whip down and undoes me, catching me as I fall. He picks me up, holding me against his chest as he strides from the room. I don't want to go to bed, not like this. I can't. But I can't find the energy to tell him, either.

We don't go to the bedroom, though, we go into the

bathroom and he dims the lights to low and carries me into the shower. He turns it on hot and slides down, still holding me, rocking me.

I curl into myself, face on my knees. There's nothing but water. Nothing but steam.

His hands start to slide on me, over broken and beaten skin, over unbruised skin, just touching me all over, jostling the plug as he goes by it. Part of me wants to push him away, part of me wants to push closer. I stay still, sort of caught between the emotions.

"It's over, Nat. It's done. Put it away, let it go."

"I'm sorry." I am. The jerk had been pure instinct; Richmond's reaction completely unexpected.

"I know. And you've said it and I've whipped you and it's over now. Let it go, Nat, it's behind us." He tilts my head and kisses me softly. I keep my eyes closed, afraid he'll see that it's not as easy for me to just pretend, that it's harder to let it go when the things you've done wrong are burning on your skin.

He growls softly, mouth on mine, lips warm, tongue hot as it pushes into my mouth. My heart pounds a little, the kiss familiar and safe, strong. He purrs, hands solid as they slide on my arms, move down to my ass. My breath stops, entire body tender, skin almost skittish. His touch is sure, hands grabbing my ass, jostling the plug still inside me. I don't move, eyes on him, waiting to see what he wants, if I can move.

"Give it to me. Give me everything."

"I don't want to do anything wrong. I don't want to disappoint you again."

"You won't, lovely." His lips cover mine. "Just give me your heart, your soul," he whispers into me.

The tears start again, I can't stop them any more than I can stop the moan. He licks them from my face, tongue sliding on my skin, hot and wet. It eases me, soothes me.

"I hate making you angry."

"No, you hate disappointing me." He kisses my eyes. "We're human, lovely, not perfect. Sometimes we both forget, hmm?"

I nod, pushing close to him, cuddling in. "Love you."

He purrs. "I know. Everyone knows. It's what makes you glow, makes everyone want you, want to be me."

"You're beautiful. Everyone would want to be you." Except me. I just want to be me.

"No, you're the draw." He chuckles. "Not that it matters. I'm me and I have you." He kisses me again, tongue pushing into my mouth, taking it, owning it.

I just let myself go, let myself relax into it.

His. Just his.

His fingers tug on the plug, pulling it out slowly, and I can feel every bump and protrusion as it slides out of me. I lean into him, moaning low, thighs spread, the offer clear. He tilts his hips, his hands holding my ass, holding me open, spread for his cock. It is nothing to lean, to take him in and settle in his lap, warm and held.

"Yes, that's it, lovely. Right where you belong." He moans, eyes on mine, hands sliding into my curls.

I nod, leaning forward for a kiss. Yes. Yes, right here. His mouth meets mine again, this kiss softer, ours.

I settle against him, our bodies just barely moving, just sliding together. His eyes hold mine as surely as his hands hold my body, holding me close, loved. I'm suddenly exhausted and melted and home and settled, all at once, body shifting slowly, enjoying the feeling of him inside me. We rock together, moving like we're one, like we're going to do this forever.

I finally lean over, rest my cheek on his shoulder, my lips on his neck. "Love you."

"Me, too, lovely." Richmond holds me close, arms around me as the rocking increases, the water splashing down around us.

I don't even know if I'm hard, if I'm wanting, the feeling of everything overwhelming. It just goes on and on, wrapping us together, each feeling sliding into the next, all of the sensations tying together into something enormous.

His lips slide on mine, his breath pushing into me. The word "come" is breathed into me, surrounds me. Pleasure flows out of my skin, my soul, my cock, my lips, just pouring from me in wave after wave. He fills me in return, long pulses that increase my own pleasure and then we're resting together, the water a caress on my skin, his breath moving me gently.

It's nothing, to just close my eyes. Drift away. Sleep.

Chapter Fifteen

There's something wrong with Nat.

He's not sleeping right. He's distracted. His focus is shot. I'm not sure what the problem is and he's hiding it fairly well. I'm not sure if anyone aside from me would even notice. But I have and I don't like it. I've asked him a dozen times what's wrong and he keeps saying nothing.

We've just had a day off and I'm hoping it's cleared his mind because we're going to play with the cane tonight, something nice and solid to focus on, to draw us together.

"Hey, Richmond? Have a good day? Gotta wash up." Nat hurries in, right before he's expected home, a little pale, a little jittery, heading for the bathroom, dat-pad a lump in his back pocket.

I frown and put down the manacles I've been oiling, following him down to the bathroom. He's sweaty, trembling a little, water running while he scribbles.

Oh, this won't do. Time for him to let me know what's bothering him. "Lovely? You want to tell me what's going on?"

"More than anything, but I can't. I promised I wouldn't, but I want to." Those eyes meet mine and I know he's not bullshitting me, not at all.

"So this is someone else's secret?" I sigh. I don't want

to order him to tell me, but if the only thing holding him back is a promise to someone else, it might be the only way.

"Kind of. Please don't ask." Those eyes meet mine, worried and stressed out.

I shake my head. "Keeping this secret is hurting you, Nat. It's hurting our time together."

"I can't break my confidentiality, I just *can't*."

"Is this secret hurting just you, or you and countless others? Nat, this isn't a place where secrets work very well."

"I know. I know, Richmond. I just... If I'm right, it could be bad, but if I'm wrong, if I get it wrong and say something, then it'll be horrible. You have to believe me, this isn't a game. I'm trying to make something right."

I want to trust him. I do trust *him,* but this involves other people and this secret is taking a lot out of him. "You have two days, Nat. Then I want this business either done or you tell me or Mal about it."

"I'll try." Nat pushes into my arms, tense and vibrating. "I didn't ask for this, but I can't stop it now."

"And you don't have to carry it alone, Nat. A promise should only be kept if no one gets hurt." I tilt his head up and kiss him hard, my hands on his hips. He opens for me, tongue sliding against mine, pushing back, pushing back.

Nipping at his lower lip, I start stripping him out of his clothes. A quick shower and then the playroom. He needs to focus, needs to feel pain and forget about this secret that's weighing him down. He needs to remember that I'm Richmond and he belongs to me.

"So glad I'm home. You smell good." His hands slide up, push into my hair.

I'm about to ask him where he went today, but I figure that'll bring up topics he'd rather not discuss right now, so instead I push him into the water, washing him quickly. Nat hums, stretching out, the soap sluicing off his fine skin.

"We're going to go into the playroom. I'm going to use the cane. I'm bringing you home."

He shivers, whimpers. "The cane? It's... So much."

"Where is your mind today? Right now? On us? Or on this secret of yours?"

"I..." Those pretty green eyes meet mine. "I'm trying, Richmond. There's so much inside me."

I kiss him softly. "You need the cane. You need to focus, to be here."

I growl and pull him from the shower. Turning off the water and drying him are a quick matter and then we're going down the hall, my strides quick and eager. He's right behind me, fingers tight and twisted in mine.

I set the lights on medium, bright enough I'll be able to see the marks come up on his back, dark enough to be intimate. "I'm not chaining you for this." No, he's going to lean against the wall and stay in place for the cane hits by pure will, need.

He nods, eyes searching mine. "You know what I need?"

"Always, lovely. Always." I kiss him, tongue pushing into his mouth, reminding him that he's mine. I can feel his nerves, but I can feel his trust too, his need. I lead him to the wall and get him leaned against it, his hands flat against the wall's surface, his body leaning slightly. "Beautiful," I tell him.

"I... Yours." He shivers when I move away, stretched and so fine.

I get the cane, taking my time, letting all his anxiety and worry slowly focus on his body, me, and the cane, let that push everything else from him. I test the cane against my palm and then through the air, letting the sound of it settle in Nat. He gasps, stilling, muscles shifting.

"Yes, lovely. It's time." I hit him with the cane, the loud crack making *my* body jerk.

His cry snaps out, skin going white before going deep, dull red.

"Beautiful." My voice is little more than a growl, the air fairly crackling between us.

"Again," I say, giving him warning before I lay another hit down across his shoulders. His fingers scratch the wall, every muscle going taut, shuddering.

"Another," I tell him. This one goes at an angle, from shoulder to hip. He's almost done, but I think he can take one more.

"Master. Master, please." I can see his sweat, his skin glistening.

"One more, Nat. You can do this. I know you can." I wait for him to acknowledge the truth of my words.

"F... for you. For you."

"For us." I hit him with the cane again, watching his skin react, watching him react. His knees buckle and I know he's about to safeword, about to break, I can feel it in the air. I'm there to catch him, pulling him down against me, sliding to the floor with him in my lap.

"Oh, lovely, that was beautiful. You amaze me every day with the way you rise to every challenge." I purr and hold him, rocking softly. I won't let him break.

"Master." The tear-stained face raises to mine, begging a kiss.

I give it to him, as in need of the connection as he is. My tongue fills his mouth, slides through it, taking him. He sobs, pushing against my chest, giving himself to me. I have one hand on his ass, the other behind his head, careful of his back, of the welts I put there. He's shaking, shuddering, pushing against me. I purr and pet and kiss, shifting so I'm lying on the floor, his body stretched out on me.

It's natural and easy to just pull out the plug and push in, taking that sweet ass. Quiet and calm against me, he just lets me in deep, lets me have him.

"My lovely boy." I fuck him with slow, deep thrusts, his body so tight and hot around me.

"Yours. Your own." He licks my skin, groaning softly, loving on me.

"Yes." My hips keep moving, bringing us together again and again, my hands sliding along his arms, his sides, squeezing his ass cheeks. He moans, shifting, riding me as he tries to avoid any burn.

"Accept it, lovely, take the pain. You know you love it." I slide one hand gently along his back. Nat whimpers, entire body rippling around me, squeezing my cock. "That's it, lovely, that's it."

Groaning, I move faster, harder, thrusting up into him with enough force to rock him now.

"I need." He rolls, biting my shoulder. I growl, fingers digging into his back. His scream is luscious, hips slapping down toward me. "Please."

I flip him onto his back, driving into him as hard as I can, just slamming our bodies together. His fingers dig into my shoulders, entire body begging and flushed, eyes focused on me. I know that he needs to come, but I make him wait, thrust wildly until I'm panting, the pleasure crawling up my back like a wild cat. Finally I give it to him, the command rough. "Come."

Heat sprays against my belly, Nat sobbing with it. His body milks my cock, pulls my pleasure from me, and I scream his name out as I fill him. Nat curls toward me, panting, moaning, shivering.

I roll again, bringing him on top of me, bringing relief to his back, and I hold him, whisper to him. "So good, lovely. Such a wonderful boy. You make me so proud."

"Love you, Richmond. I'm so tired. So tired of worrying and thinking." He cuddles, relaxed and easy against me.

"Then tell me, lovely. You don't have to carry any load alone. Tell me."

"You won't tell anyone? Even if you want to?"

"Not for our agreed-upon deadline, Nat. I won't tell for forty-eight hours." He'll tell me and I'll keep the secret because he cannot carry it alone.

"There's a top, a customer. I think he's drugging the house subs, using Risque and then threatening them if they tell, saying he'll make Mal test them, throw them out."

Fury goes through me at his words. That someone would do that, here. That the house subs, spoiled and bratty though they can be, sweet and wonderful as they are, are being abused like that, drugged.

"They have to go to Mal," I tell him.

"They're scared. The... the top has money, real money. Real power. That's why they came to me. So I could find out, because he can't ask for me."

I tighten my arms around him. "No. No one can have you. No one but me."

I shake my head. I know what I told him, but this man is a predator and he's in our home. "Nat, they have to tell Mal, they have to, before this man hurts anyone else. You and I will go with them, him, whoever is brave enough to step up. We can't go another day, another moment with this man in our midst."

Nat looks up. "No. No, what if I'm wrong? What if they're wrong? Two days, Richmond. You promised."

"What if they're wrong about what? About what's being done to them? Nat, giving the subs Risque is not only illegal, it's dangerous. Mind-altering drugs can be a part of a scene, but not against the sub's will, not without the proper safeguards and not with an illegal and dangerous substance like Risque! What if one of them dies while we knew and did nothing?"

"I don't know. I think. I... I need proof."

"I'm not saying you should tell, I'm saying they should. You or you and I can go as moral support. We can't let this happen in our home, Nat. It's wrong." I'm not going to back down and I'll tell Mal what details I know if I have to, and then he'll shut the whole club down until the truth is found out and no one will be hurt.

"You don't *understand*, Richmond. They're scared." Nat pulls away, shaking his head. "Two days."

"Then I will ask Mal to close the subs down for the next two days."

"Then he won't come in and I can't catch..." Nat's mouth snaps shut.

I growl. "You are not telling me you were hoping to bring this man down on your own?" I keep my voice calm, but I'm furious.

"Down? No. No, I just needed proof."

"We'll let Mal find proof, I don't want you anywhere near this guy. I don't want anyone near him." I get up and go to the cupboard to find the numbing spray for his back. We'll go see Mal now. Nat doesn't have to say a word.

Nat shook his head, frowning. "You gave me two days."

"That's before I knew you were putting yourself in danger! Turn around." I spray the antibiotic numbing cream on his back. The welts are beautiful and I'm sorry this is taking away from what should have been a long afterglow, but this is important. It's no wonder he's been losing sleep. "Think about it, Nat. Someone could get killed. Do you really think Mal won't believe the subs? Did you think I wouldn't believe you? No, you knew I would believe you when you told me. This can't go on."

"They won't back me up. No one will. They'll know I told, that I broke their confidence."

"Mal will come up with something." Because I don't know what to say, what to do. Only that I cannot allow this to continue for a moment longer. There isn't a worker bee sub I haven't worked with, and I will not stand by and allow even one of them to be harmed like this. "You don't have to come with me if you don't want to. You can stay here until I've spoken to Mal."

"I'm not going. I won't ruin a man if I'm not sure." Nat's got his firm and stubborn face on.

I sigh. "Nat. The club has been dealing with people like this probably since it opened, and yet I've never heard of a single bit of trouble except for the time I was involved. This guy won't even know there's a problem unless Mal gets proof, but he won't be able to hurt a soul in the meantime." I realize, suddenly, he's never even told me who it is. "What's his name, lovely?"

Nat shakes his head. "It's not ethical to tell."

I've already broken my promise to him, or at least I'm about to, so I'm not going to push him on this. Much. "And just how ethical is it to let this guy keep coming back here, drugging subs?"

"It's not. It's wrong. And I was trying to trap him. Stop him."

"Which is very noble of you, Nat, but Mal and the security personnel at the club are better equipped to do it. I'm not trying to hurt the boy who took you into his confidence, I'm trying to help."

"I am, too!" Nat turns, hits the wall with one fist. "Damn it, Richmond. One more week and I'd have taken care of it. No sweat."

"No sweat? What about the sleepless nights, the bags under your eyes? The lack of focus? The fact that if he found out you were trying to trap him he could do God knows what to you?" I take his hand and rub his knuckles with my fingers. "Enough. I'm going to see Mal."

"I'm going to take a shower. Be careful, please?"

"I'm locking the door behind me, lovely. Don't open it for anyone." I'm not the one who needs to be careful, predators like this don't go after tops.

I kiss him hard and then go, the anger just rolling through me. I head straight for Mal's office and I don't knock.

Mal looks up, frowns, communit in one hand. "What's up, Rich?"

"I've heard through the grapevine that someone is doping subs up on Risque."

"Who? Why? Which subs? Who told you?" Mal stands, fingers tapping furiously. "Get me Herc. Now. Right now."

"A reliable source. Who didn't come to you because he doesn't have proof, but he believes it's happening. And the worker bees. I don't know which ones, only that they're scared for their lives."

"Mal?" Hercules' voice comes across the comm.

"You need to be down here, Boss. Right now. We're locking down the club."

There's a growl, but the link is cut off, Hercules obviously on his way.

I take a breath, nodding. Lock down. I suspected as much without any names. The boys are safe now. My Nat is safe now.

"You'd better be ready to talk, Richmond. Hercules isn't going to be interested in playing games with you."

"I can't tell him what I don't know, Mal. Someone is drugging the subs, but there's no proof and the subs who are being drugged are too scared to come forward." Mal's got to know who told me, but there's little I can do about that.

Hercules doesn't knock, just walks in. The man has a presence, an aura that says don't mess with me. He's stunning to boot, tall, purple from head to toe and just... a top's top. "Monk's locked the place down. What the hell is going on?"

"Rich says someone's drugging the worker bees. I'm having Monk bring Nat in."

"I was hoping we could keep him out of it, Mal." Not to mention I told him not to open the door to anyone but me.

"Does he know who it is?"

I sigh and nod.

"Then he's going to tell us," Hercules puts in.

"He's worried about losing the trust of his friends."

"I don't care."

No, I don't suppose he does. I hold my hand out for Mal's comm. "I told him not to open the door to anyone. I'd better let him know to come with Monk."

Mal hands it over, Nat answering immediately. "Richmond? Someone's here."

"If the man's name is Monk, go with him. He's bringing you here."

"Richmond, you said."

"I didn't name any names, lovely, Mal guessed. Just come. These men care about the subs."

Hercules takes the comm from my fingers. Anyone else and I'd've snarled and grabbed it back, possibly initiated a fight, but this is Hercules. He is the Club. "I suggest you allow Monk to escort you here, young man, and that you be quick about." He snaps the comm off.

It isn't long before Nat shows up, fully dressed, drawn into himself. He's not the frightened boy I met at the beginning, not at all. I wait for him to stand next to me and slide my arm around his waist. I might have brought him to this, but I won't make him stand alone.

Hercules just stares at Nat. "Tell me."

Nat steps away from me, meeting Hercules head-on. "I want your word that the boys won't be blamed if I'm wrong. Only me."

One of Hercules' eyebrows go up. "I don't make deals, but I understand that you aren't presenting me with facts, only suspicions."

"One of your clients is drugging the boys with Risque, threatening them if they go to Mal. One of your bigger clients."

Hercules' only reaction is a tick in his jaw, but I've seen that tick before, I know he's not happy. "They're all big, sweetie, I need a name."

"Gent Louinto. They call him Georix."

My jaw drops and I can see everyone go still. Gent is big money, fierce. Powerful.

Hercules is the one who recovers the quickest. "Is he here tonight, Monk?"

"Give me two minutes and I'll know."

Mal shakes his head. "Kes won't need that long." Sure enough, two words from Mal and Kes is answering in the affirmative, the man fluttering furiously.

"Damnit, is he with a sub?"

"He's on the main floor with Harley, having dinner with some business associates, Boss."

Nat's getting paler and paler. "I've found traces of Risque on the palmpad of his suite and autoinjectors in his garbage, sir. I'm not making it up."

Hercules waves him quiet. "Extend the dinner, Kes. And invent an emergency — I want Harley up here before they're ready to move from the dining room."

Hercules turns to Mal. "I want all the subs who've ever worked with him drug tested. Now. I want anyone coming up positive matched with a house top, including Desmond, Hawk, Sampson, you, Richmond. I don't care if they're exclusive or have a mate, the boys need one on one by people I can trust, people who know what they're doing."

Hercules purses his lips. "Monk, go through the security tapes. If the boys are being drugged there should be some clue now that you know what to look for. I don't want Gent knowing he's under investigation — if he's innocent, I won't have him insulted."

Nat touches my hand, eyes quiet, unhappy, distant. "I'm going home."

It's a madhouse of activity, things swirling, so busy. "I'm coming with you."

"Yes, yes. Lockdown. Stay in your rooms. I'm sending the first boy who tests positive or confesses what's been going on to you, Richmond."

Hercules waves us off and I put my arm around Nat's waist and walk out with him. Nat doesn't say a word, just walks, eyes on the ground, completely pulled into himself.

I wait until we're back in our rooms and then I turn him, lift his chin. "This was the right thing to do, Nat. Those men care about the boys more than they do Gent's money."

"Yeah. I need a shower, Richmond, and a nap."

"I know." I bring our mouths together, kissing him firmly. I know he believes I've abused his trust, but I also know I've done the right thing.

Nat kisses me back quietly, then pulls away. "You'll have company tonight. Lots of it, and they won't want to see me. 'Night, Richmond. Love you."

Oh, I don't think so.

I grab his hand and tug him back. "Excuse me, Nat. You seem to be forgetting who gives the orders here."

Those eyes flash up at me, and that defiance and anger is better than the quiet. I think this is going to need a full-out assault. He needs to remember why he told me, why he came back here in the first place.

"Get undressed," I tell him, letting his hand go and watching, implacable.

"You're going to be busy taking care of other men. I'm *angry*, Richmond."

"One other man, and I *know* you're angry, but I'm still your top and you'll still do what I say."

And Nat does. Cursing and furious and throwing the clothes at me, but he gets undressed. I pick them up, fold them, still watching, making sure he knows he's my focus, now, always. Mine. I can see the stripes on him, the tension inside him. He's held it together so well, but that's not what we're about. His worries belong to me.

It's time to break him open because he's not going to do it the easy way.

"Playroom," I tell him as soon as he's naked.

He growls, storming down the hall, emotions pouring off him. "I. Am. ANGRY!"

"Louder," I tell him. "Let it out."

Nat screams, just furious, door slamming open "I don't want to be ignored! I don't want to be petted and then pushed aside! I hate that the subs here were scared! I hate that they didn't have a you to come to but they can't have you, damnit! You are MINE!"

I nod. "I am yours, lovely. All of me. And I have never pushed you aside. Never."

I don't know what to tell him about Hercules' orders sending me one of the boys who've been hurt. I've never defied Hercules before, but for Nat I'm willing to. Those boys need good, caring, strong tops to help them get through what's happened to them — and I have no doubt it has, Nat was close, really close to proving it — but maybe I'm not the right person to help anyone but Nat.

"I know. I know, but all the work I did. All the hours

and it means nothing to anyone! Do you think I just left them? That any of us just said, oh. Damn. We're submissive. What do we do? However will we cope? No." Nat turns on me, arms flying. "Jewel helped find what meds we needed. Ghost got them for us. Them. The last times Jewel and the twins stole the autoinjector. I'm supposed to meet the man who tested it tomorrow. I'm not pointless."

"Nobody ever accused you of being pointless, Nat. The things you did were dangerous. And there are protocols in place! So that no one has to risk being hurt, caught by this man and killed." I shudder at the thought. If Gent had caught any of them...

"We had to have proof!"

"There is a security team whose job it is to gather proof when accusations are made, Nat!" I'm starting to lose my cool. Now that it's over, now that Nat is out of it and the extent of his involvement is becoming clear, it hits me how it could have turned out.

"Well, obviously those men don't feel like that's something open to them!" Nat is vibrating, literally shaking there on the floor.

"No, and you didn't feel you could come to me, either," I point out.

We need a good hard session, both of us. Nat needs to break, to cry, to be held and put back together again, and I need to do it.

"I promised I wouldn't! I wanted to tell you! I wanted your help, but I promised!" Nat's voice cracks, the scream pushing hysteria.

"So you knew you could come to me. Good. Good." That's important, that we both know that.

I grab hold of his wrists and press a hard kiss on him. "I love you." I tell him. It's important he hears that, too, knows that as I take him to the center of the room and begin to put him into the cuffs.

"I'm mad. I'm tired. I want a shower and bed." He's trying to be reasonable. It's beautiful.

"But that's not what you need." I get his wrists into the cuffs, adjusting them so that he's stretched wide and high, and then begin to work on his ankles. His back is striped, the caning marks swollen, dark. It won't take long to break him, he's already so close to the edge, though knowing my Nat, he'll hold out for as long as he can before I hear the word I have never heard from him.

I strip as well, I don't want clothes to interfere later. I don't want anything to interfere. Then I pull out the wall bed and make sure the sprays and creams are in place, some water. Then I pick up the cat 'o nine tails and get settled behind him.

He's struggling, arguing, tugging at the bonds, anger flaring. "Richmond, you're not listening to me!"

"We're done talking, lovely." I don't give him a chance to answer. I just let the whip fly, watch it strike his back like nine angry snakes.

He screams, twisting furiously. "No! Richmond!"

I nod. That's it, Nat. Let it all out. All of it. I don't say it out loud, though, and I just let the whip fly again, using my full strength. He's sobbing, struggling, fighting me and the chains, screaming at me to stop, to let him go. One more blow and I hear it, his safe word, ringing through the air.

His back is bloody, his screams and cries filling the air. I drop the cat o' nine tails and go to my knees, face against his ass as I undo his ankles. My own cheeks are wet, his pain and hurt my own. His wrists are next and I'm there to catch him as he collapses.

"Let me go. No more, Richmond. No more." He pushes away, cries out as he hits the floor.

"No more, Nat. Just you and me." I pick him up and

carry him to the bed, curling up with him in my arms, rocking with him. "Sh. Sh. It's okay, lovely. Cry as long as you need to, just let go. I have you. I have you."

He struggles for just a minute longer, then crumples, sobbing softly, trembling in my arms. My own tears keep falling and I just keep rocking, stroking his arms, his cheeks, murmuring nonsense.

Finally he stills, dozing, shuddering every so often when anything bothers his back.

I manage to get one of the sprays without waking him and apply it liberally. I give it ten minutes to be sure it's numbed him properly, and then I spread on the antibiotic cream. Once he's deeply asleep I'll tie him curled in the fetal position, and then I can sleep, too, with my world in my arms.

Chapter Sixteen

I don't want to wake up. I don't want to try to figure things out. I don't want to think. And I can't seem to move.

I'm all curled into myself and sort of... stuck there. I'm warm though, so warm. And Richmond is curled around me, pressed close, holding me.

Okay. Okay, I can live with this. I close my eyes, doze in and out, still so tired.

I wake when the plug inside me slips away, Richmond quietly and softly cleaning me inside, his voice soft though I don't really hear the words, just the sounds. I don't fight him, just let him care for me. Touch me.

Another plug fills me when he's done, something large enough I know it's there, but small enough that it isn't really stretching me. Then he undoes the bindings on my legs, stretches them, massages them, and ties me back up. My arms are next, unbound, stretched, massaged, rebound. His hands are warm, sure.

It's comfortable like this. Quiet. Peaceful. "Are we okay?" Gods, my voice sounds raw, hoarse, almost destroyed, and my throat burns.

He kisses my cheek, his lips soft. "We're good, lovely. All you need to do is drift, feel, heal."

I nod, sigh and relax again, so comfortable, so quiet.

His hands slide on my back, rubbing in cream, making my back ache, but not quite hurt. The cream is soothing, though, numbing the skin and easing sore muscles. He wraps around me again when he's done, body solid and hot, safe.

"L... love you." My cheek is on his arm, resting there. Easy.

He pets me gently. "Yes, Nat. Love you." He keeps touching me, fingers light on my skin, gentle touches that slide over me.

I float in and out, unable to think, to worry, just focused on those hands. His fingers slide along my neck, pushing down between us to play with my nipples. I can feel his cock, hard, hot, rubbing against the small of my back. It makes me smile, my Richmond, always needing me, always needing to touch. His lips slide against my forehead, leaving nibbling kisses. Those make me chuckle, make me moan.

He purrs, and his hand drops to tease the plug, tugging it slowly out. I'd play with him, fight it, but I can't seem to, my body just follows his touch. He doesn't seem upset, just slides his cock in to replace the plug, hot and hard, nothing ever feels as right.

It's just like he's holding me closer, touching me deeper. There's no desperation, no freneticism.

Slowly, in and out, we move together, bodies meeting, joining again and again. He's whispering soft words that are my name, love, pride, mine. I need him. I can feel his thighs against my balls, against my ass, my cock trapped against my belly.

He keeps moving, building slowly in speed, in the strength of his thrusts, his hand sliding to play with my nipples again.

"Master." I love him. Need him.

He purrs. "Mine. My lovely. My Nat."

"Yours. Your own. For always, please."

"For always, Nat." His hips start snapping, driving his cock into me, his body still curled around mine, his hand on my chest. He's everywhere, inside and outside of me.

His order is soft, whispered across my cheek. "Come, lovely."

Heat spreads over my belly, cock throbbing where it is trapped. He groans, heat filling me, his hands petting me.

I moan, settling back down, boneless.

Still.

His.

While Nat is sleeping, I undo his bindings, leave him curled up in the bed, while I clean up Nat's clothes, the playroom. Get another earful from Hercules. I told him I couldn't take any of the boys.

I know how I feel about Nat, how I won't share him with anyone. And I'm fiercely glad that he feels the same way about me.

I head back to the bedroom, not wanting him to wake alone.

He looks pale, quiet, very fragile alone in the bed. "I was right, wasn't I? They proved it."

"Yeah, lovely. He was handed over to Planet Security this morning." I go over and sit next to him, slide my hand along his arm.

"Is everybody angry at me?"

"Well, I haven't spoken to everyone. In fact, the only one I've spoken to is Hercules, and the only one he's angry with is me."

"Why?" Nat frowns, bristling, ready to defend me.

I chuckle, smoothing the frown from his face. "Because

I told him no."

"No other subs?" Nat's eyes search mine.

"No, lovely. I won't share you, why should you have to share me?"

Nodding, settling, Nat breathes deep. "I'm hungry and my throat hurts."

I purr and stroke his throat. "Some broth should take care of both."

"I'm sorry for last... the other night. I just lost it."

"You were frustrated and hurt and angry. I told Hercules what you said, you know. About the worker bee subs not having anyone to turn to the way you did and he's got Mal and Kes on the job, to figure out a solution to that."

"Really?" Nat just gapes. "They listened?"

"Yes, lovely. I tried to tell you the other day — the people who work here are the club. They're important to Mal, to Hercules."

"I know. I tried so hard to help."

"And you did, lovely, you did." I kiss him softly. "You helped."

Nat pulls me closer, cuddling. "Good."

My hands move on him, sliding over his smooth, warm skin. Our room smells of us and sex. It feels good to be here, to be with him. "I need something from you, lovely. And this is very important."

"Anything, Richmond." Nat nods, pulls me closer.

"You must promise me if something like this comes up again, that you will come to me first. You must promise me there will be no secrets between us." He could have been hurt, killed, and I can't let him face something like that on his own again.

"Will you promise the same? No secrets between us?"

"Absolutely." I don't even need to think about it,

although there is one area... "But there will be times that I will want to keep secret what my plans for the playroom or a scene might be. That will be an exception."

Nat nods, smiles. "And if I have a surprise for you — a gift — that's okay."

I meet his smile with one of my own. "Yes, that would be fine, but this business of investigating things on your own, that needs to stop, Nat."

"It's what I was, Richmond. You know? Curiosity and the cat and all?"

"I know, lovely, and I'm not saying you can't be curious, that you can't... investigate things. But I don't like the idea of you doing it without a net like you were." I don't want to be his jailer, his parent, but this secret was eating at him, at us, and it could have gotten him killed. "I'm not asking you to report to me or anything, Nat, but if something gets serious, it starts interfering with your sleep and weighing on you. Well, then, it's time to tell me before I have to ask."

Nat's fingers slide into mine, warm and soft. "You just worry about me."

"I do. You're my world. Mine." He's the one place I'm vulnerable.

"Yeah. Yours." Nat squeezes my fingers, nods. "Yours."

I nuzzle into his neck, nosing aside the collar so I can leave a mark on his skin. Nat tilts his head, lets me have more. I bite and suck, lips and teeth and tongue working his skin, drawing the blood up to the surface, leaving a gloriously dark mark on his beautiful, pale skin. I can feel his heart pound under my lips, quick and steady. I push him back down onto the bed and follow, body pressing his into the mattress, cock hot, hard, wanting inside him. It's so easy to want him, to get lost in him.

"Yours. Master. Your own." Nat wraps around me,

holding on.

Those words make me harder than anything else, those words are like a drug. I push his legs apart with my knees, spreading him for me. So eager, so wanton, all mine. Never loved, never taken by another.

I get the plug out of him and slide right in as soon as I can. Slide right into perfection. "Nat. Oh. Mine."

"Yes. Yes." Nat looks happy, at peace. Just glowing.

I start to move, rocking with him, thrusting into his yielding, grasping body over and over again. I watch his face the whole time, my pleasure so much deeper because of his.

His hand cups my cheek. "Mine."

"Oh, lovely. From the very start."

"Yes. You waited for me to... oh..." His head tosses, cheeks flushed. "To come."

I purr, nod. "Yeah, lovely. And I'll always wait for you to come." I bend and lick across my mark on his throat. "Come."

Nat laughs, the sound a little wild as he bucks up against me, heat spraying.

My own laughter turns into a moan as his body squeezes around me. There's nothing like being inside him, nothing like coming with him.

Sated, I collapse onto him, still buried deep, right where I belong.

Home with my own, my heart. My Nat.

End.

Sean Michael

Velvet Glove, Volume IV

2781019